Love's Amber Fury

As always he ended up physically eager and mentally appalled. Their clothes lay in two disheveled piles on the floor, and Françoise laughed at him softly. "For a man who did not wish to make love to me, you undress very quickly," she said.

"I didn't say I didn't want to make love to you," Denis said. Lying as naked as a jaybird on Françoise's silk coverlet, it was all too obvious that he did. "I said it was a dangerous thing to do. But I meant it, Françoise. I can't come here after I'm married."

Françoise sat up in bed and draped herself across him. "You can." She wriggled around until she lay straddling him. "And you will." She kissed the hollows of his neck and then bit him gently. "Because I don't intend to lose a valued amusement."

BELLE MARIE
by
Laura Ashton

BELLE MARIE

LAURA ASHTON

Created by the producers of
**The Roselynde Chronicles,
Wagons West, Northwest
Territory,** and **The Kent
Family Chronicles.**

Book Creations Inc., Canaan, NY · Lyle Kenyon Engel, Founder

J

JOVE BOOKS, NEW YORK

BELLE MARIE

A Jove Book / published by arrangement with
Book Creations, Inc.

PRINTING HISTORY
Jove edition / July 1987

ISBN: 0-515-09082-4

Table of Contents

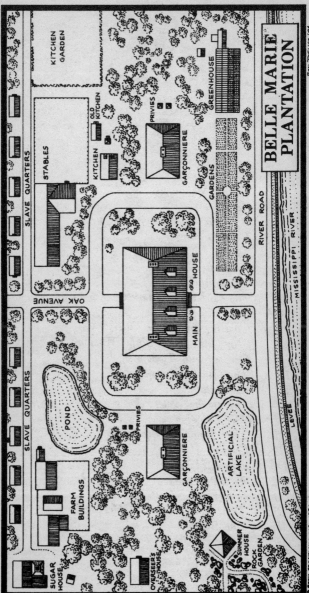

BELLE MARIE PLANTATION

Ron Toelke '84

© Bon Creations Inc. 1984

I

The

DuMontaignes

Paris, 1840

THE DINING ROOM of the marquis D'Avenal's Paris town house was brightly lit with gas lamps. Branched silver candelabrae illuminated the table, still laden with the remains of dessert, and cast flickering shadows on the eight young gentlemen gathered around it. They were all unmarried, as was the marquis, and drunk in the fashion of wealthy young men with very little else to do. Just now they were intent upon the progress of two beetles, a bronze insect and a black and gold one, which were making erratic progress down the length of the damask tablecloth.

"*Vite!* Hurry, you worthless insect!" The young comte De St. Jean said, poking a silver fruit knife at the bronze beetle.

"No encouragement allowed!" a young man who had bet on the opposing beetle, the entry of the marquis D'Avenal, protested, glaring.

St. Jean peered suspiciously at the bronze beetle, which was stumbling well behind its black and gold rival. "You ought to ask for a new beetle, Lucien!" he addressed his friend, proprietor of the bronze beetle, indignantly. "This one is missing a leg."

Lucien DuMontaigne lounged back in his chair, but his bright, dark eyes were narrowed and fixed intently on the two bumbling insects. He was very drunk, his pale, fine-boned face flushed in two bright spots on his cheeks, his black hair hanging in damp waves over his eyes. His ruffled shirtfront and white waistcoat were stained with wine. He eyed the damage distastefully before

1

raising his glass to his lips but made no answer as the marquis D'Avenal and the others who had bet on the black and gold beetle loudly protested the comte's suggestion. It never looked honorable to complain after a bet was accepted. A gentleman took his losses without whining.

The marquis D'Avenal and his guests had run out of other things to bet on when they had discovered a half-dozen beetles, drawn from winter torpor by an unseasonably warm evening, crawling on the shutters outside the brightly lit dining room, and the men had seized on them with enthusiasm. Lucien DuMontaigne had wagered an amount slightly larger than the remaining quarter's allowance that his father in America sent him, but his handsome, slightly sulky countenance was unconcerned as the bronze beetle wobbled into a pierced silver fruit dish, tried to climb it, and fell on its back. "Calm down, St. Jean," Lucien said lazily as his friend sputtered at the perfidious behavior of his beetle. "You will burst something."

"It's the principle of the thing," St. Jean said stubbornly. "Wouldn't bet on a *horse* that didn't have all its legs."

Lucien chuckled. "Next time we will have a veterinarian examine all starters."

"Interesting, isn't it, how the Americans always let us know they have more money than they need." A pale young Englishman named Reave, a quarrelsome drunk, stared at Lucien with dislike. Reave was losing money on the bronze beetle, and Lucien's disregard for its infirmities would make him look foolish if *he* complained.

Lucien raised an eyebrow with the air of one who pities a person deficient in some way. "I am not American," he explained gently. "I am Creole. From New Orleans."

"You're behaving badly, Reave." The comte De St. Jean said. "Come away before you start something." He knew that when Lucien DuMontaigne was deceptively polite, it boded no good.

Reave didn't like losing his money, and he didn't like Americans. "New Orleans?" He had trouble pronouncing it. "I met a fellow from there last week. A painter. Looked like a damned blackamoor."

"The polite expression is *gens de couleur,*" Lucien said helpfully. "Even with the demimonde, one should always be polite. They often travel on the Continent. You see, a great many of them, unlike the English, are gentlemen's sons."

"DuMontaigne, you'll meet me for that slander!" Reave lunged across St. Jean and caught Lucien under the ear with his fist. Lucien pushed his chair back, his dark eyes blazing, while the comte got a grasp on Reave's collar.

"Here now, you don't want to call DuMontaigne out!" St. Jean protested. "Not over a bug!"

"Certainly he wishes to," Lucien said, a dangerous light in his eyes. "The English are too pigheaded to back down. St. Jean will act as my second. If you can find any friends, Reave, send one of them to him later tonight. Since I believe the choice of time is mine, I'll meet you in"—he rose and consulted his watch—"six hours. It should be light by then."

"As you wish!" Reave snapped. He turned on his heel.

"Shocking behavior," St. Jean said audibly, and the Englishman's back stiffened. "Can't think why you asked Reave to dinner, D'Avenal. Now Lucien's going to shoot holes in him, and we'll have to write his family."

Reave snatched his cloak and hat from the footman, who had scurried to produce them. When the door had closed behind him, Lucien drained his glass, noted that in the meantime the black and gold beetle had crossed the finish line, and bowed to the marquis D'Avenal.

"Why are you in such a hurry to shoot Reave, DuMontaigne?" D'Avenal asked as he touched a tapestry bellpull, and the liveried footman reappeared.

"Alas, I am due to enjoy the bucolic splendors of the countryside tomorrow," Lucien said. "A visit to a friend of my father's. An old gentleman named Scarron, who is dying by degrees and intends to leave his no doubt tiresome daughter to my father's care. I *must* shoot Reave tomorrow. I am appointed to escort the girl home to New Orleans, I regret to say."

"You can't leave now. The races are next week!" St. Jean protested.

"Perhaps the old gentleman will be kind enough not to die until after the races," Lucien said. He accepted his cloak and high-crowned hat from the footman.

"Your servant, D'Avenal. I'll send you a draft on my bank."

"*Before* you meet with Reave, I do trust," D'Avenal retorted. Lucien put his hat on, chuckling.

A thin mist hung in the air, clouding the gas lamps that burned beside the marquis's steps. Lucien pulled his cloak around his shoulders and stepped into Granduncle Thierry's antiquated town carriage. As the horses clopped down the empty street, he leaned back in the carriage, thinking. The duel with Reave was of no great importance, but Monsieur Scarron could not have picked a more unfortunate month in which to die. Lucien had been planning to leave Paris to attend the races and spend the rest of January at St. Jean's country house with a convivial gathering of young bachelors, when his father's letter had arrived. Since it could easily take two months for mail to cross the Atlantic on the sailing packets, the old man had no doubt been dying for some time, but he appeared to be in earnest now, judging by the reply that Lucien had received to his inquiry as to the state of Monsieur Scarron's current health. It had been signed by a nurse or companion named D'Aubert and said only that the old man was failing rapidly.

Lucien ground his teeth. He didn't want to go back to New Orleans. He had never enjoyed such freedom as he had in Paris with doddering old Granduncle Thierry DuMontaigne, who did not go into society anymore. So long as Lucien was properly pious at home, his uncle was unlikely to hear that elsewhere his conduct was otherwise. And if his uncle didn't hear it, his father would not, which was more to the point.

Lucien considered next the matter of his bet. No doubt he could persuade Granduncle Thierry to advance him part of next quarter's allowance. Or he could sail for New Orleans and plead a bank draft lost in the post if D'Avenal got sticky. There was always a silver lining, Lucien thought, cheered. He had never found himself without a way to turn unpleasantnesses to his use. The only courses of action he did not consider were to refuse his father's orders to bring Adele Scarron home, and to admit to his father that he had bet money he did not have. Either of those would be highly unpleasant.

The carriage swept up to the steps of Granduncle Thierry's town house, and the footman pulled the door open for Lucien. Inside there were candles burning in sconces in the entrance hall and the oak-paneled library where Granduncle Thierry was dozing in his chair by the fire.

"You really ought to have gas lamps, Uncle," Lucien said, as Granduncle Thierry raised his head and adjusted his spectacles. "I damn near broke my leg coming up the stairs, and I'm sure they would be better for your eyes."

"No, I have always felt quite sure that they would explode one day." Granduncle Thierry yawned. He regarded any development since the turn of the century as something bound to explode. His thin legs were encased in knee breeches—he must be the only man in Paris who still insisted on wearing them, Lucien thought—and the cut of his coat had not been fashionable since his youth. His head nodded down to his breast, and then bobbed up again. "I do hope you don't plan to sail on one of those infernal steam vessels. No place for a lady." His chin sank down again. "Bound to explode," he muttered.

Lucien laughed. "I'm told they're damned cramped and uncomfortable. I'll send Sayer to you, shall I, to help you up to bed?" If the old fool didn't go up now, he'd doze in his chair half the night and never rise until noon. The traveling coach was ordered for eleven, and Lucien would need a little time between his meeting with Reave and his departure to explain convincingly to his uncle how it was that he had spent three months' allowance in the first two weeks of the quarter.

That explanations might be superfluous after his meeting with Reave was not even considered.

Louisiana, 1840

"A pleasant evening. And a fine thing to have one's family about." Paul DuMontaigne regarded his wife and children with real pleasure across a table laden with a vol-au-vent of crayfish, a steaming tureen of gumbo, and a whole roasted suckling pig. A simple dinner for an evening when there was no company.

"Yes, *la famille* should always be one's greatest comfort," Tante Doudouce said in her customary whisper, and Paul smiled guiltily in response because he hadn't been thinking of her. She wasn't really an aunt, but a spinster first cousin once removed. As a female she could not earn her own keep and so was "carried on" by the head of the family. The only trouble with Tante Doudouce was that she spoke either in soft, agitated chirps or in the breathiest of whispers, and so one tended to forget her, which was deplorable manners. Paul smiled at her again and admired her new cap as a penance, but it was really Sallie and the children that he had been thinking of. To a Creole, the native-born French of Louisiana, the family was the most important thing in life. It was what a man worked for, built up his land for, sweated over the planting and the cutting of the cane for. Paul's children represented the third generation of Louisiana DuMontaignes, and the second to be born at Belle Marie.

Eight-year-old Emilie, the "baby," delved with her spoon into her gumbo, deftly pushing the okra to the edges of the bowl, and retrieved a fat shrimp. She had a round, angelic face framed by a cloud of dark brown curls. "There are new kittens," she announced through a mouthful of shrimp, earning an awful glare from Mammy Rachel, five feet four inches and one hundred twenty pounds of iron-handed authority, who stood with arms folded behind Emilie's chair.

"Miss Emilie, you don't talk with your mouth full."

Eating with the grown-ups was a treat, reserved for occasions when there was no company. Emilie looked repentant.

"This is excellent gumbo," Sallie said, tasting her own. "You tell Meeow that, Testut."

"Yes, ma'am." The butler poured wine into Paul's glass and allowed him to taste it. Meeow *knew* the gumbo was good, but she had her pride, and she liked to hear it from Miss Sallie. Meeow had had another name once, but she had been Meeow ever since Lucien, then two years old, had named her for the throng of cats that always followed her. There were never less than eight or nine of them, not counting kittens.

"Whose kittens this time?" Emilie's brother Denis inquired. Denis was twenty, shorter and more solid than his father, with a pleasant, likeable face.

"Angelica's," Emilie said. "She had 'em in the soup strainer."

"Ugh!" Emilie's eldest sister, Hollis, made a face and put her spoon down. "Mama, really—"

"Well, she washed it," Emilie said.

"That'll do," Mammy Rachel said firmly. "Havin' kittens ain't a subject for table talk."

"Since your sensibilities are affected, Hollis," Paul said gravely, "I'll see that Meeow gets a new soup strainer."

Denis caught his father's eye and grinned. Family dinners always amused him, and Hollis was about as delicate as an anvil.

Only two members were missing: Lucien, in France, and Felicie, who was seventeen and in the Ursuline convent school in New Orleans, where the good sisters were, as Sallie said, "attempting to turn her into a lady, if at all possible."

Paul's gaze lingered on his wife with mingled affection and puzzlement. Sallie's trim figure and heart-shaped face were as beautiful as they had been when he had married her, and at thirty-nine there was still no gray in her golden hair. But some distance, indefinable and troubling, had grown up between Paul and his wife, and he knew, without understanding why, that Sallie was not happy, and that the distance was now so great that neither knew how to bridge it.

But tonight Paul could look with relief at Hollis, their eldest daughter. Hollis had her mother's gold hair in an even paler shade, like corn silk, gray-green eyes, and a face that was a combination of Sallie's features and Paul's fine-boned, slightly aquiline countenance. She had left her gumbo nearly untouched and was daintily toying with a slice of roast in the manner fashionable among young ladies, but she looked serene and pleased with life. Hollis was six months widowed and had only recently stopped wearing her blacks for the less somber lavender of half-mourning. There were plenty of old tabbies who would say it was far too soon for that, but Paul had hated to see his beautiful daughter in that crow's clothing, and Sallie had championed Hollis's hatred of her black gowns, saying that since she had only been married to poor Julien Tourneau for three months before he had died of a fever, six months in black was quite enough.

Julien had been ill by the time they had come back from their wedding trip. Since Hollis was only nineteen, she had come home to Belle Marie, which was, she said plainly, greatly better than living with old Madame Tourneau, who had already decided that Hollis's heart was, or should be, in the grave with her husband. Paul had supported Hollis's return to Belle Marie. She had been the belle of New Orleans before her marriage, and it wasn't natural that she should immure herself forever in widowhood.

It would be fine to have them all at home, Paul thought with satisfaction. Felicie was due to leave the convent school in June. Whatever deportment and fashionable accomplishment the nuns had been able to pound into Felicie was either there now or it never would be. The good sisters would no doubt agree that Sallie would need her more than they this summer.

Paul coughed gently to gather his family's attention. Then he nodded at Sallie and said, "My dear, I have an announcement to make."

Sallie laid her fork down. It would be pleasant if Paul would tell her things before he "announced" them.

"I have been asked—by several men who know about these matters—to run for Congress as representative from the First District."

Tante Doudouce squeaked in surprise.

"And I assume," Sallie said carefully, "that you have already decided."

"Of course. I would not have mentioned it otherwise."

Sallie opened her mouth, closed it again, and appeared to be mentally biting her tongue.

"You see, Denis," Paul proceeded to explain to the only other male at the table, "the northern railroads have begun to draw off some of our shipping—New Orleans shipping. Not so very much just yet, but there is a fear in some circles that the percentage will increase. New Orleans depends on the river traffic, and if New Orleans suffers, so will we and all the other landholders. Roman Prevost, for instance, is one of the planters who has approached me. In fact, I suspect the Democrats delegated him to do just that, since we are friends. Neither Belle Marie nor Roman's Alouette will get as good a price for their sugar in a failing port. New Orleans *must* be able to continue to attract business."

"Well, I don't see what you can do about it," Hollis said.

"Let us just say that the time for governmental reform is now," Paul said.

Denis grinned. "You are probably the only honest man they could find. Louisiana's notorious," he explained. Hollis never paid any attention to politics. "A reputation for the most corrupt government in the country won't attract Yankee shipping."

"Mmmm." Hollis let Testut remove her plate and replace it with a dish of cream and pralines. "I suppose now no one will talk about anything but politics, and all the men will smoke cigars in the library whenever there's a party."

"No doubt," Sallie said tartly. "I expect it will take a great many cigars to produce a government capable of reforming Louisiana overnight."

"Hardly overnight. But I think I had better run. The Whigs have put up Gilbert Becquerel."

Sallie's fork clattered on her empty plate, and she folded her hands in her lap as Testut set her dessert in front of her. Mammy Rachel watched her with a thoughtful eye while Paul continued.

"Becquerel's a banker. He has money, and someone with money is needed to counter him. I cannot in good conscience let Becquerel run without opposing him. He is not reliable, nor does he have the best interests of Louisiana at heart. If we want reform, we can't have Becquerel in Washington."

"Washington?" Bored, Emilie had been listening with only half an ear, but she knew the significance of that statement. "Leave Belle Marie?" Emilie could find no reason in her young mind why *anyone* would want to leave Belle Marie. It was a kingdom in itself. "And go to Washington without *me*?" she

wailed. Papa and Belle Marie, always inseparable, were essential to Emilie's world.

"I wouldn't be gone all year. Congress only sits from December to March."

"What does it do the rest of the time?" Emilie wasn't sure what Congress was or why it sat anywhere.

"Lies to its constituents," Denis said irreverently. "Not Papa, of course."

"Certainly not," Paul said. "That's why we don't want Gilbert Becquerel. Sallie, what *is* the matter with you?"

Sallie glared at him. "Let us just say I am surprised."

Paul couldn't think of a satisfactory response to that, so he turned back to Emilie. "And pretty soon you'll be old enough to go to school in New Orleans, like your sisters."

Emilie looked less than enthralled. "Do I have to?"

"You have to learn to act like a lady," Hollis said.

"Well, *you* went to school, and I don't think *you* do," Emilie said. "I saw you kissing—"

"Emilie!" Hollis, Sallie, and Mammy Rachel spoke with one voice.

"Can I take Mimsie with me?" Mimsie was Mammy Rachel's granddaughter ·and in training to be Emilie's maid.

"Yes, certainly," her father said. "And pretty soon there'll be another friend at Belle Marie for you and your sisters. I've had a letter from my old friend Jules Scarron in France. I haven't seen him since I was Lucien's age, but he was a dear friend then, and he still is. I am afraid that he is dying, and he has asked me to look after his daughter, Adele."

Emilie looked interested, and Tante Doudouce rabbity and sympathetic.

"Of course, I have written to say that she must come to us," Paul said. "Lucien will escort her."

"Of course," Sallie murmured. She had known about Adele; as a woman, Paul had considered that to be her concern. But running for office, and against Gilbert Becquerel, of all men! Paul had not seen fit to mention *that* to her until just now. Really, Paul treated her as if she were five years old. It would serve him right if there were a scandal.

Paul, oblivious to his wife's rebellious mood, took an appreciative bite of Meeow's pralines and inquired of his wife what she had been doing today.

"Painting," Sallie said shortly. She had also, of course, been seeing to the running of a thirty-room house with an indoor staff of twenty, but Paul knew that. Her painting was her escape from the thousand daily crises invariably brought to the mistress's attention. "A study of some of the field hands putting in the seed cane," she added with a touch of defiance.

Paul looked exasperated. He did not consider the field hands a suitable subject for a lady's painting and had said so before. He opened his mouth to say so again, but changed his mind. The dinner hour was a time of family togetherness. He could scold Sallie later.

Sallie returned to her dessert with a tight knot in her stomach. She and Paul would never see eye to eye, she thought. The longer she was married to him, the more Sallie wondered what Paul had wanted with her. He was a scholarly soul, and the Lord knew she wasn't. When Paul had first courted her, he had been charmed by her vivacity. Later he had seen it as childishness. *Maybe neither one of us knew what we were doing*, Sallie thought.

Sallie was a planter's daughter from Charleston, South Carolina, and there were times when she thought that New Orleans was on a different planet. She had been sixteen when she married Paul, attracted by his dark good looks, his serious manner—which had made him seem so much more grown up than the Charleston boys she knew—and his obvious love for her.

But in New Orleans Creole society, she had felt a stranger. Not that there weren't Americans in New Orleans, and if they had money, the Creoles were only too happy to marry their daughters to them. But Paul DuMontaigne was a Creole with money, and the grandes dames of New Orleans had seen no reason why he should have bestowed it upon an American bride instead of one of their own worthy daughters. Sallie hadn't been married very long when several disappointed ladies had managed to whisper in her ear that her husband had a mistress—a quadroon mistress, one of the partly black who made up the demimonde of New Orleans. That was common enough here, and the Creole wives simply pretended not to notice since there wasn't anything they could do about it, but Charleston-born Sallie had been horrified and hurt and bewildered. *Well, it was all such a long time ago*, she thought now, startled that the memory could still stab her so sharply. The woman had died years ago.

If Paul went to Washington, Sallie would happily go with him. There would be people of her own kind there, she thought wistfully. But Gilbert Becquerel—of all people to be running against!

Sallie felt faint, as if her stays were too tight across her midsection. Gilbert Becquerel. She had only to close her eyes to conjure up a picture of a handsome, florid face and a ready smile. Too ready. A philanderer's smile. *I should know,* she thought, for the outlet that she had found for her loneliness and longing to be loved without qualifications had been Gilbert Becquerel. He had been Sallie's lover for over twenty years, and she was horribly certain that Denis was his child. No one else knew or even suspected, except Mammy Rachel, who would never betray Sallie, no matter what Mammy thought of her conduct, and Mammy thought a great deal and had said it all.

Now Gilbert and Paul were going to be running against each other. The reasonable thing to do in a situation like this would be to go to bed with a sick headache and stay there, Sallie thought, nearly driven to laughter in spite of herself. What a pickle! But if Gilbert thought she would help him an inch in this campaign, he was wrong. Only one of them could go to Washington, and it was going to be Sallie.

Hollis watched a series of odd expressions flit across her mother's face, but she wasn't interested enough to speculate. She stared thoughtfully into the bowl of hothouse lilies on the table and tried to decide whether to go to Washington. Hollis had been driven almost mad by the restrictions placed on unmarried girls. She had been nearly chaperoned to death, never allowed to go anywhere without Papa, or one of her brothers, or with Mammy beside her like a bantamweight bodyguard, her white kerchief starched within an inch of its life and her black face set in an expression of unrelenting rectitude. Hollis had only married Julien Tourneau because she didn't think she could stand the restrictions any longer. When Julien had obligingly died of a fever, she had discovered that widowhood was even better than being married. The first months were ghastly, of course, since everyone had expected her to sit around weeping all day, and Hollis's ethereal blond beauty did not fare well in black. But now things were looking up.

Better yet, no one could expect her to be a virgin. Considering all the other ways in which God had seen fit to inconvenience women, Hollis thought it a blessing that one's maidenhead did not grow back from disuse. She didn't intend to remain a widow always, but she did intend to have some fun first.

Hollis had discovered that men were fun—and even easier to wind around her finger if she could actually get into bed with them instead of having just to giggle and flirt. Getting into bed was fun too, and Hollis wasn't going to tie herself to a husband until she found someone who was better at lovemaking than Julien had been. Someone like Roman Prevost, for instance, who was forty-five and had an invalid wife and so had learned interesting things from the half-black sirens on Rampart Street. She would have to give up Roman if she went to Washington, she thought, but Washington would be full of willing men with power, who made things happen. Hollis smiled silently into the lilies. Washington would be fun.

Paul and Denis, engrossed in talk of the election and of the price that André Peyraud, Paul's factor, could get for the sugar this year, didn't notice the women's silent musings, and Emilie was engaged in hiding part of her dessert in her pinafore to take to Mimsie, who didn't get nearly as good things to eat in the quarters dining room. As they rose from the table, Paul caught Sallie by the hand and waited for the family to leave the room.

"My dear, I *have* told you before that I don't like your painting the darkies. Especially not the field hands! You shouldn't even be down there!"

"I'm down there quick enough when one of them takes sick!" Sallie snapped. "And I don't notice your minding then!"

"That's another matter entirely."

"Oh, it is not! If I can doctor them, I can paint them."

"Sallie, you must realize—probably you *don't* realize, it isn't something a lady should concern herself with—but some of those field Negroes are very wild. They don't have the same ways our house folk do. It isn't a good idea to go too freely among them."

Sallie drew herself up to her full height, a wrathful, slim-waisted figure in jonquil-yellow silk spread over bell-shaped crinolines. Her blue eyes were furious, and her gold hair, normally parted into smooth bands, seemed to leap out from under her lace cap and frame her face in an aureole of wispy curls that quivered in sympathetic rage. "*Mister* DuMontaigne! I have been the mistress of this household for twenty-three years! If I do not know now which of our people can be trusted and have enough sense to protect myself, then I wonder that you let me out without a keeper. I am not a *child*!" She spun on her heel and stormed through the door, pausing only long enough in the doorway to add, "And if I were a *man*, you would like my paintings very well!"

Paul stood looking after her a moment, wondering what on earth that had to do with anything. She *wasn't* a man. And her outburst of temper just went to show that women lacked judgment.

Tante Doudouce, who had left with the children, popped in again in search of her missal for evening prayers. Seeing Paul's expression, she fluttered agitatedly out again, trailing a little shower of holy pictures across the carpet. Paul stalked away to the solace of his library. There was no point in talking further to Sallie until she came around. She never called him *Mister* DuMontaigne unless she was in a temper.

A steamboat whistle hooted through the evening air. Running feet pattered in the carriage drive as the familiar cry of "Steeeeeeamboat comin'!" floated up from the levee. Emilie passed her father in the hall at a dead run and disappeared into the dusk. Emilie never missed a steamboat. There was shouting and laughter from the garden as the household turned out to see the boat tie up at Belle Marie. One of the quarters children had been stationed on the levee to flag it down to take on the last of this year's sugar crop, bound for New Orleans warehouses.

For a moment Paul was tempted to join them, but he had no wish to go and be glared at by Sallie. He pushed open the door to his study and startled a small Nergo child who sat cross-legged on the floor by the bookcases, a huge tome in her lap.

"Mimsie! What are you doing here?"

Mimsie climbed out from under the book, guilt-stricken, and tried to make a curtsy to Paul and heave the book back in the shelf simultaneously. She hung her head. "I been readin'," she said penitently.

Paul sighed. The child had been given lessons along with her young mistress in hope that it would encourage more than a passing interest in learning in Emilie. Unfortunately the result had been that now Mimsie would risk any punishment that Mammy Rachel could devise for the privilege of five minutes alone with a book. Paul knew that he ought to report this latest breach to her grandmother, who would do her best to smack such presumption out of her, but he couldn't make himself do it. Anyone with as great a love of books as Mimsie's was in some way a kindred spirit.

Paul made as stern a face as he could manage. "You're allowed to read, Mimsie, but you're not to take my books without asking. Will you promise not to do it again?"

"Yessir!" Mimsie bobbed her head, the half-dozen braids on her small scalp standing out stiffly, like the arms of a starfish.

"All right, then. Miss Emilie's on her way to the levee, so you go and find her."

"I get her shawl," Mimsie said. "Granny'll be mad as fire, I let her out without that." She scampered from the room, lifting her calico skirts and apron in another curtsy to Paul as she passed.

Paul picked up the book that she had tried to poke back into its slot, and raised his eyebrows. *Life of Thomas Jefferson*. Good heavens.

Outside, the hubbub in the garden proclaimed that the boat had docked. Sallie's voice, conversing with the captain, floated through the open window. Paul sat down at his secretary, sighed, and wished that he understood his wife. He put on his spectacles and pulled a calendar toward him. Lucien would be home soon, with poor, bereaved Adele Scarron. They must do what they could for the girl. France had been good for Lucien, judging by his sober letters home and Uncle Thierry's reports. Lucien had spent a good deal of money, but one must, to keep up with society, and Paul had wished only to curb his son's wilder side and his taste for the wrong sort of woman. Paul would have encouraged an arrangement with one of the cultured quadroon girls who were trained from birth to be gentlemen's mistresses. He had drawn the line at the uneducated and unwashed Michelet trollops on Bayou Rouge.

Matters were different in his day, Paul thought, suddenly feeling old. Paul himself had had a quadroon mistress, and he had established his Justine in one of the little white houses on Rampart Street before he had fallen in love with Sallie Hollis in Charleston. It would have been cruel to abandon Justine, and it was unfortunate that some spiteful old tabbies had seen fit to inform Sallie of that arrangement, but it in no way lessened his love for Sallie. So Paul had neatly kept his white family in one compartment of his heart and his half-black one in another. He had given Justine a silver tea set when she had presented him with a daughter. It was the way that things were done and would certainly be a suitable arrangement for Lucien.

He would see a great change in Lucien now, Paul thought. Lucien would be steadier, more responsible, and Sallie could relax. She had known nothing about the Michelet girls, but had certainly known about the duels. In Paul's day, a matter of honor was considered settled when one swordsman had drawn first blood. Now the young fools fought to the death, and with pistols. The Americans had begun that, but the Creole sons had been quick enough to follow. And Lucien, with the supreme, misguided confidence of the young, appeared to believe that he would never die. His parents had been afraid that he wouldn't live long enough to have better sense.

The library door swung open, and Paul raised his head warily as

Sallie popped through. Her stormy mood appeared to have vanished. "You look in a better frame of mind," he ventured.

"Well, you know I don't stay mad for very long," she said frankly, "and I haven't the heart to be, just now. I've had a letter from Barret Forbes." She flourished it, and her blue eyes gleamed. "The captain of the *Sultana* was kind enough to bring it. Barret is coming in March for business in the city, and he'll be here at least a month!"

Barret Forbes was a friend from Sallie's childhood. That he had never been one of Sallie's beaux made him an even better friend now. He would have all the news from home, important and frivolous alike. Sallie nearly danced with pleasure.

"Well, that will make a houseful." Paul liked Barret Forbes. "Plan as many parties as you like, but don't start trying to marry the poor man off again."

"Oh, I've given up on Barret," Sallie said cheerfully, "unless he should take to Adele Scarron—we simply must find her a husband. But I do want new clothes if Barret's coming, I'm vain enough for that." She pirouetted happily. "And there's Felicie to dress now that she's coming out, and I'll buy some lightweight black materials to have some things made up for Miss Scarron. With no mother to dress her, there's no telling what they'll have put that poor child in."

She danced out again, leaving Paul to bless God for Barret Forbes and Jules Scarron's orphan.

"Since neither gentleman wishes to apologize"—the comte De St. Jean hadn't bothered to ask Lucien, whom he knew very well—"you will walk ten paces, stop, and turn. When my colleague here"—he nodded at Reave's second, a nervous-looking young ensign—"raises his hand, I will drop my handkerchief. You may fire when it touches the ground."

The combatants signified their understanding while a doctor stood stolidly with his black bag in hand.

". . . eight . . . nine . . . ten!"

Lucien's eyes glittered evilly, and the Englishman, who was beginning to grow sober, felt his hands start to sweat. The handkerchief fluttered, drifting lightly to the dead grass.

Two shots cracked together, and Reave dropped. Lucien lowered his pistol and waved a hand at the groom who held his horse. The doctor and the two seconds were bent over Reave. Lucien put his foot in the stirrup.

"Damn you, Lucien, don't you want to know if he's dead?" the comte shouted.

"Not particularly." He swung himself into the saddle.

"Be still," the comte grunted as the doctor tightened a bandage about Reave's shoulder. The Englishman's face was gray and damp. "You're lucky DuMontaigne had a hangover."

II

Sleeping

Water

THE PRIEST'S VOICE went on endlessly, a doleful, droning cadence against the spatter of rain. Therese D'Aubert fidgeted, her fingers clenching and unclenching restlessly inside her sodden muff. They had said a seemingly endless mass for the old man's soul in the church not an hour since. It seemed unnecessary for the priest to say it all again here. She wiggled her fingers into the opening of her reticule, tucked inside the muff, and touched the letter. It was still there. Ever since it had come from America, she had had an irrational fear that it would somehow vanish.

A hand touched her arm, and she realized that the priest's voice had ceased and that he was standing at her shoulder. She crossed herself hastily. "I'm sorry, Father Rosière, I wasn't attending. I was thinking of poor Adele."

"That's all right, my child. We must give comfort to the living as well, and you have had a great burden these past weeks. Is Mademoiselle Scarron no better?"

"No, I think not." She sniffled. The rain was giving her a cold.

"It is a great scourge, the scarlet fever. Be hopeful. Your young cousin may recover."

"I pray so," Therese said piously.

"It is fortunate that you can care for her so faithfully."

"Yes. I must go to her now." Her feet were wet and felt like ice.

"*Le bon Dieu* bless you," the priest called after her.

Le bon Dieu had blessed her when he gave her scarlet fever as a child and sent it to Adele now, Therese thought as she hurried down the muddy path from the churchyard. Her fingers touched

17

the letter again. Here was her payment for all the years as a poor
relation in Jules Scarron's household, the years of shabby dresses,
hand-me-downs from Adele, of insolence from the servants, of
sitting unnoticed at parties among the dowagers and village
spinsters, when she was only twenty-six. Here was her ticket to
America, and if she were careful and clever, she need never be
poor again.

The rain was pelting down as Therese turned off the cobble-
stoned street into the garden gate. Inside she flung her sopping
scarf and worn cloak onto the coat rack and hurried up the steep
stairs to her room. She unlocked the drawer of her desk and
pushed the letter inside. She couldn't carry it about in the house,
but she had been afraid to leave it behind her, even for a few
hours. It was addressed to Jules Scarron, from his rich friend in
America, inviting Adele to New Orleans to live. But Jules Scarron
was dead. And Adele was dying.

Therese locked the drawer again and dropped the key down the
front of her bodice as she descended the stairs. In the bedroom on
the floor below, she nodded to the nurse who sat by Adele's bed.

"Go and rest. I will sit with her."

The nurse lifted a tray of untouched broth and rustled out.

"Papa?" Adele whispered. Her young face was flushed scarlet,
and her head turned feebly on the pillow.

Therese smoothed a cool hand over her forehead. "Gone to
God, with our prayers."

"I should have been there."

"You aren't strong enough." Therese lifted the girl carefully,
fluffed the pillows behind her, then eased her down. "You must
rest. Do you want a drink?"

"Yes, please."

Therese lifted Adele's thin shoulders again and held the glass
for her. What conscience she possessed was soothed by these
attentions.

The nurse scratched at the door and beckoned. Therese laid
Adele down again and tucked the comforter about her.

"There is a visitor," the nurse whispered. "Asking for
Mademoiselle Scarron." She handed Therese a card.

"What did you tell him?"

"Nothing," the nurse said primly. "It is not for me to discuss
Mademoiselle Scarron's health with strangers."

Therese let her breath out. She slipped the card into her pocket.
"I will see him. Stay here."

The nurse settled herself in the chair. She had tended enough of

these cases in the last month to know when there was nothing
more to do but pray to God for a departing soul.

Therese ran up the stairs to her room again and unbuttoned the
bodice of her gown with flying fingers. She slipped on one of
Adele's best black dresses, filched from her wardrobe for an
emergency such as this, and smoothed her hair in the mirror. She
went down the stairs again cautiously. The servants had been
given the day off to light a candle for their late master, but one of
them might come home early. She met no one. At the parlor door
Therese took a deep breath and straightened her back.

"Monsieur DuMontaigne."

Lucien turned from moodily inspecting the dying fire and
bowed.

"I am Adele Scarron. You are kind to come."

Lucien's eyes rested on the black silk. "Your father?"

"We buried him this morning," Therese whispered. "Scarlet
fever."

"My dear Mademoiselle Scarron—" Lucien pulled a chair
forward gallantly for her.

"I had it as a child," Therese said. "A mild case. I was
fortunate. But poor Papa . . . And you must go straight back to
Paris when you leave here, Monsieur DuMontaigne. Don't stop to
dine in the village." She smiled at him shyly. "I am afraid I must
not feed you here either, but I would rather you went hungry than
chance contagion. My poor cousin is ill upstairs."

She lowered her eyes, aware that Lucien DuMontaigne was
studying her face. *A pretty enough girl,* he thought. Her dark hair
was combed into a neat plain knot, and there was something about
her eyes, light brown with flecks of gold in the iris, that suggested
less naiveté than he would have expected from a country scholar's
daughter. Her nose and mouth were a trifle thin, and she looked a
few years older than twenty, but he supposed black didn't suit her
very well.

"Did your father speak to you of a letter from my father?"

Therese nodded. "He told me that I am to go to America."

"Good. Then I don't need to explain all that." Lucien looked
relieved.

"I am grateful for your father's kindness," Therese said. "You
see, Monsieur DuMontaigne, my inheritance will not be enough
for me to live comfortably." Her voice quavered. "And I am so
very alone."

"Now, Mademoiselle Scarron, you mustn't cry. Papa will see
that you are looked after, and you won't be alone if you live at

Belle Marie, I can tell you that." Blast the woman, she was going
to start weeping. He looked around frantically for something of
more use than the scrap of black-bordered lace she had wadded in
her hand, and then reluctantly handed her his own handkerchief.

"I haven't booked passage yet, but we can sail as soon as you
can be packed."

Therese pressed her handkerchief to her eyes. "You are very
kind. Your father can be no greater comfort to me than you are
being, Monsieur DuMontaigne." She lowered her handkerchief
and regarded him gravely. "But I cannot leave Therese."

"Who's Therese?"

"My cousin, Monsieur DuMontaigne, as I told you. She is
dying."

"I thought you had no kin." Where had this cousin popped up
from? Lucien was beginning to be exasperated.

"Therese D'Aubert. A very distant cousin, on my mother's
side, and my companion. She took the fever nursing my father. I
cannot abandon her."

"I am sure that is very commendable of you."

Therese was beginning to feel that it was. Dear Adele wasn't
even going to leave her what money she had inherited from old
Jules. She had made out a will giving it to the church for their
beggarly orphan brats. "They are so hungry all the time," she had
said, as if this excused her. "They need it, Therese, while you
may find a good post without trouble."

"It will not be long," Therese said now to Lucien. "Do return
to Paris, Monsieur DuMontaigne, and I will join you within the
week, I fear."

When he had gone, she clasped her hands and sat for a long
time in front of the fire, until the thudding under her ribs subsided.
That had not been so difficult after all, and meeting Lucien
DuMontaigne here had been the most dangerous deception she
had to face. And with scarlet fever in the village, he wasn't likely
to come back.

*"Per istam sanctam unctionem et suam piissimam misericor-
diam, indulgeat tibi Dominus . . ."* By this holy unction and His
own most gracious mercy, may the Lord pardon you whatever sin
you have committed. . . .

"Amen." Adele's whisper was so faint that it could barely be
heard. Therese and the nurse and the household staff clutched their
beads as the priest intoned the final absolution. Therese felt cold.
It was oddly like watching herself die. Tomorrow she would bury

her life as Therese D'Aubert along with the body of Adele Scarron.

"Ego sum resurrectio et vita . . ." I am the resurrection and the life: he that believeth in Me, although he be dead, shall live; and every one that liveth, and believeth in Me, shall not die forever.

It was still raining. The dark, turned earth and half-wilted flowers of Jules Scarron's grave were sodden with it. A new grave lay open beside his.

"Requiem aeternam dona ei, Domine." Eternal rest grant unto her, O Lord.

The earth fell on the coffin with wet thuds, somehow more final than the light spatter of dirt on a dry day. Therese D'Aubert's gloved fingers were clenched around the letter, *her* letter now. She stayed only a moment at the graveside, and the lawyer regarded her set face with sympathy.

"You must not grieve, my dear."

"I assure you, I do not."

The lawyer sighed. "Nor must you be bitter. She did as her conscience bade her."

Therese gave him a level look. "As she said, I can always find a good post. Indeed, I believe I have. Good day to you." She turned away down the hill with the Scarron servants.

"And where will *you* go?" The housekeeper didn't even bother to call her Mademoiselle now.

"I have a post waiting," Therese said shortly.

The housekeeper sniffed. Mademoiselle D'Aubert had too many airs and graces for a poor relation.

"And now if you will excuse me," Therese said, eager for the woman to leave, "I have my things to pack. The lawyers will take possession of the house tomorrow."

When the servants had gone, carrying their own luggage with them, Therese left her cape and bonnet on the coat rack and flew up the stairs. In Adele's sitting room she forced the lock of the top dresser drawer. There were a few louis inside the drawer and she scooped them up. The jewel box was locked, but Therese had a key which she had neglected to give to the lawyers. She stood over the box a moment, thinking quickly. They would make trouble if she took anything very valuable, but the smaller pieces would not be named in the will: a small ring with a ruby, a locket with topazes, a few gold bracelets. She thrust those into her pocket with the money. In the parlor she added a small cloisonné vase and a silver snuffbox, a gold picture frame with a miniature of Jules Scarron, and a gold letter opener. There was some money in the secretary in the library, and she took most of it, leaving a few francs for effect. She mustn't take enough to put suspicions into some lawyer's head. She went back to the parlor and rearranged the pieces in the glass-fronted cabinet to fill the space where the cloisonné vase had been.

Therese ran back upstairs and pushed the things into the corners of her trunk, neatly packed with Adele's dresses. The lawyer himself had bid her take those, as being unsuitable for orphans. Therese tugged the trunk into the hall with her bandboxes to await the hired chaise, and put on her bonnet. Adele's bonnet. She tied the black ribbons under her chin and studied her face in the mirror. She smiled coquettishly, tilted her head. She might pass for twenty. . . .

Wheels rattled on the cobblestones. Therese D'Aubert climbed into the chaise, and in Paris Adele Scarron alighted.

"The cane's nearly in," Denis said with satisfaction. "We're in good time this year." The February sun filtered through the low-hanging mist, giving a faint golden glow to the newly turned earth. The black hands that followed the plow worked quickly, dropping the lengths of seed cane into the furrows with the rhythm of long practice. This was the easiest time of year, after the backbreaking work of cutting the old cane and the round-the-clock shifts of the grinding: the boiling down of the liquid secured from the crushed cane for sugar. Master and slave alike were hollow-eyed until the last of the vats was emptied.

Denis leaned his arms on his horse's withers, watching the new cane go in. "If I can sweeten André Peyraud into a good advance, we should do pretty well this year." By custom the factors in New Orleans advanced working money to their planter clients for a percentage of the profit on the next year's cane. Denis grinned at his father. "I must remember to tell Lucien what kind of whiskey André likes."

Paul chuckled. "You have the makings of a successful businessman."

"Well, I want to talk business today, Papa. If you're going to win this campaign, you're going to have to spend time on it, and that means we'll have to hire a new overseer."

"I suppose you're right." The overseer long in Paul's employ had died some months ago. "I've been putting it off," he admitted. "To tell the truth, I've been enjoying doing the work myself." He too leaned forward in his saddle, watching the cane go into the earth. New shoots would come up from each joint of the buried stalks, turning the black fields as green as grass. The earth was rich here, and the only danger was that the Mississippi, which had brought this alluvial wealth, would come again in storm time and flood it. Everywhere the packed earth of the levees held the river back. "You *are* right. Ask André to start looking." He shaded his eyes against the sun, which slanted through the bare cottonwoods along the edge of the cane field. "Hey! Daniel!"

One of the stooping figures in the cane field straightened up. Seeing Paul, he laid down his sack of cane and trotted over.

"Yes, sir, Mister Paul?"

"Daniel, I'm going to have to start looking for an overseer. I won't be able to come out every day from now on, but it may take some time to find a good man, so I'm counting on you to keep things running smoothly."

"Yes, sir, I'll do that." Daniel was a broad-shouldered man with the most even temper on the plantation and a capacity for tireless labor, but he knew his limitations. "Those darkies, they'll heed me for a while, Mister Paul, but someone bound to make trouble if you don't put a white man out here."

"Well, you see that they don't, Daniel, and you knock some heads together if you need to. But Mister Lucien's coming home, so you'll still have one of the family to take orders from."

"Yes, sir." Daniel looked troubled. "How 'bout Mister Denis, sir?"

Paul shook his head. "Lucien needs to learn the ropes. And I need Mister Denis in New Orleans. You'll do fine, Daniel."

"Yes, sir, Mister Paul, thank you," Daniel said, but he frowned as Paul and Denis reined their horses around. Mister Lucien wasn't gonna like settin' on a horse in the sun, watching the cane grow. Mister Lucien would be under a tree somewhere with a flask in his hand or chasing women who ought to be tendin' to their work, unless he had changed mightily since he went to France.

"Let's go back the long way," Denis said.

Paul nodded. He wouldn't be free to ride over his beloved land much longer. They turned away from the cane fields and into the uncultivated swampland, where their path became only a trail over the ridge of high ground that wound beside the lower reaches of Bayou Rouge. Along the banks grew cottonwood, willow, and the towering, gnarled cypresses.

Innumerable waterways, home to the wild things that had been here long before man, snaked through the marshland, changing with each flood season. If a man were willing to sit still and watch, he would see opposum, raccoon, rabbit, deer, or the quick, graceful flash of a river otter sliding into the water. Alligators, their snouts barely above the surface, searched at the water's edge for the unwary. Even this early in the year the air vibrated with the hum of insects—a thin chorus compared to the heavy, droning buzz of summer. A fishing spider, perched midstream on a water-lettuce leaf, waited for a noonday meal, and an iridescent cloud of newly hatched dragonflies zoomed overhead.

The bayou was a compromise between land and water, river and swamp. The current moved sluggishly. All day it might flow imperceptibly eastward toward Lac Fidele and, in the evening, moved by the mysterious ebb and flow of the great Mississippi delta, reverse its course seaward.

The trees had not yet begun to leaf out and the bayou looked bare and sparse, but Paul and Denis took pleasure in it. Vistas that would be hidden when the trees leafed out were open now, and it was as if one could see into the revealed heart of the swamp. From the branches above hung the ghostly gray-green curtains of Spanish moss, and in the shallows a solitary white egret perched on a log, its image doubled in the dark water below.

A faint ripple caught the egret's eye. It stabbed suddenly at the water and hopped back to its log with a young bluegill in its beak. It swallowed the fish with a quick gulp and a wriggle of its long neck, and then launched itself into sudden, startled flight as the crack of a gunshot broke the stillness.

"Damn!" Paul wheeled his horse around, looking for the marksman, but the thick tangle of leafless vine along the bayou betrayed no one. The egret flapped away overhead. "I won't have poaching on my land! Not just to put an egret plume in some woman's bonnet. Who was that, Denis?"

"At a guess, Rafe Michelet," Denis said, "but he knows better than to get caught."

"That thieving clan," Paul said, exasperated. The Michelets were a large, sprawling family headed by old Victorien Michelet, who had a slatternly wife and four children who were as shiftless as their father, and a brood of grandchildren, some of whom had probably been fathered incestuously. The Michelets had been on Bayou Rouge as long as the DuMontaignes had been at Belle Marie.

"You tell Rafe Michelet to watch where he poaches, or someone may make a mistake and shoot *him*," Paul snapped.

"If anyone shoots Rafe Michelet, it won't be a mistake," Denis said, "but I'll tell him." He doubted that he needed to. Rafe was probably still within hearing distance, lying low in the thick growth of Virginia creeper across the bayou.

A half mile farther on, a second path intersected the one that ran beside the bayou. They turned their horses onto that, riding up to higher ground, where the cut stalks of last year's corn made a gold stubble across the land. When the seed cane was in, the slaves would plant new corn here to feed themselves and the farm animals through the winter.

Paul and Denis rode by the cornfields and turned into the avenue of oaks that formed the back door to Belle Marie.

They skirted the house and drew rein in the carriage drive that led to the veranda. Between the front of the house and the river were formal gardens, laid out by Paul's grandfather and lovingly added to by his father, Paul himself, and Sallie. Mangoes, papayas, and bananas grew in profusion in the hothouses, shaded by orange trees and banks of roses and azaleas. In a shaded nook was Emilie's favorite haunt, a rock garden set about with fern, where the stones made a child-size table and chairs for her and her dolls.

She was out and about now, Paul noted, catching sight of a flicker of white pantalets and pinafore darting toward the rocks. From the speed with which she was moving, he surmised that she was hiding from Sallie and her lessons.

Denis watched her as he sang softly.

> *"In my father's garden*
> *the laurels are in flower,*
> *And all the birds in the world*
> *Come there to build their nests . . ."*

"You've always loved Belle Marie, haven't you?" Paul said abruptly.

Denis jerked his head up. The song trailed into silence. "We all do," he said carefully.

"How hard is it on you that Lucien is to have it?"

Hard enough. Lucien doesn't love it as I do. He couldn't say that. "My misfortune to be the younger." His father had an uncanny knack for reading his mind, Denis thought.

"It's bad for land to be split," Paul said. "But you'll have a full share of everything else. You and the girls will be wealthy."

Money wasn't Belle Marie. There wasn't another place on earth that Denis loved the way he loved Belle Marie. "I haven't been brooding about it, Papa, if that's what's worrying you." His square, snub-nosed face was determinedly cheerful, but Paul

wasn't sure that Denis was telling the truth. Denis, shorter and
more solid than his brother, had the look of a man who would
plant his feet on his home ground and stay there. Without Belle
Marie, he would be uprooted.

Denis slid off his horse. "I'm glad Lucien's coming home."
Better now than later. I mightn't be able to give it up later.
"Tomorrow I'll tell André to get the accounts for Lucien to go
over." Denis handed his reins to the small black boy who ran up to
take them, then strode toward the house. He was singing again,
but the light note had gone out of his voice.

"Mademoiselle Scarron, you are feeling better?"

"Yes. I am sorry to be such a trouble to you." *I am not Therese
D'Aubert, I am Adele Scarron, and it is my right to make a
nuisance of myself if I wish.* She shook away the old habit of
forced humility and dissemblance. Adele smiled at Lucien. "A
glass of wine to settle my stomach, perhaps, and I will be very
well."

She leaned back against the cushions on the chaise to display
her figure to its best advantage. Lucien DuMontaigne, she
thought, was handsome in a dark, reckless manner, but, more
important, his father was rich beyond Adele's imagining, if not
her desire. Lucien fetched a decanter from his own cabin and
poured her a glass of wine. She made a place for him to set it on
the little table beside the chaise, a vantage point from which he
could properly appreciate the curve of her breast and the
narrowness of her waist.

Adele patted the seat of the deck chair beside her. "Do join me,
Monsieur DuMontaigne. It would not cause a scandal, would it?
We are to be relatives of a sort, after all, are we not?"

"Certainly." Lucien poured himself a glass of wine. "And on
board ship, many things are more permissible." Miss Scarron
appeared to be flirting with him, and Lucien was more than
willing to alleviate his boredom with her. The only other
passengers were a bishop and two dyspeptic dowagers eating
peppermints, and Miss Scarron's trim figure and inviting smile
looked the more enticing by comparison.

"And what will you do when you return home, Monsieur
DuMontaigne?"

"Be thrown to the wolves, I rather think," Lucien said, "in the
form of my father's factor and some very dull account books."

"But one must take these matters in hand if one is to be a great landowner," Adele said, smiling at him teasingly. "Plainly you must find distraction from such tedium."

Lucien grinned. "My father doesn't often approve of my distractions."

"Are you so wicked, then? Perhaps you need a distraction to which your father could not take exception."

"If you mean the ladies, Mademoiselle Scarron, the only one my father wouldn't take exception to would be one with a ring on her finger, and that would be more boring still."

"For shame, Monsieur DuMontaigne." Adele laughed and lowered her lashes.

Lucien took her hand and kissed it. "But I am sure I could never be bored with so charming a . . . relative as yourself."

She withdrew her hand gently. "I shall find it very comforting to live among your family, Monsieur DuMontaigne, if they are as kind as you," she said, deliberately misunderstanding him. "And now I fear you must leave me and let me rest." The conversation was not going to her liking, but she had not played all her pieces yet.

Lucien bowed and picked up his hat. Adele watched him shrewdly as he left, and then curled herself up in the cushions to think. Now that the dreadful nausea had left her, she could set about making herself agreeable to Lucien DuMontaigne, but she would have to be careful how she did so. He had made it plain enough that he was not hanging out for a wife. But to be his mistress was not part of her scheme. Belle Marie had bred in Lucien the offhand confidence of one who has never been poor. Adele wanted Belle Marie.

Let him be bored a little longer with the bishop and the old ladies—then she would try again. A reckless nature was particularly vulnerable to boredom.

III

Monsieur

and

Madame

Becquerel

"YOU LOOK LIKE Felicie when she's given the nuns the slip."
Denis studied his mother's mischievous face, framed in a shirred
silk bonnet trimmed with lace and pink roses. It was tied under her
chin with a wide blue ribbon that set off her eyes.

"And just what do you know about that?" Sallie inquired
sternly. "You are not to help your sister misbehave, Denis."

Denis looked sheepish. "She had lunch with me the last time I
was in town. I rather think she wasn't supposed to, but I didn't
know it until afterward."

"Well, none of that today, mind. You can take me to see her
properly when we've finished our business." The impish look
returned to Sallie's eyes as she retrieved from her trunk a roll of
something wrapped in brown paper and tied up with a ribbon.
Denis thought that it looked just the size of a painting. He knew
what Mama did with her paintings, but he wasn't supposed to.

Sallie laid one gloved hand on his cheek and kissed him.
"When you've finished with André Peyraud, you can run along
and use your charms on the good sisters till I finish my shopping."

"You're sure you don't want my escort? The city's pretty lively
during Carnival."

"And just what masked rapscallion do you think could get
through Mammy's guard?" Sallie cast an affectionate glance at
Mammy Rachel, who was in a bedroom of their hotel suite,

29

shaking the lavender out of Sallie's shawls and walking shoes with vigorous disapproval. Mammy didn't hold with Carnival: It was much too free and French.

"You'd be terribly bored," Sallie said, "and then I shouldn't enjoy myself. I have dress goods to buy for Felicie and me and that Scarron child, and it will take all morning as it is."

She waved him on his way and picked up her reticule while Mammy slipped a shawl around her shoulders. They made their way from the hotel rooms on the third floor of the City Exchange, past the second-floor ballrooms, to the vestibule that opened onto St. Louis Street. Bidders were crowded around the auction block in the Rotunda, the central, domed chamber of the Exchange. A Negro woman in a coarse cotton shift stood stolidly while the slave dealer displayed her teeth and gums and then lifted her shift to show the rest of her. Mammy hurried Sallie out through the vestibule.

"You oughtn't come here on Saturdays. It's not fittin'."

"You know, I've never seen a slave auction. Not in all these years."

"Well, you got no idea. You got a good heart, Miss Sallie, but you got no idea."

"I suppose there are a lot of things I don't know about."

Mammy looked back at the girl on the block with sympathy, then glared at the roll under Sallie's arm as they turned out into St. Louis Street. "You know a sight too much about *some* things, if you ask me."

"Well, I *didn't* ask you."

"I'm gonna tell you anyway. I known you since your poor mama birthed you, and I ain't stupid. F'rinstance, I know you don't buy yard goods in N'Orleans. You order from France. What you want for Miss Adele is waitin' at the store already for you. Ain't gonna take all mornin' to pick it up."

"Very well, it isn't." Sallie walked briskly along the brick banquette and turned the corner into Royal. "When I've picked up the material, you're going to take it back to our rooms."

"No, I ain't."

"Yes, you are." Sallie spun around to face her. "We've had this fight before, Mammy. Don't start it again." She made an anguished little gesture with her hands. "Don't *you* ever get lonely?"

"Since my Jim died? That's been more'n thirty years. 'Course I get lonely. But I ain't found the man I thought was worth wastin' my time on, and you ain't either."

Sallie raised her brows. "Fine talk about the master."

"I ain't talkin' about Mister Paul and you know it."

Sallie set off down Royal again, her cheeks flaming. Mammy trotted after her toward the silk merchants, her white tignon starched and imposing. Despite her slight height, Mammy's basilisk stare cleared a way through the Carnival crowd in the streets. Sallie was her first charge, her best beloved, and Mammy couldn't find it in her to deny Sallie anything, even if what Sallie wanted was a no-account hand-kisser like Gilbert Becquerel. Mister Paul ought to know better, Mammy thought grimly. Mister Paul ought to get his head out of his books, where it had been for twenty-three years. She supposed, however, that it was going to stay there. Mammy glowered at a trio of lounging maskers in harlequin garb. They hastily made way on the banquette, and the women sailed by.

Denis, enjoying himself thoroughly, sipped a cup of dark coffee and chicory at a table at the Café des Refugés on Chartres Street and watched the holiday-makers. A disapproving Northerner once wrote of New Orleans, "They keep Sunday as we in Boston keep the Fourth of July." To a Creole there was nothing wrong with that. One should praise God joyously. On Mardi Gras, Fat Tuesday, which was the day before Ash Wednesday, there would be parades and mummery lasting far into the night, but already the Carnival was in full swing. The streets were full of young men dressed as Spanish cavaliers, Satan, and pirates, and a few as improbable Indians, with headdresses of scarlet and yellow feathers.

"Cordial, m'sieu?" The Café des Refugés was famous for its *petit gouave*, a cordial of its own recipe.

Denis shook his head, laid a coin on the table for the coffee, and sauntered toward the levee where André Peyraud kept his offices. The levee never ceased to fascinate Denis. It was crowded with departing and arriving passengers, sugar sacks, and baggage wagons; overhung with coal-black smoke from the steamers' stacks; and cacophonous with the clang of bells, the whirring of windlasses loading freight into the holds, the chanting of the sweating, half-naked slaves who worked them, the clatter of drays and baggage vans, and the cries of distracted passengers who had mislaid husband or child in the chaos.

Denis watched happily until his conscience prodded him along toward the factor's office. André Peyraud hung his shingle on the first floor of a tall brick building near the vegetable market, and

Denis waded through a sea of housewives with baskets on their
arms and fashionably dressed ladies trailed by three or four slaves
to carry their purchases. He skirted past a stout woman indignantly smelling a dubious cabbage, and hurried by a vendor of
mousetraps, rat poison, and toothache cures. For those who
wanted a surer cure, a dentist, perched on a platform with an
assistant and a brass band, pulled the teeth of anyone who had
nerve enough, while the brass band drowned the victim's howls.
An Indian squaw with a papoose on her back had a tray of baskets
for sale, and a peddler with three monkeys on a leash was arguing
furiously with a competitor who offered young alligators, mockingbirds, and canaries in wicker cages, and strings of dried
grasshoppers for the mockingbirds. One of the monkeys had
entangled its tether among the birdcages; while their owners
screamed Cajun imprecations at each other, the monkey was
setting the birds free. Several shoppers loudly offered their advice
on the matter, and an elegant quadroon woman, trailed by a slave,
picked her way delicately through the mess, her silk skirts lifted
only the proper inch or two from the cobblestones.

The Creole ladies ignored her, and she them. They were
enemies in the blood, and the Creole wives and quadroon belles—
whose mothers had been gentlemen's mistresses before them—
were very possibly half sisters. Denis thought, in a detached sort
of way, that the quadroon girl was lovely: With a rounded figure
and light brown hair, and skin that was pale enough that one might
never guess there was even a touch of the tar brush in her blood.
He watched her select from the best of the market's produce and
hand it to her dark maid to carry. She bought a parrot in a brass
cage, and Denis wondered if Felicie would like one of those, or
maybe a canary. He's ask Mama, he thought, when he had finished
his business with André. With that rolled-up painting under her
arm, he'd bet he knew where to find her.

"Sallie!" Gilbert Becquerel came around from behind his desk
with his hands outstretched. He kissed Sallie's gloved ones and
drew up the chair that he kept specially for ladies who might visit
him. Skirts had grown so full in the last few years that they
necessitated armless chairs. He settled Sallie in it solicitously and
spoke to the clerk who had shown her in. "Bring us a glass of the
Medeira, Lavoie, and then you may go."

The clerk, a pale, unhealthy-looking youth, brought the
decanter and a pair of glasses and departed. The outer door clicked

behind him as well. When the boss had a lady in his office and sent Lavoie away, Lavoie had learned that he would not be wanted again for several hours.

Gilbert handed Sallie a glass of Madeira and eyed the rolled-up parcel in her lap. "And what have you brought me, apart from your own sweet self?" His eyes abandoned the parcel for a moment and rested on the rosebud-shaped buttons that embellished the front of her blue walking costume.

Sallie undid the ribbons on the brown paper roll. "Apart from my sweet self, this." She handed him the canvas, and Gilbert spread it flat on his desk. "I want an honest appraisal, Gilbert."

"I never lie about things like this." Gilbert pinned the canvas down with an inkwell and an ebony ruler, then stood back to study it. It was one of her best, really quite remarkable for a woman with only the finishing-school training supposed to equip a lady to paint pretty pictures for her parlor. Somewhere Sallie had got something more. She had caught the odd marshland light that gave a faint golden glow to the newly turned earth and the stooping, muscular black backs that were bent to the furrows. A tall man, very black, almost pure African, was laying sugar cane and watching not the furrows but a café-au-lait-colored woman in a checkered tignon and a gingham dress tucked up above her bare knees. It was a very sensual picture.

Sallie sat forward in her chair, watching Gilbert intently. Her whole body throbbed with the need to hear him say that he liked what he saw.

Finally he rolled it up again and retied the strings. Gilbert Becquerel had a florid face and wavy brown hair—too brown for his fifty years—and a slightly too dashing style in waistcoats. He was also a connoisseur of art. He knew as much about it as he did about banking. Or lovemaking. He knelt in front of Sallie's chair, took her hand, and began to unbutton the blue kid gloves.

"I think it's excellent. You should stick with the slaves, the . . . underside of things. No pretty gardens for you." He peeled one glove back and kissed the inside of her wrist. A hot throbbing ran from Sallie's hand up to her throat and down between her thighs.

"You are an artist, Sallie. Paul should appreciate you more." He drew the glove off, taking the tip of each finger between his lips and tongue as it was freed. This is what she had come here for, why he had welcomed her so warmly, and they both knew it. He looked up at her and smiled.

Her eyes crinkled at him, her mouth turned up affectionately.
Gilbert was a good lover. Her other hand fluttered at his shirtfront,
but he caught it and freed it too from the glove, then put his hands
on her breasts, cupping them and leaning his head against her, the
oddly intimate gesture of a longtime lover.

Sallie untied her bonnet strings, set the bonnet on the floor, and
bent her head to his, her forehead against his hair. Even through
the heavy, stiffened canvas of her tight-laced corset, she could feel
his hands, kneading—gently at first, then harder. She caught her
breath, leaned her head back with half-closed eyes, then gripped
the sides of the chair for balance as she tried to bring her foot up to
kick off her walking boots. Her knee caught Gilbert in the chin.

"What in the hell are you doing?" He rubbed his chin
reproachfully, and Sallie laughed.

"Sorry, Gilbert. Trying to take my boots off."

He pulled them off himself, without regard for finesse, and
tossed them over his shoulder. "You're a menace. *May* I
continue?"

Sallie sighed as he reached for her again. "I wish you would."

His hands were practiced, skillful. She knew she was not his
only lover, but it didn't matter. Gilbert gave her what Paul did not:
his enjoyment of Sallie for herself, his appreciation of her
paintings, and lighthearted lovemaking without the complications
of a marriage grown distant.

Gilbert leaned forward, his elbows in the billows of her skirt,
his torso pinning her to the chair, while his well-manicured hands
opened the delicate rosebud buttons on the bodice of her gown.
When the bodice was open from neck to waist, he pushed it back
off her shoulders and kissed the rise of each breast and the hollows
of her neck. "You have the body of an eighteen-year-old," he
murmured into her throat.

"Gilbert, you're telling fibs. And it's not necessary."

"All right. You're remarkably well preserved for forty," he
said.

She laughed and bit his ear. "That's *too* truthful. And I'm only
thirty-nine. Let me enjoy it while it lasts."

His hands pushed into the layers of skirt and petticoats, between
her legs, and Sallie clutched at his clothing, pulling the cravat
away, working open the buttons of his waistcoat. Gilbert drew her
to her feet and looked down at her, a small smile of expectation on
his lips. Her face was flushed and her gold hair was beginning to
come loose from its pins. He led her into his private sitting room.

"Well, I don't see why we don't just come in here in the first place," Sallie said, laughing, "instead of getting all comfortable and disheveled and having to move."

"Goddamn it, Sallie, must you talk all the way through this?"

He locked the door. His own breathing was heavy now as he turned her around, pulled the tightly fitting bodice from her arms, and released the hooks at the back of her skirt. Sallie twisted her hips against him until her skirt, petticoats, and crinoline slipped to the carpet. Underneath she wore white cotton pantalets and white silk stockings. Gilbert pushed her into a heavy upholstered chair and slid the pantalets up her calves to untie her garters. He took the stockings off as he had her gloves—slowly, carefully, kissing her ankles. Sallie watched, enjoying herself.

When he had done, he put her feet up on the chair and knelt between them. The thin muslin of Sallie's pantalets was stretched taut over the throbbing place between her thighs. Gilbert ran a finger lightly over the muslin, once, twice, until Sallie nearly jumped out of her skin.

"Goddamn, you're beautiful, Sallie."

"You make me feel like it."

"You might tell me I'm a good lover."

"Gilbert, honey, if you weren't, I wouldn't be here."

She tugged at the steel hooks that closed the front of her corset, but he caught her hands in one of his and held them away, while with the other he pulled the corset front open. He took her left breast in his hand and stroked it while his other hand released hers and reached for the buttons of his trousers.

When they were undone, he rolled her chemise top down. He bit and sucked at her nipples while he thrust his hands under her buttocks, lifting her forward in the chair until her knees were drawn up and her toes rested on the edge of the cushion.

Sallie moaned, surrendering herself to the sensations Gilbert awoke in her. His fingers poked at a weak seam in the pantalets, then he pulled it open and slipped his fingers inside.

"Dear God, Gilbert, put yourself in me. Now." Sallie wriggled in the chair, and, gasping, they both slid to the floor. Gilbert yanked the pantalets off, flung them with the discarded corset and stockings. Still clothed, with only his trousers unbuttoned, he mounted her while she writhed under him, crying out, her hands clutching at his shirt.

Her hair had come out of its knot and lay in a luxuriant tangle under her, and Gilbert buried his face in it where it spilled over her bare shoulder. It smelled of lilacs. Gilbert clutched her to him, and they rolled together in the thick pile of the carpet while their climax mounted and broke.

Spent, he lay with his head on her breast and listened to the wild thudding of her heart. When it had slowed, he raised himself on one elbow and toyed with her hair.

Sallie grinned up at him. "You ought to put a couch in here, Gilbert. That was most improper."

"And you loved every minute of it." He pinched her backside, and she yelped and swatted his hand.

Of all his lovers, Sallie was the most alive, the most intense. And the only lady. Gilbert's other women were shopgirls, pretty quadroons, or slatterns. Sallie the artist was something extra.

She was sitting cross-legged now, her hair falling about her like Lady Godiva's, looking at her torn pantalets with mock chagrin.

"You ought to set up a mirror and paint yourself like that," Gilbert said.

"Now wouldn't that be a scandal."

"Would you sell the picture you brought today?"

"I would if I could sell it where Paul won't see it, like you did the others." Sallie didn't need the money, but she treasured the idea of someone liking her work well enough to pay for it. "I'd better tell you, though, that may not be easy. I hope you haven't sold my paintings to anybody in Washington." She gave him a sideways look.

"What have you been up to?" Gilbert asked suspiciously.

"Not me," Sallie chuckled. "It's Paul. He's going to run against you for the House."

"The devil he is!"

"Uh huh. It seems the Democrats don't think you're a fittin' person to govern us all, and they've shanghaied my poor honest husband to save Louisiana."

Gilbert looked stung. "I'm as honest as—"

"You're as honest as anyone else in politics in this state. I mean to go to Washington, Gilbert, so don't look for any help from me."

Gilbert took her hand cajolingly. "Sallie, honey, you sure *could* be a help."

Sallie shook her head. "I know I could. But you'll just have to settle for letting me keep your spirits up." She leaned forward and kissed him, her fingers tweaking at the buttons of his shirt. She prodded at one booted foot with her bare toes. "And this time take your boots off, like a gentleman."

* * *

Felicie DuMontaigne cocked an eye at the oak trees in the convent garden. A tinge of spring green was just beginning to show among the branches, decidedly too bare for her purposes. Sister Marie Josephine would catch her. Felicie ducked behind a thick trunk to think things out, prodding the base reflectively with one booted foot. She wore a plain dress of checked blue and brown muslin, considered suitable by the nuns for a young lady not yet out in society. Her golden hair was neatly braided and hidden under a brown poke bonnet which framed her heart-shaped face. Her blue eyes, very much like her mother's, were alight with mischief.

"Strawberreees! I got strawberries, red and ripe!"

Felicie pricked up her ears. The nuns always bought from the Green Sass Men, the street peddlers, and Sister Marie Josephine, who liked her *dejeuner* as much as the next woman, always came out to haggle for the best.

Felicie put her foot in a low crotch of the tree and pulled herself up to the next branch in a quick scramble. She wriggled along it and straddled the branch where it hung over the garden wall. She would very likely spoil her dress, but she didn't think Joe Spelling would mind. Another scramble brought her to the top of the wall. She cast a quick glance along the street, found with her foot the place where one brick had crumbled away, and slithered down with the ease of much practice. Sister Marie Josephine would probably make her say paternosters from now until doomsday when she got back, but in four days it would be Lent, and then there wouldn't be anything to *do* but pray for the next forty days. An invitation to watch a marionette show in Jackson Square was too enticing to turn down, and so was the open admiration of the young man who had made it. Hollis didn't have *all* the beaux, Felicie thought with satisfaction. She dropped to the banquette under the nose of a startled chimney sweep in top hat and tailcoat, his face as black as his hat.

Felicie nodded to him as if this were the way in which she customarily made her exit, dusted off her gloves, adjusted her bonnet, and strode briskly down the street.

The chimney sweep hastened equally briskly in the opposite direction. When the sisters started looking for their missing charge, he didn't want to be anywhere nearby.

"So Lucien's coming home, is he?" André Peyraud's thin, square face was unenthusiastic.

"Yes, he is," Denis said equably. "I'll bring him round to go over the accounts with you."

"If I weren't an honest man," Peyraud said sarcastically, "I'd be greatly cheered by that. The last time I saw Lucien, he didn't know a ledger from a deck of cards. Rather more familiar with the latter."

"It's been a while," Denis said. "If he's going to have Belle Marie, he's got to learn to run it."

"Hmmph." Peyraud closed his books. "Tell Paul he can draw on me for the amount we agreed on. And that I'll find him an overseer. Paul ought to leave the plantation business to you, you know."

"I'm not the eldest," Denis said shortly.

"There's no law of primogeniture in this country that I know of. Honestly, Denis, do you really think Lucien has changed any?"

"This isn't a useful conversation, André," Denis said.

"Very well." Peyraud shrugged and reached for the whiskey bottle sitting on a shelf behind his polished oak desk. "Have a drink with me."

"Not today." Denis picked up his hat. "I want to buy a present for my sister."

He strolled at a leisurely pace through the city toward Gilbert Becquerel's house on Carondelet Street. If Mama had gone to have Becquerel sell her new painting, Denis could probably still catch her there. Things were never done in a hurry in New Orleans. Denis was aware that he wasn't supposed to know what Mama did with her paintings, but he could always pay a civil call on the Becquerels and pretend to be surprised to find her there. Gilbert Becquerel was an officer of the City Bank where Paul DuMontaigne did his business, so it would not be abnormal to visit. Then he could ask Mama how Felicie would like a canary for a gift.

Denis tugged on the bell in the shaded portico of the Becquerel house and gave his hat and his card to the stately Negro butler. He sauntered cheerfully into the parlor, kissed Madame Becquerel's hand, and blinked in surprise to discover that neither his mother nor Monsieur Becquerel was present.

"I was in town, you know. I thought I'd call," Denis said, feeling a little silly.

"How kind of you." Françoise Becquerel's dark eyes regarded him expectantly, as if awaiting some further explanation. Denis became uncomfortably aware that he wasn't overly well-acquainted with the Becquerels.

He smiled, taking a seat on the red upholstered chair that Madame indicated. "To tell you the truth, I half expected to find my mother here. She made some mention of it. I wanted to ask her advice about a present for my sister."

Françoise Becquerel's nostrils flared. "I regret, Monsieur DuMontaigne, I have not seen Madame DuMontaigne today."

"Oh, well, I daresay she's still shopping," Denis said unconcernedly. "My sister Felicie's coming out this year, you know. I understand that requires a great many clothes." A rather strained silence seemed to hang in the air. "I wonder, Madame Becquerel—maybe you'd advise me." Women seemed to like being asked things like that. "Do you think she'd like a canary?"

"A . . . canary?"

"My sister Felicie," Denis said. "I want to buy her something, and I thought of a canary."

"Ah." Madame Becquerel stared at him shrewdly. This silly innocent hadn't the faintest idea where his mother really was, but Françoise Becquerel was nearly certain that she did. She had suspected for some time that Sallie DuMontaigne was one of Gilbert's women. Françoise Becquerel's lips compressed angrily. They would be at Gilbert's office. Knowing Gilbert as she did, they would be there all afternoon. She smiled suddenly at Denis, sitting awkwardly with his hands in his lap. "I am sure that she would love a canary, Monsieur DuMontaigne." She touched a tapestry bellpull beside her chair. "But do let me offer you some refreshment first. It is so pleasant to have a gentleman's company . . . with Gilbert away so often."

She sent the butler for "a glass of wine for Monsieur DuMontaigne. Two glasses." She smiled at Denis. "I shall join you."

Denis, a friendly soul, regarded his hostess with interest. He guessed her to be his mother's age, rather plumper than Sallie and as dark-haired as most pure Creole women were, and very lovely, with large dark eyes and paper-white skin. Her luxuriant hair was pinned into heavy coils above her ears. Her cap was a delicate scrap of white silk and lace, and she had pinned a hothouse flower just beneath it. She had a restful air about her. Denis thought she must be bored and set himself to be entertaining.

"It's good of you to receive me. And to offer me a drink," he added with a grin. "There's rather a bustle in the streets just now, and I walked all the way from the Market."

Françoise Becquerel smiled at him. "Then you must relax for a moment." The butler set a silver tray with a decanter and glasses on a rosewood table. "I will pour, Michael," she said, dismissing him, then smiled again at Denis. "You must stay as long as you like."

While she fiddled with the glasses, Denis looked about him. A piano, draped with various shawls and fringes, stood against the wall; and several small tables were laden with wax fruit, wreaths of dried blooms, and flowers made of human hair, all under glass domes, as well as statues, clocks, china baskets, and palmetto fans in sand-filled vases in the corners. Fashion called for clutter. Oil portraits of various Becquerel ancestors, in the powdered wigs of Colonial days or in the narrow, high-waisted dresses of thirty years ago, looked down from the walls, alternating with water-color vistas and still-life paintings of pears and dead game birds, the work of the ladies of the house.

"There." Françoise Becquerel—a thin, long-stemmed goblet in each hand—moved gracefully to Denis's chair. Her rose muslin skirts swayed as she moved, and she smelled of jasmine. She paused. "Or perhaps you would rather have whiskey? I sometimes forget that gentlemen often do."

"No, no, this is fine. Thank you." Denis took the glass. He sipped from it, and she seated herself approvingly in the chair beside his.

"You are very kind to bear me company, Monsieur DuMontaigne," she said with downcast eyes. "I confess, I was feeling lonely today." Her eyes fluttered up. "And here you are, just like a cavalier."

"A man couldn't ask for more charming company," Denis said gallantly, but he was a little startled when she laid a hand on his and leaned toward him.

"You mustn't think I complain so to every man," she whispered. "But it is a little sad for me here alone, with Gilbert at his offices so much."

"Yes, I expect it must be." Perhaps he should leave. He drank his wine.

Françoise captured his glass when he had drained it, her fingers brushing his. "You must let me give you another glassful. It is a very good wine, and I am told that it does not keep well after it has been opened." Before he could protest, she moved lightly to the table. She poured carefully, making a graceful show of her movements, and studied him under her lashes as he sat uncertainly on the edge of his chair. He was attractive in a solid way, with wavy brown hair and a strong-jawed, pleasant face. He looked to be around twenty. Inexperienced, she thought, but there was the vitality of the young about him. If she wanted a way in which to strike back at Gilbert and Sallie DuMontaigne, she could think of no more pleasant way than this.

IV

The

Marionettes

"SEE, I TOLD YOU I could do it!" Felicie arrived breathless, with a quick backward glance over her shoulder, at the foot of the steps of the St. Louis Cathedral.

"Well, if you aren't the gamest girl I ever did meet. I didn't think you'd have the nerve." Joe Spelling pushed his hat back on his head and grinned at her.

"Of course I had the nerve!" Felicie said indignantly. "I just had to get past Sister Marie Josephine."

"Is that the old religious person you had out shoppin' with you?"

"No, that was Sister Marie Celeste. She's not so careful." Felicie giggled. "Or I wouldn't have had a chance to talk to you."

"Oh, I reckon a girl like you would find a way," Joe said.

She thought his tone was a touch more enthusiastic than admiring and wondered briefly if she hadn't gone a little too far this time. But Joe Spelling was plainly a gentleman, even if she had met him at the City Market instead of being properly introduced. Besides, he was only in New Orleans on business with his brother and didn't know anybody. And the lure of the marionette show was too strong for her to resist. Felicie tucked her hand through his arm and smiled at him confidently.

"Come on, you can buy me a café before the show starts. We never get pocket money unless the nuns take us out." She drew him over to the quadroon whose stand was a daily fixture at the foot of the cathedral steps. A dark, delicious aroma of freshly ground and brewed beans filled the air.

Joe obligingly put his hand in his pocket and paid the woman
for two cups of café noir, hot and fragrant and very sweet. Other
street vendors, many of them mulattos or quadroons, had set up
their stands along the square. Joe bought Felicie a red camellia
and pinned it to her shoulder, mildly impressed with his own
gallantry. He looked around him and shook his head. "I've seen
more free niggers in one block in New Orleans than in the whole
state of Georgia! You all ain't got abolitionist notions down
here?"

"Certainly not!" Felicie looked shocked, and then decided to
forgive his ignorance. "New Orleans is very old. The *gens de
couleur* have been here nearly as long as we have. They're mostly
descended from freed slaves way back in the last century. Some of
them have done very well for themselves—send their children to
Paris to study and have big houses and their own slaves."

"Pretty high livin' for niggers," Joe said disapprovingly.

"No, *gens de couleur* doesn't mean Negroes—pure blacks. It
means—well, ladies aren't supposed to talk about it, of course,
but it means mixed blood. Mulattos and quadroons and octo-
roons."

"Well, that all means niggers to me."

"If you're going to do business in New Orleans," Felicie said,
"you'll have to understand that it doesn't. The *gens de couleur*
have a great deal of French blood." (And a great deal of very
recent French blood, but a lady absolutely *couldn't* say that.)
"Many of them live much as we do. We don't associate with
them, of course, but they're very proud of their heritage."

"Well, it's the damnedest thing *I* ever saw. And all this carryin'
on in the streets—" Joe waved a hand at a laughing trio, two men
and a girl, doing a little dance step to an organ grinder's tune.

"It's Carnival, Mister Spelling. New Orleanians enjoy themselves." Knowing Creole society as she did, Felicie was aware
that the two men would inevitably be the girl's brothers or uncles.
It didn't occur to her that Joe wouldn't know that.

"Well, I'd always heard the Frenchies were hard to get to know.
I'm sure glad to find a girl that isn't." He patted her hand. "Let's
go see those puppets you've been talkin' about."

The marionette stage was set up in the center of Jackson
Square, near the statue of the general on his improbably rearing
horse. A Punch and Judy pair emerged from behind the curtains.
They had the novelty of being painted in blackface and quarreled
with each other in Gombo, the French Negro dialect. Felicie,

giggling, translated the performance for Joe, whose French was of the book-learned sort.

At last the curtain dropped and then rose again as all the marionettes lined up to make a jerky bow. Felicie clapped her hands.

Joe slipped an arm around her waist. "You havin' a good time, honey?"

Felicie stiffened. No boy she knew would ever have taken such a liberty. For one thing, her brothers would probably shoot him. She began to feel uncomfortable. "Perhaps you had better take me back—before the sisters miss me."

"Aw now, honey, you just got here." Joe withdrew his arm from her waist, casually, as if it had never been there. "Stay and see the next show. You want some more of that coffee?"

"Well . . ." He was smiling at her in a friendly fashion. Felicie decided that he would behave himself now. Gentlemen just sometimes needed a little hint. She felt pleased with herself for being so knowing. They stayed and watched the next performance.

"And now I really do have to get back, or Sister Marie Josephine'll skin me alive."

Joe chuckled. "Well, we can't have that. But you can't go back the way you came. I just saw a passel of nuns come out of the cathedral and head that way."

"Oh, dear." Felicie looked around her uncertainly.

"You just come with me, honey." Joe took her hand and drew her away in the other direction, toward the levee. "I know a long way round. I was down here yesterday with my brother."

"Are you sure?" The rabbit warren of narrow alleys between the main streets was unfamiliar to her.

" 'Course I am." Joe tucked her hand into his arm before she could change her mind and go looking for those nuns he hadn't really seen. She was a pretty little thing. And a girl who'd climb a convent wall ought to be accommodating.

They threaded their way among the drays and hired carriages along the levee until Joe found the alley he was looking for. It cut between the blank walls of tall buildings that faced onto the levee. There were no balconies on the alley side, only back doors and low stoops. Joe pulled her into the doorway behind a stack of barrels. "Better wait a while and let those nuns get back home." He put his arm around her waist and didn't let go. "Gimme a kiss for the nice time, honey."

"Mister Spelling!" Felicie wriggled in his embrace.

"Now, don't you be a prude." Joe had come to New Orleans to have a good time, and he was determined to have it. "Give old Joe a kiss for the money he spent on you."

Felicie was beginning to be frightened. The alley was far too empty. "My papa and my brothers'll shoot you dead!" she gasped.

"I ain't goin' to be here to shoot. We're leavin' tomorrow. Now kiss me good-bye." He tightened his grip around her waist.

"No!" Felicie kicked him hard in the ankle and tried to pull away.

"Why, you little cat!" Joe twisted one arm behind her back, and pinned the other to her side. He was getting mad. She had a nerve, turning pious on him now. He pushed her against the wall, hard enough to knock the breath out of her, and kissed her before she could stop him. "You're a pretty good armful," he said triumphantly. "You just be nice. Who're you savin' it for, anyway?"

Felicie was terrified. No man had ever laid a hand on her like that. It had never occurred to her that any man would. What did he want? All she knew were vague whispers from the other girls, and a certain amount of knowledge inevitable from owning farm animals. She had never put the two together before. Now she felt sick with terror. She thrashed in his arms and opened her mouth to scream.

He clapped a hand over her lips and wrestled her down on the concrete stoop behind the barrels. The more she struggled, the angrier he got.

Felicie kicked and struggled in a mixture of fear and sheer outrage as she felt Joe's hand reach up under her skirts. His other hand was over her mouth, and she twisted her chin and bit him as hard as she could.

"Ow!" Joe howled, shaking his injured hand. Felicie managed to scream once before he put it over her mouth again, this time holding her jaws shut. She had drawn his blood, and it smeared across her cheek as she twisted harder, trying to work loose again. The sight of his bloody fingers seemed to redouble Joe's anger. He climbed on her roughly and put his free hand under her skirts, tearing at her pantalets.

One of Felicie's boots had come untied, and her kicking foot sent it flying upward. It landed just within her reach, and she lunged for it frantically. She beat at Joe's face with the hard sole, but he just hunched his shoulders and ducked down so that the blows rained on the back of his head. He hardly felt them through his fury.

"You just lie still," he grunted. His fingers twisted in the thin muslin of her drawers, and ripped. He pulled his hand away and fumbled at the buttons of his own trousers while Felicie stared at him in horror. He pulled his pants open and yanked her crinolines up in a bunch around her waist.

She couldn't see what he was doing, but she could feel his horrible sweaty hand crawling between her legs, and a sudden fiery pain as he took a tuft of hair between his fingers and yanked at it savagely. Her breath came in ragged gasps, constricted by the whalebone and lacing of her corset, and she thought she was going to faint. She writhed frantically, trying to roll away from him. Joe's hands clawed at her, and she heard his voice, thick and slurred: "I told you to lie down. And you better not go runnin' to your father afterward either—'cause there ain't none of your Frenchy boys gonna want you anymore, after what you been doin' with me!"

Françoise Becquerel leaned her head against Denis's chest. "Why, your heart is pounding, Monsieur DuMontaigne!"

"Is it?" Denis strove to sound unconcerned, but this was growing more difficult by the minute. The wine seemed to have gone to his head, or maybe it was the jasmine scent of Madame Becquerel's white skin. He was twenty this year and had never lain with a woman. Françoise Becquerel was as overwhelming as a tidal wave, and he felt as if he were drowning in her.

"I must go." The rose-colored muslin that lay against his breast didn't move.

"You needn't sound so desperate," she whispered. She stroked his chest and lifted her face to his.

"Oh, no . . . I—" His hazel eyes met hers uncertainly.

She smiled. "You have never made love to a woman, have you, Denis?"

He blushed. "I— No."

"That is no shame. You are scholarly, I think." She nestled a little closer. "Our young convent mademoiselles would have little to interest you." One finger stroked his shirtfront playfully. "And you are much too nice-minded to go with . . . women of a worse class, *n'est-ce pas?*"

Her lips brushed against his ear, and a shiver of desire ran through him. She was right about the convent-bred girls, and as for the Rampart Street sirens, he suspected it was more a matter of his being too shy to pursue one. A shyness that appeared now to be departing as if on wings, with every touch of Françoise's lips against his ear. *I ought to leave*. The thought faded away as his lips met hers, warm, pliable, inviting . . . and insistent. Her arms twined around his neck, and she pulled him to her.

A hand fluttered against his thigh and moved upward. All the unspent desire of young manhood rocked him as her hand pressed against the hardness under his pantaloons. She gave a little murmur of satisfaction under his lips and began to stroke him, moving her fingers tantalizingly up and down until he thought he would lose all control of himself.

Françoise pulled him to his feet. "I must remember that the young are impatient," she whispered. She took his hand, and he let her lead him from the room, not really seeing where they went.

Françoise opened a door at the top of a graceful stairway that spiraled up from the high-ceilinged hall. When she had drawn him inside, she turned and locked the door. This was her private boudoir, with rose silk at the windows and rose-patterned paper on the walls. A four-poster bed, richly carved of mahogany, was hung with silk curtains. It was overwhelmingly intimate, a part of herself.

Françoise turned from the door into Denis's arms, and the thudding of his heart beat in time to the quick movements of her fingers as she undid the buttons of his trousers.

"Ah!" The sound burst from Denis's lips unbidden as her hands rubbed his manhood between them. Then she turned so that her back was to him and let him unhook the fastenings of her gown and her corset cover and corset. When they had come free, she drew his hands around her and put them on her breasts. The nipples grew hard under his fingers, and a wave of fire ran through him. Françoise turned, stepping out of the rose-colored billow of muslin and lace. She raised her arms to pull the pins from her hair. Her breasts were bare, white and pink-tipped, and she wore only muslin pantalets thin enough to see the dark, inviting shadow between her thighs.

Denis's face flushed with mingled embarrassment and desire. It was too late to turn back, but he knew he didn't want to. Françoise knelt before him and began to pull his pantaloons down, slowly, inch by inch. He began to tremble. When he had stepped from the tangled clothing around his feet, she took his staff in the palm of one hand. Gilbert Becquerel was a man of exacting tastes, and Françoise had learned her lessons well. It was pleasure almost beyond description to practice them on Denis.

Denis caught her by the shoulders and pulled her to her feet, uncertainty gone, embarrassment gone, leaving nothing but desire drumming through him. He lifted her and put her on the coverlet of the bed, in the dim rose-colored light among the bed curtains. With both hands he pulled her pantalets down, and she wriggled and thrust her hips upward so that he could draw them out from under her.

He knelt above her, poised, heart pounding, and somehow stricken suddenly immovable at the last moment. Françoise smiled, and her fingers crept downward between her legs. She stroked herself lightly as if to say, *Here, here is what you want. Take it.*

Denis leaned forward, felt himself slide into those warm, clinging depths. She wrapped her legs around his buttocks and thrust her hips upward, driving him deeper, deeper. He arched his back and began to drive in and out of her. Her hips moved in rhythm with his, in mounting, aching urgency until he felt himself explode deep within her, and her body shudder against his.

She lay under him, satisfied, stroking his strong young back, liking the feeling of his young manhood within her. She wondered what Gilbert was doing with Sallie DuMontaigne. Well, here was a fine revenge, even better than she had thought it would be. Denis let out a long breath and lifted himself off her. She watched him possessively. Even now, sated, the thought of Denis's body in hers made her flush with desire.

Denis looked at the silver stars and flowers that spangled the *ciel de lit* above him. He felt drowsy and peculiarly satisfied with himself. He rolled over and kissed her because that seemed the proper thing to do. Her hair clung in dark tendrils about her face. Seen close to, her skin was not of the porcelain fineness that its color suggested, but rather thick and creamy. Her eyes were shadowed with thick lashes. She raised rounded arms above her head and stretched.

"One would never know that that was your first time, Denis." There was a purr in her voice. She reclined against taffeta pillows like a voluptuous cat. "Next time will be better yet."

"Françoise—" It seemed a little silly to call her Madame Becquerel just now. Next time? How many times could they do this and not get caught?

"Next time will be even more interesting. One acquires . . . staying power."

"Françoise, I don't think—"

"Ah, you must go and buy your little sister her—canary, was it not? Of course." She hopped out of bed and slipped her discarded camisole over her breasts. She settled the white satin corset over it and gave him a wink over her shoulder. "But first you must repair your damage, my darling."

There was something unsettling about the last affectionate term. Denis laced the corset as quickly as he could and scrambled into his own clothes, now irrationally convinced that Gilbert Becquerel would kick the door down, horsewhip in hand, at any moment. When they were dressed, she led him to the parlor and placidly rang the bell for Michael.

Michael appeared with Denis's hat, and Denis snatched it up gratefully.

Françoise Becquerel gave him her hand to kiss. "You will come back to us often, Monsieur DuMontaigne, now that you are . . . acquainted with us."

"Yes, of course," Denis mumbled. Now that he was dressed and in the parlor again, his sudden fear of discovery abated, but there was something in the way her voice tugged at him that left him uncomfortable.

Outside, he looked back at the tall, graceful house. Wrought-iron galleries like black lace stretched across the second and third floors. A flash of movement behind the French doors that led from the parlor to the second-floor gallery told him that Françoise was watching him. He turned and nearly bolted down the steps, the pleasant languor of lovemaking warring in him with the feeling that he had done something he was going to have to pay for.

"Mmmmmf!" The feel of Joe Spelling prodding between her legs galvanized Felicie to a strength he hadn't expected. She twisted her chin from under his hand again and shrieked. He tried frantically to clap it over her mouth again, but it was almost impossible to hold her down at the same time.

"You lie still!" He drew back his arm to slap her backhanded across the face when the rattle of cart wheels sounded on the cobbles at the far end of the alley. Felicie shrieked again. There was the thud of running feet, and then two heavy hands grabbed Joe by the collar.

"Hey! What you think you do, eh?" Something slammed Joe up against the side of the house, knocking the breath out of him. "This man, he bother you, mamzelle?" A large-knuckled fist appeared under Joe's nose, and he found himself looking into a tanned, weathered face and a pair of indignant black eyes. His assailant wore a voluminous shirt, and pantaloons that tucked into his boots. A thick shock of straight black hair was crowned with a woolen cap.

"Get away from me!" Joe sputtered. "That—that's my sister. I was teaching her some manners."

The water-cart man eyed Joe's open pantaloon buttons dispassionately. "You put that thing in your sister, you go to hell sure."

Felicie scrambled to her feet, feeling battered from head to toe. Tears of outrage and fear streamed down her cheeks. "I'm *not* his sister! I don't *know* him! He tried to—" She choked, sobbing. "He tried to take liberties with me."

The water-cart man drew his fist back. "I think I take some liberties with him, me." Joe reached for the knife he kept in his boot, but the other man hit him hard on the chin, knocking him into the wall. There was very little give in the cement wall, and Joe slumped against it, dazed.

Felicie wiped her eyes on the back of her hand and eyed her rescuer with satisfaction. The Acadian French of Louisiana were as prideful and short of temper as the Creoles. She hoped this one would beat Joe Spelling to a jelly.

He appeared to be considering it. "Nah," he said finally, "I kill you, it embarrass the lady maybe." He took the shaken Joe by the collar and the seat of his pants and heaved him into the alley. Joe landed sprawling on all fours, and Felicie's deliverer propelled him farther with the toe of his boot. "Too damn many Americans here. Why hell you don't all go home to Unite' States?"

Joe made a dive for his hat and backed away warily. "This *is* the United States! And I can have you arrested!"

"This is Louisiana, and I don't think you get far, I tell them what you do! You run, or I fold you up, put you in this barrel, me!"

Joe fled. The other man turned to Felicie. "What you doing out with a man like that?"

"Oh, I'm *sorry!*" Felicie turned streaming blue eyes on him. "I wanted to see the marionettes."

"Hmmph. I got a daughter, your size. She ran off, I beat her backside."

"I'm sure someone will," Felicie said penitently. "Oh, how can I thank you?" She knew better than to offer him money.

"You mind the sisters next time, behave yourself. That's where you come from, no?"

Felicie nodded.

"Than I take you back there. I am Augustin Prieur, me. First I got to collect these barrels." He brought up the water cart, pulled by a mule in a straw hat, and loaded the empty barrels into the back. There were more than a dozen of them, on various stoops, and Felicie climbed up onto the cart seat and waited for him. Augustin Prieur loaded the last barrel and handed up her missing boot. "You come home in your bare feets, the sisters really don't like it." He climbed up beside her and shook out the reins. "Hee-yup."

If Felicie had had any hopes of slipping into the convent unobserved, they were dashed as the cart rounded the corner into Ursulines Street. A flock of nuns trotted back and forth along the banquette like agitated pigeons, and Sallie's voice could be clearly heard from the corner.

"What do you *mean* she isn't here? Would someone be kind enough to tell me how you have contrived to *lose* my daughter?"

Then there was Denis, who said, "Now, Mama, you know the little devil's done it before."

Denis! Felicie started to feel faint again. How many other people were looking for her? If she had made a scandal, Papa would be furious. She hung her head as Augustin Prieur drew the cart to a halt.

"Felicie!" Sallie took in her blood-spattered cheeks and torn gown. "Oh, my darling, what's happened to you?" Denis came up beside her. Inexplicably, he was holding a canary in a cage.

"I—I—" The whole horror of Joe Spelling came back to her in a wave, and Felicie began to sob again. She tried shakily to climb down.

"Here." Denis pushed the canary at the startled nun. He took Felicie around the waist and lifted her down.

"She meet a very bad man, her," Augustin Prieur said succinctly. "So I bring her home. I do not kill him because I think that make the scandal."

Sallie had herded them all inside into Mother Superior's private sitting room, leaving Denis to devise some way of thanking the resolute Augustin Prieur. She imagined that Denis would buy him a whiskey somewhere. In the meantime there were Mother Superior's ruffled feelings to soothe. Felicie was curled in a chair with the canary and cage in her lap, and an irate Mammy Rachel in attendance.

"We are not accustomed," Mother Superior said, "to having the charge of young ladies who must be kept on a leash perhaps, to keep them from climbing the walls."

"Er, yes," Sallie said. "And since Felicie is seventeen now and is to come home in a few months in any case, it might be better, er, for everyone, if she should come home now."

Mother Superior looked as if she thought that would be a blessing directly from God.

Sallie sighed and contemplated her wayward daughter, now brightened considerably and trying to persuade the canary to sit on her finger. "After all, she has been with you for four years. I doubt that there is a great deal more that she can be taught in three months."

"Felicie," Mother Superior said tartly, "has learned to dance most gracefully. She also sits a horse remarkably well, I am told, although that is not a matter of our instruction. For the rest, she plays the pianoforte with considerably more enthusiasm than skill, and she has not the least notion of geography, other than a vague idea of the location of France. I regret to say that I do not think that the situation will improve in three months. I am an old woman, Madame DuMontaigne, and I do not think that my heart will stand the schooling of your daughter much longer."

"And if Mother Superior's hair isn't stark white under her wimple," Sallie said, "I should be very much surprised."

"Mama, I'm sorry," Felicie said.

"And so you ought to be. Come along now." The black boatmen had let down the gangway of the DuMontaigne steamboat, and Sallie hustled her aboard, attended by Denis and Mammy Rachel. Two other boatmen followed with Sallie's luggage and Felicie's trunk, hastily packed.

"You can cast off as soon as you get clearance, Sam."

"Yes, Miss Sallie." The pilot, also a DuMontaigne Negro, touched the brim of his straw hat. "You ladies want to set up on deck? It's a mighty fine day."

"Thank you, Sam."

The pilot saw them settled, tucked light rugs over their laps, and grinned at Mammy Rachel. "You want to come up front with me? I show you a mighty pretty view."

Mammy snorted. "You show me what you allus try to show me, I expect."

Sallie chuckled. "You go on, Mammy. Admire the view."

Mammy summoned up an expression of immense dignity, but she went away on Sam's arm.

"That darky's been trying to get Mammy to marry him ever since I can remember," Denis said. "You think she'll ever do it?"

"Hush," Sallie said. "You'll embarrass her. And you go away too, Denis. I want to talk to Felicie."

"Oh, all right." Denis stood up and stretched. "I'll go assist Sam with his courting."

"Thoughtful of you," Sallie said dryly. Denis looked entirely too full of beans at the moment, and unaccountably skittish into the bargain. She wondered what he had been up to, and then decided that she had better deal with Felicie first.

"Now, my girl."

"Mama, I'm so sorry."

"Whatever possessed you?"

Felicie tearfully recounted the tale of Joe Spelling. "I thought he was a *gentleman!*" she wailed as Sallie nodded grimly at her conclusion.

"And so he may have been," Sallie said with a look of distaste. "You have to understand that gentlemen—and by that I really mean just men of our class—may treat a lady one way, and another woman another. If you give them the idea that you aren't a lady, you take away your protection."

"You mean because I snuck out to meet him, he thought that—"

"Well, of course he did. Do nice girls sneak over walls?"

Felicie hung her head. "Am I ruined now?"

"Oh, my darling, no." Sallie put her arms around Felicie. "Your friend Mister Prieur came along just in time. And the sisters aren't going to tell anyone, you can bet your boots on that."

Felicie sat back, indignant. "You mean that it only counts if you get *caught?*"

"Well, that's what it amounts to, I guess. It may not be fair, but you'd better be glad of it." It would have counted if that man had raped her, all right, but Sallie still wasn't sure that Felicie really knew what he'd been trying to do.

"Well, then . . ." Felicie poked a finger at the blue fringe of her traveling cloak. "Do we have to tell Papa?"

"No, darling, I don't think we do." Paul, possibly not having as practical a nature as Augustin Prieur, might decide to go and find that Spelling boy and kill him. Or make him marry Felicie, which would be worse yet. "I'll tell Denis he's to keep quiet too. *But*—you have to promise me something."

"Yes, Mama."

"You are *never* to do anything like that again."

"No truly, Mama! I'm sorry I was so stupid."

"Well, we're all pretty stupid sometimes." Sallie hugged her. "Very well, you behave with enough propriety, and I won't tell Papa."

"Can I still go to balls?"

"If you're going to come out, you'll have to go to balls, won't you? And have a great many new dresses, and gentlemen coming to call in a *proper* fashion." Sallie's eyes sparkled. She hadn't looked forward to anything so much since she had launched Hollis into the world. What a blessing to have *pretty* daughters. "You'll find that you can do a great deal better than that Joe Spelling."

"It wasn't him, Mama, it was the marionettes. Well, mostly."

"I daresay. But you'd better be prepared for the boys chasing you, because they sure are going to."

Felicie's mouth curved into a little smile. Before Hollis got married, the house had been full of men all the time, and when they went to balls or the French Opera in New Orleans, they had flocked around her until you could hardly see her, and she'd had two duels fought over her. Felicie had been a slightly pudgy schoolgirl looking longingly at her sister's triumphs. But this year they wouldn't be doing any flocking, because this year Hollis was a widow and still in half mourning. And Felicie was seventeen and not the least bit pudgy.

Hollis was her sister, and one ought to love one's sister, but Felicie thought that if she could manage more beaux than Hollis had had, it would be a great satisfaction to her. That it would also annoy Hollis was a thought that crossed her mind.

V

Adele

"BARRET!" SALLIE CAST her bonnet to the winds and threw herself into the arms of the sandy-haired man who rose from a wicker armchair on the veranda. Barret Forbes was short and solid, with a neat, sand-colored beard and a square, amiable face.

He staggered back slightly, held her at arm's length to admire her, and kissed her affectionately. "Sallie, I swear you don't change."

Sallie patted the front of his watered silk waistcoat. "Neither do you—much."

"I'm not fat," Barret protested, "I'm just stocky."

"Sallie, that was rude," Paul said. He rose from his chair and kissed Sallie on the cheek. "How are you, my dear?" He raised his eyebrows at Felicie, who hovered, like a three-dimensional guilty conscience, beside Denis.

"I'm fine, thank you," Sallie said. "Barret doesn't think I'm rude. I've known him since I was four, and you should hear the things he used to call me. Barret knows I think he's handsome, whatever size his middle is." Sallie settled herself in a chair beside the two men. "Mammy, see if you can get Testut to find us something to drink besides whiskey."

"You tell Testut *I'll* take whiskey," Denis said. He held out his hand. "Good to see you again, sir. We didn't expect you until next week."

"The man I need to see in the city's been silly enough to get himself married and go off on his honeymoon," Barret said. "So I thought I'd loll about here until he gets back."

"Well, we're delighted to have you," Sallie said. "Barret, you remember Felicie." Felicie smiled at Barret and kept a wary eye on her father.

57

Barret eyed her admiringly. "I certainly do. Looks like you, Sallie."

Sallie sighed. "Barret, you're a lamb. I just wish I *were* seventeen. I take back what I said about your stomach." She waved a hand at Felicie. "Go and take your bonnet off, darling, and come have some lemonade with us."

Felicie nodded, kissed her father on the cheek, and scooted into the house. Paul looked pensive as her blue skirts disappeared around the doorpost. He leaned toward Sallie. "And what exactly is Felicie doing home?"

"Oh, Paul, she was *so* bored, and I couldn't blame her. You couldn't pay me to spend four years in that dreary place."

"All Creole girls are educated by the nuns. That is our tradition."

"But Felicie was due to come home in a couple of months, and I can certainly use her here, with a houseful of people." She turned to Barret. "Not you, sweetie, you're never any trouble, but Lucien's coming home with some orphaned child that Paul has somehow made himself accountable for, and there's Felicie's come-out to think of. I *need* Felicie, Paul. You know Hollis would rather be fried in oil than take a hand in the housekeeping, and Tante Doudouce is so silly, she tells the maids three things at once, and then they don't know what to do, so they don't do any of it. It will do Felicie good to learn how to keep household."

"And it'll keep her busy," Paul said shrewdly. "What mischief has she been up to?"

"Nothing very much," Sallie said airily, "though I admit the sisters were beginning to look a bit haggard. Felicie will do much better at home." She dismissed the subject of Felicie. "Now, Barret, I want to hear all the news. How is Alice?"

"Just the same," Barret said. "She thinks I'm going to catch malaria in New Orleans, and she made me pack my long underwear and fourteen woolen mufflers."

"In Louisiana, for the Lord's sake! That's Alice." Alice was Barret's unmarried sister, who kept house for him. "Now what's this about Johnny Longworth? Did they really put him in jail? Mama wrote me something about it, but she was being so discreet that I couldn't figure out what she was talking about."

"Well, he got drunk and tried to shoot his brother at the symphony in Charleston, but the bullet hit the tuba instead. You never saw such a commotion. Old ladies were screaming and fainting, and while that was going on, a pickpocket made off with three people's watches and Johnny's wife's diamond necklace, which was why Johnny tried to shoot Charlie in the first place, because Charlie gave it to Julia for a wedding present, which was terribly improper, and she insisted on wearing it anyway, so everyone assumed they were carrying on."

"Mercy," Sallie said. "I ought to go home more often."

"The best part was, they got the necklace back, and Johnny tried to give it back to Charlie, who wouldn't take it, so Johnny tried to sell it instead, and it turned out to be paste, and now Julia's mad at them both."

"Oh, heavens," Sallie said. "I must remember, if I ever see the Longworths again, *not* to mention diamonds."

Paul sipped his whiskey, listening to Barret's discourse on Charleston gossip and to Sallie's laughter. Paul was not a man given to plaintiveness, but he felt plaintive just now. It would be gratifying, he thought, if Sallie got such enjoyment from *his* company. It did not occur to him that since Sallie was not in love with Barret Forbes, it was far simpler to enjoy his company.

Adele wiped her face and neck with a black-bordered handkerchief. *Mon Dieu,* it was only the first of April, and this place was like a Turkish bath. Lucien, in a white linen coat and trousers, and a low-crowned straw hat, regarded her with some sympathy, and, she thought resentfully, a touch of amusement.

"We'll have my mother find you some sensible clothes."

Adele favored him with a baleful glance out of the corner of her eye and wiped her brow again. The little steam tug hoot-hooted as it towed them to a berth along the levee. In a two-month voyage, she had made no further headway with Lucien DuMontaigne. She could have had him into her bed with one whisper—that he had made plain enough. But she would have had nothing to show for it but the loss of that valuable property, her maidenhead. Lucien had made equally plain that he was not in the market for a wife. Adele straightened her back and dabbed at her temples with cologne from a vial in her reticule.

"Is it always this hot?" she inquired.

"Oh, it gets worse," Lucien said cheerfully. "Just wait until July."

"I think that I can bear to wait," Adele said. "I feel as if I am underwater."

"There they are!" Lucien shouted. He waved, and three figures at the forefront of the crowd along the levee waved back. His sister Emilie bounced up and down in excitement.

The sailing packet bumped gently into her berth, and the gangplank went down. Lucien hustled Adele from her seat on deck. "Come on, before we get caught in the crowd."

Denis met them at the end of the gangway, pounding Lucien on the back. A black woman in a stiffly starched apron and a white headscarf held her arms out, and Adele watched in surprise as Lucien picked her up and whirled her around.

"Mister Lucien, you put me down!" Mammy protested this assault on her dignity, but she also pulled his head down to hers and kissed him soundly when he had set her upright again. Then she backed off and gave him the once-over. A broad grin split her face. "You look mighty good to me!" Her eyes fell on Adele. "Now you introduce this child around before she thinks you been raised in the barn."

"Mademoiselle Scarron, allow me to present my brother, Denis," Lucien said obediently. "My baby sister, Emilie. And this is Mammy Rachel. You get on her good side—she's the real authority at Belle Marie."

"Your servant, Mademoiselle." Denis kissed her hand punctiliously.

"How d'you do?" Emilie bobbed a curtsy.

"Welcome to Belle Marie, honey." Mammy Rachel patted her hand.

Adele, steaming in the heat and the crowd along the levee, acknowledged Denis with a smile, automatically coquettish, and Emilie with a briefer one. A nod sufficed for Mammy Rachel. Adele swayed carefully in Lucien's direction. "I fear I am feeling a trifle faint."

"You come along with us," Denis said. "*Petite Marie's* just down the levee a piece. That's our boat." He grinned at Lucien. "You ought to see her. Papa had the boiler overhauled, and she steams along like a racehorse now. New coat of paint, too."

"That Sam, he's gone to get the bags," Mammy said. "You all come along before Miss Scarron faints dead. Miss Emilie, ladies don't stand on their heads and show their drawers."

Emilie upended herself and straightened up. She gave Adele's expression of delicate suffering a look out of the corners of her eyes. "*I'm* not hot," she announced.

"That's because the devil left you here." Denis gave her a swat on the backside. "You're not really a DuMontaigne at all, you're a jaybird. Nothing but blue feathers under that pinafore."

"Mister Denis, don't you go scarin' that baby!"

"I'm not scared," Emilie said scornfully. She skipped along ahead of them, twitching her shoulders experimentally. It might be fun to be a jaybird.

"The darkies'll tell you that all the jaybirds go to hell on Friday afternoons to report to the devil," Lucien explained to Adele. "We fully expect them to take Emilie along with them any week now."

"I see. How quaint." Sam arrived at *Petite Marie*'s gangplank hard on their heels, a trunk balanced on each brawny shoulder. Adele drew her skirts aside fastidiously as he passed.

"You've never seen darkies before, have you?" Denis said. "You want to be careful not to hurt their feelings."

"I am sure they are most loyal servants," Adele said stiffly. Privately she thought that Mammy Rachel was far too free in her manner, an attitude that would never have been tolerated in a French servant. "But they are not very . . . polished, perhaps."

"Nor are they deaf," Denis said. He strode on up the gangplank to help Sam stow the trunks. He didn't know that he thought much of Miss Scarron, but he didn't have time to worry about her now. He was more interested in getting out of New Orleans before Françoise Becquerel found out he was there and hadn't called. Denis sat down on Lucien's trunk and mentally kicked himself as Sam cast off. Françoise still enticed him, but he was beginning to regard her as a praying mantis might its true love—exotic and sensual, and very possibly too hungry.

He had seen her again when the DuMontaignes and the Prevosts from Alouette plantation had attended the French Opera. In the interval, Françoise had beckoned to him from her box and informed him delicately, behind her fan, that Gilbert would be away from the city for a week. The invitation was plain, and Denis had seen no way to turn it down. He hadn't really wanted to, he admitted, but he should have. He should have stuck wax in his ears like Ulysses and, figuratively speaking, chained himself to the mast, before he set foot in Françoise Becquerel's rose-colored boudoir again. A gentleman, she had given him to understand, did not accept a lady's favors if he did not intend to avail himself of them often.

"I wouldn't want to put you in any sort of danger," Denis had protested, striving for a gallant tone. Enclosed in the rose silk hangings of her bed, he was beginning to feel like a stud horse in a stall.

Françoise reclined languidly in the cushions, the silken coverlet exposing round, pink-tipped breasts: firm, neat half circles, delicately blue-veined. She had had three children, but each had had a black wet nurse, since like many ladies, Madame Becquerel was considered too delicate to feed her own young; it wasn't quite nice to be healthy enough to nurse your babies. She certainly exhibited stamina in bed, Denis thought, and a determination that was rapidly making him uneasy.

"The only danger, my dear Denis, would be if Gilbert should learn of us," she had said, smiling, watching him under heavy-lidded eyes.

"I couldn't chance that," Denis said. "For your sake."

"I don't believe you understand me, Denis," Françoise said. "Gilbert would never suspect me of infidelity—he is far too busy with his own. Thus I am lonely. Without this comfort, I fear I shouldn't know what to do." She sighed. "Of course, if Gilbert should learn that I had been unfaithful, it might shock him into giving me more attention. I should hate to tell him a thing like that, but if you leave me, Denis, I fear I might be distraught enough to confess." She stretched, arms over her head, and then held them out to him. "You do understand me now, Denis?"

Françoise's half-veiled threat had been plain enough for anyone to understand. Denis put his head in his hands as *Petite Marie* picked up speed. He wasn't particularly afraid of Gilbert Becquerel, other than of the agonizing embarrassment that would result. But his father! Denis thought wildly, only half laughing at himself, that he would rather change his name and go west than have Paul find out. So he had begun to hide from Françoise, pleading pressing business at Belle Marie, forgoing balls and the opera and any other place where she might find him, skulking around corners, he thought ruefully, like a pickpocket. Oh Lord, how *had* he got into this mess?

Adele was solicitously settled in a chair on *Petite Marie*'s deck, with a gratifying number of small attentions to her comfort, which a Creole woman would have taken for granted. She found herself in a better frame of mind. Unaware that the fuss with footstools and glasses of lemonade were merely the way the DuMontaignes considered that all ladies were supposed to be treated, she wondered if there might be hope for Lucien yet. She studied him out of the corners of her eyes while Emilie, settled in Mammy Rachel's lap, studied Adele.

Adele had dismissed Denis almost at first meeting. He had shown no signs of interest in her attractions, and in any case, he was the younger son. Lucien, she knew by now, would have the plantation. The green riverbanks slid by at a distance, and occasionally the wall of trees were broken by a vista of flat fields planted in waist-high cane or an avenue of towering oaks with a house, white or pastel shades, gracefully columned and balconied, at the avenue's end. Lucien named them for her as they passed.

"That's D'Estrehan there. And that's Alouette." Around a farther bend a peach-colored house with wide double stairs mounting to a front gallery appeared among a riot of azaleas. Sam, who counted the Prevosts at Alouette almost as family, toot-tooted the whistle, and the master of the house, riding along the levee road on a tall bay hack, raised his hat and waved an arm. He cupped his hands to his mouth. "Welcome home!" *Petite Marie* hooted again in reply.

Lucien, growing bored with his role as guide, seized the opportunity to drift away to the railing and call a greeting and farewell as they churned past. Adele, vexed, followed him with her eyes. Every time she thought that Lucien might be in her hand, he slid away. He wanted only one thing from her, and she thought that he had grown bored trying to get it and would seek elsewhere before he would improve his offer. She clicked her teeth together, an angry little sound, and composed her face into an air of demure coquetry as he turned back from the railing. But he didn't pause by her chair again, disappearing instead into the wheelhouse, where he could be heard cajoling Sam to let him take the wheel.

Emilie, sprawled in Mammy Rachel's lap with her white button boots dangling above the deck, twirled her empty lemonade glass between her hands and watched the newcomer with suspicion. Emilie decided there wasn't going to be much in Papa's promise of a new friend in Adele. Adele didn't look like a lady who had time for children. Emilie didn't think she wanted to be friends with Adele anyway. And it wasn't lost on her that Mammy Rachel had called her "Miss Scarron" and not "Miss Adele." Emilie slewed her head around to look up at Mammy.

"Is she going to stay long?"

"I don't know, honey, and it ain't polite to ask. Makes it look like you want folks to leave before they've got here. She's goin' to be here a spell."

"Do you like her?"

"Now that ain't my place, Miss Emilie. She's your Mama's guest." Mammy gave the unappreciated Miss Scarron a thoughtful look. "Reckon we'll just both have to be polite."

Adele caught her breath as *Petite Marie*'s engines slowed and Sam began to maneuver her up to the levee below Belle Marie. The white house, visible from the river, rose like a graceful ship in an ocean of flowers. Neatly clipped gardens ran down to the levee road. The levee was packed with people turned out to welcome home the son of the house . . . and to get a look at the French lady who'd come to stay. Adele, stepping down the gangway with Lucien at her elbow, felt herself inspected by two hundred pairs of black eyes. They were ranged neatly on either side of the garden walk, the house servants to the front, in neat uniforms and shiny boots, the field hands, barefoot mostly, behind them and hanging back shyly, clutching pigtailed, wide-eyed children by the hand. Adele, kissed by Paul and Sallie and presented to Felicie, Hollis, Tante Doudouce, and Barret Forbes, was startled to find herself also presented to the butler and the cook and a black girl called Junie, whom Sallie had promoted to be her maid.

Junie bobbed a curtsy, awkwardly, her new shoes pinching her feet. "Don' you worry, Miss Adele," she announced in an almost unintelligible patois, "I speak good French, I do."

Adele nodded, at a loss for words now that she actually found herself in the place that she had so tenaciously cheated its owners to reach. When Lucien had described it to her, it had sounded like fairyland, and the reality did not disappoint her. On the landward side were the quarters, rows of small cabins made of pine boards and mud mixed with Spanish moss, which housed nearly all the Belle Marie's two hundred black slaves. Only a trusted few— Mammy Rachel, Testut the butler, and the DuMontaignes' valets and ladies' maids—slept in the great house. A grove of pecan and walnut trees shielded the main house from the view of the quarters.

Next to the quarters were the pigpen and cattle shed, chicken house, dovecote, and a pond that was home to a family of white ducks. The kitchen itself was a separate building beside the vegetable rows, where the heat of cooking would not add to the already sultry temperatures of a Louisiana summer inside the main house, and where the danger of fire would be less. Behind the main house were the stables, where the DuMontaigne saddle and carriage horses were housed in a style considerably grander than that of the slaves.

Past the stables the oak avenue swept up to the rear of the great house of Belle Marie. The house was built of cypress, the most enduring lumber in the world, so Lucien said, and it was shaded by the oaks and magnolias planted by Paul DuMontaigne's grandfather, the rough and ambitious self-made man who had named his plantation for his only child, Paul's mother, Marie. A steep-hipped roof sloped out to shade the slender columns and wide galleries that ran around all four sides of the house on both first and second floors.

The main building was flanked by two smaller *garçonnières*, bachelor quarters where the DuMontaigne sons and male guests could smoke their cigars and play cards late into the night, or return tipsy from an outing without disturbing the ladies of the house. Like the great house, the *garçonnières* were open and airy, and tall ceilinged to catch the slightest breeze.

In the gardens to her left, Adele could see a summerhouse, a miniature of Belle Marie, built on an artificial rise where it would catch the cool air off the water. When the weather turned hot, the ladies of Belle Marie could settle in the summerhouse to sip *eau sucré* and orange blossom syrup and watch slate-blue herons wading in the artificial lake.

Paul spoke a low command, and the field hands moved back to their work and the house servants took up the baggage. Belle Marie was a kingdom in itself, Adele thought, and Paul DuMontaigne was its king. She looked up into a face greatly like Lucien's, but older, more marked with character. Jet brows rose above brown eyes and strong cheekbones. His face was rectangular, softened by a wide, sensitive mouth and the soft laugh lines at the corners of his eyes. His black hair was lightly brushed with gray. Adele observed him carefully and laid a small gloved hand in his. "You have been so kind, Monsieur DuMontaigne, to my poor father and me. His last words were of you. I feel truly now that I have come home."

> *"Drink to me only with thine eyes,*
> *And I will pledge with mine;*
> *Or leave a kiss within the cup,*
> *And I'll not ask for wine. . . ."*

Sallie and Barret were harmonizing happily at the pianoforte, while Lucien was ensconced on the settee unpacking a valise full of presents. Sallie already wore hers, a gold bracelet enclosing an ivory miniature painted with a view of Versailles. Tante Doudouce, protesting with agitated chirps that dear Lucien really needn't have remembered her, *truly,* was pinning on a new cap in front of the gilt mirror above the mantel. Paul thought that it looked as if she had it on upside down, but that was the way Doudouce tended to look anyway. With a silver humidor stocked with his favorite cigars at his elbows, Paul watched the further distribution indulgently. Anyone who traveled always brought back presents. It was a family custom, and the farther the journey, the more splendid the presents. Emilie had been allowed to stay up past her bedtime to receive her gift and had looked all during dinner as if she might burst before she got it. Little Mimsie sat on

the floor beside her, wide-eyed, knowing that there would be
something in the valise for her, too.

With a flourish, Lucien produced a doll, eighteen inches high,
with a face of delicate china, and blond china curls. She wore a
red velvet dress, white silk drawers, and a bonnet with a big red
bow. Emilie clutched the doll adoringly, put her down, hurled
herself at Lucien, and kissed him, and then clutched the doll
again. She screwed up her face, eyes closed, deep in thought.
"Her name is Madame Josette," she announced when she opened
them.

"Why not Mademoiselle?" Lucien inquired.

"Silly. Only married ladies wear velvet dresses. But her
husband's at sea," she added. Who needed him? "What about
Mimsie?" she prodded. Surely Lucien wouldn't forget Mimsie.

Lucien produced a flat package and gave it to Mimsie. "I hope
your granny doesn't get mad at me, but Emilie wrote and said it
was what you wanted."

Mimsie pulled the wrapping off and let out a soft breath of joy.
Books!

Mammy Rachel sighed. She didn't approve of Mimsie getting
ideas above her place. Mimsie read everything she could get her
hands on, and all that was going to get her was a misery later on,
Mammy suspected, wanting what she couldn't have. But it was
hard to get mad at Mr. Lucien when she had a red taffeta petticoat
with a French label in it folded over her arm. She rose, shooing
the little girls before her. "You two take Madame Josette and them
books up to bed now." She caught Mimsie by one pigtail. "And
no readin' till you got Miss Emilie's clothes shook out an' her hair
brushed."

"Yes'm."

"That pickaninny isn't going to be fit to be anybody's maid,"
Hollis said, "with her head stuffed full of fairy stories."

"Well, I think it was sweet of Emilie to write and tell Lucien
what to get her," Felicie said.

"I didn't know what to get *you*," Lucien said, "but I kind of
figured you might be too big for dolls, so I got you the same as
Hollis." He handed them each a box done up in silver paper and
presented a third to Adele. "To say welcome."

Adele took it with a smile and no illusions. Lucien must have
bought it before they had left Paris, and if it were the same as he
had got his sisters, it wouldn't a particularly good sign.

They opened the boxes to find necklaces of fine glass beads,
delicate as spindrift, green for Hollis and blue for Felicie. Adele's

were black, in tribute of her mourning. She fastened them around her neck, trying to look properly grateful.

"Very becoming," Hollis said. "And so suitable." Her green eyes rested, catlike and thoughtful, on Adele, with an expression that almost made Lucien laugh. Sister dear seemed to be finding the house rather too full of rivals, he thought, with Felicie grown up and himself appearing with little Adele under his wing. Being a widow apparently hadn't stunted Hollis's desire to be queen bee.

He presented the last package to Denis and whispered under his breath, "Reserve a front-row seat now for the cat fight."

"Well, don't stir it up," Denis said. He unwrapped a gold cigar case appreciatively. "Good of you, Lucien."

"Nothing too good for the family." The fact that the bills for his offerings were still floating about somewhere in Paris did not trouble him greatly. They would be a long time reaching New Orleans.

Sallie and Barret finished their song with a flourish and came to inspect the loot. A cheerful family buzz arose, and Adele, no longer even half listening, took in the pale satin upholstery, the thick leaf-green silk hangings, the silver tray of cakes and *eau sucré* that rested on a cherry table: all the trappings of wealth and solidity that she wanted so badly that the tips of her fingers itched. Even the sultry climate, which stayed hot well into the night, seemed less oppressive here in the high-ceilinged parlor. A small Negro boy sat cross-legged in the corner, rhythmically pulling at a rope, and the blades of a punkah fan whispered overhead. They took all this for granted, the DuMontaignes, theirs by right and birth. Adele folded her hands in her lap lest someone, somehow, see how they itched.

Jules Scarron's child was a sweet little thing, Paul thought. A little lost and lonely just now. Not much of a look of Jules about her, but that was often hard to see in a daughter. She wasn't going to be any trouble; he'd settle a little money on her when Sallie found her a husband.

"Come and have a drink with us, sir?" The ladies had retired, and the gentlemen, at loose ends, stood on the veranda, trying to decide whether to go to bed themselves.

"No, I want to ride down to Alouette and talk over this campaign Roman's inveigled me into." Paul affectionately draped an arm around Lucien's shoulders. "If I get that over with tonight, we can spend tomorrow together." Roman had an invalid wife and very little to do with his evenings. He would be awake.

"All right, we'll have a ride in the morning. Is Firefly fit?"

"Too damned fit. He threw Will last week." Firefly was a tall, rakish chestnut that had been Lucien's coming-of-age present. He was probably the fastest horse on Belle Marie and had a temperament to match.

Lucien laughed, with a reckless look in his eye. Paul thought that his son liked the horse best when it was unmanageable. "Well, wear your old breeches," he said. "Will went in the bayou." He knew Firefly wouldn't throw Lucien, though. No horse ever did.

Barret, watching their dark, fine-boned faces, head to head, thought that they were as alike as two peas, on the surface. All the same, if he were Paul, he'd put his money on Denis.

Paul lifted a hand in farewell, and the two sons and Barret strolled off toward a decanter of whiskey and the armchairs that sat on the veranda of the *garçonnière* to the right of the main house. Lucien and Denis had their rooms in the *garçonnière*, and Barret was staying in the guesthouse to the left. Paul and Sallie had encouraged Barret to extend his visit, and he had seemed happy to. Paul thought that Barret liked to get away from his sister, Alice. A trying woman, Alice.

In the stable, a sleepy groom roused himself from a bed in the straw outside the loose boxes and blinked at Paul.

"I want Molasses, Will, but you can go back to bed. I'll saddle him."

"Yes, sir, Mister Paul." Will lay back down. Mister Paul only liked to be waited on up to a point, and he usually saddled his own horse. Wouldn't make a mess of it and bring him back with a hurt, either, like some other folks' masters that Will could name. Will was proud of his place and ruled the three little pickaninnies who were his apprentice grooms with an exacting hand. The DuMontaigne saddle horses, as he was fond of informing them, were worth more than a lot of darkies on the place.

"I be glad to let Mister Lucien ride that Firefly, though," Will said darkly. "Hoss see a ha'nt in the gum tree and just upend hisself." Will rubbed his skin tenderly. There had been a rock in the water where he had come down.

Paul chuckled and swung Molasses out into the moonlight. It was a good night for "ha'nts"—ghosts. The trees lifted spectral arms to the moon, whose light turned the trailing moss to silver. It was still warm, and the air was wet and smelled richly of the lush growth overlaid with the faint hint of decay that swampland carries with it. Katydids and tree peepers made a chirping, whirring chorus all around him.

Paul kicked Molasses into a gallop along the levee road. When he turned into the gates of Alouette, he saw that he had been right: There were lights lit on the veranda, and he could see Roman Prevost's tall figure sprawled in a chair. His elbows were propped on the arms, fingertips together under his chin. Paul tied Molasses to a ring in the white brick hitching block.

Roman poured him a drink, and they settled into a companionable silence for a moment. Roman Prevost was muscular and broad-shouldered, with iron-gray hair clipped shorter than the fashion, and the tanned face of a man who spent as much time as possible out-of-doors. In evening dress, which he put on to please his wife, Eugenie, he still gave the impression of wearing riding boots. Paul and Roman had known each other since Roman's father had bought Alouette (won it in a card game, the rumor went) when Paul was seven and Roman five.

"How is Eugenie?" Paul inquired politely.

"Much the same," Roman said. "As well as can be expected."

Paul didn't pursue the subject. Roman's marriage to Eugenie had been an arranged one, in the Creole tradition. Love was expected to come *after* marriage, and Paul supposed it might have if Eugenie, who was possessed of a plaintive nature anyway, had not become an invalid in the first year of their marriage. Roman was a kind man, and he gave her every attention, but it was small wonder if he was restless. At that, maybe Roman hadn't done any worse than had Paul, who had married for love.

I didn't come here to wonder what's wrong with Sallie, Paul thought, irritated with himself. He grinned at Roman. "Now that you have talked me into this, *mon vieux,* and I can't back out, I hope you have a strategy. I warned you this wasn't really in my line."

"I noticed you handing that plain gentleman-farmer horseshit to the rest of the committee," Roman said. He snorted. "Your grandfather, old LeClerc, practically ran New Orleans."

"He didn't, however, run for *office*."

"As for the Whigs," Roman said thoughtfully, "that no-good Harrison they have put up for president has no substance. And Becquerel's a Whig. He's what we want to throw out."

"How do your reforming Democrats suggest we go about it?"

"Well, we want you to debate him, for one thing."

"Good God."

"You're a gentleman, and Becquerel's not . . . quite. Oh, his birth's all right, but there's something about him. . . . You're our kind, and if we play that up, it'll help pull some of the other landowners to our side."

"If I don't make an ass of myself."

"Your stand's clear enough. State's rights and honest politics. Protection for our class and what we've built up here, and a chance for the common man to vote his conscience and not get mowed down by the political machine."

"You don't think they're mutually exclusive?"

"Not at all."

"Then why don't *you* run?" Paul grumbled.

Roman laughed. "I'm not quite untarnished enough. None of us are." Roman had had a hand in Louisiana politics for years, and it was time to change custom. Any man with a brain knew that if New Orleans wanted to stay alive, she'd better change her reputation or lose her shipping commerce to the railroads. "It's time for new blood. You're as honest a man as we'll find. We've known each other too long for me to say that lightly, Paul." *More honest than I am,* Roman thought with a twinge of conscience. Too honest to carry on with his best friend's daughter. Hollis was too much temptation for a man with an invalid wife, but Roman was uneasily aware that that wasn't sufficient excuse. Paul deserved better from him. If it came to that, Paul deserved better than Hollis.

Hollis lay on her stomach in a tangle of damp linen, behind the mosquito *baire* that enclosed her bed, and stared thoughtfully at the pineapple carved across the headboard. It was stiflingly hot, and her thin muslin nightgown clung to her shoulders and backside, and Hollis wished vaguely that Roman were there to appreciate it. When she was sure Mammy was in bed, she was going to take the nightgown off too. Mammy would consider that a disgrace. Hollis put her chin in her hands, dismissing Mammy. It wasn't Mammy, or even Roman, that she was brooding on. It was Adele Scarron.

There was something false about that namby-pamby wench with the die-away airs and "poor me" bereavement. Papa didn't see it, Hollis thought, galled; she considered Paul her personal property as much as any of her beaux. And Denis wouldn't notice if the woman were a snake and bit him. But Emilie didn't like her, and Emilie was embarrassingly perceptive.

Well, I don't like her either, Hollis thought, *and I don't know why Papa had to go and have her live with us. She's probably just looking for a rich husband, and we don't know anything about her.*

She sat up in bed, pushed the mosquito *baire* aside, and pattered across the hooked rugs and polished cypress floor. Momentarily diverted, she stopped and posed in the moonlight in front of the cheval glass, hands behind her back, hips thrust up and forward, pubic curve outlined sharply under thin muslin. She held the pose a moment appreciatively.

Hollis abandoned the cheval glass to delve for the writing paper, quills, and ink in the little rosewood secretary under the window. Then she sat for a moment chewing the end of the quill.

The French parish priest, that was who would know. They always knew everything. What was the name of the village? Saint something. Hollis tapped her fingers in exasperation. Half the villages in France were called Saint one thing or another. St. Martin! Her green eyes narrowed triumphantly.

"Au prêtre de l'Eglise du village de St. Martin . . ."

Adele lay with her hands clasped behind her head, eyes flicking eagerly from corner to corner of her room. It was palatial by the standards of any room she had ever had to call her own, and Paul DuMontaigne had said that she must think of it as hers when he patted her hand as she ascended the stairs with Sallie and Mammy Rachel to guide her. All her gowns had been unpacked and shaken out and hung away in the cedar clothes press by Junie, who was waiting to help her undress, her black face screwed up with the effort of remembering the countless instructions delivered by Mammy on the proper conduct of a lady's maid.

Adele found being touched by black hands distasteful, but she had given no sign of it as Junie had unlaced her stays and dropped her nightgown over her head. Then Junie had brushed Adele's hair until it gleamed, tucked her—literally—into the great four-poster bed, checked the mosquito *baire* for the smallest of holes, and assured her that she would wake her with her café first thing in the morning. Adele's stiff thanks had done little to daunt Junie's cheer. White folks were peculiar, and white ladies more peculiar than any—it came, in Junie's opinion, of not bein' able to *do* nothin'— but Junie was so enchanted with her new position that the lady responsible for it could do no wrong.

The mosquito netting made the room beyond it look ethereal, wispy in the moonlight. Adele peered through the misty net, counting up treasures. The place was a haven, a room out of fairyland. And *hers*. Paul had said it was hers, but Adele felt precarious in this room, as if it might somehow be snatched away from her just as she had got it. Adele wanted it as sharply as a starving person wanted food.

If they found out her secret, they would take it away.

She sat up and wrapped her thin arms around her knees. Nothing could be taken away if she were married to it. She might also grow old and die before she caught Lucien DuMontaigne. Adele hugged her knees and thought. *Paul*. The name crept into her mind. Paul DuMontaigne, who was king of the kingdom already.

Adele's eyes narrowed, staring through the mosquito *baire* at nothing. It had been obliging of the real Adele to die. But here in this gold and white room, at the heart of everything she longed for, the new Adele thought that for this, it would not have been so hard to help her along.

And surely here in America, where the kingdom of Belle Marie was a civilization set down in a wilderness, it would be even easier to rid oneself of Paul DuMontaigne's wife.

VI

Picnic

at

Alouette

"MY GRANDFATHER BUILT these hothouses. We don't have much of a winter here in Louisiana, but we do have some. In the hothouses, this sort of thing can be grown all year." Paul gently lifted a white orchid bloom on the back of two fingers.

Adele inspected it dutifully.

"Actually my grandfather was more interested in things to eat: We grow pineapples in here. But Sallie likes to keep flowers year round. There's a vase of them in every room in the house, fresh every day."

"I know. There are lilies in mine this morning. Lovely. Do you know, Monsieur DuMontaigne, I don't think that, except for the time I spent with Papa, I have ever been so happy as I have been here this last week?"

"Well, I'm glad of it, my dear. And you must call me Paul. We're family of a sort. Cousin Paul, if you like."

"Very well then, Cousin Paul." Adele gave him a sidelong look and a smile. "Tell me about the sugar cane. Lucien tried to explain it to me, but I am afraid I am very stupid. I didn't understand it at all."

"Well, come outside then, and get a breath of air." Adele followed him gratefully. It was stifling in the glassed-in hothouse.

"Come and admire the azaleas. They do grow wild here, but these are cultivated." He settled her on a white marble bench in front of a massed bank of them, scarlet and pale pink. Paul stood facing her and put one boot up on the end of the bench, leaning his arms on his knee.

"Sugar cane is the wealth of every planter here, and the bane of his existence. It is a tropical plant, you see, and Louisiana is a subtropical country. So the cane never fully matures. One must cut it at the last moment, and then cut it all in a great hurry before it spoils. Too much rain, too little rain, the wrong temperature—it rots. Cotton is more stable, but the land is too wet for it this close to the river. And sugar is better money."

"And then, it is . . . ground up?"

"It's really put through rollers to squeeze the juice out, and then the juice is boiled for syrup, and crystallized."

"Then sugar supports . . . all this?" Adele's hand made a gesture inclusive of house and gardens and the acres stretching away beyond.

"I've money in a few other ventures," Paul said. "It pays to have a safety valve. But without the cane, no, there would be no Belle Marie."

"You love it greatly, do you not, Belle Marie?"

"Very dearly," Paul said, touched that she should notice. "There will always be DuMontaignes here." He patted her hand. "And you will always be welcome among them. And now, I should take you in. It's going to pour in a minute." The air had thickened, and the sky overhead shimmered with water. A few warm drops fell on her hand.

"Come on." He took her hand. She picked up her skirts with the other, and they raced for the house.

Across the garden, Adele saw Tante Doudouce frantically trying to gather up her prayer book and tatting in a large unmanageable bundle that trailed skeins of thread about her feet. In a family like the DuMontaignes a spinster kinswoman was always welcome, but Adele had not failed to notice that they all called her "poor Tante Doudouce."

If I do not marry this man, I shall be like that, she thought.

Denis and Lucien, riding along beside the cut that drained the lowest of the cane fields, merely pulled their hats a little lower over their eyes against the rain. They carried waterproofs rolled up behind their saddles, but the effect inside them was very much like a steam bath. It was more comfortable just to get wet.

The field hands, hoeing weeds in the waist-high cane, dropped their tools and ran gleefully for the canvas shelter at the end of the field. It was dinnertime anyway, and if they were lucky, the downpour would last a while.

A woman from the kitchen dipped greens, pot likker, and peas out of two kettles, and a small girl followed behind her with a basket of bread. Big Daniel, the slave acting as temporary overseer, dipped his bread in the pot likker and watched the rain come down. It made the cane grow, but it sure did make the weeds grow too. It would be more than two months before the cane could be laid by—tall and thick enough to be left to choke out the weeds on its own.

A light chocolate-brown woman sidled up to Daniel, tin plate in her hand. "Aw now, Dan'l, I can't get no strength from this. You give me somethin' good to eat, I show you what I can do." She licked her lips suggestively.

Daniel pushed her away, not without a certain amount of regret. "You quit struttin' your shape at me, Celeste. Won't do you no good." He grinned at her. "Mister Paul say he gon' hire a new overseer by an' by. Maybe you get lucky again."

Celeste sat down with a pout. Mister Jim, the last overseer, used to give her good things to eat and lighter chores than chopping cane just for coming to his house at night. With Mister Jim gone, Celeste was aggrieved to find herself treated like everyone else.

A tall black man with the face of a nearly pure African changed places to sit beside her. "If you hungry, I give you my bread," he said. "You stay 'way from Dan'l."

Celeste shrugged. She bit into the bread, strong white teeth making neat indentations along the edge. She moved so that her bare leg rested against him. "You don' own me, Gabriel. You ain't even married to me."

"I would be," Gabriel said.

Celeste tossed her head. She'd rather be dead underground than married to Gabriel. Celeste liked to have the men coming around; that was power. Gabriel wouldn't stomach that for a minute if they were married—he didn't like it now, when it wasn't his business. She rubbed one bare foot against him. "You come round tomorrow." Tomorrow was Saturday, a free day. "Maybe I give you somethin' you like just as well." Maybe she wouldn't too. She'd decide tomorrow. If he started trying to teach her his dreary old stories again, she'd find someone else. Who wanted to hear about Africa? Africa sounded worse than anything Celeste had ever heard of.

Gabriel finished the remains of his dinner, knowing what she was thinking. What he wanted with a no-account, loose woman like Celeste, he didn't know, but want her he did. She was in his skin as much as the stories that he saved and treasured so fiercely, his only legacy from his African father. "That's your heritage," he had tried to tell her. "Same as white folks look to France, we got to look to Africa, an' be proud."

"I ain't proud of nothin' 'cept I don't have a face as black as a coal bin," Celeste snapped. "You go teach the pickaninnies, you want to, leave me alone." What was the use of going around proud, saying your granddaddy was a king in Africa? It was the white man who had the power and having white skin that got you somewhere.

Denis cast a thoughtful eye on Daniel, who was watching the squabbling couple with uncertainty. The darkies would be getting out of hand pretty soon if André Peyraud didn't find them an overseer, and then the new man would waste a lot of time getting them in shape again.

"Papa wants you to get a feel for the place again, Lucien. You'd better start here, until we get an overseer."

"So Papa mentioned," Lucien said. He yawned. "Do you know, Denis, I believe I'm getting wet." He swung Firefly's head around, sitting the red stallion easily, as Firefly kicked and curvetted, seeing spooks in the wet cane.

Denis kicked his own horse into a canter and swung him across Firefly's path. "This is going to be *yours!* Don't you care enough to see to it properly?"

"Why, yes," Lucien said lazily. "I can't say I have a burning desire to play overseer. Much too hot, and it interferes with my day."

"And what happens when Papa's gone, and you have to run it yourself?"

"Why, then I expect I can hire you, can't I?"

Denis made an angry grab at Firefly's reins.

Lucien's eyes flared. "Take your hand off my horse!"

"Not until you listen to me!"

They sat glaring at each other in the pouring rain, straw hats sheeting water. Finally Lucien gave a small shrug. "I don't want to quarrel with you, Denis. We used to be friends."

"You mean I used to cover for you to Papa," Denis said grimly.

"Come now, I made the first move. It's your turn." That was how they had settled boyhood fights. If one made an overture, the other was honor bound to take it. Denis decided to ignore the fact that Lucien only made overtures when it suited him.

"Will you listen?" Denis entreated.

"Yes, yes. Say your piece."

"Just this." Denis looked Lucien square in the face, hazel eyes stubbornly meeting Lucien's impatient black ones. "You're going to have Belle Marie whether I like it or not, and I won't stand by while you run it into the ground."

Lucien cocked an eyebrow. "Jealous, baby brother?"

"Shut up, Lucien. You *will* learn to manage it properly, because if you don't, I will knock you down and push your face in."

He dropped Firefly's rein and kicked his own horse up the road, aware of the field hands' interested eyes on his back. Lucien chuckled and followed him.

For the next three weeks Lucien inspected every inch of Belle Marie with his father and brother, Paul showing him the past year's improvements with pride. Denis had the grimly purposeful air of a school teacher with a reluctant pupil.

Sallie, watching them, couldn't decide whether she was viewing family togetherness or a neatly constructed bomb that was getting ready to go off. She loved all her children, but couldn't help thinking that if only one son could have Belle Marie, it should be the one who loved it best. But how could she say that to Paul, when she *knew,* if he didn't, that Denis wasn't his?

When Roman Prevost brought an invitation to a picnic at Alouette, in honor of Adele's arrival, Lucien's homecoming, and Barret's visit, Sallie accepted with heartfelt thanks. A day of idleness and good company might defuse the bomb. At any rate, Denis wouldn't knock Lucien down at it.

The only fly in the ointment on the day was a worried Mammy Rachel, who had come to tell her that Meeow had a fever.

"Send for the doctor, and I'll go and see her." Summer fevers were not to be taken lightly.

"I done sent," Mammy said.

"Felicie, get me my bag." Like most plantation mistresses, Sallie nursed the sick herself, with Mammy's help and, lately, Felicie's.

"I've got it, Mama. Is Meeow going to be all right?" Of all the black folk on Belle Marie, Meeow was second only to Mammy in the DuMontaigne children's love. She spoiled their dinner appetites with illicit cakes and let them help on baking days. The best stories of Felicie's childhood had been told by Meeow, her arms white to the shoulders with flour, amid an enthralled audience of children and cats.

"Well, we aren't going to know until we see her," Sallie said, but she looked worried too. Meeow aside, she couldn't trust Hollis to see that Adele had a good time at the picnic. *Why everything at once?* she thought, distracted.

Meeow's round black face was dry and hot to the touch. She lay on the cot in her cabin with her "cures" hung above it: chinaberries and toadgrass, and a gris-gris of bits of red wool and what Sallie, resolutely ignoring it, thought was a chicken head.

"My spells don' do me no good, Miss Sallie," Meeow said.

"Well, they may yet," Sallie said. She knew better than to take them down. "And we'll see what the doctor says."

"Won't be no good, Miss Sallie. It's done got me."

"Nothing's 'got you' until you're dead from it," Sallie said briskly, beginning to feel relieved. She had been afraid of yellow fever or malaria, but it didn't look like either. "Who else is sick?"

"One of the babies in the quarters is down with the chicken spots," Mammy said.

Sallie unbuttoned Meeow's dress in search of spots. A dead frog was bandaged tightly to her chest. Sallie lifted it gently. "I think this has done its work." That might be more than Doctor Leboeuf would stand for. Three little pimples were forming on her stomach. "Well, you're a bit old for it, Meeow, but I think you've got chicken pox."

"I ain't got no baby disease," Meeow said. Chicken pox was beneath her dignity. "The Lord gon' take me sure."

"No He isn't." Sallie looked at Mammy. "I don't like to leave though, not till Doctor Leboeuf has seen her. Just in case." It would distress Meeow if her white family waltzed away to a picnic while she was sick. And the Lord only knew what she'd dose herself with while Sallie wasn't looking.

"Let me stay, Mama," Felicie said. "I've had chicken pox."

"Well . . ."

"And I'd better have Doctor Leboeuf check all the pickaninnies too, and try to quarantine the ones that have got it," Felicie said, taking charge, "or some of the other big ones will get it, and you know it's awful to catch it when you're grown. Poor Meeow." She bent down and kissed the cook sympathetically. "I bet you feel terrible." She smoothed the coverlet over Meeow's ample frame, ignoring the fact that she could feel more charms and whatnot under it. "I'll send you a nicer pillow than this one. And Mammy, you get her some lemonade to drink."

Sallie blinked at her daughter in mild surprise. Then she got up and put her arms around her. "My darling girl, I believe you're growing up. All right, if you want to stay, you may. You come on to the picnic when the doctor has gone. I'll tell Will to harness the gig for you."

As she left she heard Felicie's voice, cheerful and reassuring. "Now you do what Doctor Leboeuf tells you to, because what on earth are we going to eat if you stay sick? You know that Sissie can't cook." Sissie was the kitchen maid. Meeow never trusted her with anything more complicated than shelling peas.

"Sissie?" Meeow changed her mind about dying. "Don't you let that fool in my kitchen. You borrow a cook from Mister Roman, you hear, lessen you *all* want to die!"

The picnic at Alouette might have been better described as an outdoor banquet. The long trestle tables were laid with white linen and Eugenie Prevost's best silver. There were fruit ices, pastries, and cold soups, and barbecued meat roasted whole over spits outside the kitchen. A quartet of musicians played under the towering magnolias, and the drive was lined with carriages and saddle horses. The garden thronged with company. The older men talked politics, crops, and horseflesh. Their wives, like a colorful flock of birds in scarlet and deep green, sat on the veranda or under the shade trees, and very little escaped their attention. Marriages and betrothals, births, deaths, and misbehavior were all commented upon, sorted out, and speculated over. Young men in summer suits paid court to girls in flower-petal muslins. The children—girls in short crinolines and pantalets, boys in short pants and wide lace collars, and the littlest boys in dresses— darted in and out while their mammies watched them benevolently from their own corner of the garden.

Mammy Rachel was keeping track of Emilie, and Hollis, left to keep track of herself, sat demurely, for the moment, on a bench under an oak tree and rested her green eyes thoughtfully on Roman Prevost. Her lips curled into a little smile. She could see only his back through the crowd of the picnic party, but every line of it was familiar to her. He had taken off his coat in the sweltering heat, which even the shade of the old magnolias did little to abate, and Hollis could see the muscles rippling down his back under his linen shirt. For a man in his forties, Roman's body was still strong and wiry, his legs slim in neat breeches and polished boots. Hollis watched him as he passed behind her father and Barret Forbes and appeared again bending over the chaise, where his invalid wife, Eugenie, was propped, with Tante Doudouce and the old Fontaine sisters to form her court, and a small Negro boy to hold her parasol. Eugenie was a pale, thin-lipped woman who had taken up ill health as one with an aptitude for music might take up the piano. She subscribed to the theory that a lady should always be the center of attention. If one couldn't command that attention with beauty, one could do it by being a nuisance.

Hollis didn't care for Eugenie. She had the belle's natural scorn for the wallflower, augmented by the fact that she knew Eugenie disapproved of *her*. Hollis eyed Roman pensively. She had come to the Prevosts' picnic prepared to be bored, but now she was beginning to get an idea. Roman was being excessively attentive to his wife and the old misses Fontaine, but Hollis knew that he was well aware of her.

The shadows of the magnolias played across the front of his breeches, defining perfectly, from Hollis's vantage point, the bulge beneath the fabric. Really, men's clothing was indecently informative.

They ought to wear crinolines, Hollis thought, giggling, *so we couldn't tell what they're thinking*. She made the prissiest face she could and nodded gravely to Eugenie and the misses Fontaine, then let one eyelid drop in the ghost of a wink as her gaze met Roman's. His eyebrows rose, but the elderly Fontaine sisters appeared not to notice. They bowed to her in return, with a faint hint of disapproval. *Old cats*. They had been "surprised that dear Hollis was out of mourning so soon," and were no doubt informing Tante Doudouce so, judging by the helpless, twittery look on her face. Hollis eyed the misses Fontaine with glee. If they only knew what she had been up to since Julien had succumbed to his fever. Now that she was out of those horrid black gowns, it was even better. Lavender, the color for half-mourning, suited her pale blond coloring to perfection.

Hollis turned a little so that Roman could get the full effect. *I'll do it*, she thought. *Right under the poor old things' noses*. She flicked an eye at Roman and slowly drew her index finger across her throat and down the swell of her breasts and saw that he was taking due notice. To slip away from a picnic party and make love with the host within spitting distance of nearly every stiff-necked old frump in Louisiana would be amusing. And she was practically certain that she could get Roman to do it, against his better judgment, which would be even more fun.

She looked her best today, Hollis knew, and her best was very enticing. Her white throat and shoulders were bare and dipped invitingly into a froth of lavender ruffles across the low neck of her gown. Under it her breasts were milky white, rounded and firm, with small pink nipples just the color of the ribbons in her camisole. Hollis had noticed that as she was dressing this morning and had thought then that she couldn't have made a better match if she had gone naked into the yard-goods shop to do it. Roman always noticed things like that and paid attention to them the way he paid attention to every part of her body.

Hollis felt herself growing flushed and warm under her crinolines, and then a tight, almost painful sensation began to take hold of her. She willed Roman to look at her again. He did, and she stood, swaying her bell-shaped skirts back and forth a little to intensify the sensation. She smoothed their ruffles with small white hands so that the stiff crinolines underneath pressed against her. She twisted her slim hips, rubbing herself against the crinolines.

Eugenie was gossiping languidly with Tante Doudouce and the misses Fontaine, and Roman edged away from them and moved smoothly through the crowd toward Hollis. He picked a julep and a glass of iced lemonade off a tray being passed by Jacob, the black butler, and handed the lemonade to Hollis with a courtly bow.

"If you were a mare, Hollis, I'd say it was time to send for the stallion. *Mon Dieu,* you are indecent." He whispered in her ear so that no one else could hear him, and Hollis saw with satisfaction that his face was flushed under his tan, and his voice was thick.

"You make me think indecent thoughts," she said mischievously. She peeped at him from under her pale lashes and then deliberately flicked a small pink tongue out and ran it slowly across her lips.

Roman eyed her with exasperation, feeling the stiffness that had come unbidden at the first sight of her grow worse. The very thought of Hollis made his blood run hot, and there was a devil in her that delighted in provoking him at the most inopportune moments—such as a picnic for a hundred people given in honor of her father's guests and her brother's return from France, and where Roman was the host. The quartet struck up a lively air, and under cover of their music Roman whispered, "Behave yourself, or I will spank you."

"Punishment for my naughty thoughts? You'd have to take my clothes off to do that." Hollis leaned against him, enjoying the feel of the hard muscles under his shirt. He held the frosted glass of julep in one hand, and the other hung free at his side. She drew the tip of one finger across the palm of that hand. "Would you like to spank me?"

Roman tensed with a sudden intake of breath that was evidence of his desire, if she needed any other than the dark flush on his face and the telltale bulge under his breeches. Hollis sparked a blaze in him, then quenched it with exquisite skill. He wondered where she had learned that. Certainly not from Julien. Roman decided that Hollis's skill was simply born of her appetites. A God-given talent, no doubt.

Hollis moved closer, so that the bell of her skirt hid the movement of her hands. She put her long fingers on his breeches, stroking the outline under them. He backed away, gritting his teeth.

"Stop it, Hollis."

Hollis looked amused—she enjoyed watching him squirm. She made another prissy face as two girls her own age strolled by, arm in arm. "Agnes, *chérie,* that is the prettiest gown!" They passed, and Hollis leaned against Roman again, chuckling. "I bet no one ever undressed *her* at a picnic."

She leaned back against the trunk of an ancient oak and put her hands up to fiddle with one of the ivory combs in her hair so that Roman should have the full benefit of her figure. The shadows dappled the white skin of her breast, and her waist was only a shade over eighteen inches. With no one but Roman to watch her, her thoughts were very plain on her face. Roman felt caution slip away from him as he gave in to the urge that was beginning to overpower him.

"Now how in the name of God am I to make love to you at a party?" he said, his voice husky.

"The old summerhouse," Hollis said. "No one goes there, and the path is oyster shells. We'd hear anyone coming." The summerhouse was at the other end of the gardens behind the box hedge. No one would walk that far in this sultry heat for no reason.

Hollis tugged briefly at his hands, then darted away into the shadows of the boxwood. Roman followed, desire coursing through every vein.

The summerhouse was overgrown, and where once the ladies of Alouette had sat in their summer muslins to savor lemonade and gossip, now the Spanish moss hung in gray-green folds like bed curtains. The strands of moss made shifting, aqueous shadows in the air as Roman strode up the sagging steps, following the flicker of lilac that was Hollis's skirt. For a moment that was all he could see of her, a ruffled flounce in a pool of pale sunlight, and then her face looked out at him from the shadows, her lips moist, her gray-green eyes hungry, her cheeks and neck suffused with color. Hollis let loose the passion within her like an animal off its leash. There was no calling it back.

"Watch," she said. "I like you to watch me." She turned her back so that he could see her small hands slowly, deliberately parting the hooks of her gown. As the last one came open she smiled at him over her shoulder. The ruffled lilac slipped to the floor with a stiff rustle as her crinolines came with it. Roman could see her slim waist and the round curve of her hips under thin pantalets. She moved languidly, with a mermaid's grace in the watery light, as if she heightened her desire deliberately now by holding it at bay. She posed for him, leaning against a moss-grown column, her hands tucked behind the curve of her hips, a wanton statue come to life. He caught his breath. "*Mon Dieu, you are so beautiful.*"

"That's why you're here, Roman," Hollis said. "Because I'm so beautiful."

He feverishly stripped off his shirt. Her hungry eyes slid over his chest, paler than the tanned skin of his face and neck. She slipped into his arms, and he held her, crushing her to him, drinking in the scent of her, lavender like the discarded gown. His hands fumbled in the ribbons of her camisole, and he picked the tiny buttons open and drew it down her arms. Hollis rubbed herself against his swelling manhood, the lavender scent mingling with the female smell of desire and willingness. Her breasts swelled above the lace and whalebone of her corset, and he buried his face in them, nibbling at the soft skin while his fingers wrestled with the knotted corset strings.

"Mmm mmm, can't do that," Hollis whispered. "I can't get back into the corset without Mammy to lace it. You'll just have to make do with the rest of me." Beneath her passion there was one cool, detached island that let lust run free and still protected her from its consequences. She took his hands and put them at her waist, on the laces of her pantalets instead. She wanted to feel his hands inside them, stroking, exploring. She gasped as Roman jerked savagely at the strings, and the pantalets slid away in a tangle of muslin and lace. His hands slid urgently down her belly to lose themselves in the curling blond hair below. For a moment she knew she was in danger of losing control of him and of the situation. Hollis gave her body thoroughly to her lovers, but the control must be hers.

"No, not yet. You're hurting me!"

"Goddamn you, Hollis." This time she was going to find out he wasn't a lapdog. He picked her up and laid her flat with a jolt in the shadows on the floor, standing up again only long enough to strip off his own boots and breeches. His manhood stood out before him, stiff, jutting out at her angrily.

She sat up in the sea foam of discarded crinolines and took him first between her hands and then into her mouth, moaning a little as she did so.

Roman rocked back on his heels, his hands clutching at her shoulders as pleasure throbbed through him. He stroked her throat, feeling the muscles move under his hand, but careful with the last vestige of good sense left to him not to press hard enough to leave a bruise. Her father and brothers were drinking juleps at Roman's picnic on the other side of the boxwood hedge, which added, he found, spice to the encounter. Certainly it seemed to for Hollis. Her mouth moved expertly, her eyes heavy-lidded. Her shoulders swayed as if to some erotic music, the swell of her breasts rising and falling. Her hips twisted slowly, wanting him, postponing one pleasure for another. Finally she sat back, panting for breath and licking her lips.

Roman grinned at her. His mouth felt heavy. "You shouldn't know how to do that. And you're indecently good at it."

"Roman! You know I wouldn't do that for any man but you!"

Roman ignored that. He knelt, still shaking. Hollis seemed content now to let him do what he wanted. He lifted her breasts out over the top of her corset, pinching them so that the nipples stood out. He rubbed them lightly with his forefinger, and a little moan came from deep in her throat.

"I want you now!"

He pushed her down flat again and began to play with her, his fingers in the soft curling hair between her thighs, postponing now, as she had done, the final delicious moment. Her slim hips began to twist on the floor, beckoning and urgent. Hollis moaned louder. Roman buried his face where his fingers had been, and put his fingers over her mouth to make her be quiet. She sucked at them greedily and spread her long white legs apart in the tangled muslin as far as they would go, her feet arched against the floor. He licked at her wet pink flesh as his passion mounted still higher. Then he lifted his mouth away and straddled her. "Roll over, Hollis."

Her eyes snapped open. He bent and kissed her belly. "I *said* I would spank you."

Her eyes, under heavy lids, glittered suspiciously. Roman slid his hands around her waist and lifted, moving himself to one side.

He turned her over. Her white, rounded buttocks were small, firm, and inviting. He pulled her across his lap and stroked the mounds, taking them firmly in his hands. "You have been a disgrace to your family all afternoon," he said, grinning.

He squeezed and kneaded. Hollis squirmed under his manipulations, and he lifted his legs, wedging her tightly between his knees and torso.

"You don't get away that easily. This is for ladies who don't act like ladies." One slap. "To teach you decorum." Another slap, a bit harder, turning the smooth white cheek pink. "Until you learn to behave." Three rapid slaps.

"That hurt!" Hollis tried to right herself, but Roman would not let her. Instead he leaned down and bit her. Then he squeezed and kneaded again, ran his hands between her legs and under, finding the source of her pleasure. She looked at him over shoulder, writhing. "Make love to me, Roman. I want you. I want you now."

He rolled her from him and knelt above her, sweating in the sultry shadows of the summerhouse. Hollis's face was flushed deeper now, and her hands pulled at his shoulders. Roman entered her in one swift stroke. As he thrust deep inside her he looked into those gray-green eyes, hoping to read something there, but there was only a hot desire. The urgency in him was too strong to care. He drove hard, again and again, until a tearing cry burst from her and she gasped and sank sharp teeth into his shoulder like an animal. He rode her harder, passion-driven, until his own climax exploded in frenzy, wave after wave, and he lay heavily on top of her, his mouth dry and his dark hair wet with the heat.

After a moment she pushed at him, and he rolled off her.

"I knew I could make you do it," she whispered with satisfaction. "I'll always be able to make you, won't I, Roman?"

He had the feeling that their lovemaking had been a battle for dominance. He wasn't sure who had won. "What if your father came looking for you?" he said.

"It would never occur to Papa that his daughter might be tumbling like a field hand in the summerhouse," Hollis said. She sounded as if it was partly that that had excited her, but she made a pious face. "I know that things would be different between us if they could. That you'd have me honestly, marry me." Her voice prodded him from drowsiness.

"Yes, of course," he murmured, sleepy now with the heat and satisfied desire. It was the expected answer. But a good Catholic could not divorce his wife. Roman found that he was grateful for that. Hollis in bed—or his summerhouse—was one thing. But he would as soon take an alligator to wife.

A small hand crept out and stoked his flaccid organ.

"It's too hot, Hollis. And I'm too old."

Hollis rubbed her face along his thigh. She bit him gently. After a moment Roman found that he was not too old, after all.

VII

The

Michelets

ROMAN DUCKED AROUND the far end of the boxwood hedge, feeling furtive and a trifle silly. Hollis had disappeared in the opposite direction and would shortly be found sipping *eau sucré* on the veranda with the gently bereaved air of a widow. Hollis would have done very well on the stage, Roman thought, chuckling, and it would have afforded her far more scope for her other talents.

A gig clip-clopped up the drive, and he turned to greet the late arrival. A small Negro groom hopped down from the gig. Roman blinked in surprise as a girl in an afternoon dress of cream-colored lace and blue-figured muslin handed the child the reins and buggy whip and stepped out onto the carriage block. She gave him a friendly smile and an impishly questioning look out of the bluest eyes he had ever seen.

"Good heavens! Felicie? Pardon, *Mademoiselle* Felicie!" Roman swept her an elegant bow.

Felicie looked delighted. "You didn't recognize me. That proves I *have* grown up!" She held out her hand. "How do you do, Monsieur Prevost?"

Roman kissed the little kid glove. "I do very well now that you are here. And as you're so grown up, I expect you're old enough to call me Roman."

"Oh, marvelous. That *will* frost Hollis."

Roman gulped. "Er, why?"

"Oh, she gives herself such airs, being the eldest," Felicie said. "It's aggravating, having Hollis calling all the gentlemen by their first names, while I'm still saying Monsieur This and That."

"I see."

Felicie gave him another dazzling smile. "And it's especially gratifying because you're so much older."

Roman appeared to be choking on something, and Felicie looked repentant. "Oh, dear, I didn't mean you're old." She studied his craggy, tanned face and salt-and-pepper hair. He had gray eyes. He was Papa's friend, but Felicie hadn't ever really *looked* at him. "I only meant that you aren't a *boy*, like—"

Roman burst out laughing. "You're getting in deeper, Felicie! You'd better stop and start over entirely. Tell me why you are so late to the party."

"Well, Meeow has the chicken pox," Felicie confided, setting herself to be entertaining to her host, "and she's absolutely certain that she's going to die, of course, and trying to cure it with dead frogs and chicken heads. Mama thought she'd better come to the party with Adele, because Adele doesn't know anyone, so I stayed until Doctor LeBoeuf came, and made sure Meeow took her dose of medicine, and then I hid the rest of it. She always tries to take it all at once, and you just can't convince her that lots isn't better than some."

"Good for you," Roman said approvingly, and Felicie beamed at him. How nice of Monsieur Prevost—how nice of Roman—to have a party today. Felicie felt marvelous. The blue muslin was her new best afternoon dress, and a new wide crinoline gave her skirts the fashionable bell shape. There were new blue slippers on her little feet, and Mammy had dressed her gold hair in a grown-up style, very smooth over the forehead, with two braids looped below her ears, and a knot of curls at the nape of her neck. She inspected the picnicking crowd happily, as if to be sure that everyone was having a good time. She could see Mama fanning herself in the shade with some other ladies, and Denis head to head with Valcour Aimée discussing, judging by their known interests and extravagant gestures, some new piece of experimental refining machinery designed to blow the whole state to kingdom come. Lucien, on the other hand, looked bored and sulky, skulking on the outskirts of the party. It must be dull for him here, after Paris, although personally Felicie didn't see how anyone could find such a nice party dull. Adele Scarron didn't seem to be having a very good time either. She was talking with Papa instead of the people her own age.

"Checking up on them all?" Roman inquired.

Felicie grinned. "I just want everyone to have as good a time as I'm having. Mama says I'm going to grow up to be a busybody if I don't watch out."

Roman smiled, touched that this cheerful child should have so much care for everyone else's happiness. "I'm glad you like my party. Even in my, er, ancient company."

Felicie looked up at him. "I like your company very much."

The sunlight gilded her gold hair and brows. It gave a rose-gold glow to her cheeks and throat. Her blue eyes sparkled up at him, and Roman's heart turned over in his chest. Youth and happiness stood before him, he thought, like a very young bird perched on a limb, wings half-spread. He remembered her as a chubby schoolgirl in the full sleeves and short skirts of a few years back, which had become her most dreadfully. What on earth had happened to her?

Roman stood speechless, in love for the first time in his life, terrified that it might show, and almost certain, with Felicie's bright face upturned to his, that she stood on the brink of the same discovery. A silent warning beat in his brain: *Be careful. There is Eugenie. You are married. Felicie must marry.* Felicie must not be allowed to fall in love with him, not go to her own wedding desperately wanting him instead.

He took her arm, unable to make himself part from this new discovery so soon, but grimly making his voice light and avuncular. "A host is supposed to keep track of things. Come along and keep track of them with me if you like."

Hollis had an excellent vantage point from her seat under the magnolias. The four young men in attendance on her were too intent on squabbling among themselves for the privilege of bringing her a plate to see her gray-green eyes, demurely lowered, snap open and freeze on the tall figure of Roman Prevost with Felicie on his arm.

Nor did their passage go unnoticed by Sallie, from her chair on the veranda. At Felicie's arrival, the gossips' gallery tipped forward avidly and announced that it could find no fault with younger Mademoiselle DuMontaigne.

"But she is *belle*, Sallie! A breaker of hearts."

"Soon she must marry, before all the young men fight duels!"

"Ah, the offers you will have! How lucky she is," the old ladies sighed. "She may take her choice."

Sallie fanned herself contentedly and noted how the young men's eyes followed Felicie's progress. Then she saw the look on her daughter's face. It was upturned to her escort's, lips slightly parted, interested, earnest, blue eyes shining. Felicie beamed with a delight whose source was all too evident, if as yet unrealized. *Oh, no,* Sallie thought. *Oh, no, not Roman.*

* * *

Lucien drained the sliver tankard in his hand and kicked idly at the base of a white column overgrown with a tangle of Virginia creeper. He was growing steadily more surly and bored. His friends were all dancing attendance on the girls. Lucien had no taste for simpering belles who were his sisters' friends. The price tag on them was too high. Even Adele had made it clear what the cost of her compliance would be. Lucien had no desire to pay for his amusements with a wedding ring, especially not for the little amusement that the convent-trained mademoiselles would offer, although he did rather doubt that Adele Scarron came into that category. But he sure as hell didn't want to find out badly enough to marry her.

Lucien took a quick look over his shoulder. None of his loving family seemed to have its eye on him at the moment. He ducked around the corner of the house into the drive and slipped Firefly's reins loose from the ring in the hitching block.

"Lucien, *mon amour*, so long you been gone, *hein*? Why hell you not come see me sooner?" Tassie Michelet unbuttoned her dress with enthusiasm, exposing ample breasts restrained only precariously by a grubby camisole.

Lucien pulled her down to him, biting them, and the pirogue rocked in the water. Yellow-flowered butterweed grew up around it like daisies in a meadow. Tassie pulled off what little underclothing she bothered to wear and tugged at Lucien's breeches. He made a grab at them as they came off and stuffed them where they wouldn't go overboard. Tassie was a tall girl, big-boned and large-footed. Her face was sensual, if none too clean, with a wide mouth and large eyes under a tangle of dark hair. She straddled Lucien, and he grunted with satisfaction as she wriggled down over him. Tassie never wasted much time on preliminaries. She made a long-drawn noise, interrogation sliding into contentment.

"Ah, he just the same, him." She slid her hands under Lucien's buttocks and arched her back.

"What did you expect?" Lucien ran his hands over her, exploring ribs and belly.

Tassie giggled. "He fall off maybe, you don't use him enough."

Lucien made a grab at her breasts and pinched her. She yiped, ran her own hands up between his thighs and began to stroke his staff at the base as she moved herself up and down on it. Lucien groaned, eyes half-closed, hands squeezing and stroking now. Tassie leaned forward, knees on the pirogue floor, feet tucked up against his hips. She braced her hands on either side of his head and began to lick his ear. She smelled of sweat and fish and bayou water: a personification of Bayou Rouge. Lucien wrapped his arms around her back and pulled her down flat on top of him, lifting his hips to drive himself deeper into her. Tassie's bare legs stretched out beside his now, her feet braced against the rocking of the pirogue.

Christ, we must look a sight, Lucien thought, but there wasn't anyone likely to come along except for some other member of the Michelet clan, and old Victorien Michelet didn't give a damn who screwed his daughters. Lucien suspected he did it himself.

He groaned and thrust upward a final time, then fell back as satisfaction flooded through his loins and then ebbed exquisitely away. Tassie twisted herself on him and lifted her head, her dark, tangled hair making a curtain around their faces, so that he could watch her as she came to her climax. The wide mouth stretched in an amorous, hungry grimace, and then fell slack, sated. Lucien was not much given to introspection, but he thought then that that was what Venus must look like. Neither the marble maiden nor the fat voluptuary, but merely Tassie Michelet in a pirogue.

Tassie, unaware of her significance as a symbol of sexuality, pulled herself off Lucien and lay down beside him, scooping up a handful of bayou water to douse them both.

"Ah, she is hot work, that."

"I brought you a present," Lucien said. He rummaged in the covered basket he had set in the pirogue and fetched out a bottle of wine and a box wrapped in gold foil. "Chocolates."

Tassie tore the wrapping off greedily. "Lucien, *mon amour,* I tell you, you stay away too long," she said, her mouth full of chocolate. Tassie and her equally obliging sister Sukie would usually sleep with him just because they liked it, but chocolates clinched the matter.

Lucien pulled the cork out of the wine and tipped the bottle up, the dark red wine running down his chin. He wiped his mouth with the back of his hand and passed the bottle to Tassie. "How's your family?"

Tassie swallowed and grinned at him. "Bigger by one. I told you, you stay away too long."

"The baby I saw? That yours?" That made her second.

"A fine boy, him. Gon' be strong."

"Who's the father?"

Tassie giggled. "How hell I know? You maybe."

"Oh no. Not me. Remember, I've been gone too long."

Tassie took another drink of wine. "Maybe not you. *I* don't know."

No one knew who had fathered most of the Michelets. They had been a parish scandal for years. Most of the Cajuns—Acadian French driven out of Nova Scotia by the British, for whom they still harbored a black hatred—were hardworking, pious folk. The Michelets made a chancy living from the flotsam and jetsam of the river, supplemented with poaching. Occasionally they sold a load of wood—when it wasn't too much trouble to cut it—to the steamboats that stopped to refuel along the Mississippi. Victorien, the current patriarch, and his wife, Estelle, had four children: Rafe, Sukie, Tassie, and the youngest girl, Ermandine. There were grandchildren of varying ages. Tassie had two, and Lucien had lost count of the ones belonging to Rafe and his wife, who seemed to be perpetually big-bellied. She was some sort of cousin, too—no one but a relative would be willing to marry a Michelet. It was probably only the new blood that the girls brought in that kept them from all being spavined and witless.

Tassie licked the chocolate off her fingers and ran them through Lucien's hair. They were still slightly sticky. Lucien caught her wrist and put her forefinger in his mouth. He ran his other hand under her belly, fingers probing in the damp hair between her thighs. He held her tight by the wrist as she began to wriggle. The more she squirmed on his fingers, the higher his excitement mounted. Tassie was lust personified: unwashed and unadorned, but cheerfully uncomplicated.

"Lie down." He maneuvered carefully in the small boat to get her under him, while she complied, giggling. She grabbed his staff and tugged at it, propping her feet on the sides of the pirogue. He put both hands between her legs and grinned as she began to writhe against them. But Tassie was interested in lovemaking games only up to a point. Then what she wanted was him inside her, as deep as he could get. It amused Lucien to keep her waiting, trying to fight her climax because he liked it better when he was in her. He put a hand between her breasts and held her down, still prodding her with the other one. "You'll just have to do it twice," he panted, "because I'm going to make you do it this way."

She writhed against his probing hand, back arched, brown eyes glaring at him, and he laughed. Pushing her over the edge when she didn't want to go was almost enough to make him climax himself. Tassie writhed again as his fingers manipulated her.

Suddenly her knees sagged apart in acquiescence, and he could see the muscles tighten in belly and thighs. The hidden valleys under the dark bush of hair were hot and wet, and he felt her skin grow taut beneath his fingers. Deliberately he flicked his thumb back and forth. He throbbed from head to toe as Tassie throbbed beneath his hand. She seemed to explode under him, clenching and unclenching around his fingers. He pulled his hand away and mounted her swiftly, driving deep into her.

"No," she panted, still quivering, trying to pull away. "Not now." Her breath was ragged gasps.

"Yes, now." He slid out of her and pushed in again, moving quickly, lightly, prolonging her climax until slowly it began to mount again. He felt his own coming with it. They writhed together in the pirogue, entwined. The boat rocked dangerously and upended. As his passion reached its peak, Lucien felt himself drenched in swamp water.

"Ah! Christ!" He surfaced, sputtering.

Tassie, wet hair plastered to her face, was righting the pirogue. She pulled herself into it deftly and held the paddle out to him. "Some fine lover, you," she announced. "Get in. I know man was eat by alligator once."

"You go swimming?" Victorien Michelet, taking his ease in a hammock composed of four kinds of string, raised his head enough to inspect his daughter and Lucien. "You catch bad things from those water. *Rafe!*"

Raphael Michelet emerged from the cabin. His bare chest was scarred with the reminders of a few old knife fights, and he had the bright dark eyes of an intelligent ferret. He laughed when he saw Lucien and made a welcoming gesture with his arm. "You try to drown him, Tassie? Defend your virtue, *hein*?"

Tassie made every effort to clip her brother across the ear. Rafe ducked and smacked her backside, and she vanished into the cabin. Rafe pulled a clay jug from under the front steps and sat down on the stoop with it. The Michelet cabin was of weathered board, on pilings, and it listed dangerously. A torn red shirt served as a curtain at the front window, and the stoop was further occupied by a pair of hounds that looked as if they had been put together from sections of other dogs. Rafe took a swig from the jug and passed it to Lucien.

Lucien tilted his head and drank cautiously. Victorien distilled it himself from whatever was on hand.

Rafe chuckled. "Don' tell me you sink my pirogue, man."

"Just my dignity," Lucien said. A scream of laughter from the cabin informed him that Tassie was regaling her sister with an account of the afternoon.

"Sukie, she be glad to see you too, her," Rafe commented. He held out his hand for the jug. "You come hunting with me instead, before you wear it out."

"I'll do that. How are you doing?"

"All right, me. I make sixth *bébé* for wife this year." Rafe drank. "Or somebody do. And I find good place to catch birds. Only trouble is, she's on your land. It's good thing you come home, maybe. Your father, he don't like me so much."

"Maman says," a clear young voice announced from the doorway, "you better shoot *something* tonight, or you don't eat."

Lucien looked over his shoulder and encountered a pair of enormous brown eyes in a delicate face. Glossy brownish-gold hair hung down to her waist. She was barefoot, but she was wearing what must be the only clean garment in the Michelet house. "*Bonjour,* Lucien."

"*Bonjour* yourself. Which one are you?"

"I'm Ermandine," she said. "You remember. Dinah."

"She grow up," Rafe said. "Pity she don't get good sense with it."

Dinah ignored him. "Maman, she say welcome home. She come out, but she don't feel so good."

"That's quite all right," Lucien said gravely. Estelle Michelet never "felt so good" if whatever was required of her involved movement. He looked at Dinah with growing interest. She must be fifteen, or maybe sixteen, this year. Someone with more quality than old Victorien had sired her, that was plain. Her bare feet were fine boned and delicate, and her figure was slim, less buxom than Tassie's, with a quicksilver grace to her movements. Lucien patted the weathered boards of the stoop beside him. "Come and talk to me."

Dinah shook her head. "No, I got work to do."

"Listen to the princess, her." Sukie poked her head out the window, grinning. "You don' want that one, Lucien. She think she Cinderella. Someday these prince, he come take her off from Bayou Rouge. You come see *me* next time—I don' drop you in the water."

Sukie disappeared again amid shrieks of laughter. Dinah stood her ground stubbornly.

"You say *bonjour* to Denis for me? He is healthy?" Dinah asked.

Sallie had always forbidden Denis and Lucien to play with the Michelet children, but naturally that hadn't stopped them. Dinah had tagged after Denis like a puppy. "He used to carve you dolls, didn't he?" Lucien said. "I'll bring him next time." He smiled up at her. "I'll bring you a present too. What do you like best?"

"No!" Dinah backed away. "*Pardon,* Lucien, you are very kind, but not."

Lucien shrugged and took a last drink out of Rafe's jug. As he swung up onto Firefly's back he heard old Victorien Michelet shouting at her from his hammock, "I got fool for a daughter, me. What hell you saving it for?"

Dinah snatched a homemade broom from the clutter behind the cabin and applied it to the porch until finally Rafe got up and moved just to get out of her dust. He picked up his gun and set off, with the jug in his other hand. Dinah glared after him, and then at her father.

When she had swept the porch, she put the broom away and stared at the cabin despondently. A clean porch wasn't going to make a hovel anything but a hovel. She smoothed her skirts, carefully washed in the rainwater barrel. And a clean dress wasn't going to make her any better, either.

Dinah turned down a path into the woods, in the opposite direction from Rafe, her bare feet making neat tracks in the damp earth.

"Dinah! Come and help with *bébé!*" Rafe's wife shouted at her from the back stoop. Dinah shook her head. She disappeared behind a curtain of green ash trees.

Half a mile farther on there was another path, which was really no more than a muskrat trail, and a little clearing at the end of it, where a finger of the bayou ran suddenly out of the tangle of palmetto and vines. Dinah sat down on a log and put her chin in her hands. A red-winged blackbird was perched on a palmetto frond, head cocked, regarding her with a beady eye. It would be fine and simple to be a bird, Dinah thought. Birds didn't worry about their clothes or where they lived. And sparrows didn't fall in love with red-winged blackbirds. They just naturally mated with other sparrows and liked it.

I don't even talk right, Dinah thought. She had tried to learn, aping the Prevosts and the DuMontaignes, but her sisters and even her mother had jeered at her for it. What was the good in a Michelet talking like a DuMontaigne anyway? Denis was grown up now. When people like the DuMontaignes grew up, they didn't come back to the girls like the Michelets, unless they came back the way that Lucien did, prowling like a tomcat, him.

Dinah crossed herself. *Holy Mother Mary, you just let me see Denis sometimes, talk to him, I don't ask for nothing else.*

VIII

The Girl

in the Market

"LUCIEN. GOOD OF you to join us." Paul's raised eyebrow was
eloquent.

I've cut it a little too fine, Lucien thought. The company at
Alouette was getting ready to leave. Sallie was already settled in
the carriage, looking exasperated. Barret Forbes was pretending
not to notice, studying the much admired architecture of Alouette.
Emilie was asleep in Sallie's lap, and Mammy was tucking Hollis
and Felicie into the carriage beside their mother and Adele across
from them. Tante Doudouce, who kept running back to say
bonsoir to someone she had forgotten, reappeared now, face
flushed and cap slightly askew on her gray curls, and beamed at
Lucien.

"There now," she announced to Sallie, "didn't I tell you the
dear boy would turn up? He can't have met with an accident, not
here at Alouette, I said, and I'm sure that he is only off smoking a
cigar with his friends, gentlemen do like that. . . ." She trailed
off, perhaps noticing for the first time that Lucien was on a horse.

"It is considered good manners," Paul said, "when one is a
guest of honor, to remain at the party." Paul let his eyes rest long
and thoughtfully on his son, making it plain that he noticed that
for some reason Lucien had found it necessary to change his
clothes.

Lucien conjured up a rueful smile. "I am sorry, sir. I thought
Firefly was showing a bit lame, and I wanted to— Well, he took a
fall with me, and I thought I'd better change."

"Get yourself home!" Paul snapped. "I won't stomach being

lied to. I know perfectly well where you were, and I don't intend to discuss *that* in front of your mother and sisters. You've embarrassed me enough for one day."

Lucien's mouth twisted into an irritated line, but he didn't reply. He wheeled Firefly around and sent him clattering down the carriage drive. On the levee road he overtook Denis, driving Felicie's gig, and drew rein beside him.

"Bad timing," Denis commented. "You met Papa, I presume."

"And got a chewing out in front of Barret and the girls, and anyone else within earshot," Lucien said malevolently. "He seemed to know where I'd been. Do I have you to thank for that, Brother dear?"

"*I* didn't know where you were," Denis said, "and I said so, too. What I thought was another matter. Been slumming, Lucien?"

Lucien glowered at him. "Not you too."

"I'm hardly in a position to point fingers," Denis said. He ran a hand through his hair, leaving it standing up on end. "Get in, Lucien. I've got to talk to you."

Lucien raised his eyebrows in unconscious mimicry of his father. He tied Firefly to the back of the gig and climbed in beside Denis. "What have *you* been up to?"

"Oh, God," Denis said. He was silent for a moment. "Worse than tumbling those Michelet tarts. I don't want Papa to find out, but I'm getting a little desperate. How does one, er, *dis*entangle oneself?"

Lucien looked interested. "From whom?"

"Think of the worst possible person."

"Eugenie Prevost," Lucien said.

"Don't be an ass. Gilbert Becquerel's wife," Denis said dolefully.

"G—" Lucien eyed his brother with something approaching respect. "How in the name of Mary and Joseph did you manage to put it to Gilbert Becquerel's *wife*?"

"I—I rather think she put it to me," Denis said. "I'm not sure what happened. One minute she was telling me how nice it was of me to call, and the next, we were upstairs in her bed."

Lucien let out a hoot of laughter.

"It isn't funny. I can't shake her."

"Baby Brother, you must have a great natural talent."

"How the hell should I know? I never did it before."

Lucien hooted again.

"Oh, shut up," Denis said irritably, "and give me some advice from your . . . varied experience."

"But I don't seem to have your fatal attraction for middle-aged females. They almost never fall in love with me."

"Damn it, she isn't in love with me. I think she's using me to get back at her husband. Becquerel has a name for philandering. He dyes his hair," Denis added, as if this somehow compounded the crime. "She says if I leave her, she'll tell her husband everything. To get his attention."

Lucien gave a long, low whistle. "That surely would do it."

Denis reached in his pocket and produced a note, addressed to him in a feminine hand, full of loops and curlicues. Silently he handed it to Lucien.

Françoise Becquerel had couched her invitation to revisit her boudoir in such everyday terms as to be wholly unincriminating. In light of their previous conversation, however, it amounted to an order.

"You see what I mean?" Denis asked gloomily. "Now I know how poor old Molasses feels." Molasses was Paul's saddle horse, much sought after at stud.

Lucien leaned back in the gig, shaking with laughter. He handed Denis back his billet-doux. "I'm sorry, I just can't help it. If you're looking for advice, I haven't got any. You'd better go and enjoy it. She looks a nice enough lapful. A little plump maybe—"

"Go to hell," Denis said without any real animosity. "I should have known you wouldn't be any help. You never want to get *rid* of them."

"Well, that's all the advice I've got," Lucien said. "Don't take it if you don't want to. You could always make a clean breast of it to Papa. It surely would take his mind off me, now wouldn't it?"

I made a mistake, Paul thought, watching his elder son's receding form. *The devil take Lucien, I should have known better*. Well, hindsight was a very marvelous thing, and it had by now occurred to Paul that the year's stay in Paris had not curbed Lucien's reckless habits. Paul snorted, wryly amused in spite of himself. He could as profitably, he thought, have sent a fox to a poultry yard to learn a vegetarian diet. He eyed the two figures in the gig ahead. Well, Lucien was going to learn. He had to. Therefore he would.

"Mama, I don't know why you let Felicie wear that dress. It's positively indecent." The Belle Marie ladies were squeezed into the carriage. Hollis eyed Felicie with disfavor across her mother's lap. The sleeping Emilie had been transferred to Mammy, seated opposite them between Tante Doudouce and Adele. It was unnecessarily cozy. Sallie wished she were, like the gentlemen, outside on a horse.

"Mama—"

"I heard you, Hollis. Felicie's dresses are not your concern."

"Well, I think it's too low in the neck. It doesn't look *nice*."

"Oh dear, do you think so? Well, perhaps, a little . . . at the shoulders . . ." Tante Doudouce fluttered in distress.

"It is *not*," Felicie said. "Mama, it isn't any lower than Hollis's."

"I'm older."

"You're a widow. You have to wear ugly *purple*. That's not my fault."

"Well, it looked just *awful*. Everybody was *staring*."

"They'd stare at you if you had anything to stare at." Felicie was triumphantly aware of being slightly better endowed than her sister.

Sallie had had enough. "Stop it, both of you!"

Hollis and Felicie glared at each other and subsided.

Now what? Sallie thought. Hollis didn't usually bait her sister like that. Hollis needed something to do, Sallie thought, and since she didn't seem inclined to do anything around Belle Marie, she had better marry again as soon as she decently could. Sallie looked at Felicie, who was gazing dreamily out the window. Felicie too. Before she did anything like falling in love with someone as completely unavailable as Roman Prevost.

Adele's gold-flecked eyes rested with amusement on Hollis. Adele was perfectly aware that Hollis didn't like her—and astute enough to have a fair idea of why Hollis was picking a quarrel with her sister. Though what either one of them wanted with a man who was married, Adele couldn't fathom, since she couldn't reasonably picture either of them disposing of Eugenie Prevost. Little Felicie was too innocent, and Hollis did not have the stomach for it. But so long as Hollis spent her abundant cleverness on outwitting her sister, so much less time would she have to think of why she did not like Adele.

Adele smiled, very sweetly, and leaned forward to pat Felicie's hand. "*Petite,* I think the dress is *charmante*. So very becoming to those blue eyes."

* * *

"I never saw anyone so nicey-nice!" Hollis cast a venomous glance at the closed door across the hall from her own as Mammy Rachel unlaced her stays. "That Adele talks like she has a lump of sugar in her mouth, and I just can't bear a two-faced woman!"

"Is the pot callin' the kettle black?" Mammy muttered. She stood on tiptoe to lift the loosened corset over Hollis's head. "I see you, lookin' pious as a deacon and castin' your eyes where they got no business to be."

"I have *no* idea what you're talking about," Hollis said airily. She inspected her reflection in the mirror.

Mammy picked up a silver-backed hairbrush and appeared to be deciding whether to use it on Hollis's hair or her backside. "Your mama may not know what you up to, and I ain't gonna tell her, 'cause I ain't gonna break her heart, but don't you think *I* ain't got eyes. *I* know why you been snipin' at your sister."

Hollis turned and looked at Mammy over her shoulder. She picked up the discarded gown. "I want you to sew some ruffles inside the front of this dress."

Mammy snatched the dress away. "I will not. I never heard of such a thing!" Hollis glared at her resentfully, and Mammy's face softened. "Hollis honey, you got just as nice a shape as Miss Felicie. And it ain't good for you to be takin' on 'cause a *married* man's been talkin' to your sister instead of you."

Hollis snatched the dress back. "I'm nineteen. That's old enough to do what I want. Give Felicie your lecture. I don't hear you scolding *her*!"

Mammy folded her arms. "Felicie's just a baby. You ain't. Felicie got no idea, and it's gonna stay that way." Like Sallie, Mammy Rachel suspected that Felicie hadn't really *thought* about why she had had such a good time in Roman Prevost's company. And the good Lord forbid that Mammy Rachel was going to tell her.

"*I* don't like Adele either," a young voice said from the doorway, and Hollis and Mammy spun around.

"How long have *you* been there?"

"Miss Emilie, you get in bed!"

"I bet if you sprinkled salt on her, she'd go right up in flames." Emilie padded across the floor in her bare feet and sat on Hollis's bed. Her hair was skinned tightly back into two plaits, and her brown eyes gleamed from under the lace bed cap. "That's what you do with a loup-garou."

"Well, whatever she is, she ain't no werewolf," Mammy said, relieved that Emilie seemed more interested in Adele's possible satanic origins than in her sister's indiscretions.

Hollis giggled. "Let's sprinkle her with salt and see." She didn't mention her own investigations. Her letter to France had not yet received an answer. Anyway, incriminating information was most useful when no one else knew about it.

"She's been makin' up to Lucien," Emilie said chattily, "but I think she gave up on him, 'cause now she's makin' up to Papa."

"That gal sure do know what side her bread's buttered on," Mammy muttered. Mammy, by mysterious ways of her own, knew that, like poor Miss Doudouce, Adele Scarron had practically no money of her own. She doubted that Adele was as resigned to that situation as Miss Doudouce was. Mister Paul would give Adele some money if she married. How much was strictly up to him.

"Well, I just can't bear the way she acts like a poor little orphan and just dies away every time Papa looks at her," Hollis said.

"Maybe you mama marry her off to somebody," Mammy said. She shook out Hollis's nightgown. "In the meantime, you quit specalatin' 'bout her, Miss Emilie. Ladies don't specalate 'bout other folks' business."

"I'm not a lady yet," Emilie said.

"Pretend you is disguised as one."

Emilie retired to her bedroom to discuss with Mimsie how best they could shake salt on Adele Scarron without occasioning comment. She decided to heed Mammy's advice. It never did to let a loup-garou know you were watching it.

Hollis was less easily swayed. The assault on two fronts to her hitherto acknowledged position as the belle of the family grated on her. She watched jealously as Felicie, dressed in an elegant scarlet habit with a jaunty black velvet jockey cap supporting her veil, went riding with her father and Roman Prevost. It was no consolation that Adele Scarron proved to be afraid of horses and cut no great dash on an old tub of a mare. Paul dropped back to escort her, leaving Felicie to gallop ahead with Roman. Hollis, who had ensconced herself in the garden with a parasol and a book, had an excellent view of this pairing off.

That her mother and her mammy were too preoccupied with plans for Felicie's first social season to pay much attention to Hollis did nothing to improve her mood. She took it out in baiting Felicie, and Felicie, who had no more tolerance for that sort of thing than most sisters, responded in kind. In the presence of both sisters, Adele Scarron adopted a saintly expression that set Hollis's teeth on edge, and counseled them to make peace in a manner guaranteed not to produce it. With only Hollis present, Adele was less chatty, being content to regard her coolly with a look in her eyes that Hollis was astute enough to recognize as well-concealed dislike.

By the end of May, as Lucien had predicted, the prospects for a hair-pulling match were excellent.

Barret Forbes, who had spent a lifetime letting his sister Alice's daily list of complaints and tribulations roll over him unregarded, found the atmosphere at breakfast a trifle too pointed even for him to ignore. Sallie poured the coffee with determined cheerfulness, and Doudouce was her usual silly self. *Bless the woman,* Barret thought. *If Doudouce had been present at the fall of Pompeii, she would have been worrying about what the sulfur in the air was going to do to the silver.* When Denis said that André Peyraud thought he had found them an overseer, Barret hastily announced that he would like to see New Orleans one more time before he left.

"Do, Barret," Sallie said. She glanced meaningfully at her daughters. "And I can't say that I blame you. But don't forget you've promised to come back to us this fall for Paul's election."

"I shall certainly be here," Barret assured her. An election in Louisiana was generally even livelier than a Mardi Gras. "I wouldn't miss it for worlds."

"I thought I might just duck out before the hostilities commenced," Barret said to Denis as they relaxed with cigars in the salon of the *Petite Marie*. "I was expecting derringers at ten paces over the bacon and eggs. What's the matter with the girls?"

"God knows," Denis said. He hadn't paid them much attention, but he was unspeakably grateful for Barret's decision to join him. Françoise Becquerel could hardly expect him to visit her towing Barret along. Denis hadn't informed her that he was coming to New Orleans, but lately he had begun seeing Françoise behind every bush, like a hobgoblin.

They made their way through the Market to André Peyraud's office with Denis jumpily expecting to see his nemesis bearing down on him at any moment.

"My God, what a beautiful woman!"

Denis started, and then got a grip on himself. Françoise was pretty enough, but she wouldn't elicit that tone of voice from Barret Forbes. He looked and saw the same quadroon girl that he had seen buying a parrot the day that he had been so ill-advised as to request Françoise's advice on the subject. Really, the woman who'd caught Barret's eye was too light for a quadroon, Denis corrected himself mentally. Probably an octoroon. She had curly light-brown hair, elegantly looped and braided, and creamy skin and a lovely, impish face. She reminded Denis a little of Emilie.

Barret was staring in patent admiration.

"You can meet her at the Quadroon Ball," Denis said, "if she isn't already taken. But she won't give you the time of day unless you offer a permanent arrangement."

Barret watched her silently for a moment. She moved lightly, gracefully, chatting amiably with the shopkeepers. Her black maid trailed behind her, basket on arm. "How can you tell she's colored?"

"Well, she's not wearing a bonnet," Denis said. He grinned. "It's the law. The ladies pushed that one through—they thought the quadroons were getting uppity. The colored women have to wear a tignon. But they make the most of it." The girl's head scarf, unlike the stiffly starched white ones that Mammy Rachel wore or the gingham one of her black maid, was of the same shot silk as her gown, and it was ornamented with a ruby brooch. It showed a good deal of curling hair and a pair of ruby eardrops.

"She's a gentleman's mistress," Denis said, "or she will be. Probably also a gentleman's daughter. I feel sort of sorry for them. Their mamas and aunts auction them off to the highest bidder, just like *they* were. Sort of a family profession."

"What happens to the boys?" Barret asked.

"They don't fare as well. Sometimes the father buys them a farm upstate somewhere or sends them to France to live. They're an embarrassment here. If they want to marry, they have to marry blacker than they are. The quadroon girls won't have anything to do with them."

"I suppose, if one is businesslike, there has to be a premium on white skin," Barret said. His voice sounded suddenly strained.

Denis shrugged. "Isn't there everywhere?"

"Come on," Barret said abruptly. "We'll be late."

André presented for Denis's inspection a New Englander named Harlow McCamy. He looked to be about thirty, with a round, freckled face and reddish sandy hair. His unprepossessing appearance was more than offset by glowing references from two New England farmers and a more recent one from a Louisiana sugar grower. Letters of character from a former teacher and a headmaster testified to a classical education, which would appeal to Paul.

Denis tapped the letters in the palm of his hand. "Impressive. I take it from these that you left your former position with no ill will. Why *did* you leave?"

"They were small farms, Mister DuMontaigne. As I told Mister Peyraud, they really weren't big enough to need an overseer on a permanent basis."

"Have you any experience overseeing black hands?"

"No, they farmed with free labor there—mostly meaning the old man and his sons. And me." McCamy smiled. "I learned to understand sugar from a slightly closer viewpoint than I really wanted to."

"Well, it doesn't hurt to have the darkies know that you've cut cane yourself. That way you know when they're slacking. You're from Vermont, Mister McCamy. Do you have any prejudice against slave labor?"

"Do you mean, am I abolitionist?" McCamy shook his head. "I wouldn't apply for the position if I were."

"Do you think you could handle a black crew?"

"Certainly."

"Married, Mister McCamy?"

"No!"

The word spilled out hastily, and Denis thought that McCamy's voice went up in pitch just a little. He wondered why, but the man's personal life wasn't his business unless he was a drunk. Jilted by some girl in Vermont probably, Denis thought with sympathy.

"Well, my mother likes to have a married overseer," he said. "Thinks it makes a man more stable. But maybe it's just as well. Most Yankee women don't really like it down here. I tell you what, McCamy, you'd better come back with us and talk to my father. The final decision's his. But I'll give him my recommendation. Bring your bags. You'll need to stay the night."

"Thank you very much." Harlow McCamy held out his hand. "I'll be ready as soon as I collect my things from the hotel."

Denis, who wasn't going to be happy until he had put a few miles of the river between himself and Françoise Becquerel, hustled them on board the *Petite Marie* with a speed that Barret complained made the wind rush in his ears. Privately he thought it was probably just as well. In his pocket was a querulous letter from his sister Alice, demanding to know if he had deserted her entirely. Barret knew that he should have gone home three weeks ago, if only because he was having such a good time at Belle

Marie that the longer he stayed, the harder it was going to be to put up with Alice. Of all the ways in which he could occupy the few days left before his departure, pursuing an introduction to an octoroon girl he had seen by chance in the City Market was about the looniest. Despite these glimmerings of good sense, Barret acknowledged to himself that that was what he was strongly tempted to do, and Denis's haste to go home was no doubt sent by Providence to keep Barret out of trouble.

"Thomy, is my aunt up yet?" Claudine Belloc unpinned her tignon before the gold mirror in the salon and pushed a few errant pins back into her modish looped and braided hair.

"She just ring, Miss Claudine," Thomy said. "Tea tray be here in a minute."

"Good. I'm famished." She laughed at Thomy's expression of horror. "And don't tell me that ladies aren't supposed to be famished. I expect I can control myself." She waved a hand at the parcels on the Sheraton table under the mirror. "Delilah, take these things upstairs and see if Tante Clélie needs help dressing." Clélie took a two-hour nap every afternoon, from which only fire or flood would have deterred her. Her maid, who was even older than she was, did the same.

Delilah gathered up the parcels and Claudine's tignon. Thomy eyed her burden suspiciously. "Where's your parasol? I don't see no parasol."

"Merciful heavens, Thomy, you're a butler, not my governess."

Thomy stood erect, his thin black face sculpted in dignified disapproval. "Miss Claudine, you go out without your parasol, you'll freckle sure, and Miss Clélie, she have something to say about it. You want to make your come-out with ugly freckles on your nose?"

"I don't want to make it at all," Claudine muttered rebelliously.

Delilah, mounting the staircase with Claudine's purchases in her arms, shook her head. Miss Claudine didn't know when she was well off. Soon some white gentleman would be buyin' her a house and carriage with fancy harness.

Delilah deposited the parcels in the armoire in Claudine's room and went to lace Tante Clélie's small imperious figure back into her corset, while Miss Clélie's maid, Allie, tottered about with a hairbrush. Some folks seemed to do all the work, while other folks took naps.

Tante Clélie, garbed for the afternoon in bottle-green silk from the best modiste in New Orleans, black silk mitts, and a quantity of jet jewelry, entered the salon to find her niece eating ham sandwiches.

"Ah, *mon Dieu,* you wretched girl, you will get spots on your face and look like a cowslip! *Not* ham!" The rebellious expression on Claudine's face told Tante Clélie that this had not been the best approach. "The watercress is nice, *petite,*" Tante Clélie said hopefully. "Try the watercress."

"There's nothing *to* watercress."

"Ah? That is good. There is *supposed* to be nothing to *you.*" Tante Clélie's face softened. "Your figure is most elegant, *chérie.* It is important—ah, most important—that it should remain so. Your future, you understand that it could hang on such a thing as this. We have but one weapon, and that is beauty."

Claudine put down the ham sandwich and bit penitently into watercress. It wasn't fair to vex Tante Clélie so. Tante had done everything she could for her. It wasn't Tante's fault that what Claudine wanted wasn't Tante Clélie's to give.

"Ah, that is my good beautiful girl." Tante Clélie bent and kissed Claudine on the cheek and settled herself at the tea table. Her bright dark eyes regarded her niece affectionately. "All the years of lessons, all the governesses, all the clothes—you will not let them go to waste, no? It is what your poor Maman wanted. And your Papa, he has said to me he is most pleased with you."

Claudine thought that that was gratifying, but not quite enough to make her turn cartwheels. She should consider herself lucky to know her father at all, to speak to, that is. There were many of her friends who only knew their fathers' names; many fathers who did not bother to visit now, so many years after they had first formed their connections with the mothers.

"He comes as often as it is prudent, you know," Tante Clélie said, watching her face. "And he has given me some money for you, money of your own, so that you need not choose a rich man. If there is one of modest means who is pleasing to you . . ."

Claudine made an irritated little gesture. "I am under the impression that it is *I* who am to be chosen. Very much like the slave market we are all at such pains to distance ourselves from!"

"Claudine Belloc!" Tante Clélie was outraged. "In our veins is some of the finest blood of France and Spain. You will not speak thus to me!"

"I'm sorry, Tante."

"I do not understand what it is that you want!" Tante Clélie said, exasperated.

"I do not want to be a woman kept by some man! Who will stay only so long as I practice those oh-so-interesting things you have told me about in the boudoir, and who will leave anyway when he marries some white woman. Who, despite my fine aristocratic blood, can't marry *me*!"

"I see." Tante Clélie pursed her lips. "You are envious. You wish to be white. Then think of this: You will have a better life than most white girls. Your man will choose you for love and leave you only because he must. He will leave you wealthy, and when that time comes, you may suit yourself in the matter of another man, if you want one. And your children, they will be light like you. They may, if they wish to go elsewhere, cross the line, *be* white. For them, it could be as you would have it for you."

Claudine looked at Tante Clélie with respect. That was the closest the old lady would ever come to admitting that she was darker than her niece, just dark enough for there to be no doubt about what blood was mixed with her aristocrats'.

Like Claudine's mother, Clélie had been a gentleman's mistress. Her lover had left her title to the little white house on the ramparts where they had shared housekeeping as well as another piece of property in the business district. Clélie was a shrewd woman, and she had managed very well. She had four slaves of her own now, and this much grander house. When Claudine's mother had died, Clélie, far too old to feel comfortable as a mother, had taken the child anyway, reared her, loved her, rejoiced in her beauty, and had her schooled in three languages and all the feminine accomplishments that Creole girls laid claim to. With one addition: Claudine, whose virginity had been most carefully guarded, knew, unlike the Creole girls, how best to please a man when the time came to lose it—all to the end that she should make a good match, a marriage in all but name with a man who would provide for her.

Claudine poured her aunt a cup of tea from the delicate silver pot, making, from long practice, a graceful show of wrist and fingers.

Tante Clélie nodded her approval. "Very pretty."

Claudine smiled at her affectionately. "I'll try not to vex you, Tante." When she was very small, after her mother had died, Claudine had thought that when she was grown, her father would come and take her away to live with him. It was only when she was old enough to understand the world that she had realized that he would not. Could not.

* * *

Paul laid his spectacles on the desk and rubbed the bridge of his nose. They pinched, and after ten years of wearing them, he still found it aggravating that he couldn't read without them . . . or write a letter that didn't look as if it had been scrawled with his left hand. He had too damn many letters to write. Letters to men who controlled votes. However much the Democrats wished to do away with that sort of influence, they had better make use of it this election, he thought wryly. And letters to men with money. A candidate who financed his campaign entirely from his own pocket could hardly claim to have the populace behind him.

Paul ran his hands through his hair. This sort of thing was not his style. *Maybe I shouldn't have let Roman talk me into this.* Certainly it was too late now. And Sallie wanted it, Paul knew that. Little Adele had offered to serve as his secretary. Maybe he should let her.

There was a tap at the door, and Testut ushered in Harlow McCamy.

"Thank you, Testut. Where is Lucien?"

Testut gave the master a wary look. "Mister Lucien, he saddle up that Firefly hoss, sir."

"I see. Mister McCamy, I wanted my elder son to be present at this interview, but since he seems to have mistaken the time, we'll— The hell with it!" Paul pointed a finger at Testut. "You tell Will to go find Lucien and tell him from me that he's not too old to thrash. And if he's gone to Bayou Rouge, I'm going to do it!"

"Yessir." Testut made a speedy departure.

McCamy looked hesitant. "Perhaps another time . . . ?"

"McCamy, if I hire you, you'll discover our peculiarities soon enough. Sit down."

McCamy sat.

"My son Lucien has spent as much time sauntering about France as I am willing to allow him, and he is now to learn to manage Belle Marie. It will be your unfortunate duty to teach him to manage a sugar crop."

McCamy's mouth twitched. "I see."

Paul began to warm up to him. "Lucien will undoubtedly give you more trouble than the darkies will. They are a good lot by and large—I don't keep troublemakers very long." Paul put his spectacles back on and studied Harlow McCamy. "Since you have never managed darkies before, you may come to me or to Denis for advice at first, as long as they don't know you have. Your qualifications are excellent, Mister McCamy. My only qualm is whether or not you can manage the field hands."

"I'm certain that I can."

"They're childlike in many ways, but they have their dignity, and it is precious to them. The overseer who remembers that has little trouble. There will be transgressions, I warn you of that. You may punish them as you see fit up to a sentence of ten lashes. Anything over that has to be approved by me. I might add that I have never approved it. There are better ways to handle men than with a whip."

"I concur, sir."

"Tell me, McCamy, what do you do for amusement?"

"Well, I—I read, sir. Quite a lot. Not very much else, really."

"I think you may suit. If you would like to borrow from my library here, you may feel free."

"Thank you!" Harlow McCamy's eyes lit up with real enthusiasm. He had been eyeing Paul's bookshelves wistfully and seemed almost as pleased with that offer as with the realization that he was being hired.

"As to your other duties, I require only that you make an extra man at dinner parties when my wife needs one, refrain from courting my daughters, and go to church on Sunday. We are Catholic, as are the slaves here, but I don't object to your attending another church."

"I am in the habit of it, sir. My family were Presbyterians."

"Were?"

"I have no kin." McCamy seemed to be choosing his words. "My father . . . left us when I was quite small. And my mother died some time ago. She hadn't been . . . well for a number of years. It was a blessing, I think."

McCamy's freckled, bookish face had grown reserved, almost frozen, and Paul declined to pry. He thought that Harlow McCamy was not an entirely happy man, but Paul didn't require jollity, only good service.

"I'll have someone show you about. You'll have the use of a mount out of the stables and a small house to yourself."

A house to myself, Harlow McCamy thought. He gazed around the cheerfully furnished parlor with almost frantic gratitude. He was alone. He could bar the door if he wished, perhaps bar out the things that crept into his sleep at night. The house was a haven, a refuge after the years of boardinghouses and beds in some farmer's attic, shared with the farmer's sons; of footsteps and voices in the dark, and whispers and laughter outside the door; the years of places that reminded him, with such instinctive terror, of his mother's house.

McCamy walked into his dining room. A blueberry pie had been left on the table by Meeow, recovered from her bout with "chicken spots" and eager to assure the new young man of a welcome.

Beyond the parlor was the bedroom, comfortable and solitary. A patchwork quilt was laid on the bed and around it was the necessary mosquito netting. McCamy let out a little sigh and found that his hands, which had been shaking, were stilled. There would be no fearful things to keep him company in a bedroom like that.

IX

Dinah

DENIS AND LUCIEN tied their horses to the railing and slung their
game bags over their shoulders. A retriever and a spotted setter
padded at their heels.

Rafe Michelet was waiting for them on the cabin stoop in the
lingering twilight, shotgun across his lap. Two bluetick hounds
and a red-spotted one with a chewed ear waited with him, front
paw hanging off the edge of the stoop, eyes fixed hopefully on the
shotgun.

Old Victorien was asleep in the hammock, from which he
appeared not to have moved in the last two months. A battered hat
covered his eyes and nose, leaving only a gray-stubbled chin
protruding. The cabin was dark.

"Where are the girls?" Lucien asked.

Rafe shrugged. "They go off, make quilt for Cousine Odalie.
She get herself married next week."

"I'll send her a wedding present," Lucien said. "What would
she like?"

Rafe grinned. "Clothes for *bébé*. She gon' have twins, her.
That priest, he give them no peace till they get themselves married
with each other." Rafe stood up and tucked his gun under one
arm. He fished the jug out from its usual spot and passed it to the
DuMontaigne brothers. "Is good to see you again, Denis. Your
papa, how he do?"

"He says he'll shoot you if you touch his egrets again," Denis
said equably. He wiped his mouth and passed the jug to Lucien,
and they set off with the dogs lolloping silently ahead of them into
the dusk.

At twilight the silent heat of the bayou began to stir and rustle, as the night creatures roused themselves from daylight torpor. The chirping of crickets faded into a vibrating chorus of frog song, the deep resonant hum of bullfrogs overlaid with the voices of the tree frogs, and the staccato sound of a night heron echoing from the dark water. Bats swooped, raccoons and opossums prowled through the underbrush, and the deer and swamp rabbits came out to feed. Behind them came the reclusive predators of the swamp: black bear, bobcats, red wolves, and sometimes a cougar, ghostly silver in the moonlight.

The DuMontaigne dogs trotted behind Rafe's hounds, interested in the night smells, but with a faint attitude of going slumming. Rafe, on the other hand, was shooting for the pot, and his hounds were businesslike in their forays into the underbrush.

The jug went round again as they walked. "I hear your papa got him a new overseer," Rafe said. "A Yankee, very pale, like someone he is bleach him, and he walk with just a little limp, yes?"

"I suppose it wouldn't be tactful to ask what you were doing on Belle Marie when you happened to see him?" Denis said.

"I shoot a little rabbit, maybe catch a turtle, me. Your papa, he don' mind that."

"Not as long as your rabbits don't have feathers." Denis couldn't help liking Rafe. Raphael Michelet was as much a part of the bayou as the herons, a form of wildlife himself. "Why so interested in our overseer?"

"Not me," Rafe said. "Tassie. She come with me, and she see this overseer, her. She give him li'l smile. Then this overseer, he run like wet cat." Rafe grinned in amusement, white teeth glinting in the dark. "Tassie, she is insult. Want to know, is this overseer, he like boys, him? Or is she get ugly?"

"Au contraire," Lucien murmured, and Denis burst out laughing.

"You tell Tassie poor old Harlow was just overwhelmed," Denis said, giving another whoop of laughter. Poor Harlow—he had probably never seen anything like Tassie.

"I don't know," Rafe said. "Man look like he got a ghost under his hat."

A cacophony of yelping and baying from the thickets ahead cut short their speculation. "My Emile, he got somethin' now," Rafe announced.

Emile's businesslike baying announced that they had certainly treed something. The three men pushed their way through the thicket to find a bobcat, furious and ears flattened, perched on the broken-off trunk of a dead gum tree. Rafe's hounds ringed the tree in a professional manner, while Denis's retriever bitch Annie barked excitedly, and Lucien's setter hurled himself dementedly at the trunk, apparently trying to climb it. Rafe raised his shotgun just as the setter, in a burst of frenzied enthusiasm, hooked his hind claws in a snag a few feet off the ground and launched himself upward. The bobcat came down over the setter's back and disappeared in a frothing mass of dogs.

"Goddamn!" Rafe lowered his gun, then dived out of the way as the bobcat erupted from the melee and came straight at them, hounds in hot pursuit. A bobcat, when it was good and mad, didn't stop for very much. Denis's retriever and Lucien's setter dusted themselves off and galloped after the disappearing hounds.

That was when something seemed to snap in Emile. Abandoning the bobcat, he turned on the amateurs who had been foisted on him. The bluetick hounds reversed course with a communal snarl, which indicated that they would far prefer biting the DuMontaigne dogs to having another crack at the bobcat. In another moment, all five dogs were entangled like a medieval manuscript border, each one biting some portion of the next.

"Goddamn!" Rafe yelled again. He directed a pair of well-placed boots, shaking off the hound that transferred its grip to his right ankle. Lucien and Denis collared a dog apiece and sat on them. Rafe's hounds retired to the far side of the gum tree to lick their wounds and glare balefully at the interlopers.

"I need a drink, me," Rafe announced.

Lucien was still sprawled across the heaving setter, who appeared to want another go at Emile. Lucien sat up, one hand through its collar, and held out the other for the jug. "Me too. Sorry about that. Christ, what a dogfight!"

Denis hauled Annie to her feet and dragged her over to the other two. "Sit still, you moldy bitch." Annie licked his face and sat. Denis hooked an arm around her neck, and Lucien passed him the jug.

They sat catching their breath, panting like the dogs in the dark. "Those dogs," Rafe said finally, "they made good alligator dog."

"Alligator dog?"

"Sure. You throw 'em in for bait. Now we got to wait a while, hour maybe, till my dog, they remember their business." He tilted the jug again. "He's good thing we bring these jug, *hein*? I tell you 'bout Cousine Odalie and the knife-sharpen man, and how they break his wagon once, while we wait."

* * *

> *"Un petit bonhomme pas gros qu'un rat,*
> *Qui battait sa femme comme un scelerat—"*

> *"A little man no bigger than a rat,*
> *Like a rascal he beat his wife with a bat—"*

Three voices were lifted in slightly drunken harmony. They had, by dint of tying the DuMontaigne dogs up with a rope, managed to bag an opossum, four rabbits, and a muskrat, and had heard the story of Cousine Odalie and the knife-sharpen man, which, as Denis had said, was worth at least five rabbits to the connoisseur.

The Michelet cabin came into sight. A lantern in the window proclaimed that the female relations had returned from Cousine Odalie's quilting party. Denis and Lucien tied their game bags and two of the rabbits behind Lucien's saddle, and Rafe presented Maman Estelle with the rest.

"Ah, bon!" Estelle, seated on the stoop, inspected the contents of the game bag with approval. "I make me little fur hat too, yes." Estelle Michelet was broad and big-boned like Sukie and Tassie and considerably heftier. She wore a faded gingham dress, an old jet brooch apparently donned in honor of Cousine Odalie's party, and a pair of Victorien's boots, having, as she explained, lately cut her foot on an oyster shell. Denis thought that the addition of a muskrat hat would be something to see.

"Dinah!" Estelle shouted through the door. "Fin' me my pipe, she's on the table, an' come see who is visit!"

Dinah handed her mother a corncob pipe, and Estelle poked a stick into the lantern to light it with.

"Bonsoir, Denis," Dinah said gravely.

"My Dinah, she grow up some," Estelle announced between puffs. "See how you like her now, *hein*?"

"Maman!" Dinah's fine-boned face, thrown into high relief by the lantern light, flushed dark. Denis decided suddenly that only a man who was blind in both eyes would not like the way Dinah looked now. He hadn't seen her in nearly a year, and something had certainly happened. Dinah brushed past him down the steps, her lower lip between her teeth, and he trotted after her.

"Don't let your mama embarrass you." He caught her wrist, and she stopped, looking at her feet.

"My whole family, she embarrass me."

"Mine too sometimes," Denis assured her.

"Your maman," Dinah said with a baleful glare at Estelle on the porch, "she don' tell mens to look at your sisters' shape, no."

"Not exactly," Denis said. "Mama just tells them how well she cooks—and this means Hollis, mind you, who doesn't know which end of a spoon to stir with—and how she just *loves* little babies. And all the time you can see the word "marriage" written in big blue letters right round her eyes."

Dinah chuckled, but she said ruefully, "Good Cajun boy don't want to marry Michelets."

Dinah hadn't ever really looked like a Michelet, he thought, with her slender, graceful figure, and her earnest, if often misguided, efforts to pattern her speech on his and Lucien's. There must be somebody to marry Dinah. It wasn't fair. He put his arm around her. "He'll come along, honey. I promise."

Dinah gave him a sideways look. "Maybe." She seemed disinclined to comment any further.

Denis could hear his brother's voice and Rafe's and Victorien's from the direction of the old reprobate's still. "If Lucien drinks any more of your father's corn squeezings, I'll have to tie him on his horse," he said. He lifted her onto the vacated hammock and sat down beside her. "Talk to me."

"What about Lucien?"

Denis shrugged. He was a little drunk himself.

Dinah kicked her bare feet at the ground, making the hammock rock gently. "Maybe one day I go away, be singer in the opera, me. Then it don' matter I don' marry." She gave him a quick grin to be sure he understood that this was all dreaming. "Maybe I run 'way with gypsy wagon, tell fortune." Dinah drew her hair across her face like a veil and lowered her eyelashes at him mysteriously. She laughed and then sighed, sober again.

Denis studied her profile, delicately etched by moonlight. Her hair was a dark shadow that flashed gold as the hammock swung. "Dinah, how would you really want to live?"

Dinah gave him a frank look. "With man who don' make *bébé* for some other woman. You think I find him?"

Denis slipped an arm around her and pulled her head down onto his shoulder. Françoise Becquerel receded conveniently from his mind. "Yeah, I think you'll find him." He kissed the top of her head.

Dinah held her breath. She leaned lightly in the crook of his arm, felt his lips brush her hair, afraid to move for fear he might vanish. Things you wanted desperately had a way of doing that when you reached for them, she had found.

"Dinah honey, how old are you?"

"Sixteen," Dinah said.

"Where'd the years go?" Denis murmured. He tightened his grip a little, fearful that she might run away. "Remember the dolls I used to make for you?"

"I still have them," Dinah whispered back. "I take them out sometimes." They were hidden where the children couldn't find them and spoil them.

"They weren't all that great," Denis said. "One leg always came out longer than the other." Poor kid, they were probably the only dolls she'd ever had.

"You make them," Dinah said, "so I don' care."

Denis dipped his head so that he could look at her face. "Is that why you kept them?"

"I talk to them," Dinah said, feeling stupid and a little ashamed. "I ask them how you do. Pretend they been to see you."

"Dinah . . ."

She lifted her head a little, and he kissed her, lips meeting hers gently, carefully. She moved in his arms, and a small hand crept up along his back. With his newfound knowledge, courtesy of Françoise Becquerel, Denis thought that she kissed like someone who was trying it out for the first time. He drew his mouth away from hers and kissed her eyelids and then the end of her nose. She leaned her head against his with a little sigh of contentment, and they rocked gently in the hammock, heads together, watching the golden wink of fireflies floating in the trees.

"Denis!" Lucien's voice, impatient and querulous, came from the darkness.

"Damn!" Denis said.

"Where the hell are you? These damn boots have rubbed a blister on my heel, and anyway the jug's empty. Let's go home."

Denis hopped out of the hammock before Lucien could see him with Dinah and draw any conclusions. He kissed her again, quickly, in the dark. "I'll be back."

"*Denis!*" Lucien called.

"Wait a minute," Dinah whispered. She flitted toward the cabin.

Annie got up from the cool spot she had dug for herself under the hammock and wagged her tail as Lucien's setter appeared.

Lucien untethered the horses and tossed the reins of Denis's bay at Denis. "We'd better wake somebody up to clean those rabbits, or they won't be fit to eat by morning."

"You can't wake some poor darky up at two in the morning to clean rabbits," Denis said.

Lucien raised his eyebrows. "Well, *I'm* not going to do it. What the hell have we *got* darkies for?"

"Never mind." Denis decided he'd do it himself. Lucien smelled like old Victorien's still. He'd probably cut his thumb off. And Denis wanted to think about a few things.

"Denis!" Dinah pattered down the porch steps with something wrapped in a scrap of blanket held in one arm. "Here. Your little sister, maybe she like this." Denis peered down and saw a pair of bright black eyes in a black highwayman's mask peering back. The little raccoon chirruped inquiringly as Dinah held him out.

"Rafe, he shoot his maman," Dinah said, "two, three week ago. He is tame like a kitten." Her brown eyes pleaded with him, and Denis decided that a raccoon was exactly what Emilie needed.

He tucked the little creature in the pocket of his shooting jacket, where it curled into a ball and began a contented singsong noise like a purr.

Dinah let out a sigh of relief. "I couldn't bear it if Rafe, he shoot him, no." She patted the pocket. "You be good, *hein*?"

Denis thought that that was highly unlikely. "He won't be any trouble at all," he said gallantly. "Emilie will love him."

Dinah watched wistfully as the horses trotted into the dark. Lucien was singing again, some American song Dinah didn't know, and Denis's jovial tenor joined in.

"Mister Frog went a-courtin', he did ride,
Ah-hah, ah-hah!
Mister Frog went a-courtin', he did ride,
A sword and pistol by his side,
Ah-hah, ah-hah!"

Dinah sat back down in the hammock. *You wish for things, the danger she's maybe you get them*, she thought. Yesterday Dinah, if asked, would have said that if she thought that Denis DuMontaigne might love her, there wouldn't be much else on the earth she could ask for. Now she thought she was stupid like the jaybird, yes. They couldn't marry with each other, no, not even if Denis wanted to, him, and he wouldn't. DuMontaignes, they married rich like themselves with a girl.

Dinah stilled the hammock with a jolt. She folded her hands in her lap and thought hard. She had always done anything Denis wanted. She had climbed trees she was afraid of, jumped creeks to follow him, and got stung by bees stealing honey, all because Denis had said, "Come on!" If he wanted her now, he could have that too.

An' I don' cry when he leave, no, she told herself sternly.

Because he would. Denis was a man who would want to marry.
One day he would marry somebody else.

Until then she would take what she could get and be thankful.
And that was sinful, yes, but Dinah decided that she would have a
long time to be forgiven for it, afterward.

It was a wakeful night. The sky, which had been clear an hour
ago, was clotted with dark clouds, and the air was still, hot and
humid, like a roof pressing down—the sort of night when people
sleeping turn in their beds, dreaming of things they want or things
they fear.

In the quarters under the nut trees, Gabriel rolled over,
stretched, and went to stand in the cabin doorway. It was way past
curfew. He had that Celeste on his mind, and it was no use telling
himself she wouldn't do him no good because he already knew she
wouldn't. She was on his mind anyway, just as if he'd been
hoodoo'd. Maybe he had. Celeste wasn't above getting what she
wanted any way she could. She didn't want him, but maybe she
liked seeing him squirm, to get back at him for trying to teach her
things about Africa that she didn't want to know.

A flicker of illicit light caught his eye. Celeste was up too, or
someone in her cabin was, and she'd get a licking if that new
overseer caught her. Gabriel slipped out the door, and black skin
melted into black shadow. Gabriel didn't care if he got a licking.
He wasn't sure if he cared if Celeste did, but he wanted to see her.
There were better women on the place to want, but he wanted
Celeste. He'd wanted her so long, he guessed he was used to it by
now.

"What do you think you're doin'?" Gabriel whispered when he
spotted Celeste, crouching just inside the cabin door, doing
something with a thing in her lap by the light of a candle in a
cracked plate. She stuck whatever it was under her apron as the
door swung open. Gabriel blew out the candle before she could
get to it.

"That curtain ain't closed all the way."

"What you doin' here?" she hissed.

He grabbed her by the wrist and dragged her outside. "Some
highfalutin' yellow woman got a candle burnin', gonna get her
backside burnt."

She smiled slyly. "You come all this way jus' to save my
backside?" She kept her hands under her apron.

"Gimme that!"

She tried to wriggle away, but he put a hand under the apron and wrenched the thing out of her fingers. "Who you put a conjure on?" He turned the little figure over in his hands, half expecting to see himself. It was crudely made of clay, with a scrap of cloth for trousers, but the face had been painted white with chalk, and it had pale straw for hair.

Celeste snatched at it. Gabriel flung it on the ground in disgust, and she dived after it.

"He ain't been here a week, and you're already schemin' how to get your ass in his bed!" Gabriel glared at her.

Celeste clutched the figure behind her, out of his reach. "I ain't had no better offers!"

"You have plenty, you stick with your own kind like you meant to!"

"Who's meant to? My mama sure ain't, or I 'spect I'd look like you!"

"They's worse things to look like," Gabriel said stolidly. "That last boss—I know what you did with him, an' maybe that was *his* idea, but now you're lookin' for it, and it ain't right."

"And it ain't your business!"

"Ain't I tryin' to make it my business?" He took her by the shoulders and shook her. "You settle down and marry me, stay away from that white man!"

Celeste leaned against him. "You sure would like that, wouldn't you?" She rubbed her face against his cheek.

"You know I don't want nothin' but for you to marry me." Gabriel's voice was husky.

Celeste pushed him away suddenly and danced out of reach. "Well, I reckon you're just too black for me." Her voice was mocking.

Gabriel's big fists clenched and then unclenched again. "And I reckon you ain't black *enough* to suit me," he growled. "And you ain't gonna get any whiter from climbin' into white beds at night. Woman ought to be proud o' what she *is*. You ain't actin' no better than them Rampart Street whores." He turned on his heel.

Celeste stood looking after him. A half smile flickered across her mouth. There was a satisfaction she couldn't put a name to when she pushed Gabriel over the edge. It wasn't the anger she enjoyed; it was the power to provoke it. But marry Gabriel—huh-uh. She was gonna be the overseer's woman again. Celeste clutched the little conjure man, and the crudely modeled phallus stuck out grotesquely.

> *"Tell us, what was the bride dressed in?*
> *Ah-hah, ah-hah!*

> *Tell us, what was the bride dressed in?*
> *A cream gauze veil and a brass breastpin.*
> *Ah-hah, ah-huh! Oof!"*

Denis dumped Lucien down on the bed and pulled his boots off. "Ebenezer, you awake?" he called out to the sleepy slave who served as valet to them both and slept on a pallet in the next room.

"I is now," Ebenezer said grumpily, appearing in the doorway and rubbing his eyes.

"Well, get Mister Lucien into his nightshirt."

"You all stay out mighty late with them no-account Michelets," Ebenezer grumbled. "*Specially* when you say, 'Don' wait up.'"

"That was when Mister Lucien was operating under his own steam," Denis said. "Just be glad you aren't cleaning rabbits."

"Rabbits?" Ebenezer gave him a wary look. "I ain't no kitchen hand."

"Try telling that to Mister Lucien if he takes it into his head you're gonna clean 'em," Denis said cheerfully. "You just be glad he passed out."

"Hummph."

Denis picked up the game bag and left Ebenezer to shake Lucien out of his coat and trousers as best he could. The kitchen was dark except for the glowing heart of the banked coals in the fireplace. Denis tripped over a cat and lit the candle Meeow kept by the door. He dumped the contents of the game bag on the scrubbed oak table, lit the oil lamp above it, and proceeded to skin the rabbits, whistling under his teeth and kept company by a ring of interested cats. Presently the little raccoon, which had been peacefully napping in Denis's jacket pocket, stirred, poked its nose out, and climbed up his chest, clinging to his jacket buttons with small black hands. The cats craned their necks forward like snakes and hissed in unison. The raccoon chittered back at them. Denis detached it from his jacket buttons and upended it under the light. "He" was a she. Denis stuck her back in his pocket and found a cold biscuit for her to eat, hoping that she wouldn't feel compelled to wash it first. It had just occurred to him that Dinah's gift was going to have to spend the night with him. Poor kid. Dinah had too soft a heart to be a member of that family. She sure as hell didn't look like a Michelet either, with those fine bones and that brownish-gold hair, the color of fallen leaves. And fancy her keeping those poor, bedraggled dolls all those years just because he had made them.

When the rabbits were skinned and gutted, Denis chopped up

the offal for the cats and stuffed the meat in a pot to take to the root cellar, where it would stay cool till morning. A faint crunch of footsteps on the oyster-shell walk made him pause with his hand on the latch. Harlow McCamy was walking from the direction of the overseer's house. He didn't appear to be going anywhere in particular, and his arms were folded across his chest as if he were cold.

"Everything all right?"

McCamy jumped, and then looked sheepish as he recognized Denis on the kitchen steps. "Yeah, fine. I just . . . couldn't sleep. It's that kind of night."

"That it is. Probably gonna storm like hell in a couple hours. Don't get caught out in it, or my mama'll make you a dose of coat grass tea. There isn't anything worse to drink this side of the bad place."

McCamy chuckled. "I'll remember." Denis raised a cheerful hand in farewell, and McCamy looked up at the sky. One more good rain and the cane could be laid by. Already it rippled like an island sea, lapping at the edges of the orchard and gardens. As soon as the cane no longer needed weeding, he could put the hands to cleaning out the ditches, mending the fences and levees, and bringing in the corn and the small cotton crop planted on drier ground. McCamy bent his mind to that, although tentative dates for each picking were already noted in his book. An owl hoo-hoo'd somewhere in the trees and a mockingbird hoo-hoo'd back at it. McCamy shivered, a twitching of the muscles that was fear. He knew why he couldn't sleep; he was afraid to—afraid of the devouring phantasms that had suddenly crept into his bed again.

It had begun with the girl by the stream. She had been leaning over among the rocks, with a net to catch crayfish in her hand, tangled hair falling about her face and her skirts tucked up around her thighs. Her bodice was open almost to her waist, and she had doused herself with water so that the thin calico clung to breasts grotesquely large, like damp pillows that could engulf and smother him. She had run her tongue over her lips and smiled, showing sharp, hungry teeth, and Harlow turned and fled, through the tangled Virginia creeper and back into the waist-high cane. Her voice followed, mocking him, until it seemed to come from all around him. He stumbled and fell, scrabbling among the thick stalks, trampling the cane underfoot. The voice pursued him, seeming to wrap about his legs, and he fled headlong until he fell on all fours, heart pounding, at the far edge of the cane field.

That night the dreams had begun again: dreams of towering

female forms, with open mouths and monstrous breasts; dreadful mouths, gaping wetly, which would devour him if he didn't run. It was always the same dream, which Harlow had never been free of. Everywhere he went, he had hoped it would be different, but the Furies followed him. And when he woke, his leg hurt. He had broken it somehow as a child—exactly how was vague—but the dreams always made it ache.

Harlow huddled into the cane chair that Meeow kept beside the kitchen door and put his head in his hands. He had thought that she was dead. He had buried her. *Lucille McCamy, Beloved Mother.* It was carved on her stone in Vermont. But when he looked at a woman, any woman, he knew that she was still there . . . waiting for him to sin, waiting for him to anger her. Then she would catch him and beat him, her night robe offering terrifying glimpses of dangling breasts and naked legs, until whatever man she had with her that night shouted at her to come back to bed. And then Harlow would creep into his own bed and listen to the horrible noises that came through the wall—wet sounds and thick, grunting breathing. The next night the man would be gone, and there would be another one.

When he was old enough to go away to school, Harlow had fled to the place as to a haven. His school had been the only refuge whose walls had kept his mother out.

Even after he had run from the girl by the stream, he had thought that the overseer's house would be safe, a male place locked and shuttered against women. But the other man had sinned in that bed, sinned and made animal noises there with a black woman. Harlow had sent her away when she had knocked on the door, but she was in the bed anyway, he could feel her there when he lay down, as black as a devil in the night, her four black limbs the four posters of the bed, her mouth open to swallow him.

He hid his head in his hands, curled into a ball in the chair, until the pouring rain came down.

Harlow sat up and looked at the sky. Lightning sheeted across it, and the crack of thunder followed after. Best to get indoors. He trotted toward his house.

He should check his book again, to be sure of the best dates for laying the cane by. He wouldn't want to make a mistake his first season here. This was a good post, with good wages and a fine, private house to himself. And Paul DuMontaigne was generous with his library. He would read a little before he went to bed. Harlow yawned. There was something else he should see to this month. Oh yes, he must write to the preacher at home and remind him about the flowers for Mother's grave. A son should remember things like that. Harlow sighed. He missed his mother; it was a pity she had died so young.

X

Courting among

the Otters

DENIS SWALLOWED THE last bite of his steak and eggs and inspected the dishes in the center of the table. "Pass the marmalade, Adele, if you please. Mama, are there any more biscuits?"

Sallie shook the little crystal bell that sat by her plate. The butler materialized immediately. "More biscuits, please, Testut. Denis, that's your sixth. Where on earth are you putting them?"

"I'm hungry," Denis said.

His tone had a touch too much nonchalance, Sallie thought, and she looked suspiciously at him, and then at Emilie, who was watching Denis's plate from across the table with round brown eyes and open mouth. As she watched, it happened again: A little black hand came up and felt around on the plate. Finding no biscuits, it investigated further. It patted at the tablecloth beside the plate. Sallie laid her fork down and watched with much the same expression as Emilie's.

Felicie, seated between Lucien and Emilie, started to speak, but Sallie, her blue eyes alight with mischief, shook her head at her daughter. Tante Doudouce and Adele, seated on either side of Denis, sipped their breakfast coffee unsuspectingly. The hand patted farther along the tablecloth, and Sallie thought she caught a glimpse of bright eyes and whiskers in the shadow of Denis's carefully arranged napkin. Tante Doudouce set her coffee down, and the little black hand patted hers.

The coffee cup shot upward as Doudouce threw up her hands and shrieked. A masked black face popped up from Denis's lap to

see what the commotion was about, and Doudouce rocketed from
her chair as quickly as a woman in a full crinoline could.
Confronted with a shrieking elderly female with her hands clasped
firmly across her eyes and her feet doing a sort of tarantella, the
little raccoon scrambled up Denis's chest to his shoulder and then,
perhaps feeling that that wasn't far enough, launched itself onto
Adele's head.

Adele screamed, the pot of marmalade upended itself in Hollis's
lap, Hollis screamed, and Sallie, Emilie, and Felicie collapsed in
helpless laughter.

"Get it off me!" Adele demanded, so furious that her teeth
chattered.

Denis detached the raccoon and tucked it under one arm, where
it chittered to itself with curious whirring noises. Denis cast an
apologetic glance around the table.

His father favored him with an awful glare. "I trust you are
sufficiently amused, Denis. If so, you may remove the creature
from the breakfast table."

"Oh, don't be so stuffy, Paul." Sally wiped her eyes. "I haven't
seen anything so funny in years. Doudouce, darling, it's all right.
It's only a raccoon."

Doudouce took her hands away from her eyes. "Oh, dear, when
it just leaped out at me like that, I declare I thought it was the devil
himself."

"You ain't so far off," Mammy Rachel said grimly. "Miss
Emilie, you an' Miss Felicie sit up an' behave yourselves. Mister
Denis, where you get a raccoon?"

"Yes, do favor us with an explanation," Paul said. Adele had
sat down again gingerly, and Paul shot her a look of concern. "My
dear, are you all right?"

"Quite," Adele said. She gave Denis a look of loathing and
willed herself to smile angelically at Paul.

"Well, I'm not," Hollis announced. "If anyone is interested,
my dress is spoiled." She glared at Adele. "Nobody but a ninny
would take on like that."

Adele refrained from answering, although she looked as if she
had a great deal to say.

Felicie, under no such compunction, filled the breach. "I
wouldn't worry about it, Hollis. That dress never did become you
anyway."

Lucien, who had been lounging in his chair watching the
upheaval with amusement, meeowed softly under his breath, and

Paul turned to him. "Restrain your natural inclination to stir things up with a stick."

"I'm sorry," Denis said contritely. "I didn't mean to cause a riot. The raccoon's a present for Emilie. I wanted to surprise her."

"You have succeeded," Paul said dryly.

"I think she's adorable," Felicie said.

"Yes, *charmante*," Adele agreed with every sign of sarcasm.

But the sarcasm was lost on Emilie. "*Charmante!* That's a wonderful name! I'm going to call her Charmante." She looked up at Mammy Rachel. "Can I go get her?"

"I don't 'spect I can stop you," Mammy said. "Mister Denis, if you wasn't too big, I'd whack your bottom."

"I may yet," Paul said, but a smile was beginning to twitch the corners of his mouth. He would remember to his dying day the morning that the devil had tried to hold hands with Tante Doudouce. "How did you happen to acquire a raccoon?"

"Dinah Michelet gave it to me." Knowing his father's views on the Michelet girls, Denis hastened to explain. "The youngest girl, Ermandine. She's about sixteen now. I don't know where the Michelets got her, you'd swear she wasn't a member of the same family."

"I think we can imagine where they got her," Paul said, "which we will not discuss." Estelle Michelet had had quite a following in her youth, some of them, regrettably, gentlemen.

"No," Denis said hastily. "Anyway, she's a pretty little thing, and she works hard."

Sallie raised her eyebrows. "I don't really think I've ever heard the word *work* used in connection with the Michelets." She didn't care for the enthusiasm with which Denis described this youngest daughter as "a pretty little thing."

"Dinah's different," Denis said. "She's got a soft heart. Rafe shot this little baby's mother, and Dinah raised her from a kitten, or whatever you call them. She gave her to me for Emilie because she was afraid Rafe would shoot this one too."

Emilie looked indignant. She scooped the raccoon into her arms protectively. "Well, I think somebody ought to shoot *him*."

"A sentiment shared by many," Paul said.

Emilie sat down again with the raccoon in her lap. She gave it a slice of melon off her plate. Charmante flipped herself onto her back and twirled the melon with all four feet while Emilie watched, delighted.

Mammy Rachel appeared to be counting up the number of clean pinafores Emilie would require daily with a raccoon living in her lap. "Is that critter housebroken?" she inquired suspiciously.

"Dinah says she is."

"I don't imagine the Michelets care much if a raccoon does its business in the house or not," Lucien remarked.

"Well, Dinah would," Denis said. "Perhaps you don't remember the conversation." A glare at Lucien informed him that if he did not wish his condition of the night before—and his undoubted hangover this morning—to be mentioned publicly, he had best mind his own conversation.

"You're mighty protective of little Dinah all of a sudden," Lucien said.

"Sure," Denis said amiably. "Come on, Emilie, let's go see if we can't get Uncle Jem to make you a basket for Charmante to sleep in." Uncle Jem was a lame Negro who did a thousand odd jobs on Belle Marie. He kept a sack of candy in his pocket and a store of fascinating tales in his head. His workshop was a favorite haunt of all the children, black and white.

Emilie put Charmante on her shoulder and tucked her hand into Denis's. They departed, with Charmante peering back over Emilie's shoulder, possibly marking in her memory the location of the breakfast table.

Sallie knitted her brows, again wondering whence came Denis's sudden interest in "little Dinah."

Paul, Denis, Lucien, and the new overseer had ridden out to the cane field before breakfast and pronounced that the cane would be officially laid by in two days, in time for Independence Day. July fourth was the traditional date, but the vagaries of the cane often made the laying by come later. This year the Fourth of July festivities and the celebration that marked the laying by would coincide, and every soul on the place who wasn't actually in the cane field was baking pies and mending best dresses in anticipation. The Prevosts at Alouette and the DuMontaignes at Belle Marie had held joint Fourth of July celebrations for years. There would be a fish fry on the river for everyone, fireworks on the levee, and a dance in the sugarhouse, which was being swept and cleaned and decked with calico bunting for the occasion.

Uncle Jem was nailing a new sole on one of Mammy's best shoes when Denis and Emilie arrived. "You have a seat on them new benches I make for the fish fry. What you chillun up to?" Denis was still "chillun" to Uncle Jem.

"We need a basket, Uncle Jem," Emilie announced.

Uncle Jem inspected Charmante. "You ain't get one of my picnic baskets I just made, for that coon."

"Just a nice basket I can put a cushion in," Emilie wheedled. She plodded herself down, knowing that Uncle Jem would come up with something. "Tell me a story," she suggested.

"What kind story?"

"Tell me about Fourth of July."

"Well, it got somethin' to do with a big war a ways back, but I don't rightly know what. An' somebody run around on a horse warnin' folks the 'Mericans was comin'."

"No, they didn't," Emilie said. "It was the English that were comin'. The Americans did the warnin'."

"Well then, supposin' you tell *me*." Uncle Jem tapped the last nail into Mammy's shoe and wiggled his fingers inside to make sure it hadn't come through the insole.

"Well," Emilie said, trying to remember her sketchily studied history, "the Yankees took all the Englishmen's tea and threw it in the river."

Uncle Jem put the shoe down. "Who'd do a fool thing like that? I never knew a Yankee yet what wasted anything."

Denis sat on a bench with his back against the workshop wall and thought about Dinah while Emilie and Uncle Jem argued Revolutionary history. There was something about Dinah—what she'd had to put up with, and how Sukie and Tassie had not been similarly affected.

Little Mimsie arrived in a flurry of running feet, her hair neatly tied up in a dozen braids and her backside smarting. Mammy Rachel, noting Mimsie's absence, had gone looking for her with fire in her eye, found her ensconced with a book in the privy, and sent her briskly about her business.

Uncle Jem produced a candy drop apiece for the little girls, and he and Emilie laid their debate before Mimsie for arbitration. Mimsie, Uncle Jem had been interested to discover, knew more than most grown folks he could name. He looked at Emilie. "An' some white chillun," he added pointedly.

"It wasn't the river," Mimsie said. "It was Boston Harbor, an' they dressed up like Injuns an' threw all the Englishmen's tea overboard off a ship 'cause they were mad about havin' to pay taxes on it, but that ain't why we have Fourth of July."

"It ain't?"

"Fourth of July's when they signed the Declaration of Independence. Thomas Jefferson wrote that, and he's about the smartest man that ever lived."

"I don' care what kind of decoration he wrote, he ain't no smarter than General Jackson," Jem said. Andrew Jackson, the hero of the Battle of New Orleans, was popularly supposed to walk on water in Louisiana.

"It wasn't no decoration," Mimsie said. "It was a de-*clare*-ation. That's a piece of paper that said we shouldn't belong to England no more."

"Well, we didn't belong to England, we belonged to France," Uncle Jem said, exasperated. He turned to Emilie. "You understand any of this?"

"No, sir," Emilie said. It was considered rude not to say "sir" to anyone older than you were, black or white. "Why don't you tell us about how the peacock got the owl's eyes on his tail instead?"

Denis watched Mimsie with troubled sympathy. There might be something in the prejudice against teaching a slave to read, he thought. Some plantation owners flatly forbade it, although the DuMontaignes never had. However, Denis thought Mammy was right: It was likely to give Mimsie a misery when she grew up. Like Dinah, Mimsie knew about too many things she couldn't have. Just now she was content to read about them in books, but when she was grown, like Dinah, she would not be. Even if she gained her freedom, she wouldn't fit into the world she had found in her books. *Damn!* Denis thought. That wasn't going to happen to Dinah. He stood up and headed for the stable.

"Denis! We don' expect you again today!" Dinah yanked off the apron in which he thought she had killed a chicken, and bundled it up behind her back.

"I . . . I just wanted to let you know the little coon was a success with my sister," Denis said, feeling suddenly tongue-tied.

"Well, actually it started a riot at the breakfast table, but Emilie loves it."

"Oh dear, I don' stop to think, maybe he make trouble," Dinah said.

"Don't worry about it," Denis said. "We need livening up. By the way, he's a she."

"She find her a friend, you'll be liven up more than you want, maybe," Dinah said dubiously.

Denis laughed. He held out his hands to her, stopped, embarrassed, and stood looking at her uncertainly. "How are you today, Dinah?"

Dinah smiled. Her face lit up. "I'm glad to see you, me. You come with me, I show you somethin' I don' show nobody else."

* * *

"Over there," Dinah whispered. A brown otter head poked up from the tangle of vine along the water's edge. Denis and Dinah sat still, hardly breathing, and the otter wriggled up on the bank. It looked at them with beady, inquisitive eyes for a moment. Apparently finding the silent interlopers no threat, it chirped and flowed up the bank like living water. Dinah showed Denis where the otter slide was, and as they watched, two others followed, launching themselves from the high point down a twisting course and into the water. The bayou formed an almost motionless pool at the bottom of the slide, and the three otters frolicked in it joyously.

"Nobody he don' come here but me," Dinah said. "They are my otters, them. Now I give you half interest." She chuckled. "Make up for give you raccoon, maybe."

"Thanks." Denis put an arm around her waist. "Will we shock the otters if I kiss you again?"

Dinah's brown eyes beamed at him. "Not if you don' make noise, no."

He touched his lips to hers, acutely aware that there was very little under Dinah's dress but Dinah.

She sighed and moved a little in his arms. He kissed her again, very gently, fearful that, like the otters, she might vanish. Her brown-gold hair rustled against his cheek. He touched it lightly with the back of one hand. *"Feuille morte."*

"What?"

"That's what they call that color hair, like fallen leaves." He rubbed his face against it. "Dinah, can I see you again?"

Dinah made one last grasp at her conscience. "Your mama, she don' like it."

"I don't care," Denis said stubbornly.

Dinah laid her head on his shoulder. "Then you come. I don' think I get along without you, now."

"Drink to me only with thine eyes. . . ." Denis warbled cheerily at his reflection in the mirror while he adjusted his cravat.

Lucien lounged in the doorway with a sardonic expression. "You're mighty bucked up. I didn't think you set so much store by these jolly family outings." The prospect of a Fourth of July fish fry left Lucien cold.

"Oh, I am," Denis assured him. "I plan to lead the tug-of-war personally. I was hopin' you'd take the other team so I'd have the pleasure of pullin' you into the river."

Lucien considered that. "What'll you bet me?"

"If you lose, I don't hear another word out of you about Dinah."

Lucien's eyebrows rose. "You aren't really courtin' that child? I thought you had enough complications in your life."

"I surely do." Denis picked up his wide-brimmed straw hat. "So I don't need you stickin' your oar in."

"What if you lose?"

Denis wasn't above blackmail. "If I lose, I won't mention to Papa that you've been cavortin' in pirogues with Tassie Michelet."

"You've got a nerve. I don't see any particular difference between us."

"There's a big difference between Dinah and Tassie, and if you weren't a lunkhead, you'd see it too."

Lucien hooted. "I suppose your intentions are honorable."

"You bet." Denis had come to that conclusion this morning. Sure, he wanted Dinah; but he wanted her in a way that wasn't going to make her unhappy. "Once everybody here gets used to the idea, I'm gonna go courting with a ring in my pocket."

"The last trump's gonna sound before Papa gets used to that idea," Lucien said frankly. "He'll lock you up till you get your wits back."

"You just leave that to me," Denis said. He was as aware as Dinah of what his family's reaction would be, and Paul's opposition was going to be small beer compared to his mother's: Of all her children, Denis was the closest to Sallie, and he was aware that his own quietly stubborn nature was an inheritance from her. But one of them was going to have to give in eventually, and this time it was going to be Sallie. Denis would wait, if he had to.

They descended the stairs to find most of the family milling in the hall. Sallie and the girls carried parasols and wore broad-brimmed straw bonnets and gloves to protect their hands from the sun. Emilie, who hated gloves, had pulled hers off and was swinging them in her bonnet, which she held by the strings. Denis lifted her up and kissed her. "Ready for watermelon and ice cream? You put those gloves on, or you'll get freckles, and Mammy'll dip 'em in lemon juice and make you wear 'em to bed." He remembered Hollis and Felicie protesting this treatment.

Emilie sighed and drew her gloves back on. "I'm already in disgrace," she whispered.

"What have you done?"

"It wasn't me, it was Charmante. She found a bowl of fruit in the dining room, and you ought to see the rug."

Denis noted that a certain amount of complaint was still emanating from the next room. He poked his head through the doors.

Mammy and Testut were indignantly sweeping mango rinds into an empty bowl, muttering to themselves. A silver pot of disheveled-looking roses sat in a small lake in the middle of the mahogany table. Testut mopped it up with a cloth while Mammy squatted down on the Aubusson carpet to collect a further array of seeds, rinds, and a squashed persimmon, which apparently Charmante hadn't cared for.

"You just wait till I get my hands on the no-account animal, washin' its dirty feets in my flowers."

"And stainin' up the table Mister Paul's granddaddy brung all the way from France," Testut said.

"It's mushed a 'simmon clean into this rug," Mammy announced grimly from under the table.

"That's what come of havin' wild animals in folks' houses."

"It do." There was a certain difference of opinion between Mammy Rachel and Testut as to who really ran Belle Marie, but on some matters they were prepared to present a united front. Mammy caught sight of Denis in the doorway. "An' *some* people oughta of known better."

Something rustled behind the floor-length curtains, and the culprit streaked across the floor and up Denis's boots. Testut flapped his rag at it. Denis scooped up Charmante and fled.

The carriage drive was lined with saddled horses, wagons for the house servants, and a carriage for the ladies. Some of the field hands had been down at the bayou all night setting out their fish baskets and getting the pits ready to roast a pig and a lamb. The spring wagon was loaded with vegetables, pies, cakes, watermelons, and buckets of ice cream, which Meeow had sat up all night churning. Mammy was to drive that wagon, with Meeow beside her. Adele's maid, Junie, Mimsie, and Emilie were sitting in the back, in charge of seeing that nothing went overboard on the way.

"And seein' that nothin' goes into nobody's stomach, neither," Mammy said sternly. "*In*cludin' raccoons." She glowered at Charmante, who was peeking out from under Emilie's skirts.

Sallie had decided to ride, and Denis trotted his horse alongside hers. "You look very elegant, Mama."

"Thank you, dear." Sallie rode Briar Rose, her little copper-colored mare, almost every morning, and she had an extensive wardrobe of riding habits. This one was of pale-blue broadcloth, with gold braiding sewn military fashion down the front.

"I wonder if I could borrow old Buttertub tomorrow," Denis ventured. Buttertub was the family name for Butterfly, the fat old mare that Sallie had retired last year. She had a placid disposition and all the speed of a tortoise.

"Whatever for, darling?"

"I thought I might teach young Dinah to ride," Denis said. "She'd like to learn, and God knows she'll never get the chance any other way."

"I suppose so," Sallie said, distracted by the sight of Roman Prevost riding beside the carriage and leaning down to talk to Felicie through the window. *Roman ought to know better,* Sallie thought. If only she had been sure that he *did* know better, she would have given him what-for. What held her back was the suspicion that Roman—like Felicie—might still be oblivious as to why they found each other's company so congenial. If so, the last thing Sallie wanted to do was push him into the realization. But *was* Felicie oblivious? Lately Sallie had thought she looked unhappy, the way a girl might look, for instance, if she had fallen in love with a man who was married.

". . . and you'd like Dinah, Mama," Denis was saying.

"Really, darling?" Sallie said vaguely, with her eyes on the carriage. *Damn Roman.*

There was a great deal of food, and Denis managed to sample all of it, although he felt a bit like old Buttertub as he lined up at the head of his tug-of-war team. Mammy kept an eagle eye on the girls, being of the opinion that no real lady ever ate a square meal in front of gentlemen.

The two teams lined up on either side of a small creek that fed the bayou, Denis and Lucien as opposing captains at the head of the teams and the strongest of the slaves behind them. The captain's position was the most vulnerable, and pride spurred each team on not to allow the master to be pulled into the muddy water. There was the added incentive of a drink of whiskey for each man on the winning side.

Paul fired a pistol to signal the start, then sat back to enjoy the competition.

"Come on, Denis! Pull, Daniel, don't let them get you!" Felicie, feeling that a dunking would do Lucien a world of good, cheered unashamedly for Denis.

"What a savage you are," Roman said, amused. "I'm glad I'm not out there instead of Lucien."

"Oh, then I'd cheer for *you,*" Felicie assured him.

"Would you now?" Roman regarded her affectionately. *I ought to have my head examined,* he thought, aware of Hollis regarding him from the next table with all the conviviality of an adder.

The twenty men on each team heaved at the rope.

Lucien's line staggered forward, bent their backs to the rope, and dragged it back again, towing Denis toward the water.

"Heave!" Denis shouted. He dug in his heels and pulled. He was going to drop Lucien in that creek if it killed him.

Lucien's team faltered as Denis's men redoubled their efforts. The two teams seesawed back and forth, neither ever quite getting the other into the water. The Belle Marie Negroes and those from Alouette shouted advice and waited gleefully for the first splash. Lucien's arms were beginning to ache, and the knotted rope was chewing up his hands. The water in the creek was more like muck. Lucien was beginning to wish he hadn't worn his new boots.

"All together now!" Denis yelled. "Heave!"

Lucien flung himself backward frantically. "I'll give every one of you a new suit of clothes if we win!" he shouted.

"All right, you shiftless darkies," Daniel bellowed behind Denis. He tightened ham-fisted hands around the rope. "You all want all them *other* shiftless darkies struttin' around in tall silk hats and fancy waistcoats? I purely don't think I could *stand* it!"

They fell to at that, laughing and hooting at Lucien's team. Slowly they inched backward. Lucien teetered on the creek edge. Denis gave him a wicked grin and jerked the rope one more time. Lucien slithered forward and sat down suddenly in the water.

"Keep pulling!" Denis yelled. "They've *all* gotta get wet before we've won!"

Lucien, cursing fluently in French and English, struggled to get up again as the rest of his team was hauled over the edge on top of him.

"Come on, Mister Lucien." Gabriel, just behind him, hauled him to his feet. "Oh, Lord, I think we done had it!" Behind them, the rest of their demoralized team had slackened their grip and were being towed rapidly through the mud. Lucien and Gabriel dived out of the way.

"Lord have mercy, I don't think I ever saw a better sight," Denis said, watching his brother pour mud out of his boots. He was none too clean himself, having landed on his backside when Lucien's team suddenly let go of the rope. His white shirt was wet with sweat and smeared with stains. It was worth it. "Daniel, you tell our boys I'll match my brother's offer—a shirt and a pair of pants apiece as soon as I can get 'em."

When everything in sight had been eaten and all the children had been rounded up from the creek and woods and counted, it was nearly seven o'clock. The party moved back toward Belle Marie. The benches were set up again in the garden, and Paul and Denis and Harlow McCamy took the fireworks up on the levee and prepared to singe their eyebrows in the name of patriotism and independence.

Roman candles soared and burst over the Mississippi River, like cascades of fiery chrysanthemums falling toward the water. The audience in the garden watched wide-eyed, sleepy children cradled in their laps. The more prudent had picked spots with a clear path back toward the house; you never knew with fireworks. The year that a rocket had turned around and chased Mammy Rachel was still being talked about. That was the year Sis Rachel had become a religious woman, Testut always maintained.

Denis gingerly set up the finale. It had been ordered from China, and on the bright red paper that it was wrapped in was printed mysterious, unreadable instructions. "Better duck, McCamy. These things have a mind of their own." He hoped he had it right-side up. He touched a match to the fuse and hopped out of the way. It spit and crackled, then suddenly erupted into the night sky. A shower of sparks rained down into the water, and in the air a red, white, and blue rose unfolded. Its petals spread outward above their reflection in the dark river, and a small gold center burned brightly for an instant after the rest had gone out.

Emilie sighed. "That was the best ever." She snuggled sleepily against Mammy Rachel's bosom. Charmante, her full, furry stomach stretched like a drum, was asleep beside her, her ringed tail over her nose. Emilie yawned. "Can I go to the dance?"

"Go to the dance? You can't even stand up. High time you chillun was in bed." Mammy prodded Mimsie, who was leaning against her knee, and stood Emilie on her feet. Mammy looked down at the little raccoon with an exasperated eye. "You too, I s'pose." She scooped it up, and it burrowed into the crook of her arm. She scratched its head resignedly. "I don't recall askin' the Lord to send me any more babies, but it appear I got one. You keep them hands where they belong, an' maybe you grow up without bein' somebody's hat."

A platform had been built at one end of the sugarhouse for Uncle Jem and his fiddle. The slaves from Belle Marie and Alouette were ready to dance reels until dawn. Beside the platform a table was laid with a midnight supper and a bowl of punch, to which Paul had personally added a bottle of whiskey.

The DuMontaignes came to start off the dancing, accompanied by Roman Prevost, who knew that his wife would be in bed long ago. Uncle Jem struck up a Virginia reel.

Roman bowed to Hollis, whose beautiful, bad-tempered face gave every indication of an imminent explosion. "Would you care to dance?"

"I'm just so happy you condescended to notice me, I could die!" Hollis said witheringly.

Roman decided that flattery was the better part of discretion just now. "I always notice you," he said. "And don't pout, because it'll spoil that pretty mouth."

Hollis looked at him sideways, as if debating whether or not to allow him the privilege of a dance. "It did seem to me at the picnic that you were more interested in babies out of the schoolroom."

"I'm just polite," Roman said. "Which is more than I can say for you. How anyone so beautiful can have such a nasty temper—"

Hollis appeared to be mollified. She didn't mind if he thought she had a nasty temper so long as he thought she was beautiful. She laid her hand in Roman's with a triumphant glance at Felicie.

The sets were beginning to form for the reel. Felicie shrugged and commandeered Harlow McCamy. Since Denis was dancing with Sallie, Paul gave his arm to Adele Scarron.

"You needn't stay if you're bored," he whispered as they danced down the line, "but we always start it off. The darkies would be hurt if we didn't."

Adele had never understood why the DuMontaignes, who *owned* their servants, should be so careful of their sensibilities. But by now she knew Paul well enough not to say so. When her place at Belle Marie was secure, she would let him understand that these Negroes were far too free in their ways. They bowed, circled with linked arms, and then passed by the shoulder, as the fiddler called the steps. Adele smiled up at him as they moved down the line again. "Have you given any more thought to letting me help you with this election? The correspondence alone must be fearfully tiring for you."

"If you're certain it wouldn't be too dull for you." He was sure that Sallie would consider it exceedingly dull.

"But *non*," Adele said eagerly. "I should find it fascinating. And I must thank you in some way for your kindness."

The fiddle scraped into silence. Paul, bowing over Adele's hand, saw that Sallie and Denis were standing in the middle of the dance floor and appeared not to have noticed either the last measures of the music or its cessation. Sallie had her hands over her mouth, and Denis looked embarrassed and stubborn.

"Denis DuMontaigne, you will *kill* me, you surely will!" Sallie's voice was loud in the sudden silence of the fiddle. The dancers all pricked their ears up interestedly.

Lucien, who had been lounging by the punch bowl, looked at Uncle Jem. "You'd better play something else," he suggested.

Uncle Jem looked disappointed, but he put his fiddle to his shoulder. Sallie dragged Denis toward the door. "I never heard of anything so disgraceful!" Sallie's voice carried across the floor, "and I flat forbid it, do you hear me? I wouldn't let you marry a Michelet if she were the last female on this earth!"

At this interesting announcement, Hollis and Felicie abandoned their partners in midstep and followed their mother and Denis.

"My dear, you'd better excuse me." Paul kissed Adele's hand briefly, nearly missing it, and headed for the door. Just inside it he collided with Mammy Rachel. "I suppose *you* know all about this," he growled.

"Well, I don',"" Mammy Rachel said, "but I 'spect I'm gonna, an' so is everybody else for four miles, the way Miss Sallie's carryin' on. You better quiet her down some."

"On the contrary," Paul said grimly. "I intend to do a little shouting myself."

Outside, he found Denis standing under the pecan trees, trying to get a word in edgewise.

"You're going to break your father's heart!" Sallie said.

"Now, Mama—" Denis began.

"I just don't understand why." Felicie looked distressed. Nobody respectable ever married the Michelets. "She isn't *good* enough for you."

"Everybody'll think you ruined her," Hollis hissed. "Everybody'll laugh at us."

"Shut up, Hollis," Denis said.

"I won't! Those trashy Michelets don't care *what* they do! I bet she's been in bed with everything with pants on from here to—"

"Hollis!" Sallie snapped. "You mind your mouth!"

"I won't!" Hollis shrieked. "I'm not going to have any trashy poor-white Michelet slut for a sister-in-law!"

Denis lost his grip on his temper. He grabbed Hollis by the shoulders. "You say one more word like that about Dinah, and I'll shake you till your teeth rattle!"

"Papa!"

Paul detached Denis from Hollis, and the combatants stood glaring at each other. "Hollis, if you can't conduct yourself like a lady, you may leave," Paul said. He looked from her to Felicie. "You may both leave anyway. Go to bed!"

Hollis stalked off. Felicie hesitated. She put a tentative hand on Denis's arm. "Why throw yourself away?"

"Honey, I'm not." Denis patted her hand. "Now go to bed and let me face the music." He gave his father an embarrassed grin.

"You picked a hell of a time for an announcement like that," Paul snapped, unmollified.

"Well, I tried to talk to Mama earlier," Denis said, "but she wasn't listening."

"It didn't occur to me that you were trying to announce an engagement," Sallie said caustically.

"I am," Denis said. "But I'm not planning on getting married right away. I have to give Dinah time to get used to the idea."

Paul snorted. "I doubt that that will take very long. Here's an idea for *you* to get used to: My son is not going to be entrapped by a scheming—" He bit back the words that occurred to him first. "By a woman of that kind."

"You've got it all wrong. I haven't done anything with Dinah. What do you think I am? And Dinah's about as worldly as Emilie."

"So are you," Paul said. "I can't lock you up, Denis, but I'll tell you this—if you sneak off and marry a woman who'll embarrass you for the rest of your life, you'll regret it, and you won't be able to undo it."

"I'm not going to *want* to undo it."

"Yes, you will!" Sallie's hands fluttered in agitated explanation. "Oh, Denis, I knew a girl back home in Charleston who ran away and married her father's overseer. He was an uneducated man. He didn't know how to behave, and nobody would receive them. She was just *cut off* . . . from her family, her friends, everyone she knew. The last time I saw her, she was twenty-five and she looked forty, and they lived in a horrible little house because no one would give him a job after that." She pulled at her husband's sleeve. "Paul, we can't *let* him!"

"Mama, I'm not going to run away anywhere and marry Dinah. I'll marry her when I can do it at Belle Marie, and when she'll be welcomed like one of the family." His mouth set in a stubborn line. "However long that takes."

"It will take considerably longer than you've got," Paul said, "unless you plan to outlive your brother and your sisters as well as your mother and me. You have neither my permission nor my blessing. I won't forbid you to see the girl, because I *want* you to see her, and to think honestly about how it would be to present her to our friends as your wife. But I flatly forbid you to mention the subject to your mother again."

"Well, *I* don't!" Sallie snapped. "Denis, I *want* to know what you're thinking. And the good Lord knows I want to know what you're *doing*." She gave him a level look. "If at all possible, before you do it."

Denis laughed. "I promise. I guess a dance wasn't the best place to pick, but I wanted to get it over with."

"It's not over," Sallie said tightly. "I don't want you to feel you can't talk to me, but I can't give you my blessing."

Denis shrugged. "Then I'll have to wait."

As Denis walked away through the trees, Sallie put her knuckles to her mouth. "Oh, Paul," she said, "not Denis too. I don't think I can bear it. It's so awful to want someone you can't have." Felicie and Roman Prevost. Her and Paul. And now, she had begun to think, poor Paul and Adele Scarron. The girl had been making eyes at Paul across the table. *I could stop that,* she thought drearily, *but what would be the use?* It wouldn't make Paul stop wanting Adele; it wouldn't make him want her instead. "I'm tired, Paul," she said suddenly. "It's been a long day. Stay and dance if you like. I'm going to bed."

Paul looked after her sadly. *To want someone you couldn't have* . . . He wondered who Sallie wanted. For a moment he thought of going to her room anyway; she never refused him. Then he sighed, went back into the sugarhouse, and asked Adele Scarron to dance again.

The agitated voices in the upstairs hall woke Emilie. She climbed out of bed and tiptoed with the raccoon tucked under one arm like a doll.

"Miss Emilie, you get back in bed this minute!"

Emilie turned to find Mammy Rachel, hands on hips, in the doorway of the connecting room that Mammy shared with Mimsie.

"An' put that coon back in its basket, 'fore you get fleas an' I don't know what all."

"Charmante hasn't got any fleas," Emilie said, having no idea whether the raccoon did or not. "What's going on? Why is Hollis screeching like that?"

"An' well she might," Mammy said grimly. "I might as well

tell you, 'cause everybody on this plantation's gonna know 'bout it by tomorrow. Probably everybody in the state of Louisiana, if Mister Roman don't make his darkies keep their mouths shut. Your brother Denis he tell your mama he gonna marry that no good poor-white Michelet child, that's what."

"Dinah?" Emilie looked interested. Dinah had given Denis Charmante, and was thus on Emilie's list of favored people.

"An' don't you go tellin' your mama I told you," Mammy said. "Now you get in bed, an' if you're fixin' to sleep with that coon, you and me's gonna bathe her in feverfew tea tomorrow."

"I don't see what everyone's yellin' about," Emilie said. "Dinah's nice."

"Honey, you ain't old enough to understand," Mammy said. She cocked an ear toward the hall. "I got to go do somethin' with Hollis 'fore she wake Miss Doudouce. I purely ain't up to talkin' to Miss Doudouce."

Emilie pattered back to bed obediently. She could understand that. Tante Doudouce always listened to the first half of what you said and not the second half, and so lived in a state of perpetual confusion.

Emilie pulled the mosquito netting closed and listened to Hollis's voice go up two notches as Mammy went in. Emilie snuggled down with Charmante clutched in one arm, and Madame Josette in the other. "Everybody's so busy yellin' about Denis," she told them darkly, "they've forgot all about Adele. They'll be sorry when she hauls 'em off to Bayou Goula an' bites 'em. They'd better watch her."

XI

*"An Unsteadfast,
Sinful Woman"*

LOUISIANA'S AUGUST HEAT was not to be imagined by anyone who had never endured it. Slaves from farther north, whose masters had not allowed them to acclimatize themselves gradually, often died in the fields, and the death rate for the white population was not much less. Malaria and yellow fever were an ever-present threat, as were a myriad of diseases caused by spoiled food and bad water. Garbage rotted in a matter of hours, and in New Orleans the gutters smelled so bad that Sallie flatly refused to go into the city at all.

Indoors, slight relief was obtained from the punkah fans, which were swept back and forth overhead by pulling on a rope. The littlest Negroes were set to this task in the summer, and none of the ladies was ever without a fan in her hand. In the daytime all the windows and doors stood open, in the hope of catching a breeze off the river, and the maids spent their days in constant pursuit of the insects that hopped and zoomed in from out-of-doors. No one was ever particularly surprised to find a grasshopper in his teacup or a firefly swimming lazily through the darkness of a bedroom. Everyone, children included, sat up late in the relative cool of the veranda because it was simply too hot to sleep.

The blue-green cane grew thicker and taller with each torrential downpour, which left the ground steaming like a teakettle. Harlow McCamy came out his front door at six o'clock on a morning that was already hot and gave orders to start bringing in the cotton in the upper fields. The field hands could work till noon, he judged, and after that he'd slow the pace. A horse clip-clopped by and

Harlow raised his hat to Sallie DuMontaigne, out for her morning ride. Later, if it weren't too hot, she might come out to the cotton field with her easel and her paint box and a little darkie to set them up for her. She would find an unobtrusive spot and spend an hour or two painting the pickers in the field. Paul DuMontaigne didn't like that, but it wasn't the overseer's business to tell tales on the mistress. He hoped fervently that she *would* come, as protection from the devils that pursued him.

Celeste sauntered by him, a canvas cotton sack slung over one shoulder and resting on her hip. Her skirts were tied up around her knees. A red tignon bound her hair tightly, accentuating toffee-colored skin, a full mouth, and slightly slanting dark eyes. She grinned at him, showing little white teeth, as she passed. She licked her lips.

"Mornin', Mister McCamy. You don't look like you slept too well."

"It is very hot," McCamy said stiffly. "Get about your work, Celeste."

Celeste appraised him. The man must be a fool. She'd done everything but tuck herself into his bed at night, and he had yet to take her up on it. And she thought the rest of the field hands were laughing at her.

"It sure is hot." She undid two buttons of her dress and fanned herself with one hand. "But I got somethin' I bet make you sleep better at night." She pulled the dress open a little wider, exhibiting a dark swell of breasts. She took a step toward him.

"No!" McCamy flung himself backward with unmistakable revulsion. He slipped on a rock, and his bad leg buckled under him. He righted himself, scrabbling at the air. The other Negroes had stopped to stare, and he whirled around to face them. "Get to work!" he hissed. Unnerved by the flaring light in his eyes, they fled into the field.

Celeste's eyes opened wide. The overseer knew what she was offering, all right; he just didn't want her. She thought he was afraid of her. She laughed and eyed him malevolently. A silly little sister-boy like that wasn't never gonna want her, and she wasn't never gonna get no privileges or good things to eat. And that Gabriel was gonna laugh at her.

"I bet you just don't know what to do with it," she whispered. "Look." She lifted her skirts deliberately, thrusting her bared hips forward. Her thighs glistened with sweat in the sultry air. "That's where it goes if you can make it stand up long enough. Ain't you even gonna try?"

"Get to work!" McCamy's voice rose in pitch. He felt as if he was strangling. "Get to work before you get a whipping!"

"Huh-uh." Celeste shook her head at him. She dropped her skirts but didn't bother to button her dress. "You ain't gonna whip me, not an' have every hand on the place know you got a tool in your pants you can't use. You can't, can you? That's your trouble, ain't it, Mister McCamy?"

"Get into that field, you whore!"

Celeste went slowly into the cotton rows while McCamy stood trembling behind her. His skin felt clammy, and his stomach heaved with nausea. He turned into the cotton and vomited.

"What you talking to the boss about?" Gabriel asked suspiciously.

"Ain't none of your business." Celeste stripped the cotton bolls with quick, nimble fingers while Gabriel stood, hands on hips, glaring at her.

"That white man don't want you," Gabriel said slowly. "I seen the look in his eye. You leave him be, Celeste, or you're gonna make trouble for everybody."

Daniel came down the row toward them. "I make trouble for the pair of you, you don't get to work," he said, but he looked sympathetically at Gabriel's dark, set face. When Gabriel had moved away down the row, Daniel grabbed Celeste's arm. "If you don't want him, why don't you leave him alone too, 'stead of hanging him on a string like you do?"

"Ain't your business either," Celeste said. She gave him a quick smile, teeth just bared, over her shoulder. " 'Less maybe *you* want to try some out?" It was a perfunctory suggestion, more out of force of habit than anything else. Daniel was married, and he preached at prayer meeting every Sunday. She pulled at the cotton angrily. "*I* can't help it if he keep comin' around. *I* don't ask him."

"You don't send him off neither," Daniel said. "You're an unsteadfast, sinful woman, Sister Celeste, an' if you don't ask God to loosen up the hold the devil's got on you, you're goin' to hell sure."

"I ain't at prayer meetin'," Celeste said. She flicked an eye at the slight figure of Harlow McCamy.

"I seen what you're trying to do to Mister McCamy," Daniel said, "an' it's about as safe as poking at a snake."

* * *

Harlow McCamy thrashed in the tangled bedclothes, his skin wet and clammy, his eyes open and staring. Every night since Celeste had begun her unrelenting pursuit he had had the dream. Now the dreadful forms that haunted him were back, as black as the alien and disturbing force that emanated from the Negro women. They terrorized him even more than white women—to Harlow there was an animal sexuality in them, a primitive nature closer to the earth, without the shield of the thousand conventions and pretenses behind which white women hid their sex. Dark hands reached out for him, like black earth pulling him into the ground with the growing cane. Mouths that bent to kiss opened and swallowed him.

She was there in the bed. If he closed his eyes, she would wrap those dark arms around him. McCamy sat up with a stifled scream and flung himself to the floor. A large insect rattled against the windowpane, attracted by the candle, which McCamy, uncontrollably fearful of the dark, had left burning on the night table. A pitiful and terror-stricken figure in the crumpled nightshirt and cap, he pulled himself into the candle's small circle of light. Arms wrapped around his knees, he sat there until morning.

"Good morning, Mister McCamy." Sallie raised her riding crop to Harlow as she passed him on her usual morning ride. Unsettled by his pallid countenance stretched taut over bones thrown somehow into high relief, she looked back at him over her shoulder. "Mister McCamy, aren't you well?"

"Yes, I'm fine," Harlow said too quickly. He took a deep breath. "Very well, thank you, ma'am."

"Well, you look awful to me," Sallie said frankly. "You send for Doctor Leboeuf if you don't feel better. You've got to be careful here in the summer—the heat can be very debilitating."

"I—I'll remember," Harlow said. He turned away quickly. *She knows*, he thought, choking. *They all know.* Imagined laughter battered at his ears.

Harlow forgotten, Sallie turned Briar Rose onto her favorite path, a trail that crisscrossed the bayou on old wooden bridges. It was Denis who burdened her mind this morning. Cheerful, *stubborn* Denis, who refused to back down. Her best beloved (although Sallie admitted that to no one, not even to herself), who was going to ruin his life. It was bad enough to watch Felicie, who, Sallie realized, was now pining for Roman Prevost, and Paul spending his time with that shallow, selfish French girl who would no doubt break his heart. But, dear God, not Denis too!

And what about her? It was only the unhealthiness of New Orleans in the summer that kept her from going to Gilbert, but did she really *want* Gilbert? She would be glad enough to part with him if she and Paul were going to Washington. Why didn't she mind parting from Gilbert more? Was her admitted irritation at having Adele Scarron stuck under her nose prompting her to long for Paul again? He'd already had one mistress when he married her. She should hardly be surprised if he took another one, she supposed.

"This was supposed to be such a wonderful summer," she said despairingly to Mammy later, as she brushed Sallie's hair and repinned it before dinner. "Lucien and Felicie home and Paul running for office—I thought that was going to be exciting, but all he does is shut himself up in his study. Paris didn't help Lucien at all, and Denis and Felicie are unhappy—I swear there's something on Denis's mind besides that Michelet girl."

"Too many folks thinkin' the grass is greener on the other side of the fence, I reckon." Mammy studied Sallie with concern. "Honey, you'll fret yourself into a illness worryin' about them chillun."

"And Hollis," Sallie added. "Hollis is so edgy, she makes me wonder what *she's* been up to." Sallie made a face in the mirror. "And what kind of example have I been setting for her?"

"I ain't gonna argue with you there," Mammy said.

"No, I'll bet you're not. Even Mister McCamy looked like the hoodoos were after him this morning."

"Hmmph." Mammy Rachel had a low opinion of Yankees. "That Mister McCamy, he ain't got much *to* him, if you ask me." She poked the last pin into Sallie's hair and set tortoise-shell combs into either side, just above her ears. Mammy kissed Sallie's cheek affectionately. "You eat your dinner an' cheer up, honey. Mister Paul, he tells me Mister Barret's comin' back."

Sallie brightened. "Yes, the end of next month. He says it's to see Paul campaign, but I think Alice is driving him crazy. I don't know why he doesn't get married."

"Maybe he can't find no lady what wants to be driven crazy," Mammy said. "That Miss Alice is a tryin' woman."

"And maybe he's too set in his ways now. We aren't so young anymore." She made a face in the mirror. "Do I look all right?"

"Honey, you gonna look all right when you is older than me," Mammy said. Sallie had the sort of beauty that aged with grace. "Now you go eat your dinner. I'm gonna see do that Jem got my Bible fix yet. I might wanta pray some, the way things is goin'."

* * *

Mammy Rachel's Bible lay on the table between wooden clamps. Jem was putting a new cane seat in one of the chairs from *Petite Marie*, while Sam, the boat's pilot, leaned against the wall, watching him. Mammy Rachel settled herself in an already-mended chair and pulled her boots off. "I declare, my feet be two sizes bigger'n they was this mornin'. You fix my Bible, Jem?"

"I put a new bindin' on," Jem said. "You done split the old one right down the back."

Sam grinned. "You been prayin' too hard, Rachel. You plumb wore it out."

"I know a few folks what could use a little *more* prayin'," Mammy said, "'stead of shootin' dice on that steamboat."

Sam bent over the back of her chair. "Maybe I'm just needin' a good woman t' show me the way."

"Father Fortier, he show you the way in church on a Sunday iffen you ain't sleep through it every time," Mammy said. "Ain't nothin' stoppin' you from prayer meetin' here in the evenin's, neither."

"I 'spect I need inspirin'," Sam said. "Rachel honey, why don't you put them boots back on and take a walk with me? Mighty pretty down on the river this evenin'."

"I might at that," Mammy said. It was her evening off, and Junie had charge of Emilie. She collected her Bible, thanked Jem, and walked with Sam down to the levee.

"Ain't hardly seen you all summer," Sam said, looking sideways at Mammy Rachel. He folded his arms to admire the river in the twilight.

"I been busy, what with guests an' Mr. Lucien, an' the Frenchwoman, an' I don't know what all."

"Too busy for me?"

Mammy Rachel sighed. "You got winnin' ways, but you ain't steadfast, Sam, and I'm too old for a fly-by-night man."

"I ain't!" Sam said, insulted.

"You is. You got a good heart, an' you done talk me into bed with you so easy it embarrass me, but I marry you, I won't know a peaceful night, wondering what devilment you up to."

"Well, the river, he's mighty pretty, so you walk with me a little more anyway," Sam said. He slipped an arm around her waist. "Long as you're feelin' so old tonight, I'll restrain myself."

They strolled along the footpath that ran beside the levee road. It was a courting sort of evening, and they weren't the only couple out to look at the river. Daniel and his wife, Riar, were sitting on the jetty where the steamboats tied up. *Petite Marie* bobbed in the water beside them, and Sam eyed her fondly.

"Prettiest lady I ever saw, and a sight more accommodatin' than some," he remarked.

"What you mean is, she can't talk," Riar said, laughing. "Evenin', Sam. Evenin', Sis Rachel."

"Evenin', Sis Riar, Brother Daniel." Mammy Rachel put a touch of formality in her greeting. There were marked degrees in the social scale between the field hands and the house servants, but Daniel preached at prayer meeting every Sunday evening, which Mammy attended as a firm believer, and this elevated his status somewhat in her eyes. "How you doin' this evenin'?" she inquired.

Daniel's expression was troubled. "Sis Rachel, it seem to me the world's got powerful ungodly, what with folks forgettin' they place. Let alone—"

"Daniel, you hush!" Riar shook her head at him.

"I can't," Daniel said stubbornly. "I done look at the problem every which way, an' I can't see how to come at it."

"Then hush up about it!" Riar hissed. "Mister McCamy hear you, I don't know what happen!"

"Things go on the way they is, *somethin'* gonna happen," Daniel said. "Sis Rachel, she might can see what we oughta do 'bout Celeste."

Mammy folded her arms in disapproval, but she shook her head. "That Celeste been sinful since the day she been born. The devil's gonna come for her one of these days, an' we better leave her to him."

"But it ain't the usual problem," Daniel said. "She been after Mister McCamy since he got here, but he act like he scared of her. Now he goin' round like there was ha'nts after him. She push him too far, she gonna bring bad times on all of us."

"He ain't as scared of her as I is of you tellin' tales 'bout Mister McCamy," Riar said tightly. The overseer's power over the field hands was nearly absolute and generally unquestioned.

Mammy frowned. Her influence with her white family was large, but there were some things that she knew better than to interfere in. She bent a steely eye on Sam, who had been listening with the interest of one whose work did not come under the overseer's supervision. "You ain't heard none of this," she informed him.

"Now you know I ain't no gossip," Sam said. "Mister Paul, he oughta sell that Celeste, though."

"Mister Paul ain't ever sell but three darkies that I know of," Mammy said, "an' one of them was to a man what owned the girl's husband, so's they could live together. You know as well as I do he ain't gonna sell Celeste long as her mama's livin'." Celeste's mother was elderly and not in good health. Celeste paid as little attention to her as possible, but Paul would never separate them. "It ain't my place to tell Mister Paul anythin' 'bout this," Mammy said, "but Celeste don't know that. You keep out of it, Daniel, and I see what I can do."

As an upper house servant, Mammy Rachel had little contact with the overseer. Like most black house servants, she considered the white overseer, especially if he was a Yankee, to be a person of little status. When she went out to the field the next morning, on the pretext of borrowing two hands to help her "turn out" the best parlor and shift the heavy furniture, she was appalled. Even at a distance, McCamy's skin looked pallid, his pale eyes haunted and dark-circled. He was screened from the Negroes in the field by a stand of oak trees, and it looked to Mammy as if he were hiding there. As she approached, Celeste darted between two trees and stopped a few paces from him. McCamy flinched and backed away as if she had struck him. Neither noticed Mammy Rachel, and she stood still, feeling that she was observing something tormented and unhealthy in them both.

Celeste spoke, and the taunting note in her voice, but not the words, carried down the field to Mammy. Celeste lifted her skirts in unmistakable invitation. McCamy put his hands out as if to push her away. His eyes were wild and not quite focused.

That man's gonna go over the edge, Mammy thought. She rustled the dry cotton stalks with her skirts and strode toward them. McCamy whirled, whether seeing her as a deliverer or as a witness to a private and painful humiliation, Mammy wasn't sure. "*There* you is, Mister McCamy," she said briskly. "I need you loan me two of your boys for the afternoon, if you can spare 'em."

Harlow fought for what control he could muster. His hands shook. "I— Why yes, certainly." He fled round the trees toward the men in the field.

Mammy advanced on Celeste. "I seen you," she said grimly. "I seen you with your skirts up like a whore."

Celeste narrowed her eyes. "You mind your singin' an' your prayin'. Leave me alone."

Mammy lifted a hand and smacked Celeste across the face. "I been prayin' for your mama to get her health back, but now I think the Lord bless her if He take her home to Him afore she see you clear!"

Celeste's eyes blazed, but she held her hands at her sides with clenched fists. She wasn't about to admit it, but Mammy scared her—not much, but some. "You ain't got *no* say over me! You just fill up with spite 'cause you ain't young an' you ain't pretty no more!"

"Pretty is as pretty do. Inside you is twisted up like a ol' snake. You leave that man alone 'fore you start somethin' you can't stop!"

Celeste appeared to consider. "Maybe I do. Maybe I don't, too. Ain't gonna be 'cause you tell me!"

Mammy raised her hand again, and Celeste turned and ran back into the field and fell to picking cotton. Mammy watched her dubiously. If she had made any impression on Celeste at all—and Mammy had her doubts—it would fade in a day or two. Celeste was not the sort of woman to set the fear of future punishment above her immediate wishes.

The heat shimmered visibly, its ripples distorting black hands and faces out of their accustomed form. Harlow McCamy stood beside the ditch that ran between this field and the next. He reached a hand toward the bridle of his patiently waiting horse, pulled it away again, reached back, stopped, and looked wildly around him, upward at the brazen sky, then out across the open fields. He reminded Mammy of a nocturnal creature caught abroad in daylight. Mammy Rachel had as little respect for the white man who had charge of Negroes and couldn't handle them as she had for the man who mistreated them. It seemed to her that both displayed behavior unbecoming the race that, by fortune, had been given command over another.

She waved an arm at the two burly slaves that McCamy had called out of the cotton field, and they trudged after her back toward the house. They seemed delighted to have been let off cotton picking. "Y'all can start with that pi-anna," she told them lest they have any illusions about taking it easy in the second-best parlor all afternoon.

Parlor and piano were occupied when they got there. Felicie was playing "Au Clair de la Lune" unhandily and brooding into the array of shawls and clocks and wax flowers that decorated its top.

"That's all right, honey, you go right ahead," Mammy said when Felicie stood up.

Felicie shook her head. "No, I have a headache anyway." She wore the lightest of muslin gowns, but her cheeks were flushed.

Mammy put her hand on Felicie's forehead suspiciously. "You come out on the gallery, I get you something cold to drink." She added over her shoulder, "An' I want all this here furniture out on the gallery. An' carry it, you hear? No shovin' it and scarrin' up the floor."

When she returned with a glass of orange-flower water, Felicie took the glass with an absent expression, but didn't taste it.

"You drink that 'fore you faints!"

Felicie smiled wryly at Mammy and drained the glass. "You know I never faint."

"Wouldn't hurt none if you did," Mammy informed her. "A lady's s'posed to be delicate, an' ladies what is delicate faints."

"Well, you'll just have to give up on me. I'll never get married anyway, so it doesn't matter."

Mammy was indignant. "Don't you let me hear you talk like that! I knows what's wrong with you, moonin' after a man what's married! I'd be ashamed of you if you wasn't just a baby and don't know what you doin'!"

"I do know what I'm doing," Felicie said glumly, "and I didn't do it on purpose. I thought it would be *fun*, coming out, and having all the boys come courting." Her eyes lit briefly. "And they do, too, Mammy, you've got to admit." She sighed. "But I just can't get interested in them. They all seem so young, wanting to fight duels over me. Half of them were wanting to fight duels over Hollis two years ago."

"That don't mean they ain't in love with you now."

"But I just can't seem to be in love with them. Not with . . . with somebody better right under my nose." There seemed to be an unspoken understanding that Roman's name was not to be mentioned.

Mammy put her hands on her hips. "Well, you better start tryin'. You want to end up like poor Miss Doudouce?"

"No," Felicie admitted. "But maybe I will anyway."

"No you ain't," Mammy said firmly. "Not if I has to find you somebody to marry my own self. They's plenty more men than the ones what lives around here. Maybe I ask Mister Barret to look around."

"Don't you dare!" Felicie said, mortified.

"Well, I'm gonna, if you don't perk up some an' stop lookin' like a dead fish what just buried its best friend!"

XII

Debate,

with Tomatoes

BARRET FORBES GRINNED at Paul. "I'm sure you'll confound the enemy handily. I wouldn't miss watching you do so for anything."

"I wish I shared your confidence," Paul said. "I let Roman and his henchmen talk me into this debate, and I'm wondering if they ought to lock me up in my room like poor Tante Zizi, who thought she was François Villon and simply couldn't be let out loose at all."

"I'm sure you'll do admirably," Sallie said, "even if you don't consider it suitable for me to come and listen."

"Now, Sallie, we've been through all that."

"Yes, haven't we?" She wrinkled her nose at him. "Since women aren't considered intelligent enough to vote, I suppose it doesn't matter." She laid down her napkin and rose from the breakfast table. "Come along, Felicie."

"I didn't say you weren't *intelligent* enough—" Paul called after her.

Sallie ignored him. She didn't really *want* to vote; it struck her as being slightly common. "We'll see if Madame Lolo has your dress ready for a fitting," she said airily to Felicie. Madame Lolo was the quadroon modiste hired twice a year to spend two weeks at Belle Marie sewing for the ladies. "Hollis, you and Adele come along too, please. We'll leave the gentlemen to more important matters."

Hollis, who didn't particularly care whether her father debated Gilbert Becquerel or shot him, so long as he won his election, was happy to consider more interesting matters elsewhere, but Adele departed reluctantly, with a little backward wave of her hand at Paul, indicating her knowledge of woman's proper place but of an otherwise burning interest in his political career.

Barret eyed her askance. Unfortunately, with Lucien and Denis also present, there didn't seem any tactful way to ask Paul about his and Adele's relationship.

"Well, I intend to go with you," Lucien said, chafing under the boredom of a summer wasted, being forcibly reintroduced to the working side of the plantation.

With some exasperation Paul watched Lucien happily tucking into a plate of eggs and thick, home-cured bacon. It would be so much simpler, and probably more profitable, to turn matters back over to Denis, but Denis deserved better than the privilege of serving as his brother's land agent. *If I win,* Paul thought, *Lucien will have to sink or swim.* He hoped to hell Lucien could swim. There was no backing out of this campaign now.

Denis, prodding unhappily at the mess he had made of his uneaten breakfast, announced that he thought he'd come along too. Unlike Lucien, Denis really wanted to hear his father's debate with Gilbert Becquerel—in spite of his fear of bumping into Françoise Becquerel.

When Sam tied up *Petite Marie* at the levee in New Orleans opposite Jackson Square, Roman Prevost was waiting for them at the City Exchange, where Barret and the DuMontaignes had booked rooms. Three men whose faces were masked by the identical trio of cigars, mustaches, and important expressions converged on Paul with much back-patting and hand-shaking and bore him off to be instructed in the fine points of routing Gilbert Becquerel.

Denis grinned. "He's probably in more danger from the audience than from Becquerel." New Orleans political meetings were lively affairs, and the voters often came armed with tomatoes.

"We'll stand near the door," Lucien said. "Papa's on his own. I'm going to go and find a drink. Barret, are you coming?"

Barret looked embarrassed. "I, uh, I thought I might do a little shopping in the Market. Presents for your mother and the girls." He also thought he might see the beautiful octoroon girl there again, but he felt too silly to admit that she'd been on his mind that long.

"Denis?"

"No, I think I'll stay here and read." Denis looked sheepish. It sounded lame even to him.

Lucien hooted. He knew perfectly well why his brother was afraid to show his face on the street.

Lucien and Barret departed on their separate errands, and Denis settled into an armchair with a volume of Byron. Thank God he'd thought to bring something to read, to give his excuse at least a shaky verisimilitude. He opened the book at random. *Don Juan:*

> *What men call gallantry, and gods adultery,*
> *Is much more common where the climate's sultry.*

Good God! He closed the book again and decided to forget about Byron.

There was a tap at the door. Expecting another of his father's Democratic henchmen, Denis ambled over to open it. A small Negro boy in an elaborate scarlet uniform stood outside. He proffered a sealed envelope to Denis.

"Is you Mister Denis DuMontaigne?"

"Yeah." Denis took the envelope reluctantly. It smelled unnecessarily of scent, and he thought irritably how like Françoise it was to dress her page up like a Louis XIV footman. He dug in his pocket for a coin to give the child. "Are you supposed to wait for an answer?"

"No, sir. Madame, she just say was you here, I'm s'posed to give you that there message."

"I see." When the boy had departed, happily clutching his bonus, Denis sat down again and opened the letter with the enthusiasm he would have accorded a basket of hornets.

"Françoise, you must be mad!" Denis set his hat on the parlor table and looked at her with exasperation. She had apparently given the butler, Michael, the day off, and that in itself boded no good.

Françoise pouted prettily. "You do not care for me anymore." She poured a glass of wine from the crystal decanter on the table and offered a second glass to Denis.

"At this hour of the day?"

Françoise shrugged and raised her glass.

Denis watched uneasily. She was starting to drink more and more, always out of the same delicate fluted goblets. She always referred to them as "my grandmother's fine old glasses" and seemed to feel that as long as she drank out of those, it didn't really count.

He couldn't flat out say that he wished she were at the bottom of Lake Pontchartrain, and he was enough of a gentleman to feel a certain responsibility about their affair, but he also felt like he had his feet in glue. *I've got to get loose*, he thought desperately. There was Dinah. "I do care, Françoise, but this is dangerous. You don't really want your husband to find out; you know you don't."

Françoise had a look in her eye that gave Denis very little hope of agreement. "I have told you," she said flatly, "I will *tell* him, if necessary."

"What good would that do you?"

"He would certainly pay more attention to me than he does now. Gilbert is not a man who would accord to his wife the privileges he takes for himself."

"You mightn't care for the attention," Denis said.

Françoise shrugged again. "It would be an improvement on none at all." She poured herself another glass of wine.

"There's another complication," Denis said desperately. "I'm going to get married."

Françoise raised her delicate brows. "Oh?"

"And of course after that—"

Françoise put her glass down. She twined her arms around Denis's neck, so that her pretty face was tilted up to his. She smiled and kissed him. "There is no *of course*"—she kissed him again—"about it." Her skirts swayed as she pressed herself against him. "Now be sensible and come upstairs." Another kiss as she nestled closer. "Don't be pious, Denis. You know that you would like to."

The maddening thing was that when he had her in his arms, rubbing herself against him like a cat, he *would* like to. The youthful ardor of a twenty-year-old body obstinately refused to subjugate itself to more cerebral dictates. Françoise drew her fingers down the nape of his neck.

As always he ended up, physically eager and mentally appalled, in Françoise's bed. Their clothes lay in two disheveled piles on the floor, and Françoise laughed at him softly. "For a man who did not wish to make love to me, you undress very quickly."

"I didn't say I didn't want to make love to you," Denis said. Lying as naked as a jaybird on Françoise's silk coverlet, it was all too obvious that he did. "I said it was a dangerous thing to do. But I meant it, Françoise. I can't come here after I'm married."

Françoise sat up in bed and draped herself across him. "You can." She wriggled around until she lay straddling him. "And you will." She kissed the hollows of his neck and then bit him gently. "Because I don't intend to lose a valued amusement."

"Damn it, Françoise, you can't force a man to make love to

you," Denis protested. "And you can't stiffen his cock for him if it's not in the mood," he added crudely.

Françoise laughed at him again. "Denis, *mon ami*, that is not your problem." She sat up again and positioned herself over him, and he had to admit that it wasn't.

She took his hands and put them on her breasts, and in spite of himself he kept them there.

She was breathing heavily, and her pale cheeks were flushed. "So you will come and visit me, yes, when I want you to? Because if not"—he pinched her breasts, half-angry, half-passionate, and she squirmed with pleasure—"then I will tell Gilbert, yes?" *And I will get such pleasure out of telling him who you are*. But not as much pleasure as she got from Denis, not quite.

Gasping, Denis pulled her down to him so that her face lay in the hollow of his shoulder. He put his hands on her buttocks and pressed upward with his hips, driving himself deeper into her. Even as his passion mounted and burst, he wondered how in the name of heaven he was going to get away from her.

Denis got back to the City Exchange with five minutes to spare, before an early dinner—time enough to save him from Lucien's taunts, if not his suspicions. It was still hot in September, and Denis was dripping with sweat, having set as fast a pace away from Françoise Becquerel as he could manage. He stripped off his shirt and splashed fresh water into the basin from the pitcher on the washstand. He bathed his face and chest with it, dried himself with the luxurious towel provided by the hotel, and was setting the studs into a clean shirt when Lucien and Barret arrived, having met on the Exchange steps.

"You'd better change if you want to get dinner before the doings start," he informed them amiably. "Papa's already gone down."

"I trust you spent a pleasant afternoon," Lucien said. "You look a mite disheveled."

"I took a nap," Denis said, refusing to be baited.

"You need dinner," Barret said. "Go and dress, Lucien." He disappeared into his own room across the hall in search of his evening clothes. He hadn't seen the girl in the Market, and he was feeling restless.

In the dining room of the City Exchange, they found Paul still surrounded by the mustachioed trio who were giving him last-minute counsel.

"Stay off the presidential election if you can."

"No, stay off Van Buren, but hit Harrison if you get the chance."

"Try not to let 'em tangle you up with Van Buren. Tell 'em you're here to get Paul DuMontaigne elected because Louisiana needs honest government in bad times."

A waiter arrived with steaming bowls of crayfish bisque, and the men behind the mustaches continued their conference between spoonfuls.

"We're not talking parties here so much as DuMontaigne versus Becquerel. Never mind what the Yankees are doing, Louisiana sets her own style. The Democrats have come for states' rights, so use that."

"Gentlemen!" Paul laid his soupspoon down, and the advisers eyed him attentively. "We've been over all this. What I should like now is to eat my dinner in peace." He picked the spoon up again and saluted them with it. "With your permission."

The trio fell silent, but they looked dubious. They wanted Paul's name and reputation to beat Gilbert Becquerel with, but they didn't trust a man this new to politics to know what he was doing. There was no telling what an amateur might take it into his head to say once he got going.

"How are they holding up?" Denis slipped into a seat at the end of a row, beside the third adviser, and cast his eyes over the crowd in the rotunda of the Exchange.

"They're restive," the man said. "We'll get some votes from the men that count"—he nodded at the front rows—"but the boys in the back like a little more excitement to their politics."

Paul, looking like the gentleman farmer he was, and Gilbert Becquerel, wearing a distressingly bright flowered waistcoat and bearing an indefinable air of hair oil and polish, were seated on a dais at one end of the rotunda. A blue cloud of cigar smoke overhung the room, its smell mingling with those of beer and of the audience itself. Behind the top-hatted front rows were shopkeepers, bank clerks, and other solid citizens, and behind them was an eclectic mixture of Cajuns, Irish, Germans, Kentucky flatboatmen from the river, and even an Indian or two. It was in the rear ranks that the tomato-throwing element was generally to be found.

"How many of these guys can vote?" Denis asked.

"You got to be a property owner, of course, but you'd be surprised who turns up on the rolls as a property owner. Becquerel's slung a good bit of money around in this crowd."

"To boo my father?"

"Oh, they'll do that anyway. Becquerel too, if they get bored. Nah, the free beer is just to remind 'em of who takes the best care of 'em when it comes time to vote."

"Which most of 'em aren't entitled to do," Denis said with disgust, "although they'll probably get away with it. I'm beginning to see why you want to elect my father."

"Your father's a sight too upright for my money," the man admitted, tugging his mustache. "You gotta know when to scratch the other man's back in this business. But we don't want Gilbert Becquerel. We gotta sweeten up our reputation in New Orleans if we're gonna keep the shipping coming in strong. A man like your father's a credit to his class; makes it easier to get his point across."

"I see." It all sounded a lot less altruistic to Denis than it had when Roman Prevost had explained the same thing. He listened to his father with interest.

The first topic to arise was the ever-touchy question known as states' rights—for lying behind that question, like the hidden base of an iceberg, was the issue of slavery. Even those Southerners who thought that slavery would eventually have to go knew that it would mean economic ruin if it were rammed down their throats by the free states. Paul DuMontaigne and Gilbert Becquerel were in agreement on that point.

What mattered was which man could better ensure that his viewpoint was given proper attention in Washington. Monsieur Becquerel found it hard to believe that Monsieur DuMontaigne would find himself at home in Washington in these fast-paced and tricky times. Monsieur DuMontaigne, for his part, found it hard to believe that a political party whose slogan promised a jug of hard cider and a log cabin to drink it in was capable of being entrusted with the future of Louisiana.

Monsieur Becquerel informed Monsieur DuMontaigne that he was naïve. Monsieur DuMontaigne informed Monsieur Becquerel that honesty and naïveté were not synonymous, a fact that might have escaped Monsieur Becquerel since he appeared to have little acquaintance with either.

The audience sat up. This was more like it.

The next topic was the matter of governmental reform. Paul proposed a number of changes that made good sense and very tedious listening. Then Paul swept an eye over the audience and let it linger on the back rows as he condemned the rampant irregularities in the voting rolls.

An irate mutter answered him, and the man beside Denis groaned and put his head in his hands. *Amateur!*

Gilbert Becquerel looked greatly cheered. "We are running for the Congress of the United States. These are matters I intend to leave solely to our state legislature, where they properly belong."

"If we wish reform to be made," Paul snapped, "then we must set an example, at whatever level we serve. Our shipping comes downriver from other states, which look to our performance in Washington, as well as at home, as a measure by which to judge us. Shipping is our lifeblood. Prosperity from our shipping will bring prosperity to every man in this room."

Shouts of agreement from the front rows greeted this, and the rear ranks settled down a trifle. Prosperity was a word with a magical quality. Every man liked to think of it as his right, if he only voted the right leader into office.

"Prosperity," Paul said, driving his point home, "will serve the citizens of New Orleans longer and better than free beer on election day."

The mustachioed man next to Denis took his head out of his hands. He thought maybe their man was getting the hang of this.

As the debate progressed, however, Denis realized that the rear ranks were growing restless again. Hands began to creep into coat pockets. A burly flatboatman across the aisle meditatively tossed a ripe tomato from hand to hand, and his expression said plainly that these two had been jawing for three solid hours and nobody had started a fight yet. This wasn't his idea of politics.

The debate's sponsors, on the dais behind the candidates, also appeared to take note of their constituency's frame of mind. Gilbert Becquerel, waxing eloquent on the future of "our beloved Crescent City," was ruthlessly interrupted in midmetaphor.

"Monsieur Becquerel, I am afraid that you are out of time. Monsieur DuMontaigne, you have five minutes to respond, and that will conclude the evening."

Observing the tomato faction and recalling that the tougher element occasionally threw potatoes instead, Paul said that he felt he had said all that he had to say, but would be pleased to allow Monsieur Becquerel to use the time instead.

That was where Becquerel made his mistake. Overestimating the tolerance of the rear ranks, who had been wooed with largesse from his campaign, he took up where he had left off.

"Aw, now, he done said all that," someone announced. There was a rising murmur of agreement. He was their man, but it seemed a pure shame to waste a good tomato. A loud splat announced the current sentiment of the crowd, and the top hats in the front rows ducked down as one man.

"Time to go, kid," said the adviser in the seat next to Denis. They dived for the floor, and Denis noted that his father was there before him, looking elegant and unstained. Gilbert Becquerel had not been so fortunate. He brushed by them in the doorway, pausing only long enough to glare at Paul and Denis. His flowered waistcoat was adorned with a red tomato splotch, glowing brightly like a cabbage rose among the bachelor's buttons.

"Goddamn, Gilbert, you oughta knowed better!"

"Hell, a man wears a waistcoat like that, he's askin' for it!" Hoots of laughter followed him.

Becquerel glowered at the supporters who trotted beside him. "DuMontaigne was a hell of a lot better prepared than you thought. Haven't you fools got anybody who knows what's going on?"

"No spies in DuMontaigne's camp, if that's what you mean. His people are pretty loyal."

"Goddamn it, find someone who's not. They can't all be incorruptible," Becquerel said. It wasn't any use asking Sallie, but there were plenty more people at Belle Marie, and the odds were good that somebody had an ax to grind. "What the hell do I pay you for?"

"I almost felt sorry for him, in his nice new waistcoat," Denis chuckled.

Paul dropped into a chair in their suite upstairs. "A sight to gladden my heart, I must admit." Paul put his arms over his head and stretched. "I may be too old for this business."

"We were thinking of popping over to the Orleans Ballroom," Denis said. "You haven't seen the sights, Barret, until you've seen that one. Will you join us, Papa?"

Paul shook his head. "No, I've got a speech I want to work on while it's fresh in my mind."

"All right then, don't wait up for us." Denis collected his top hat and gloves. Skulking inside had proved no defense against Françoise, so he might as well go out. The Orleans Ballroom was the one place he could think of where she wouldn't be lying in wait for him.

The entertainments at the ballroom in a wing of the Théâtre d'Orléans were officially known as the Bals du Cordon Bleu, but no one except the proper *tantes* and *mamans* who presented their daughters there ever called them anything but the Quadroon Balls. Here the beautiful daughters of the *gens de couleur* made their bow to the society of their unique world. The women were all quadroons, or lighter; the men were all white. The gentlemen paid two dollars admission, double the price of the white balls. No colored men were admitted, ever, not even brothers.

Compared to the Quadroon Balls, the white balls of New Orleans were boring affairs. It was a rare gentleman of that city who did not slip away from his female relations to spend his evening in the Orleans Ballroom when the dates of white and quadroon affairs conflicted.

The lilting music of a waltz filtered out into the lamplit air of Orleans Street as Denis, Barret and Lucien approached. Barret eyed the building with interest. The wide, low façade was plain to the point of ugliness, but there was an air about it proclaiming that within was beauty. Across the front, an ironwork balcony overhung Orleans Street, and behind it the moving shadows of the dancers could be seen against the windows.

The ground floor was divided into private card and reception rooms, and the stairs were crowded with men in evening dress. Lucien, Denis, and Barret paid their two dollars and mounted the broad stairs to the second-floor ballroom. Inside, the ballroom was as elegant as the building façade was plain. The walls were paneled and inlaid with intricate patterns, lined with statuary, and hung with paintings in gilded frames. The dance floor, three thicknesses of cypress wood topped with a layer of quarter-sawed oak, was as smooth as glass and renowned as the finest in the country. Crystal chandeliers cast a sparkling light on the spinning dancers.

The girls were beautiful enough to take a man's breath away, Barret thought. Their skin ranged from soft chocolaty brown to pale cream. In the rustling of silk and taffeta, their gowns dipped and swayed as they danced.

In stiff gilt chairs along one wall sat the mothers and elderly sponsors, also in evening dress, their dark eyes watchful like grandes dames at any ball. Champagne, the best, was served, as well as brandy, absinthe, and excellent food. The orchestra was always the finest, the girls the most refined, the most beautiful. When a man showed interest in a girl, the sponsors put their heads together. Who had known the young man's father and uncles? Had they been generous? Had they position? There were standards to uphold.

Barret and the DuMontaignes stood for a moment just watching the whirling dancers. The music swept to a close, the partners bowed to each other, laughing, and the men led the young ladies back to their mothers, or, if an understanding were in the making, out into the warm shadows of the gallery.

"There." Denis poked Barret in the ribs. "Isn't that the one?"

Barret turned slowly, pretending he hadn't been looking for her. She wore a gown of pink taffeta scalloped with white lace and stood fanning herself next to a tiny dowager in a plum silk gown. The dowager wore a pearl necklace that was probably worth as much as her house and observed Barret with an imperious and calculating eye. Barret hastily looked away.

"Not bad," Lucien murmured. "A little *ingenue* for my taste, but *belle*. I'll get you an introduction if you want to dance with her."

"No," Barret said quickly.

Lucien just grinned and strolled off. Barret was too stodgy. Lucien accosted the young Creole who had just returned the girl to her basilisk of a chaperone. "*Bonsoir,* Michael. Do me the favor of an introduction. That is, if you are not—?"

"Not at all," Michael said cheerily. "Delighted to oblige. Mademoiselle Belloc, allow me to present to you Monsieur Lucien DuMontaigne. Lucien, Mademoiselle Claudine Belloc and her aunt, Madame Clélie Belloc."

Tante Clélie's eyes snapped up to Lucien's face. *Mon Dieu.*

He bowed to her. "Madame, is it permitted that I dance with your niece?"

Tante Clélie nodded warily. It would not do to make *le scandale.* Claudine was an intelligent girl. She would know how to handle matters. If not, then there must be a word in his ear. . . .

XIII

The

Quadroon Ball

THE ORCHESTRA STRUCK up again. Lucien put his arm around
Claudine's waist and swept her into the center of the room. She
spun lightly on her feet. Lucien could see why poor Barret had
been staring. Certainly a very pretty girl, although a trifle too
innocent for his taste—if innocent weren't a contradiction in terms
for a quadroon *sirène*. She had been taught to dress well—the pink
silk became her admirably. No doubt the old sphinx in the pearls
chose her clothes.

"I have not seen you here before, m'sieu," Claudine said
nervously.

Now, why on earth should he make her nervous, Lucien
wondered. The light laugh and the flirtatious eye she had bent on
young Michael were not in evidence. "I just thought I'd look in
for an hour or two," he said. He smiled down at her, and his eye
was caught by the brooch that pinned a spray of rosebuds to the
low neck of her gown. It was a tiny fan of gold filigree, with three
ruby drops pendant from it. His eyes narrowed, and then he
looked over her shoulder gleefully. No wonder the old lady had
been giving him the fishy eye.

"That's a charming brooch, Mademoiselle Belloc. Most unusual."

"It was my mother's," Claudine said. Surely there was no harm
in telling him that much. "It was made from an earring. She
couldn't wear earrings, you see. They irritated her skin. My father
saw this in a jeweler's window and knew that it was just the sort of
thing she liked, so he had a brooch made from it."

"How very thoughtful," Lucien said. He refrained from cackling out loud, but it wasn't easy. No doubt her father hadn't seen fit to mention that since he'd found himself with one earring left over, he had had *it* made into a brooch for his wife. Waste not, want not. Lucien had seen that little gold fan with three ruby drops adorning his mother's dresses often enough.

Lucien and Claudine whirled in and out among the other dancers, Claudine still looking uncomfortable, Lucien gazing dreamily over her shoulder with half-closed eyes, his lips curled into a small smile. She knew who he was, or if she didn't, he'd bet the old aunt did. There were other DuMontaignes in the world, of course, but Lucien was well aware of his resemblance to his father. For a minute he contemplated making an offer for her, just to see what they would do. A most embarrassing situation.

"You dance charmingly, Mademoiselle Belloc. You are *ravissante*. I am *enchanté* that I came here tonight."

"You are too kind, m'sieu," Claudine murmured. The brown eyes were downcast, the impish face studiously wooden.

She does know, Lucien thought. *She's wondering how one tells a hopeful lover that he is addressing his half sister.* He chuckled silently and cast an eye across the room. The old aunt was still watching him, the plum-colored plumes in her hair upright with disapproval. If she had to warn him off Claudine, she would probably tell his father that she had done so. Lucien decided that the amusement derived from stirring up the henhouse tonight would be more than counterbalanced by his father's irritation afterward.

Lucien spun Claudine around as the music whirled into the finish of the dance, then tucked her arm through his and escorted her, not to the row of chaperones seated along the wall, but up to the unsuspecting Barret Forbes.

"Mademoiselle Belloc, allow me to present to you as a most desirable partner, Mister Barret Forbes of Charleston. Barret, Mademoiselle Claudine Belloc."

Claudine smiled at him, and Barret threw caution to the winds. "I would be honored if you would dance with me, Miss Belloc."

"You must ask my aunt, m'sieu," Claudine said.

"That's the old dragon in plum silk," Lucien said helpfully.

Claudine gave him an appraising look. She began to have the feeling that Lucien DuMontaigne wasn't as unaware of their connection as she had thought. Why he should present her to his friend from Charleston, she wasn't sure. She looked Barret over. He was about forty, she thought, with sandy hair and beard and a face more pleasant than handsome. His brown eyes regarded her with admiration, but also with something more. Empathy perhaps. Some sort of understanding. A man whom one felt instantly one had known for a long time, Claudine decided. A kind man, and by the spark in his eyes as he looked at her, a loving man. Things might not be so bad with a man like that. But from Charleston . . . Claudine could see no future in that, and she had been very carefully taught to consider the future.

Barret offered her his arm. She would worry about the future when it got there, Claudine decided rebelliously. "Come with me, M'sieu Forbes, and I will present you to the dragon," she whispered.

Lucien found Denis drinking champagne. "You look particularly smug," Denis observed. "What have you been doing?"

"Introducing Barret to our half sister," Lucien said cheerfully.

Denis's plate landed at his feet in a splash of crabmeat and Haviland china. "Good God." He peered at the girl who was presenting Barret to her aunt. A footman scooped the wreckage of the crab cake into a silver dish, unnoticed. "Are you sure?"

Lucien took a glass of champagne in each hand and nodded toward the long windows that opened onto the gallery. Denis followed his example. He thought he was going to need it. On the gallery, Lucien chuckled quietly in the darkness. "Our upright papa would appear to have sown a scattering of wild oats in his day."

"How do you know?" Denis demanded.

Lucien laughed again. "Papa gave Claudine's mother, who is thankfully now deceased, a brooch made out of one of a pair of earrings, and then had the spare one made up for Mama. Or perhaps the other way around, but I wouldn't bet on it. You've seen it—the little gold fan thing with the ruby drops."

Denis drained one glass of champagne and started on the next. "And I thought she reminded me of Emilie," he said faintly.

"So she does," Lucien agreed. "Quite a family resemblance, once you look for it. I expect I made quite a stir in the chaperones' corner." He grinned.

Denis glared at him. "So you found it amusing to introduce her to Barret. Damn it, did you stop to think of Mama?"

"No," Lucien admitted. "Why should I?"

"Because if you stir up something that's going to make Mama unhappy," Denis said, "I will beat you to a jelly."

"That's the second time you've threatened me since I came home," Lucien said lazily, "but you still haven't done it."

"You haven't pushed me far enough," Denis said.

"I trust I shan't. Brawling is so common, and one can hardly call one's brother out with a pistol." Lucien drifted off to the card rooms, not overly alarmed. He had never taken Denis very seriously.

Denis, thinking of the satisfaction he'd get from pushing his brother's face in, glowered after him. He was far more irritated with Lucien than with his father, who appeared to have been the soul of discretion, if one didn't count having given away one too many brooches. Introducing his father's octoroon daughter to his mother's oldest friend could not by the wildest stretch of the imagination be thought discreet. Damn Lucien anyway.

Denis eyed the dancers apprehensively through the open window. It wouldn't do to tell Barret—that would unfairly humiliate Sallie, even if she never found out about it. He noted that the chaperones were also showing a certain interest in the couple. He considered telling the girl's aunt, but, contemplating that formidable row of dowagers, his nerve failed him.

The dowagers were taking an interest in the gentleman from Charleston.

"A guest of the DuMontaignes—a very old friend of Madame's family, I believe."

"Ah, and wealthy. A great deal of land, I have heard, and planted in rice."

Information and comment hummed back and forth. The ladies made it their business to know these things.

"He carries himself well. Most elegant in his dress."

"Ah, but so old. Surely he is past the age of being interested in our Claudine."

"And a friend of the DuMontaignes. Unwise, perhaps, to allow a connection there?"

Upon reflection, Tante Clélie thought the same thing. She had been so relieved to find that young Monsieur DuMontaigne was not taking an interest, that she had perhaps been hasty in welcoming his friend Monsieur Forbes. She had no intention of admitting that now. "I do not believe that anything will come of it," Tante Clélie said regally. "I have not heard that he has the intention of settling here, and he could not take Claudine with him to Charleston. No, he is merely enjoying a pleasant evening with a pretty girl."

"Very handsome," Madame Patrick, the most redoubtable of sponsors, declared. "I do not think a man should be too young."

"A trifle dull for a girl so young, perhaps, but a steady man. That is most important."

Madame Patrick inspected the subject of their conversation once again as he swept by with Claudine in his arms. "He has excellent hands," she pronounced. "One can always tell a gentleman in that way."

Barret, happily oblivious to this analysis of his qualifications, was lost in his dance with Claudine. His black patent slippers and her pink satin ones twirled and glided under the spangled light of the chandeliers. Punkah fans suspended from the ceiling made a breath of air that stirred the crystal drops so that the light swam like stars on the polished floor. The girls in their pastel ball dresses looked as ethereal as fireflies against the black and white of their partners' evening clothes.

Claudine leaned back against his supporting arm as they spun to the music. Her brown wavy hair was pinned into a knot at the back of her head and dressed with a coronet of pink roses. Her pink dress was cut low across her breast and shoulders, and she had that warmly colored skin most often characterized as peaches and cream. She smiled, transforming a proper young lady's face into one of elfin charm.

"I had no idea, M'sieu Forbes, that gentlemen learned to waltz so well in Charleston."

"I like to dance." Barret grinned at her. "I also find that it is a telling point in my favor with the ladies."

Claudine tut-tutted at him comically. "And with all those points in your favor, M'sieu Forbes, you have never married?"

"I have a sister who unfortunately provides me with more company than I really require."

Claudine gave a gurgle of laughter. "Do you make a long stay in New Orleans?"

"As long as I can."

"To escape your sister, of course."

"Of course," Barret said gravely, but that wasn't what he meant, and he didn't think Claudine thought it was either.

"You must be sure to see all the sights," she informed him. "The cathedral, of course—most elevating. And watch the ships come into the harbor. And there is the opera. That is our passion here."

"Do you like the opera?" inquired Barret, who loathed it.

"Most certainly."

"Then I shall be there. And what else is there to see in New Orleans?"

"The theater." Claudine made a wry face. "And us, of course." She glanced around the shimmering ballroom. "We are one of the sights. You mustn't miss that."

"Not for worlds," Barret said, with such unexpected seriousness in his voice that she looked up at him curiously. His gray eyes met hers, and a little jolt ran through her. He was not at all what she had envisioned, but she realized as he tightened his arm about her waist that it would be fatally easy to love this man.

Their steps slowed as the music stopped, but he stood with his right arm still encircling her. Her gown was laced tightly about her tiny waist, but above and below it her breasts and hips made round, feminine curves. He thought with affection that she would probably be plump when she got older and was startled to find himself thinking as if it had already been decided that they should get old and plump together.

"I did not mean to sound . . . acid," Claudine said. "I have a very good life, and truly I did not think that you came her to stare at us."

"No, I know you didn't," Barret said. His eyes smiled into hers, and Claudine thought again, *He understands. He understands what it is like to be us. How does he know?*

"Will the dragon permit you to walk on the gallery with me?" Barret whispered.

"I think so. If I take a glass of champagne." She lifted one from the waiter's tray as he passed and led the way onto the rear gallery, where they could look down on the flagged courtyard and the moonlit gardens.

"Why champagne?" Barret inquired when they had found a quiet spot and were leaning against the filigree of lilies that adorned the wrought-iron railing.

Claudine giggled. "Tante Clélie says that a glass of champagne is most useful when conversing with a gentleman who may become amorous. It is so sticky, you see, and it spills so easily. You hold it before you, thus, and if he wishes to embrace you, he must ruin his nice evening clothes."

"I see," Barret said. "Are you permitted to drink it instead, or is it only to hold me at bay?"

Claudine set the glass on a table. "Sometimes one finds one doesn't need it at all."

He smiled and slipped an arm around her shoulders, and they listened to the mockingbirds. Finally Claudine said that Tante Clélie would be looking for them.

"She will be making discreet inquiries into your intentions if you keep me out here any longer."

"I don't know what they are," Barret said honestly. "But I want to see you again. Am I permitted to call on you?"

"I will go tidy my hair," Claudine said, "and you must ask Tante Clélie. That is the way it is done."

Barret pulled her to him and kissed her quickly. "To give me strength," he murmured.

Claudine laughed and disappeared through the window into the crowd on the dance floor. Barret caught a glimpse of her pink skirts going through a door at the far end of the ballroom, in the company of another young woman. He sighed and approached the row of old ladies who were all regarding him with avid curiosity.

"Madame, would you grant me the favor of a few words with you?"

Tante Clélie rose. She laid her gloved hand on Barret's arm. "You may procure me a cordial, M'sieu Forbes, and I shall be charmed to converse with you in the courtyard. A very pleasant night, don't you think?"

"You have made a conquest! I can tell!" A light-brown girl in a gown of emerald green tugged Claudine through the door of the ladies' dressing room. "Is he American? Who is he?"

"He's from Charleston," Claudine said airily, with her heart in her throat. "I daresay nothing will come of it, so you are not to tell everyone, Mimi."

"Ho-ho, you grow cautious." Mimi made a face at her in the gilt mirror that hung on the wall, then pushed the camellias that adorned her dark hair more firmly into her curls. "Why should he speak to your aunt if nothing is to come of it, slyboots? Eh?"

"I couldn't go to Charleston with him," Claudine said, "and I don't expect he wants to move here. Oh, it just isn't fair!"

"Pooh, *chérie*. There are more fish in the river. Younger ones, too."

"Younger ones get married," Claudine said darkly. "And then where are you?"

Mimi giggled. "Rich, with a house of my own. It is a much better system than getting married, *I* think. This Monsieur Forbes is rich, everyone says. Aren't you burning to know what he is saying to your aunt?"

"Of course I am." Claudine put her hands across the front of her gown. Her stomach felt fluttery. "I just don't know what I *want* him to be saying. There are too many complications."

"Now then, M'sieu Forbes," Tante Clélie said when she was comfortably seated under a potted palm in the lantern-lit courtyard. "You wish, I think, to speak of my niece." She cocked a bright dark eye at him, reminding Barret of a shrewd, plum-colored bird.

"I would hope for Madame's permission to call on her," Barret said.

"To call on her." Tante Clélie appeared to consider. "You are not from New Orleans, M'sieu Forbes. You must understand that my niece must make a permanent alliance. And that she will have—I will be frank—only a season or two in which to do so, before she will be considered to have died on the vine. She must not be seen entertaining gentlemen who wish only to come calling. What precisely do you propose?"

"I don't know," Barret said helplessly. "I will be frank also, Madame. I did not come here tonight with any intentions at all. I need time to think, to . . . to see what may be arranged."

"I am not at all sure that it can be," Tante Clélie said. "It is my understanding that things are not done in Charleston as they are here. I should not wish you to take Claudine there, M'sieu Forbes, where she would have only the company of women of an unmentionable sort. Claudine is descended from the finest bloodlines of France. She has been educated as a young lady of quality and must have a suitable arrangement. Also I should wish to know more of your background, M'sieu Forbes." Tante Clélie sipped her cordial and eyed him expectantly.

Having heard of the thoroughness with which the girls' guardians investigated their prospective protectors, Barret was not unprepared for the question. In Charleston, it would have been considered the height of impertinence, but this was not Charleston, and Tante Clélie was like no other colored woman Barret had ever met.

"My family has lived in Charleston for well over a hundred years, Madame. I have money, and I am unmarried. I am an old friend of the DuMontaignes of Belle Marie, with whom I am staying just now."

"Yes, so I am informed." Tante Clélie spoke thoughtfully into the small crystal cordial glass. "There may be a matter of which we must also talk. I am not sure." She looked up at him. "Very well, M'sieu Forbes. Claudine wishes you to call upon her, or she would not have sent you to me, so I shall permit it. But you must understand that some sort of arrangement must be proposed, or the connection broken very shortly."

"Thank you, Madame." Barret rose and bowed. He escaped with the sensation of having been given the once-over by an expert.

There was no sign of Claudine in the ballroom, and Barret suspected that etiquette demanded that he should not meet with her again until he called on her formally. The guardians must have time to ferret out a prospect's circumstances.

Wondering exactly what he *was* proposing, Barret went in search of Denis and Lucien and a drink of whiskey, in whatever order he happened to come upon them. Admittedly, he thought, he had had Claudine on his mind since he had seen her in the market last summer. Admittedly, he had come here tonight hoping to see her again. But he hadn't thought further than that. Everything that had happened after Lucien had introduced them had had an otherworldly quality about it, as if each step had been the only logical one, while simultaneously some dimly protesting part of his mind kept trying to tell him that it wasn't.

Denis was also in search of Lucien. It was growing late, and they were to make an early start home tomorrow. Maybe together he and Lucien could pry Barret out of the ballroom before he did anything irreparable.

As he had anticipated, Denis ran Lucien to earth in one of the card rooms on the lower floor. These were inhabited by the gentlemen who were interested in the spectacle and a convivial evening's entertainment but were not in the market for a mistress. Lucien and Michael Auzot were playing vingt-et-un, with a half-empty bottle of whiskey on the table between them. Denis thought Michael looked as if he were barely sober. Lucien didn't appear to be drunk, but Denis recognized the bright glitter in his eyes. "We ought to go find Barret and clear out," Denis suggested. "We've a hellishly early start to make in the morning."

Lucien didn't move. "No need to be so uncivilized. *Petite Marie* makes fourteen knots. I can't see any point in getting home for breakfast."

"Fourteen knots?" Michael looked affronted. "That tub? Come now, DuMontaigne, *Ariel* could pass your boat with half a fire going." He had a new boat, Denis remembered, of which he was inordinately proud. Denis glanced warily at Lucien. Michael was also inordinately touchy on the subject.

Lucien was looking interested, and the glitter in his eyes had grown more pronounced. "Denis, how fast would you say that flatboat of Auzot's is?"

"I wouldn't," Denis said. "Shut up before you start a fight." Drunken duels had been fought for a lot less than that.

"Who wants a fight?" Lucien said.

"You appear to be looking for one," Michael said stiffly.

"Not at all," Lucien said. Another night he might have fought Michael just for something to do. Tonight the compulsion was uppermost to bet on something with more scope to it than vingt-et-un. "I'll race you, Auzot, you and your leaky sieve. New Orleans to Baton Rouge."

Michael narrowed his eyes. "What stakes?"

"Five hundred dollars," Lucien said before Denis could think of an argument to stop him. Denis looked at Lucien suspiciously. He had an idea Lucien didn't have five hundred dollars.

"That's not enough," Michael said. "Five hundred dollars and that chestnut of yours. Against five hundred dollars and my matched pistols." He chuckled. "The ones you've been coveting, DuMontaigne."

"Done," Lucien said. "In . . . shall we say four days? I won't get home until tomorrow."

"That will serve." Michael Auzot rose unsteadily. "Your servant, DuMontaigne. Keep my horse exercised for me."

Lucien poured himself another drink. Denis snatched up the whiskey bottle and poured one of his own. He regarded Lucien with exasperation. "I don't suppose you have five hundred dollars," he commented.

"I don't suppose I'll need it." Lucien tipped his glass up and drained it. Denis was still holding the bottle. Lucien looked at him pointedly until Denis shrugged and set it down again. Lucien poured another drink.

"I expect you have some plan for explaining to Papa how you happen to have arranged a race for *his* steamboat? Not to mention betting a horse that was your coming-of-age present. You really ought to be ashamed of that."

Lucien raised an eyebrow. "And you can't wait to tell him."

"You've been so busy tonight, I wouldn't know where to start," Denis said sourly.

"Then you *aren't* going to tell him?"

"Damn you, Lucien, how can I not?"

Lucien shrugged. "Well, it won't serve any purpose. I can't back out of a bet. Even Papa won't ask me to."

"No. You have a talent for starting things that nobody can back out of. One of these days, you bastard, you're going to do something you can't live with."

Lucien laughed. "I'm not the only one, little brother. How's Madame Becquerel these days?"

"Shut up!" Denis hissed. There were far too many people milling about. Michael Auzot was still in the far doorway with an interested crowd around him. Several other young gentlemen were making their way toward Lucien, and there was already brisk wagering on the outcome of the race. Lucien was right about one thing, Denis realized: He couldn't get out of it if every idiot in New Orleans had already laid a bet. Denis sighed. He didn't care much for tale-bearing anyway. "All right, I won't say anything, but it's sure as hell going to come to Papa's attention if you lose five hundred dollars and that horse."

"I won't," Lucien said. Auzot's steamboat was fast enough, but steamboats were tricky beasts. They had a tendency to explode if pushed too far. Michael Auzot didn't have the nerve for a steamboat race. Lucien was betting on that as much as he was on the boat.

XIV

Requiescat

THE NEXT MORNING Barret and the DuMontaigne men strolled up from the jetty through the still-lush September garden and found a distracted Sallie on the veranda, in a navy blue calling costume and a dark bonnet. She was pulling on a pair of dark gloves and appeared to be trying to talk to Mammy, Hollis, Felicie, Meeow, and Testut simultaneously.

"Paul, thank goodness you're back!" Sallie turned to him with relief. "Paul, Eugenie Prevost is dead."

"Eugenie? Good God!" Paul couldn't admit to any extraordinary fondness for Eugenie, but she had gone along so comfortably in her ill health that everyone had assumed her to be one of those tenacious invalids who invariably lived to be ninety.

"Apparently her heart just gave out," Sallie said. "Nobody knew there was anything wrong with her heart. I'm going over there now and see what I can do to help Roman. I'm going to take Mammy with me. Hollis, I want you and Felicie to stay here and look after Emilie." It would have been most unsuitable to take Felicie, and Hollis had an odd look about her too this morning, which Sallie didn't want to pry into just now. "Testut, we're going to have to put up some of the people who'll come for the funeral, so you'd better have all the rooms turned out. Meeow, you pack up anything you can that'll travel and send it over to Alouette."

Will drove up with the gig, and Sallie and Mammy got in. Sallie leaned out again to kiss Paul on the cheek. "Mercy, what next?" she whispered. "I expect you'll want to call on Roman later. Poor man, it must have been an awful shock."

Felicie watched as her mother tapped Will on the shoulder and the gig crunched down the oyster-shell drive. Could you kill somebody by wishing she weren't there? Felicie wondered. And how awful it was if you just couldn't help a little ripple of happiness when somebody said she was dead. Felicie felt hollow inside, terrified that somebody might be able to tell just by looking at her that she was glad that Roman's wife had died.

Troubled by no such twinge of conscience as her sister's, Hollis merely considered Eugenie's death a favor bestowed on her by fate. She was busy making plans, in which a suitable dress for a second wedding figured largely.

Adele had been standing in the parlor watching through the window. The house would be in upheaval for weeks, she thought. She had been at Belle Marie long enough to know that the Prevosts and the DuMontaignes were friends of long standing, and to know something of the circumstances of Roman Prevost's marriage. Monsieur Prevost's change in status should effectively occupy Hollis, Adele thought with satisfaction—Adele had formed a fairly accurate idea of what Hollis's relations with Prevost had been—although in the long run Adele thought that she would put her money on little Felicie. But what mattered to Adele was that Hollis and Felicie would be occupied, Sallie would have a houseful of guests, and no one would have time for Paul DuMontaigne except Adele. Paul must be dependent on her *before* she took any further steps.

Adele let the curtain fall into place and went out into the entrance hall, and across to Paul's office.

She would take care of his correspondence this morning, and he would be flattered and grateful that she had remembered it amid the morning's confusion.

Kyrie eleison
Christe eleison
Kyrie eleison

Father Fortier, in a black cope, stood before Eugenie Prevost's coffin. It was stiflingly hot in the church, and the ladies' black gowns and bonnets made it worse. Sallie thought drearily that she hadn't been so depressed since they had buried Julien Tourneau. She glanced at Hollis, wondering if this were bringing back grim memories of her husband's funeral. But from Hollis's expressionless profile, Sallie had the impression that whatever Hollis was turning over in her mind, it wasn't Julien Tourneau.

"Deus, cui proprium est misereri semper et parcere . . ." O

God, to whom it belongs to have mercy and to spare, we humbly entreat You for the soul of Your handmaid Eugenie, whom You have summoned today from this world. . . .

Roman, in the front pew, muttered his responses in a low voice, and his craggy face looked drained. Sallie hadn't realized that he had so much gray in his hair. Whatever his relations with his wife had been, her unexpected death had left him shaken. What would he do when that wore off? Felicie, on Sallie's other side, was chalk white under her bonnet, and she seemed to be trying to make herself as small as possible.

In the rear of the church the Negro slaves wept loudly, chanting their responses with enthusiasm. Eugenie Prevost had not been particularly dear to them, but they felt that a funeral wasn't a funeral without some shouting.

"Anima ejus, et animae omnium fidelium defunctorum per misericordiam. Dei requiescant in pace," Father Fortier intoned. May her soul and the souls of all the faithful departed through the mercy of God rest in peace.

"Amen."

Paul, Denis, and the other pallbearers rose and lifted Eugenie's coffin. She would be buried in the family graveyard at Alouette, and the hearse was waiting at the church door, drawn by two black horses with black plumes in their bridles.

The horses moved slowly. The carriages of the family, friends, and what appeared to Sallie to be half the population of New Orleans followed. Louisianians gave great ceremony to death and delighted in putting on mourning for the most distant of kin. Roman and the gentlemen would escort the coffin to its grave, while the ladies would alight at the Alouette plantation house to await them. As a rule, Creole ladies did not attend funerals at all.

In the best parlor at Alouette, everyone milled about exclaiming over the somber beauty of the black wreaths and the black-veiled mirrors, the clocks properly stopped at the hour of death. Ah, and poor Roman—the shock! It quite made one's heart flutter to think of it. They were having an excellent time.

"Miss Sallie, you want that coffee pot brung in now?" Jacob's black face bore an uncertain expression. Roman's female relations had all been giving Jacob conflicting orders.

"Yes, thank you, Jacob, I think we'd better. And some sandwiches, too, if you please. We'll keep the rest of the meal until the gentlemen get back."

"Yes'm." Jacob departed and reappeared with the coffee pot, a silver urn that held a full gallon and was used only at weddings and wakes. Mammy followed him with trays of sandwiches, which she set on a long sideboard against the wall. Roman's *tantes* and *cousines* all told her to rearrange them, each suggesting a different location. Mammy said "Yes'm" and put them where she thought they ought to go. One of the Negro girls from Alouette began to pour steaming café noir into Eugenie's best cups, and the *tantes* and *cousines* all stopped trying to take charge long enough to drink it.

With the ladies at least temporarily settled, Sallie looked around for Felicie and found her sitting in a window seat, staring out at the row of black carriages in the drive.

"My dear child, you're going to make yourself sick if you go on like this. Whatever is the matter?"

"I'm scared," Felicie whispered. "Mama, I'm just terrified. I wished she was dead, and now she is!"

"I see." Sallie looked at her daughter's anguished face. "Really, truly dead, or did you just wish that Roman weren't married?"

"That Roman weren't married." Felicie hung her head. That was bad enough to admit. "But it's the same thing, isn't it? There wasn't any other way he could get *un*married."

"Well, I don't think you need to worry about it. We can't wish people dead, thank goodness, or everyone would possibly all fall down at once. It was probably a little sin to wish you could have him instead of Eugenie, but not like really wanting her to die. You can ask Father Fortier about that if you want to, but I think he'll tell you the same thing."

"No, if you think it's all right, Mama, then I feel better."

"Good," Sallie said briskly. "Now I want you to try to stop looking so doleful. I see the gentlemen coming back. You go and offer your condolences to Roman."

"I can't!"

"You'd better. If you don't, he won't understand. And what's more, every old lady in the room will start trying to figure out why."

"All right." Felicie gritted her teeth. As Roman came in, she put her hand out to him. "I'm so terribly sorry, Monsieur Prevost," she muttered, and fled before he could answer.

Roman started to follow her and found himself outflanked by Hollis. "My poor Roman." Hollis took his hand. Her voice was low, uncomfortably intimate. "So unexpected for you, such a shock. But a merciful release for poor Eugenie, don't you think? I remember we spoke only last summer of the sadness of your situation."

Roman had had almost no sleep in the last two days, but Hollis's voice snapped him out of his lethargy. She was being reasonably discreet because there were too many people listening, but there was no mistaking her meaning. She expected him to marry her. And how like Hollis to bring it up at the first opportunity, even if that was Eugenie's funeral. Roman groaned. He looked around and realized that Felicie was nowhere to be seen. He looked grimly at Hollis.

"You are kind to be concerned. I fear I am still too much overset to think of the future."

Hollis's eyes narrowed. "But of course," she said sweetly. "We must talk another time . . . soon. Whatever your circumstances, I have always known that you would behave in an honorable fashion."

"Certainly," Roman said. His female relations, and Eugenie's, eyeing Hollis askance, descended upon him tearfully, and Hollis retreated. There was a stone bench under the willows in the garden, and Hollis allowed three young gentlemen to persuade her to sit there with them. A funeral was a social occasion, and it was a rare one at which a little courting didn't take place on the side. She wasn't going to stand in the parlor like a wallflower, she thought, furious, while Roman made a big show out of crying over his wife.

Barret, standing in a corner with a plate of chicken sandwiches and a large glass of whiskey for which all the returning gentlemen had immediately made a beeline, decided that he had done his social duty. He had carried shawls and reticules, propped old gentlemen into carriages, and returned to Belle Marie when they were half a mile down the road to the church to help Tante Doudouce find her smelling salts. At Alouette, he had seen Eugenie buried and prayed wholeheartedly for her soul. The wake looked as if it were just getting going, and he doubted he'd be missed. He stepped through the open windows onto the veranda and untethered the horse he had ridden from Belle Marie. It was a pleasanter day outside than in, and he could be in New Orleans by midafternoon.

* * *

Tante Clélie's house on Toulouse Street was a pale yellow building of plastered brick, ornamented with the delicate tracery of wrought-iron balconies. Barret presented his card at the door and allowed himself to be inspected by a tall, thin butler with the face of an elderly tortoise, who appeared to be starched within an inch of his life.

"I see if the ladies to home," he announced, having shown Barret into a well-lit and graceful entrance hall with a floor tiled in marble. After a moment he reappeared, possessed himself of Barret's hat and walking stick, and threw open the doors to the parlor.

Tante Clélie was seated at a card table, upon which she had dealt out a game of solitaire. Claudine, in a gown of pink and yellow flowered muslin, was setting stitches in an exquisite piece of silk embroidery. They both looked up as he entered, and Barret's heart flipped as Claudine's brown eyes met his and her face crinkled up into a smile. She held out both hands to him. Barret kissed them and then dutifully kissed Tante Clélie's as well.

"You are punctual, Monsieur Forbes," Tante Clélie observed. It had only been two days since the ball. "Pray sit down. Would you care for a glass of sherry?"

"Thank you." Barret took a deep breath. "I came, Madame, to assure you that my intentions are serious." He heard the soft sound of an indrawn breath from Claudine. "That is, if Mademoiselle Belloc is agreeable."

"Mademoiselle Belloc is agreeable," Claudine murmured.

"But I don't know how the devil I'm going to manage it yet," Barret said, abandoning a formality that was evidently a considerable constraint on him. "Would you be willing to trust me until I think of something?"

Tante Clélie looked thoughtful. "For a certain time, yes," she said finally. "You have the reputation of a man who makes good on his word."

Barret stroked his mustache, smiling into his hand. It appeared that a certain amount of checking up had been done.

"But only for a certain time," Tante Clélie said. "A few months, Monsieur Forbes." She rose. "I will permit you to sit with Claudine for half an hour. More would not be respectable. And there is a certain matter of which Claudine wishes to speak to you herself." Tante Clélie made a stately exit as Thomy appeared with a tray bearing a decanter and glasses. When he had also departed, Barret looked hesitantly at Claudine.

"Did you mean it when you said you were agreeable?" he whispered. "I don't want you forced."

"No, it's just that there is something that I have *got* to tell you first." She had an air of wanting to get it over with.

Barret wondered what was so awful that she would have to steel herself to tell him. He reached over and pulled her head down onto his shoulder, inhaling the scent of lilacs. "What have you done?" he whispered. "Murdered someone?"

"Don't be silly," Claudine said ruefully, "*that* wouldn't have anything to do with you. No, it's worse. Paul DuMontaigne is my father."

Barret nearly burst out laughing at her conviction that an embarrassing parentage was worse than a murder. But he had to admit she had a point. Blast Paul and his youthful indiscretions anyway. And not so youthful, now that Barret thought about it— Claudine wasn't any older than Felicie.

Barret kissed the top of her head. "I don't care if your daddy was Attila the Hun. That's Paul's problem."

"It will be your problem if someone makes a scandal about it," Claudine said unhappily. "Tante Clélie wanted to tell you, but I said she must let me do it. I will understand if you wish to change your mind."

"Well, I don't," Barret said stubbornly. "Claudine, honey, I don't know what the hell I'm going to do about you, and Paul is the least of my worries, but I'm going to think of something." He sat her up and looked into her troubled face. His gray eyes were earnest and his face made youthful by emotion. "You've been on my mind every minute since I met you. If you think you can stand me, that's all that matters."

She put her hands on either side of his face. "We are taught to tell very flattering lies," she said solemnly. "But I don't *want* a man I must lie to for years and years. So I will tell you truthfully that I like you very much. I feel at peace with you, comfortable with you. I will love you very dearly, Barret, if only you will love me."

He took her hands and kissed the palms of them, and then pulled her into his arms. "I already do," he said into her hair. It was a new emotion to him, sharp and biting and unfamiliar, but he knew that it would mellow with time, becoming an understanding, a companionship of the heart. "I'll think of something," he said again. There would be some way open to them, there must, he thought fiercely, cradling her against him. Claudine wanted him, by a miracle, so Claudine should have him. She had put up with enough other losses in her life.

Felicie leaned wearily against Sallie's shoulder in the upstairs hall at Belle Marie. "Mama, I'm so tired. Would it be all right if I just went to bed?"

Sallie pulled off her bonnet. "It's been a long day. I've told Testut to send trays up to anyone who wants to rest in their room and not come to supper." Testut had loved that. Every visitor seemed to be as old as the hills and as deaf as a post, and they would all ask for something different. He would have to put up with it, Sallie thought. She'd put up with them all day.

Hollis gave her sister a baleful glare as their mother went into her own room. "Why don't you just faint?" she inquired acidly. "Then *everyone* could come and cosset you, and you wouldn't have to put on an act for Roman Prevost."

The injustice of that goaded Felicie from under the oppression of her conscience. "I didn't! Why can't you manage to keep your attention off anything in pants that comes your way? You had every boy at the funeral bringing you coffee and fetching you a cushion, just like it was a party! Anyway, what business of yours is Roman Prevost?"

Hollis smiled and struck a nonchalant pose. "Oh, none."

"Good." Felicie opened the door to her room.

"None that you need to know about anyway," Hollis laughed languidly.

Felicie paused with her hand on the doorknob. "What do you mean by that?"

"I told you, nothing that Little Sister needs to know about. Now that Eugenie's dead, Roman's not going to be interested in a baby like you anyway."

"You don't know what Roman wants!" Felicie snapped.

"I know better than you do! He doesn't want a simpering little die-away miss out of the schoolroom. You don't know what *any* man wants!"

"And I suppose you do because you spent six months being married to a man who spent most of his time gettin' ready to die!"

"I know what Roman wants," Hollis said distinctly. "I know *just* what Roman wants."

A year ago Hollis's hints would have gone over Felicie's head, but in between she had been nearly raped by Joe Spelling. She stared at Hollis. "I don't believe you."

Hollis grinned. "Felicie, honey, that's a matter of complete indifference to me. But if you're counting on marrying Roman, I wouldn't order my wedding dress just yet."

"The subject has not come up," Felicie said stiffly. "He just buried his wife today."

Hollis chuckled. "Eugenie's been dead for years, he's just been waiting for her to fall down."

"That's not true! Roman's an honorable man!"

"Honor's not much fun in a bed."

"Hollis Tourneau! You better not let Mama or Mammy hear you! And I just flat don't believe you. Roman wouldn't do a thing like that. And if he had, well, he wouldn't—he wouldn't talk to me the way he has."

Hollis scowled at her sister. Roman hadn't "done a thing like that" lately, but as far as Hollis was concerned, that wasn't going to make any difference. "You *better* believe me," she said, "because you're right about one thing—Roman's an honorable man, all right. And honorable men don't ruin a woman and then not marry her."

Felicie's face went white. "If anybody ruined anybody," she said between her teeth, "I know who started it. And I'm just so ashamed to have you for a sister I could die."

"What a pity," Hollis said. "Then I don't expect you'll want to be a bridesmaid." She swept into her own room before Felicie could reply, and the door clicked behind her.

Felicie stared miserably after her. She was horribly afraid that Hollis was telling the truth. And if she were, what would Roman do? An honorable man *ought* to marry Hollis. And Hollis's sister ought to want him to, because of the family honor. Felicie pushed her door open and sat down at the dressing table, waiting for Mammy to come and unlace her. She decided she wouldn't give a dime for the family honor if it meant that Roman had to marry Hollis.

Sallie dropped her bonnet on her bed and stood thoughtfully, hands on hips, staring at nothing in particular. She wondered what Roman was going to do now, too, and whether or not she could tactfully ask him.

Sallie looked at the bed with dissatisfaction. She had been intending to try to nap—everyone else seemed to be exhausted—

but she had the fidgets. She pulled her painting apron, a voluminous white canvas garment that covered her from head to toe, out of the armoire, tied it on, and went into the sitting room that served as her studio.

A cheerful jumble of easels and canvases, with an oilcloth rug much stained with paint—this was Sallie's private domain.

She pulled back the cloth that covered her newest canvas. The painting, almost completed, showed the flat bayou lands under a sullen sky, leaden with rain clouds. Three blacks worked in the foreground, their swinging hoes biting into the wet, rich earth, chopping the weeds from the cane rows. There was warmth and intensity to the figures that contrasted sharply with the gray, lowering land behind them.

Sallie stared at the canvas dispassionately, and slowly the painting took foremost place in her mind, pushing Felicie and Roman and a thousand other problems to one side. She opened the paint box and began to squeeze stripes of flake white and green earth onto her palette.

"My dear, I should have thought you would be lying down."

"Mmmm?" Sallie, intent on her palette, didn't look up for a moment. When she did, she saw Paul's face registered mild surprise and then a thin-lipped disapproval as his eye fell on the canvas.

"I found I wasn't tired," Sallie said briefly.

"I should have thought you would be ready to drop," Paul said, "after all you've done the last few days. Surely you would be better off resting than playing about with paints."

Sallie turned back to her canvas with clenched teeth. How like Paul to come and poke at her now, when she had had all she could stand for one day. "I am not 'playing about.'"

Paul glared at the canvas with patent disapproval. "I should like to know what else you call it," he snapped. "You *know* I don't consider it suitable to have you going out in the cane fields like a darky."

"Holy Mother Mary in heaven, I'm tired of being suitable! I'm sick to *death* of being suitable. And if you think all these old ladies are going to be shocked at my being up here painting darkies, you can just tell them that I went mad and you had to lock me up!"

Sallie glowered at him over her palette. Her nose itched, and she rubbed it with her hand, leaving a smudge of flake white. Paul glowered back. They had been married twenty-three years and had had five children together. When a crisis came—Eugenie's death or Denis's lunatic desire to marry a Michelet girl—Paul and Sallie stood together and dealt with it. When the crisis ebbed, it seemed that all the old resentments were still there.

"Of all the silly, childish—" Paul stopped, exasperated. "You aren't going to come down to dinner like that?"

"I'm not going to come down to dinner at all," Sallie said balefully, "if you keep on at me. My painting is my business, Paul. It's not yours just because you're married to me. I have to have something that's my own. What in hell"—she stared him in the eye, daring him to object to her language, too—"do you think I'm going to do, draw pictures of darkies on my napkin and scandalize all your fat old aunts?"

"I *never* know what you're going to do," Paul retorted. "Your behavior is irrational, even for a woman."

"Mister DuMontaigne, I have just organized a funeral and a wake for the Lord knows how many people, made sure they were all met at the boat, found places for all of them to stay, made sure nobody got left behind at the church or stranded on a levee somewhere, and I have managed to stay rational throughout, which was a good thing, because Roman was quite obviously incapable of doing it himself."

"Things like that are women's business," Paul said. "No one would expect Roman to know what needed doing." And what did that have to do with her painting? Sallie continually lumped together subjects that had no connection and then got angry because he refused to admit that she had proven anything.

"No, but you expected *me* to know!" Sallie said.

"Naturally. And you did an excellent job of it," he added, trying to placate her, with no real idea of how the argument had taken this turn.

"But you don't expect me to know how to behave myself at dinner!" Sallie's voice was growing shrill, and she was plainly not mollified.

"I didn't mean that literally," Paul said. "I only meant that— that"—Paul lost his temper too—"that your goddamned paintings are unsuitable for a woman of breeding!" he shouted.

Sallie put the palette down. She wiped her hands on her apron. "Go away, Paul. Just go away before I get any madder." Her voice shook.

Paul turned on his heel. "Very well. Come down when you are more in control of yourself."

The door closed behind him. After a second or two the palette splattered against it.

Paul and Sallie appeared at dinner several hours later wearing twin expressions of determined graciousness, and none of their guests seemed to notice anything amiss. They had been married so long that they had learned to cover heartache automatically.

The next morning the house was still in a state of hospitable confusion, and the master and mistress found it easy to go their separate ways. Some of the houseguests were making ready to leave. Others appeared to have settled in for the rest of the month. Hospitality in a large plantation house was limitless—guests stayed as long as they chose. Tante Doudouce and a flock of *tantes* and *cousines* had settled in the morning room over coffee and *beignets*, for what Paul referred to with amusement as a *gumbo ya-ya*—a Cajun expression that meant that everyone talked at once.

Sallie was poring over the latest fashion pictorials from Paris with the younger ladies, and Paul had taken three old gentlemen shooting, in the hope, he said, of preventing them from shooting each other by accident. No one noticed that Lucien, Denis, and *Petite Marie* were missing.

Denis had at first washed his hands of Lucien's race, but after Lucien and Sam had taken *Petite Marie* downriver at first light, Denis had grown progressively more fidgety all morning. Finally he had stalked out to saddle his horse. He could watch the race from the levee road, he thought, although what purpose that might serve, he couldn't say.

Lucien, aboard *Petite Marie*, clapped Sam on the shoulder. "We've got a fine day for it."

"Yessir, Mister Lucien." Sam gazed up at a cloudless sky. "A fine day. We gon' beat the pants offa that *Ariel* boat."

Tall columns of black smoke, from *Petite Marie* and *Ariel*, which was berthed a few spaces down the levee, rose into the air and blended into a canopy above them. Already the levee was crowded with sporting-minded gentlemen who had bet on the race's outcome and with anyone who liked steamboats, which appeared to be most of New Orleans.

"Where's my horse, DuMontaigne?" Michael Auzot, standing on *Ariel*'s deck, shouted across the water.

"And my pistols?" Lucien shouted back cheerfully.

A call from the boiler room indicated a full head of steam, and Sam backed *Petite Marie* into the river. The big freight and passenger steamers always cast off between four and five in the afternoon, so now, at barely two o'clock, the racers had the channel to themselves. *Ariel* backed out of her own berth, and the two boats lay a moment side by side, with the pent steam shrieking through the safety valves and the black clouds rolling from the chimneys above them. A gun boomed from the levee, tall columns of steam burst from the 'scrape-pipes of both steamers, and *Petite Marie* headed up the river with the DuMontaigne pennant—green cane stalks on a dark ground—snapping from her jack staff, and *Ariel* close behind her. Both had a full load of wood and would stop for nothing but more fuel between New Orleans and Baton Rouge, a journey of some twelve to fifteen hours, depending on the vagaries of the river and the talent of the pilot. Paul had had Sam trained by an experienced Mississippi pilot, and Sam knew the river with the familiarity that another man would have with the carriage drive that led to his own front door. When no one needed *Petite Marie*, Sam took her out every two or three days anyway, to look at the river. The Mississippi was treacherous, snags and sandbars shifting constantly, landmarks eroding as the river ate away at the bank. Formerly clear channels could silt up in a few days, and sometimes the river even changed overnight, abandoning a horseshoe loop for a straighter channel.

Slack water lay along the Mississippi banks, while the current in the center ran the swiftest. Boats going downstream took advantage of the current; those heading upstream worked as close to shore as possible. The leadsman called the depth continuously as *Petite Marie* wriggled her way past a series of reefs:

"Mark three! Quarter less three! Half twain!"

Ariel followed close behind her, and the pair of them skimmed like dragonflies over the shallow water. Steamboats were shallow-draft ships anyway, and the small private boats of the plantation owners drew even less water than the commercial steamers.

Sam looked over his shoulder. *Ariel* was inching up behind them. Just before the next bend there was a snag, jutting up under the shallow water like a hook set out to fish for steamboats. It was a familiar hazard to both pilots, and *Ariel* was already beginning to cut into deeper water. Sam put the wheel down and stood on a spoke, and *Petite Marie* swung into her "marks," the exact spot on the river where the channel lay clear to open water. The two steamers came into the center of the river neck and neck. Sam pulled on his bell ropes. He was answered by faint jingling below in the engine room, and *Petite Marie* picked up speed.

Lucien glared at *Ariel* keeping pace beside them, her azalea blossom pennant snapping in the wind. "Come on, Sam, she'll make better than this!"

"Huh-uh, Mister Lucien. You leave me pilot this here boat. I push them boilers as fur as they'll go. Don't you worry—that *Ariel* boat, her pilot don't know the river like I do. His massa ain't let him go out an' look at it 'cept when massa's got a mind to go somewhere. Makes him cut cane instead."

Lucien lapsed into silence, but he paced and fidgeted about the pilothouse, looking at his watch and across the river at *Ariel*.

Both pilots swung their boats and began to make for an island chute, a shallow-water passage that would cut off a great deal of distance. Sam nosed in ahead of *Ariel*, and they could hear Michael Auzot swearing. The river was rising, and there would be just enough depth for *Petite Marie* to get through, but it was tricky. And there was no going back. The chute was too narrow to turn in, and too crooked to back out. Sam swung the wheel gently, maneuvering through landmarks visible only to himself.

"Starboard lead!"

The leadsman's voice sang back, "Mark twain! Quarter less twain!"

Sam pulled on the bell ropes, and their speed slackened. Steam began to whistle through the gauge cocks.

"Eight and a half! Eight feet! Eight feet! Seven and a half!"

"Stan' by," Sam said through the speaking tube to the engineer below.

"Seven feet! Six and a half! Six feet!"

"Now!" Sam shouted through the tube. The bells jangled wildly. "Let her have it!"

Petite Marie hung an instant on the tip of the reef, there was a grinding shudder as she slid over, and then a whoop from Sam. *Petite Marie* came out of the cut into the clear water of the river again.

"Ain't I tell you, Mister Lucien, you leave this here boat to me? We get lucky, that *Ariel* boat'll stick fast and sit there till the Lord send her some high water!"

Lucien laughed. He looked over his shoulder at *Ariel* laboring through the cut as *Petite Marie* picked up speed. Lucien stepped up to the wheel and nudged Sam aside.

"I'll take her for a while now. I want to beat that bragging bastard personally!"

Sam looked dubious, but he was a slave, which didn't give him much ground to stand on. "I dunno, Mister Lucien. This here river ain't so accommodatin', even when he's lookin' peaceable."

"It's clear water for the next five miles except for Sugar Point," Lucien said. "You know that."

"Yessir, but the river, he can silt up fast when he take a mind to."

"Well, I know a reef when I see one, and I can skirt Sugar Point as well as you can." He grinned over his shoulder at *Ariel,* still wallowing through the cut, and tugged on the bell.

Sam shook his head and sat down on the bench at the back of the pilothouse. Sam knew better than to risk Mr. Lucien's anger. He sat, arms folded, and watched warily as Lucien spun the wheel, straw hat back on his head and plainly enjoying himself. Singing, Lucien began to turn *Petite Marie* at the approach to Sugar Point.

There was a sandbar under every point, where the water that came down around it formed an eddy and allowed the sediment to sink. Fine lines on the face of the water branched out like the ribs of a fan. Lucien knew that they were little reefs. A skilled pilot would run them close, just missing the ends of them. Lucien swung the wheel farther, still singing, but the tune was growing jerky. Sam gritted his teeth. If Mister Lucien didn't stop showin' off, he was gonna be on the sand.

Lucien knew it too, but *Ariel* had successfully negotiated the cut and was just behind them now, and if Michael Auzot saw him give the wheel to Sam, Lucien would never hear the end of it till doomsday. And if he cut too wide around the reef, *Ariel* would slip through on the inside and into the lead.

Lucien swung over, easing past the reef. He'd run this water before, just last month, and it had been easy then. *Petite Marie* slid over what he thought was the last of the Sugar Point bar, and Lucien pulled the bell for more speed. There was a shuddering impact and a grinding sound. They'd struck a sandbar.

"Back her!" Lucien shouted. "Goddamn it, *back her!*"

Sam was off the bench and tugging at the wheel, but it was too late. *Petite Marie* bucked, shivered, and sat where she was.

"We done run aground," Sam said unnecessarily.

"I can tell that, you black fool!" Lucien shouted. "Get her

off!'' The fact that he had done it himself was not improving his temper. He swore at *Ariel,* churning away upriver, showing them her heels.

Sam was already out of the pilothouse, shouting for the rest of the crew. Setting a spar to lift them off the sand was not the easiest task under any circumstances. He hoped to hell Mister Lucien would stay and do his complaining where he was damn at and not decide to come help.

Since Lucien did not feel that it was any part of his business to take off his coat and get in a sweat, Sam's wish was granted, but Lucien, pacing back and forth in the pilothouse like a caged cat, was in a towering temper by the time *Petite Marie* finally floated free.

"I want every bit of steam you can give her, and this time I mean it!'' he snapped.

"Mister Lucien, them boilers won't take no more'n what I give 'em already!'' Sam was hot and grimy from getting the boat afloat, and his own temper was on the edge of boiling.

"You give me any more airs,'' Lucien growled, "and I'll sell you down to Plaquemines Parish for a cane cutter! Now get me a head of steam!''

"Yessir!'' Sam picked up the speaking tube. Lucien couldn't sell him and he knew it, but he could make life mightily uncomfortable. Sam wasn't sure whether he was more afraid of Lucien DuMontaigne in a vengeful mood or of the pressure in an overloaded boiler.

Petite Marie began to churn after *Ariel,* making better headway now, her pennant flying jauntily. Slowly she narrowed the gap, drew up to a quarter mile behind *Ariel,* and hung there.

"Come on! Come on, damn it!'' Lucien nearly danced in impatience. "If we don't catch her now, we won't do it. Some of those channels up ahead are one steamboat wide.''

"I know,'' Sam said. He spun the wheel and edged into the best water. "We get lucky, that pilot on that *Ariel* boat, he'll put 'em aground. Mighty tricky water comin' in a few miles.'' He gritted his teeth. Better tricky water than too much pressure in those boilers. The pressure of the steam moved the pistons that turned the paddle wheel, but the boilers could only stand so many pounds per square inch before they ruptured and blew everybody around them clear to hell and scalded them to death. If there was one thing Sam didn't want no truck with, it was a chancy boiler.

"Goddamn it, I'm not waiting around to 'get lucky'!'' Lucien's eyes glittered dangerously, and Sam saw, now with real fear, that Lucien had had a flask tucked into his coat pocket, and, as Lucien raised it to his lips again, that it was nearly empty.

"Mister Lucien, you ain't thinkin' straight. You—"

"You mind your manners, you ignorant nigger!" Lucien snatched the speaking tube out of Sam's hand. "You give her everything you got, you hear," he shouted into it, "or I'll take the hide offa every one of your lazy backs!"

XV

Fire

on the

Water

DENIS, RIDING ALONG the levee road upriver of Belle Marie, saw *Petite Marie* begin to close on *Ariel*. They made a pretty sight, with white railings as fanciful as the wrought-iron ones that embellished New Orleans's houses. *Petite Marie* was painted a butter yellow behind the white railings, and the pilothouse that sat aft of her smokestacks was adorned with gilded curlicues. A gilded iron "DuM" swung between the smokestacks, and her paddle box had been painted with a vista of Belle Marie plantation. The furnace doors were open, and Denis could see the glare of the fires, even in bright sunlight. Her churning wake made a froth in the broad muddy water of the Mississippi as she bore down on *Ariel*.

Denis drew rein and leaned on his saddlebow. A flicker of movement in the pilothouse caught his eye, and he squinted into the sun. He could see arms gesticulating wildly. A dark face in a white shirt that must be Sam was pushed away by a slimmer, straw-hatted figure.

Then a shimmer of distortion rippled through the air, the way heat rippled over a cane field in the summer. It was almost invisible, just a queasy, slightly askew sense of something out of kilter. With a roar the whole forward third of the boat sheered away from the stern, rose in the air, toppled, and fell backward with a dreadful booming crash. The chimneys turned end over end, broke apart, and plummeted in a rain of jagged steel into the rest of the boat.

199

"Oh my God!" Denis was off his horse, frantically pulling off his coat before the last of the wreckage had ceased to fall. He scrambled on all fours up the steep, grassy side of the levee. As he dove into the water, the boat began to burn.

Lucien had only an instant, as he saw the chimneys shudder and lift into the air, to know what had happened. Sam screamed, tried to run from the pilothouse, and was drawn through the glass of the shattered window by the force of the explosion. Lucien frantically muffled his face in the lapels of his coat, pressing the cloth against nose and mouth as he felt himself lifted, battered by a hurricane of flying debris like a wind out of hell, and hurled downward forty feet into the boiler chamber.

There was scalding steam everywhere, and the black firemen who tended the boilers lay writhing on the floor or already were still, their lungs destroyed by the steam. Lucien's heart drummed in his ears, and unconsciousness began to pull at him. He fought it back, scrabbling in terror-stricken blindness for clear air. He shouldered his way through a door half-ripped from its hinges. A jagged edge of metal clawed at his coat. Reeling, he wrenched away, ripping his coat open down the back. With the lapels still pressed to his face, he stumbled through. There was live steam everywhere. Lucien plunged through a shifting mass of firewood, staggering and falling, afraid to open his eyes, and unable to use his hands for balance for fear of taking the coat from his face.

His foot came down on a rolling log; he thrashed through the wood, and fell into empty air. Muddy water closed over his head.

Denis, swimming for the now flaming boat, saw *Ariel* stop, turn, and begin to churn back downriver. *Petite Marie* was a mass of flames on the water. A dead body floated past him, the face scalded beyond recognition, its legs tangled in the gilded insignia that had hung from the chimneys. Only the broad shoulders and the tattered shirt told Denis that it was Sam.

Denis began to tread water, pushing his way through floating, fire-blackened debris. There was no sound but the roar of the flames as the current swept boat and wreckage downstream. Denis knew there would be no going aboard what was left of *Petite Marie*. The fire would eat her to the waterline in minutes, and anyone still aboard was already dead. There wasn't much chance, he knew, horror-stricken, that *anyone* had come out of that explosion alive. They were drifting into faster water, but Denis fought the current anyway, searching doggedly as his arms and legs grew weary. He had to find Lucien, or Lucien's body.

He found two more bodies, but they were the black corpses of a fireman and the mate. The mate had a crowbar driven clear through his chest, and the fireman had plainly been killed by the steam: His bare chest was a raw, angry red. Denis let them drift away in the muddy current and resumed his search. Odd things floated by, a nightmare parade of everyday articles rendered horrible by their juxtaposition to death: a chamber pot, a red velvet chair from the salon, a breadboard from the galley. In a jumble of floating logs he caught sight of a white hand and began to swim toward it.

His chest burning, Lucien clawed his way to the surface. He opened his mouth, gasping, into the air. Spots swam in front of his eyes as he drew in breath after breath. The crackle of fire came from close overhead, and he looked up to see the boat burning. A flaming board dropped from the wreckage of the stern, and Lucien fought his way through the water away from it. He was battered by the sea of floating firewood that had rolled after him through the hole in the hull.

"Lucien!" His brother's voice came faintly above the crackle of the fire. *"Lucien!"*

Lucien wasn't even sure he had heard it at all, but he gasped out "Here!" choking and spitting water. A hand and a face came through the sea of logs and pulled him free.

With Denis supporting him, Lucien kicked away from the burning boat toward the shore. He wondered vaguely where Denis had come from, and then wondered if he were going to faint. There was a high whining in his ears, and the sunlit water danced spottily in his eyes. Somewhere behind them a bell sounded.

Denis got one arm under Lucien's shoulders and waved the other at *Ariel*. The crew had lowered a dinghy, and Michael Auzot and two crewmen stepped into it. "Here!" Denis shouted. "Auzot! Here!" The dinghy's oars dipped in the water, and it skirted cautiously through the wreckage toward them.

"Dear God," Auzot said as they came alongside. "Here, lift him in." He put out a hand to help Denis after. "Anyone else alive?"

Denis shook his head sadly. Now that he was in the dinghy, his tired muscles seemed to have turned to straw. "I don't think so," he said wearily. "But we must look anyway."

"We'll do that," Auzot said. "Is that your horse on the levee?" Denis nodded.

"Can he ride? Can *you*?"

"I can ride," Lucien said quickly. He slumped against Denis on the dinghy's seat, but he was beginning to realize that he was unhurt.

Denis poked at him suspiciously and decided that he had no hidden wounds. "We can ride," he said grimly. Now that he knew that Lucien was unhurt, he was beginning to be coldly, lastingly angry. The memory of Sam's dead, scalded face floated in his mind.

"I'll put you ashore," Auzot said, "if you're sure you can make it all right, and we'll pick up the dead." He shook his head, gazing at the carnage on the water. "As many of 'em as we can find."

Dripping, Denis climbed up onto his horse and hauled Lucien up after him. "I'll get you home and send for Doctor Leboeuf," Denis said, "and then I'm going back to help Auzot."

With the terror of the explosion fading, Lucien began to shiver. He felt cold, and his teeth chattered. The extra strength that fear had lent to his body ebbed away, leaving only indignation at this miserable turn of fate and a natural disinclination to take the blame. "Who overhauled those boilers?" he asked angrily.

"The same firm that built the damn boat!" Denis snapped. "They aren't proof against fools."

"I told Sam not to push her so hard," Lucien said.

"Lucien, I just don't want to hear it," Denis said. He remembered the arguing figures in the pilothouse.

"I'm lucky to be alive," Lucien said sullenly. "We had Sam trained by the best man on the river, and look what happens. And that fire crew wasn't any better. These damn niggers haven't got enough brains between 'em to run a steamboat."

Denis's fists clenched on the reins, but he remained obdurately silent. At Belle Marie he dumped Lucien unceremoniously on the veranda and turned his horse around. Someone had to go and help search the river, and he'd rather do that, Denis thought, than face Mammy Rachel and the firemen's widows. At the end of the carriage drive, he reined his horse around again. Mammy deserved better than that from him. Denis tied the horse to the hitching block and mounted the steps to the house. Lucien was nowhere to be seen.

Paul stared at Lucien. His face was incredulous. Lucien had been explaining very carefully exactly why nothing concerned with the accident had been his fault. A brusque gesture of Paul's hand cut him off in midsentence.

"I would suggest that you don't tell that story to the women whose men aren't going to come back," Paul said. He took off his spectacles and rubbed the palms of his hands over his eyes. "I'm not inclined to listen to much more of it myself." He put his spectacles back on and looked coldly at Lucien through them. He had not invited him to sit.

"Tell Will to get Firefly out," he said brusquely. He picked up a pen and drew a sheet of writing paper toward him.

"I beg your pardon, sir?"

"You bet this horse on the outcome of the race, did you not? You can hardly be said to have won."

"The race wasn't finished!" Lucien protested.

"Auzot turned back because you blew up a steamboat and killed five men. A gentleman settles his debts. He doesn't use another man's death to weasel out of them." Paul finished writing and took up a sheet of blotting paper. "I am assuming that you don't have five hundred dollars."

Lucien was silent.

"This is a draft on my bank for that sum." Paul held the paper out. "Tell Will to take it to Auzot with the horse."

Lucien took the draft. "That's very generous." The expression on his father's face kept him from protesting further.

"Don't feel that I'm letting you off without responsibility," Paul said. "You're going to pay me back, Lucien."

"Of course, sir, just as soon as I get my next quarter's allowance."

Paul ignored that. "I won't put a price on the men you killed. For them, you will come with me and apologize personally to their families. And to Mammy," Paul added, aware of her connection with Sam. "That one should be the hardest, I imagine." He looked his son in the eye. "I want you to be ashamed of yourself, Lucien. If you aren't, I don't know what's going to become of you."

"Yes, sir," Lucien muttered, feeling pent up and furious. He had his explanations thought out, neatly arranged and convincing. It was maddening that his father wouldn't hear them, wouldn't let him explain them to Mammy. He could have convinced her that it wasn't his fault or convinced her enough to *say* that it wasn't, which was enough to soothe Lucien's conscience.

Paul watched these thoughts flicker over his son's face and read them accurately. *What am I going to do with you?* he thought desperately. *How am I going to make an honorable man of you?* "I'm not inclined to wait for your allowance," he said aloud.

"The boat was insured, but you owe me five hundred dollars, and you're going to work for it."

"Help McCamy, you mean?" Lucien said. "Certainly, sir."

"I don't need two overseers," Paul said. "Nor do I consider a man who would bet money he didn't have as fitted for the post. You will go to mass every day for two weeks to pray for the men you killed. After mass, you go into the fields. You're going to cut cane, Lucien, until I judge that your wages equal the money you bet."

"Paul, you'll kill him." Sallie's face was troubled under her black bonnet, the same bonnet she had worn to Eugenie's funeral. They had buried Sam and the other four today in the slaves' graveyard behind the quarters.

"No," Paul said. "But it may drive some honor into him. What will become of him if he has none?" Paul's face was tired, sharply lined.

He looks old, Sallie thought with sympathy. It would come nearer to killing Paul than Lucien, she thought. Lucien was his firstborn, the one on whom all his hopes were placed. She wanted to take Paul's hand, but she doubted it would comfort him.

"Do you have any better idea?" Paul asked wearily.

"No." Sallie shook her head. From the quarters she could hear the Negroes keening, a wailing that rose and fell, alien and uncomfortable to white ears. They would mourn all night. Their white owners had attended the funeral, but Sallie knew that they would not be welcome now.

As dusk fell, the mourners left the graveyard. They filed solemnly, still keening, through the wooden picket gate, with Daniel at their head. Riar had her arm around Mammy Rachel. The social gap between them had narrowed in their grief.

Rachel looked back over her shoulder at Sam's plot. *Maybe I shoulda married him,* she thought. She couldn't see where it would have done any good. But if she had, she'd feel like she had a better right to mourn. Rachel looked almost enviously at the two widows. Their faces were tear-streaked, as stark as dark carvings.

An' I sinned with him, too, Rachel thought. *The good Lord knows I was lonesome, but I oughta married him if I was gonna do that.*

"The Lord, He allus forgives, does we ask Him," Riar said. She had a pretty good idea what was troubling Rachel.

"I got time to ask Him," Rachel said. "But Sam, he gone to

stand before the Lord tonight, an' he don' need one more sin on his soul."

"Don' you fret, Sis Rachel. Sam was a good man. The Lord He know that. You gotta trust. What else gon' get us through?" The hope of heaven made life bearable.

The procession wound its way from the graveyard to the sugarhouse, where the prayer meetings were held. Daniel took his place at the head of the room, and they began to sing. Paul had had hymn books printed for them, but most of the slaves couldn't read. They knew the songs by heart.

"Gonna lay down my burden, down by the riverside
Down by the riverside, down by the riverside.
Gonna lay down my burden, down by the riverside.
Ain't gonna sin no more . . ."

Lucien sat on the veranda with his chin on his fist, listening to the singing. Mammy hadn't spoken to him since yesterday morning. She would come round, he knew, but it was the first time in his life that he could remember her deserting him. He felt oddly defenseless.

He wasn't the only one missing Mammy. Emilie sat weeping quietly into her sheets with Charmante curled at her feet. She had wanted to go to the mourning, but Mammy wouldn't take her, although she had taken Mimsie.

Hollis sat in the parlor grumpily trying to sew a flounce back onto the dress she wanted to wear tomorrow. She stuck the needle into her thumb, sucked at it, and swore. Adele, sitting across from her, raised her eyebrows in a shocked way that made Hollis want to slap her.

Denis poked his head into the parlor and backed out again. Neither of the girls looked to be in a good mood, no doubt because there was no one to wait on them—every slave on the plantation had gone to the mourning. Denis prowled into Testut's pantry in search of a drink for himself and Barret. The house felt echoingly empty without the chatter of black voices. The pantry was unfamiliar territory, but Denis found a bottle of whiskey and two mismatched glasses and took them back to Barret, who was sitting on the veranda with Felicie. Denis noted without much surprise that Roman Prevost had joined them. If Roman wanted to come courting Denis's little sister, Denis didn't mind, as long as Roman was discreet about it while he was still wearing black. Denis greeted him quietly, since he suspected that Roman hoped to avoid apprising Hollis of his presence. Hollis had been making a dead set at Roman ever since Eugenie died.

"I can scare you up another glass," Denis offered, "if you aren't particular what it looks like. Papa gave everyone the night off to go to church. It's a good thing you didn't come to dinner," he advised him. "Mama and Felicie cooked it."

"I'm sure it was excellent," Roman said.

"It was terrible," Felicie said. "There was too much onion in the chicken, and if the biscuits had been round, you could have played tennis with them. Adele said it was disgusting, and where were the servants, and things were not done so in France."

"I have always felt that a guest should help around the house," Barret said, amused.

"That's more than Adele does," Denis said, "although I suppose she isn't exactly a guest. I'm afraid we're stuck with her. That woman is never going to be able to understand why Papa gave all the darkies the day off."

"If she is going to live in Louisiana," Roman said, "she had better learn."

"It does seem strange without them," Felicie said. She wanted Mammy, who could have looked at Roman and known without asking him if Hollis was telling the truth. Felicie just couldn't make herself ask Roman that.

Denis looked at Felicie's hopeful face and the expression on Roman's and was strongly tempted to take himself and Barret off and leave them alone, but he couldn't do that. It would be too improper. For the first time he was grateful for Dinah's irregular family.

"Madame de Vries is singing this Tuesday, in *Robert le Diable*," Roman said to Felicie. "Would you and your mother and family like to hear her with me? I'm afraid it will be very dull—I can't receive company yet." Almost as passionately as they loved the opera, New Orleanians loved to visit between the acts.

"I shouldn't mind that," Felicie said. All she wanted was Roman's company. She wondered if there were any way to persuade Hollis to stay home. She doubted it. Even with all the dreadful things that were happening—everyone in the family knew about Paul's edict concerning Lucien—Felicie couldn't help feeling that life was a wonderful adventure if it had Roman in it.

"Then that's settled," Roman said. "Denis, I believe I'll have that drink. Monsieur Forbes, do you care to join us at the opera?"

"I'm afraid I'm otherwise engaged on Tuesday," Barret said, thinking of his promise to accompany Claudine and Tante Clélie to the opera on Tuesday. He was willing to endure an opera for Claudine's sake, but no one else could have dragged him there with a team of wild horses. He sipped his whiskey, lit a cigar, and thought about Claudine. Hell of a time in his life to fall in love, he finally decided.

Roman and Felicie sat and watched the moon come over the oak avenue, while Denis went to find another glass. The singing in the distance had changed again to that fearful, keening wail.

"It's hard to believe that that's darling Mammy," Felicie said. "And Testut and Uncle Jem and Meeow."

"We don't truly know them," Roman said. "We think we do, but there is a face that they put on for us that must be like a mask."

"It's a little frightening," Felicie said.

"Don't let it trouble you, petite. Tomorrow they will seem ordinary again."

"Nothing has seemed very ordinary since this spring," Felicie said. "Not even you."

He smiled at her sideways in the dark. "That is because we have only just met each other. We never took notice before."

"I was awfully afraid that I was going to be sorry that I had," Felicie said slowly. It was the closest she would come to mentioning Eugenie's death—or how it would have been if Eugenie hadn't died.

"We have been given a second chance, petite," Roman said. "*Le bon Dieu* always has a reason for that, so we must use it. One never throws a gift back in God's face."

"No," Felicie said, comforted. "No, one couldn't do that. It's a relief to think of it that way."

XVI

The

Grinding

LOUISIANA WAS NEVER truly cold in the winter, but fall was the pleasantest season. Shortly after Roman's opera party, the slackening rainfall and the faint crispness in the air brought Paul, Denis, and Harlow McCamy out of bed with an eye to the thermometer before they had even shed their nightshirts. Every morning the three of them rode solemnly into the cane, poked, tested, broke off a stalk, and conferred seriously together: the annual race between the weather and man's judgment.

On October 15, the grinding began. Lucien, scowling blackly, stalked into the field with a cane knife in his hand, amid the high-pitched giggles of the Negro girls, muffled not very successfully behind their hands. He ignored them and began cautiously to strip his little patch of cane and cut it. A cane knife was a razor-sharp machete with a hook at the end, an instrument that demanded respectful use. The Negroes moved with a practiced rhythm, singing as they worked, not because they particularly enjoyed cutting cane, but because it lightened the labor. The cane stalks were bent down, the knives flashed in swift strokes, stripping the leaves from one side and then the other. A third stroke lopped off the unripened joints at the top of the stalk, and a fourth severed it at ground level. Straw hats and bandannas bobbed up and down, and the sun reflected off the long blades as the cutting ate its way through the field.

For the first half hour Lucien worked out his temper on the cane. After that he ached too much to care. Shoulders and forearms grew steadily stiffer, his spine shrieked at the unaccustomed bending, and the boots he had worn felt like vises on his feet. Sweat dripped into his eyes and stung the scratches on his hands.

After four hours there was a twenty-minute respite for a meal of corn bread, pot liquor, and beans, which he ate hunched in misery, without the strength to move from where he had laid down his knife. The adult slaves worked two eight-hour shifts each, and Paul had decreed that Lucien should work one. He had been in the field since first light, and at dusk he staggered into the house and stripped off his filthy clothes, with barely enough strength to eat his dinner before he fell into bed. He was past anger, past arguing with Paul, grimly trying now just to endure. In the morning, with his cramping muscles bent nearly double, he went into the field again.

Paul watched him go with a feeling of desperation nearly as strong as Lucien's. He was well aware of what he was putting his son through. Cane-cutting was backbreaking work, even for a slave who was used to it. It would nearly kill Lucien. But it might temper him into something better than he had been. Paul sighed. At the very least it would teach Lucien that every action had its consequences, even for the privileged.

Paul closed his study windows and turned back to his secretary. He slammed his fist on the desk top in a pent-up fury. That was a lesson that might save Lucien's life one day, but it was not enough to make him fit to be the master of Belle Marie. Paul was beginning to fear that he could not, *must* not, give Lucien his birthright.

The sight of the master's son laboring with a cane knife had been funny the first day. On the second, Lucien's gray face and the look of dull agony in his eyes told the field hands that, if they were wise, they would pretend not to see him at all. For a few more days there was a vengeful satisfaction in watching Lucien, responsible for five slaves' deaths, sweating it out in the cane field, but by the end of the week even the Negroes had begun to feel that he had paid in full. Lucien might have been a ghost, unseen by the field hands and ignored by Harlow McCamy, who was greatly disinclined to give him any orders. A sullen pride and a very real fear of his father kept Lucien working.

As the cane cutters moved through the field, they were followed by slaves who loaded the cut stalks onto two-wheeled carts for mules to drag to the sugarhouse.

At the mill the cane was fed into the new steam-driven press and crushed between iron rollers. The cane juice ran into kettles heated by heavy furnaces that swallowed load after load of wood cut earlier in the season from the swamps. The air was thick, misty with steam and overpoweringly sweet, as the juice foamed into a succession of ever-smaller kettles, to extract the last possible drop of water from the remaining syrup.

When the syrup had boiled down, the cooling masses would be poured into tanks to crystallize. The molasses residue that was drained off was barreled and sold or used on the plantation, and the brown-sugar crystals were loaded into hogsheads and shipped to André Peyraud in New Orleans.

The unending labor went on for weeks, leavened for the slaves by extra rewards—drinks, presents, and a ball at the end—and for the DuMontaignes, by sugarhouse parties, where the children made molasses taffy and the grown-ups drank a smoking punch of syrup and whiskey. Anyone who felt poorly was hustled off to the sugarhouse to breathe the vapors, said to be a sure cure for ills of all kinds.

Emilie, Mimsie, and a fast-growing Charmante were underfoot everywhere, riding on the cane carts or the mules that pulled them, being shooed away from vats of boiling syrup, or watching the raw cane being fed into the rollers.

Denis, when he could snatch a few minutes away from the work, slipped off to Bayou Rouge to pay illicit court to his Dinah. Alouette plantation was in the middle of its own grinding, and Roman Prevost became a less frequent caller. Hollis contented herself with keeping as many young men at her side at the sugar parties as she could manage, and Felicie and Sallie spent their time planning the grand ball that would celebrate the New Year and, everyone hoped, Paul's election to Congress. Barret, as a guest, had no duties, and if anyone besides Denis noticed that Barret too was slipping away with increasing frequency, no one thought anything of it in the chaos of the grinding.

Paul took Adele on a tour of the sugarhouse, and the sticky sweet air, the heat, and the smell of sweating bodies made her ill. She kept away after that, working on Paul's correspondence and an unexpected problem that had risen in her mind: If Paul won his election, would he want a French wife unfamiliar with American customs?

Adele mulled that over as she wrote out the letters that Paul had given her to copy in her fine, copperplate hand. She didn't particularly *want* to go to Washington. It was Belle Marie that she wanted. And she knew that, as Paul's wife, if he went to

Washington and left her here with his children, she would not have a pleasant time of it.

Adele laid down her quill and wiped her hands on the dark apron she wore over her morning dress. There would be company again after lunch—coming from New Orleans to watch the grinding. *Mon Dieu,* these Americans made a party of anything.

Mammy was straightening Sallie's embroidery floss in the parlor. Adele called out to her as she passed the door, "Go find Junie to help me dress." She continued up the stairs without bothering to wait for an acknowledgment.

Mammy put her hands on her hips and glowered after her. Some folks were mighty above theirselves, ordering other folks around what didn't belong to them. She put her head out the window and shouted at a passing pickaninny: "Fin' that Junie an' tell her to get herself upstairs!"

"Yas'm," a male voice floated back lazily. Mammy went back to the basket of floss. If the pickaninny found Junie, that was just fine. And if he got sidetracked and didn't, that wasn't Mammy's department.

Adele, upstairs in her room, ground her teeth listening to this exchange, and twisted around like an eel, trying to unhook her own dress. The DuMontaigne children ordered Mammy around in the most cavalier fashion, and she did anything they asked. With Adele, Mammy invariably passed the request on to a lower-ranked black. And the other servants were just as bad. It never occurred to her that the DuMontaignes gave their orders with affection and respect and thus reaped willing service.

Junie trudged up the stairs reluctantly. As far as her new position was concerned, the bloom had worn off the rose a long time ago. Junie would have waited on a kinder mistress with unstinting devotion. Adele had earned only disgruntled servitude.

Adele shifted irritably while Junie laced her into a black-silk afternoon dress. When Adele had gone, Junie held the discarded muslin morning dress up against herself in front of the cheval glass. Most white ladies gave their maids their discarded clothes, when they were a little worn or the ladies were just tired of them, but Miss Adele never did.

Adele was unaware of her shortcomings in the eyes of her maid. She assumed that the servants were inclined to treat her with scant respect because of her poor-relation status. Consequently she became more aloof until all the Negroes decided that that Miss Scarron, she wasn't never gonna do no good here, an' Miss Sallie, she better marry her off quick.

"Yeah, she sho' had," Testut said, " 'fore that Miss Scarron, she give Mister Paul the glad eye anymore."

"You hush up!" Mammy Rachel said. "Mister Paul, he never do a thing like that!"

"White folks ain't no better'n any other folks," Testut said forthrightly, "when it come to sin an' fornication. She spend her whole time doin' up his letters an' things."

"That don't give you no call to slander her," Mammy said, but it didn't carry much conviction.

With a party planned for the afternoon, the family ate a lunch of jambalaya served on the sideboard, so that Testut could have the dining table to lay out china for afternoon tea. At two o'clock they strolled down to the levee to meet the steamboat chartered to bring their guests from New Orleans. Lucien, given an afternoon's respite so that he could grace the party with his presence, was scrubbed and dressed in clean clothes, with elegant gloves on his blistered hands. The guests consisted mostly of business associates and anyone of influence who was considered to be wavering politically between Paul and Gilbert Becquerel. Most were accompanied by wives and children. A number of them had never been to Belle Marie before and, but for their usefulness this election year, would not be there now. The trio of political hands who had advised him before his debate were there. You had to admit, they said among themselves over beakers of smoking syrup punch, that DuMontaigne didn't give himself any airs. And that little wife of his—just the right touch. She'd do fine in Washington.

"Yep, she sure would. Don't you think so, Miss Scarron?"

Adele turned to find that the little frog-faced man beside her had been eavesdropping on the advisers' conversation.

"I hear Mrs. DuMontaigne's from Charleston, too," the man continued, grinning. "One o' the best families. Some good connections there."

"I expect so," Adele said disdainfully. Singing Sallie's praises did not interest her, and furthermore this was not a person with whom she wished to converse.

His next remark changed her mind for her on that score. "You don't look as interested in DuMontaigne's winnin' this election as a loyal little niece oughta be."

"I am not his niece," she said stiffly, but she gave him a wary look.

"Well, you're livin' here," he said cheerfully. "That's about the same. Cheer up, honey, there might be other folks that would like to see DuMontaigne take a beatin'." He seemed to have taken her lack of denial as a confirmation. "Why do you want him to lose anyway?"

"That is my affair. *If*, of course, I do wish him to lose," Adele said cautiously.

"Well, we'll just take that as read, shall we?" the man said. "*Why* ain't my affair—as you say. But you an' me might have a little talk. My name's Bill Ewing, in case you don't remember it."

Adele inclined her head to indicate that indeed she didn't, but when he extended his hand, she took it and allowed hers to be shaken.

He grinned at her again. "We oughta get along fine. Mutual interest, as they say. Why don't you an' me take a little stroll down to the garden?"

Adele sniffed. "M'sieu Ewing, surely you have lived in New Orleans long enough to know that that would not be proper. I may walk with you a little distance out of earshot, but not out of sight."

"Suit yourself," Ewing said.

Adele wished they could have gone farther; she had no desire to be seen conversing with so unprepossessing a man as Bill Ewing. His trousers were of a large green checked material and his coat was a brilliant green of a slightly different shade. A bright yellow waistcoat added to the froglike effect. Emphatically not a gentleman.

She gave him only the tips of her fingers to escort her down the path, as if she feared some contagious disease.

"Now, Miss Scarron, I'm gonna put my cards on the table," he announced when they had traversed a suitable distance, "because you're about my only hope in this crowd. The Whigs have got a lot of reasons for not wantin' Paul DuMontaigne in Washington, startin' with upsettin' the balance of things, if you take my meaning. Things have been goin' on just fine in New Orleans for a lot o' years, and there ain't no call to go messin' around with it." Adele's expression remained unchanged: interested, wary, and about as stiff, Ewing thought, as a church statue with a poker up her ass.

"And in what fashion do you think I could help you, M'sieu Ewing?" He obviously wanted her help, or he wouldn't be telling her this. Men like Bill Ewing didn't waste their time. "Assuming that I would consider such a thing," she added primly.

"Oh, I expect you would," Ewing said. "Mister DuMontaigne seems to be relyin' on you pretty heavy. *This is my invaluable assistant, Miss Scarron,"* he said, aping Paul's Creole accent. "Now how come you're doin' all that if you want him to lose?"

"That is not your business!" Adele snapped. "And I have told you, M'sieu Ewing, I did *not* say I wished him to lose!"

"All right, all right." Ewing held up his hand. "Let's just *suppose* you want him to lose. Well, you couldn't do better than to be lettin' me know, quietlike, what's in all them letters you copy, and just who DuMontaigne's meetin' with."

"M'sieu Ewing, just exactly *how* did you get invited to this party?"

"Oh, I'm a man with connections," Ewing said airily. "DuMontaigne would like to swing me to his side, but you get one honest idiot in the government, an' the next thing you know you're hip-deep in 'em. I made up my mind to go with Becquerel. He may be crooked, but you always know what he's gonna do."

"I see." Adele's thin face turned thoughtful, and her gold-flecked eyes rested calculatingly on Bill Ewing. "Are you not afraid I will tell Paul DuMontaigne this?"

Ewing shrugged. "Tell him all you want." He began to drift away. This French girl was a mite too shrewd. Bill Ewing would have preferred to work with someone stupider, but there wasn't anyone else available. He looked at her over his shoulder and shook his head. "You won't get anywhere trying to blackmail Bill Ewing. I just thought we might do each other a favor, that's all."

"Wait a moment, M'sieu Ewing." Adele took a step toward him. His manner was appalling and far too familiar, but politics in New Orleans did not appear to be a gentleman's business. This frog-faced man might well be able to outflank Paul's advisers.

"Yes, Miss Scarron?"

"Naturally, I must make a few conditions." She spoke lightly to indicate that these would of course be negligible, and Ewing chuckled. He thought he'd keep a pretty sharp eye on her "conditions."

Adele extended a regal, black-gloved hand. "I am sure that an agreement between us is possible, M'sieu Ewing. Now you may walk me back to the sugarhouse before we attract attention."

Lucien watched their progress with sardonic amusement. Bill Ewing would only be snubbed by Adele, Lucien thought. Paul wouldn't like it, either; Bill didn't have the qualifications to court a member, even a courtesy member, of the DuMontaignes. Lucien cast a disdainful eye over the rest of the company. There were

rather too many Bill Ewings present. Hearty politicians with stout
wives who had the wrong accents.

Looking saturnine and unpleasant, Lucien leaned against one of
the upright beams that supported the roof of the open shed where
the boiling was done. A couple to whom he had been introduced
upon their arrival approached him, marveling at the steaming vats
of syrup.

"Just so interesting! Don't you find it so, Mister DuMontaigne?"

"Not particularly," Lucien drawled. "But then sugar isn't a
novelty to me."

"Oh. No, no I suppose it isn't, but so—so exciting," the
woman stammered, unsure of whether she had been snubbed or
not. She backed away hesitantly and bumped into a black slave
carrying a bucket of smoking syrup. "Oh!"

"Perhaps if you stood over here." Paul came around from the
other side of the vat with Denis and drew her gently out of the
traffic pattern. "Denis, why don't you explain to the Adamses
how the boiling is done?" Paul shifted the couple into Denis's
charge and hissed in Lucien's ear: "If you can't contrive to be civil
for an afternoon, you may go back to the cane field! I didn't let
you off to amuse yourself by being rude!"

Paul stalked off, and Lucien ground his teeth, listening to
Denis's cheerful voice conversing with the vulgar Adamses.

Lucien had always had a faint scorn for his brother, but he had
never actively disliked him until it had occurred to him that Denis
wanted Belle Marie, and that with the disaster of *Petite Marie*
Lucien had overstepped the bounds of what their father would
tolerate. Since then Lucien had suffered the growing conviction
that if their father went to Washington, he might well leave Denis
in charge of Belle Marie, and that if he did that, Lucien might not
be able to wheedle him into giving it back. Lucien had never
wanted to run Belle Marie, but he most certainly wanted to inherit
it. If Paul left Belle Marie to Denis, Lucien would be a
laughingstock. That had dawned on Lucien at about the same time
as the thought that he might finally have pushed his father too far.

"Here, try these, Madame Adams." There was a rustle as
Denis dipped his hand into a barrel of shelled pecans. "Tie one of
these bits of string around it, and just dip it in the tank. Careful
now, the sugar's hot."

Lucien listened resentfully as his brother bent his natural
friendliness on the Adamses. Paul wouldn't be quite so taken with
Denis, Lucien reflected, if he knew that Denis was busily

cuckolding Paul's election opponent. Nor of course would Gilbert Becquerel care much for the knowledge. Lucien straightened up as the possibilities of that occurred to him.

Lucien slipped through the crowd. As he passed the Adamses, he surprised them with a suddenly charming smile.

You have a friend who wishes you to know that your wife has taken a lover. . . .

That should do the trick, Lucien thought, blowing on the ink to dry it. No names mentioned, no names signed. How much better, Lucien reflected, simply to leave matters to Monsieur Becquerel. Paul, if informed of Denis's entanglement, would give him a lecture and then help him cut the connection. Gilbert Becquerel, on the other hand, might shoot him.

XVII

The Demons

in the Cane

You have a friend who wishes you to know . . .

GILBERT BECQUEREL HELD the letter by one corner and lit it with his cigar. When it was well aflame he dropped it into the fireplace with a grunt of irritation. So Françoise had found an amusement. She had had a look of malicious triumph lately, which he had put down to some other small coup scored over one of the circle of friends with whom she waged a constant rivalry over minor matters.

If she thought he was going to be complaisant about having a pair of horns hung on his forehead, she was much mistaken. Gilbert considered Françoise to be his property in the same fashion as his house or his horses.

Gilbert shook the bell on his desk. The clerk, Lavoie, poked his head in.

"Has Bill Ewing shown up yet?"

"Yessir, Monsieur Becquerel. He's in the front office."

"Send him in. And bring us a bottle."

When Ewing appeared, Becquerel waved him to a chair. Ewing sat and gave the candidate of his choice a cheerful grin. "I think we got what you need."

"What I need," Becquerel grunted, "is a stick to beat my wife." He would not have admitted Françoise's faithlessness to a social equal, but Ewing didn't count. Conversely, Ewing needed to know—that sort of thing could affect an election if it got out. Becquerel noted Ewing's expression of worried interest. "I'll tell you in a minute. What have you got?"

219

"A woman," Ewing said. "Funny how they seem to crop up." He wondered what indiscretion Madame Becquerel had committed. If a man didn't keep a better eye on his wife than Becquerel kept, Ewing thought, he had to expect it. A man who spent all his time chasin' whores was just bound to make his wife a little touchy.

"Who is this woman?" Becquerel inquired irritably.

"Lil' French lady," Ewing said. " 'Bout the same character as a copperhead snake if you want my opinion, but she's livin' with the DuMontaignes, and she don't want Paul DuMontaigne to win."

"Why not?"

Ewing shrugged. "She wouldn't tell me and it don't make any difference to us. Some family spite, I reckon. But here's the kicker—she's copyin' letters an' whatnot for DuMontaigne. Keepin' his calendar. She'll pass it on to you through me, and that'll give us a handle on where to work first."

"It had better. DuMontaigne's making too much headway to suit me. I wouldn't have thought there were that many fools in New Orleans."

"Don't worry," Ewing said. "Old-style politics ain't dead in New Orleans yet. We'll swamp DuMontaigne, as long as nothin' we don't know about don't come up at the last minute. Now what the hell's this about your wife?"

Becquerel took a watch on a gold chain from his waistcoat pocket and studied it for a moment. Then he looked up and regarded Bill Ewing's froglike countenance with irritation. "She's got a lover," he said bluntly.

"Who?"

"If I knew who, I'd call the son of a bitch out," Becquerel informed him, "and I wouldn't need to tell you."

"Well, how'd you find out?"

"Some public-spirited citizen," Becquerel said dryly. "I want you to have someone watch my wife, and when this man is there, let me know, and I'll deal with it. Nobody else, understand?"

"I thought the idea was to hush this up," Ewing said. The voters would stand for a lot, especially when you bribed them, but a man who couldn't control his wife looked a damn fool.

"Well, what the hell do you expect me to do?" Becquerel said. "Shake his hand?"

"All I know is, you fight him and the boys in the saloons won't give you one vote if you lose."

"I won't lose," Becquerel said grimly, "and the boys are real fond of seein' justice done. Now go do what I told you. And get

me some information out of that girl of DuMontaigne's. We've got
to know where we stand."

Adele laid her quill down and pushed her chair away from
Paul's desk. The day's correspondence was neatly stacked, ready
to be taken in a postbag to the levee. The flag was always out for
any boat bound for New Orleans to stop and pick up the post from
Belle Marie. The mail seemed to flow unendingly. Adele ran a
hand over her forehead.

"You mustn't tire yourself with this." Paul bent over her chair.
"I should *hire* someone—I'm too new to this. I didn't realize what
a volume of correspondence it takes to run for office."

Adele smiled up at him. Hire a secretary? Certainly not, not
when she found the position so useful. "I enjoy it." She patted his
hand to assure him of her earnestness.

They made a fine tableau, backlit by the lamp on the secretary.
Very picturesque, Sallie thought with gritted teeth, as she passed
the study door. Why should she be so hurt? It didn't seem fair,
after all these years, that it should hurt now to see Paul falling in
love with Adele. Or into whatever he was falling into, Sallie
thought: discontent with herself, or comfort with Adele, who,
with no other duties, had time to spare for Paul's campaign. Oh,
damn Paul! He wasn't going to get anything from Adele but
heartache. So why should he make her, Sallie, miserable with his
dreadful little love affair now? Sallie picked up her skirts and ran
up the stairs, surprised at the bitterness of her feelings.

She sat at her dressing table until she felt less like slapping
Adele. She was a fine one to point fingers. But she had never
flaunted Gilbert Becquerel in Paul's face. *Well, you had a child by
him,* her conscience pointed out briskly. There was no getting
around that. She didn't love Gilbert. Was Paul in love with Adele?
If so, what then? He wouldn't leave Sallie for her. He would just
go along as he was and be miserable.

Oh, very fine. Having established everyone's thorough unhap-
piness, Sallie gloomily regarded her reflection in the mirror.
Maybe she ought to fight that woman for Paul. *I'm still pretty,* she
thought. *Prettier than Adele.* But what was the point of fighting
for the affections of a man who had fallen out of love with her
years before?

I haven't got time to worry about it, Sallie thought. There were
six more parties before the election, and Adele as sure as fire

couldn't manage those. *I'm going to get Paul into Washington,*
Sallie thought. *That's what I'm going to do. And I'll worry about
the rest of it afterward.*

Paul saw Sallie's blue skirt flick past the study doors and braced
himself, more guiltily than he would have expected for a man who
hadn't actually done anything, to explain why he appeared to be
holding hands with Mademoiselle Scarron. But Sallie's footsteps
continued along the hall and up the curving staircase with only the
briefest of pauses.

Paul felt oddly deflated. He had braced himself to meet his
wife's accusations with righteous indignation, but she hadn't been
annoyed enough even to make one. Paul sighed. He supposed that
that only told him something he had already known.

He looked back at Adele. She was gazing up at him with an
expression that Sallie hadn't shown him in years—mingled
admiration and affection, and an earnestness untainted by years of
quarrels and awkwardness. Paul squeezed her hand. "Come out in
the garden for some air before you give yourself a headache with
my dreary letters."

Adele rose with a smile. She had only a minimal affection for
Paul, but she wanted his name and his possessions with a passion
equaled by few lovers.

In late October the garden was past its best show, but banks of
chrysanthemums were still blooming, and scarlet Virginia creeper
climbed trees and fences. The scent of woodsmoke and burning
leaves drifted on the crisp air. In the kitchen garden the pumpkins
and squash would be ripening. Paul steered Adele that way.

"This is my favorite time of year. Sallie likes the spring, but
fall is my season. I don't think even the flower gardens are a better
sight than that." He pointed at the ranks of yellowing corn stalks
with pumpkins glowing orange between them. A rabbit darted
through the vines, saw them, and flattened itself under a pumpkin
leaf. Paul watched it indulgently.

Adele studied Paul curiously. She had the impression that he
liked watching his kitchen garden better than he would like being
a congressman. It might, she was beginning to think, be boring to
be married to this man.

"It is very lovely," she said, trying to understand how Paul
viewed a scene that to her seemed no more beautiful than a
haystack or a farm wagon or any other utilitarian object. To Adele,
beauty was a grand house or a formal vista of fountains and
flowers. Beauty was that which had cost money.

"I am glad that you are learning to like it here," Paul said.

"*You* are here," Adele said. She lowered her eyes and whispered softly, "How could I not love it here?"

She stood, eyes downcast, as if embarrassed to have spoken in such an unseemly fashion. Paul put out a hand in reassurance. His fingers brushed her cheek and the stray tendrils that had escaped from the neat dark bands of hair over her ears. Her lashes fluttered up, then down again. Paul took her hand.

Emilie, Mimsie, and Charmante, coming up through the trees toward the kitchen in hope of pralines, caught sight of them and skidded to a halt in the shadow of a stand of yellowing corn. Emilie pushed Mimsie back into the corn and gazed at her father, wide-eyed and indignant.

"What you doin', Miss Emilie? You know we ain't s'posed to be in here!"

"Hush!" Emilie hissed. "I want to hear what they're sayin'."

"Who?"

"Papa and that Frenchwoman."

As they watched, Paul took a step closer to Adele, bent, and kissed her hand.

"Come on!" Emilie said furiously.

"Where we goin'?"

"To find Mammy." If anyone could put the interloper in her place, Emilie was sure it was Mammy Rachel.

"Granny say she goin' to see Meeow," Mimsie said hopefully. She was more interested in pralines than in mixing, possibly to her future discomfort, in the master's business.

"Well, we'll look there first," Emilie said. An enticing, sugary smell drifted from the kitchen. Charmante scampered ahead. She liked pralines as well as the little girls did.

Mammy Rachel was just going up the kitchen steps, a basket over her arm, when Charmante bounced up the steps behind her. Two fat cats were sleeping on their backs in the doorway, paws in the air. Charmante trotted across them and they sat up suddenly and cuffed at each other, each assuming the other to have disturbed its repose. Charmante had no time for cats. She climbed up the table leg, where Meeow was rolling pastry, and popped her small black face over the edge.

"*Miss Emilie!*" Meeow put her hands on her hips and yelled through the open door. "You come git that coon! I done tol' you the last time that raccoon is too onstreperous to bring in folks's kitchens."

"Yes, ma'am. I think she was lookin' for pralines."

"*Hmmmph*. Her an' a few others I know. All right, you chillun git a handful out o' that there jar and git out o' here 'fore I make me a raccoon pie."

Mimsie dived for the jar of pralines, and Emilie, remembering a more important errand, sidled up to Mammy Rachel. "I was lookin' for you too," she whispered. "We gotta do something about that Adele."

"What you think I can do 'bout her?" Mammy inquired. "An' just what is it you think needs doin'?"

"Papa was kissin' her hand," Emilie whispered, outraged. "An' she was givin' him that *look* she has," she blurted and ran out the door.

Mammy Rachel looked after Emilie thoughtfully. That Adele was up to something, Mammy was certain, but she couldn't for the life of her figure out what. No one but a much bigger fool than Adele would entertain the notion that Paul DuMontaigne might divorce his wife, and Mammy Rachel didn't think Adele was a woman who would want to be somebody's mistress.

Mammy stooped down, picked up her basket, and grinned at Meeow. "Will you give me some cold pie for Mister Lucien?"

"You're a forgivin' soul, Sis Rachel."

Mammy sighed. "I known Mister Lucien since the day he was born, lot longer'n I known Sam. I can't turn my back on somebody what was my baby. Not no way. Not forever, I can't."

Meeow nodded. "I reckon not."

Meeow packed cold meat pie and pumpkin tart into Mammy's basket for Lucien, and added a jar of homemade blackberry wine.

"You take the boy that. Dan'l, he tell me Mister Lucien just about dead when he come off work the first day."

When Mammy got to the cane field she thought that Lucien looked like he was just about dead now, but under the sweat and grime she could see that he was beginning to toughen up. There were muscles in his arms that hadn't been there before, and the raw places on his hands were beginning to turn to callus. He didn't look up as she approached, just kept cutting doggedly with a rhythm that was starting to approach that of the field hands. Only when she halted in front of him did his eyes appear to focus on her boots and the hem of her stiff, starched apron. The knife slowed and came to rest against the ground. Lucien carefully straightened his back. His face was hollow and the black hair hung dankly over dark-circled eyes. He watched her doubtfully, as if he thought she might have come to assure herself that he was paying a proper price for her Sam.

"I ain't come to give you a lecture," Mammy said. "I 'spect you done had that." It was the first thing she had said to him since Sam died.

Lucien dropped the cane knife. He stood uncertainly. He had an irrational urge to lay his head against her breast and have her tell him, as she had done so often in his childhood, that he wasn't wicked, he just needed to school himself. "Schooling yourself" had had the comforting sound of something that could be done later, that didn't have to interfere with your life now.

"I'm so tired," he said slowly. "I wake up tired."

"A cane field's a fine place for the Lord to sweat the sin out of a man," Mammy observed.

"But I didn't mean for the boat to blow up." He knew better than to blame it on Sam to Mammy Rachel. "I didn't want all this to happen."

Mammy sighed. "You never did, honey. But you didn't want it *not* to happen very hard, neither. All your life you been heedless of other folks, an' a man can't live like that. Maybe this here's your last chance to grow up." She shook her head, watching Lucien's weary face. It wasn't gonna work. As soon as Mister Paul let him loose out o' that cane field, Lucien would be the same again. *It must be I done somethin' wrong, but I raise him just like Mister Denis*.

Mammy Rachel held out the basket, contents neatly covered with a napkin. "I brung you somethin' to eat. An' Meeow send some o' her blackberry wine."

Lucien nearly snatched at the basket. He kissed Mammy on the cheek. "You tell Meeow her blackberry wine tastes better than champagne after what I've been eating out here," he said. His old easy charm wiped the uncertainty from his face. He hugged Mammy, sat down, and began to wolf down the cold meat pie.

Mammy watched him unhappily. He was hers, her baby just as much as he was Sallie and Paul's, and she loved him. His hands shook as he ate, the twitching of muscles pushed beyond their strength. Lucien wiped his mouth on the back of his hand. He drank the wine, and when Mammy handed him the pumpkin tart, he ate it ravenously. When he had finished, he saw Harlow McCamy watching him. Pride forced Lucien to his feet. He picked up the cane knife and gritted his teeth as pain shot up his back. "Has Papa told anybody how long he means to keep me out here?"

"He ain't say," Mammy Rachel said, "and I ain't sure I don't think you oughta stay out here the rest o' the season," Mammy said. But she couldn't bear the hollows under his eyes or the dull, dogged look that came into them as he began to swing the cane knife. "You learn to school yourself, an' I talk to Mister Paul. But you gotta learn. You can't put it off no longer."

"I promise," Lucien grunted. "Just talk to Papa. He'll listen to you." He would have promised anything to escape from the cane. As Mammy picked up the empty basket, a stirring on the far side of a pile of cut cane caught her eye. Harlow McCamy stood backed nearly against the stalks, as if pursued. His voice came clearly on a rising note of panic that was shockingly revealing, like a man stripped naked of all his proper protections. Another voice, female laughter, floated mockingly over the cane.

Mammy put the basket on her arm and started for them almost at a run. Celeste stood facing McCamy, her chocolate-brown face twisted scornfully. "Master don' know what a sissy-boy he done hired, do he?" she inquired malevolently. She lifted her skirts, showing lithe brown legs. Mammy, coming around the corner of the cane pile, saw McCamy's face. The corners of his mouth twitched, and his eyes were staring at something that appeared more dreadful than the spiteful girl in front of him.

"All master's other overseers, they like me plenty," Celeste said, her voice rising. "You got the right to use any woman here if you want to, long as you man enough. But you ain't, is you?" Celeste's voice was shrill, and she watched with satisfaction as McCamy's face went chalky. Every nigger on the plantation had laughed at her 'cause she'd bragged how she'd get the new overseer to courtin' her and not have to cut no more, and then she couldn't do it. Well, they could laugh at him now. Celeste wasn't afraid of McCamy—he was afraid of her, too afraid to whip her. Celeste had a predatory instinct that recognized McCamy's fear and drew her on to hunt him into madness.

The other Negroes stood watching warily. Gabriel's face was rigid with shame. He stared straight ahead at Celeste. A short burst of laughter from one of the younger men was silenced by Daniel.

"You get out o' here. You all get out o' here!" McCamy was like a loaded gun. If he didn't strike Celeste, he might take out his terror and his vengeance elsewhere.

McCamy stiffened as another hoot of laughter mocked him, this time from Lucien. The master's son leaned on the handle of his cane knife, watching the overseer's discomfiture with satisfaction. McCamy had seen Lucien filthy and humiliated. Lucien took a distinct pleasure in watching him held at bay by a woman who didn't need anything more than to be turned over his knee and then given the screwing she'd been asking for.

"Man what can't use the tool the Lord give him oughta be grateful for a chance to practice a little," Celeste said distinctly. She lifted her skirts again and thrust her hips at him. "Ain't you got nothin' in those pants?"

Gabriel brushed past Daniel's protesting hand and loped across the edge of the cleared field to Celeste. He shook her by the arm. "You come back along o' me! Can't you see the man's near crazy?" he hissed in her ear.

Celeste jerked her arm away. She spun to face him. "You jus' wants me your own self!" She laughed and stamped her bare feet in an angry little dance in front of him. "But you ain't man enough either, is you? You an' all your stories 'bout Africa! You ain't any more good to a woman—"

Mammy Rachel stared into Harlow McCamy's face, aghast. She had never seen a fear like that. Whatever he saw, Mammy thought, wasn't only Celeste but some nameless terror out of his own mind that took Celeste's voice and outward form. She dropped her basket, spun Celeste away from Gabriel, and smacked her hard across the face.

Celeste's eyes blazed. She clenched her fists as Mammy Rachel, who was half a head shorter, hit her again. She lifted a hand to retaliate and met Mammy Rachel's eyes. Slowly Celeste lowered her hand. Mammy Rachel was a power on Belle Marie.

"You're tryin' to make trouble for every black person on this place, an' that ain't gonna be tolerated," Mammy said crisply. "You get yourself back in that field and stop slackin' off your work, or the Lord help me, I'll tell Mister Paul to sell you at an auction." Mammy turned on Gabriel. "An' you is too good a man for a slut." A cautious look over her shoulder showed her that McCamy, attention diverted from himself, stood staring blankly past them, perhaps fighting still with whatever horrors crowded his mind. Mammy pushed Celeste and Gabriel away from him, toward the field.

Celeste went sullenly. She glared at Mammy Rachel over her shoulder from narrowed eyes. "You ain't own me!"

"You ain't worth ownin'! I never thought I'd see the day when one o' Mister Paul's darkies act like that! I see you do it again, I take a whip to you iffen nobody else do!" Mammy Rachel advanced on Celeste with upraised hand, and Celeste retreated into the cane.

Mammy picked up her fallen basket and gave the field hands a look that said that the show was over and they'd better quit their slacking. Avoiding looking at Harlow McCamy, Mammy Rachel walked past him as quickly as possible and strode with set determination toward the house. When Mister Paul went in his study after dinner, Mammy was gonna make him listen to her. As a rule she didn't try to interfere in the way the field slaves were handled. But Mister Paul had to get rid of Celeste, or that Yankee overseer, or both. A man who couldn't handle field hands hadn't any business on Belle Marie.

Celeste looked over her shoulder at Mammy Rachel's retreating back. "You get away from me!" she screamed at Gabriel. Her face stung where Mammy had slapped her, and her pride stung worse. In a foul temper she picked up her knife and began to slash at the cane with it.

Retching, McCamy leaned with one hand on the waist-high pile of stacked cane. His stomach knotted itself into a tight ball of pain. The Negroes backed away into the windblown cane, whispering, eyes wide and frightened. Even Lucien turned away from the figure that was bent double beside the cut stalks. The sky was lowering, ominous. A few drops of rain spattered down, but McCamy didn't move.

Slowly the Negroes picked up the rhythm of the cutting.

"Cut high, cut low,
Swing fast, swing slow . . ."

The chant was off-balance and jerky. Cane stalks fell, tangling on the ground. Apprehensive eyes looked backward at the overseer. The rain began to sheet down. They grumbled at it but didn't cease their cutting. The harvesting couldn't stop for rain. When they looked back again, McCamy was gone. In the downpour, no one noticed that Celeste was gone too.

Lightning spread through the sky along the flat horizon. Thunder rumbled on its heels, and the wind bent the cane stalks nearly flat before it. Harlow McCamy huddled in the tall cane like an animal looking for a burrow, his knuckles in his mouth. His mother's voice and form came out of the thunder at him, naked, with a stick in her hand, beating him to the ground. Frantically he scrabbled for a refuge among the stalks.

"You can't hide here." Celeste stood over him, her eyes narrowed and venomous. "There ain't no place you can hide from me." She dropped her cane knife and pulled at the front of her

dress. Her black breasts hung wet and glistening. McCamy
mouthed terror-stricken words that rushed away into the wind.
Celeste pulled her skirts up to her waist and spread her legs.
Harlow felt himself falling into some yawning hell from which,
once it had closed around him, there would be no returning.

The lightning crackled jaggedly above them. Beyond the uncut
cane that screened McCamy and Celeste, the Negroes wrestled the
wind for the cane stalks while the ground turned into a quagmire.
The master's orders were to bring the field hands in if there was
lightning, but McCamy hadn't come to order them out of the field,
and they were afraid to leave.

"Go away," McCamy screamed at Celeste, but she advanced
on him. He stumbled and dropped to his knees, and she put a hand
between his legs. "Maybe I see if they's anything in there," she
hissed in his ear.

Harlow screamed in real terror as she touched him. He pushed
at her, and she fell backward into the mud, skirts crumpled up
under her, knees apart. Deliberately she reached down and stroked
herself between her legs, her eyes on him. She twisted her hips in
a slow, malignant dance of sexuality. "You want it, don't you?"

He backed away and her other hand shot out and caught his.
"Take a good long look."

Harlow trembled. The rain beat into his face, and on its wings
came the demons, hands outstretched for him, fanged mouths
open to swallow him, wet, rain-slick legs spread to smother him.

"No!" He screamed and grabbed the fallen cane knife, slashing
at the demons. Celeste saw his contorted face through the rain and
knew with a swift lurch of fear that she had pushed him too far.
She let go of his hand and tried to wriggle away, but the movement
caught his eye and the knife came down again. The last things she
saw were his pale, hunted eyes and the cane knife, sliding toward
her out of the rain.

The booming thunder faded into the distance, and the rain
slackened. A faint trace of sunlight filtered through the cane.
Harlow, on hands and knees, his hands buried nearly to the wrist
in the black mud, opened his eyes and looked about him with
growing dread. Celeste was sprawled beside him, her throat and
breasts hacked into gaping wounds, ghastly and bloodless, that
ran with rainwater into a sodden pool of pink among her tangled
clothing. Harlow became aware of something in his hand, and
looked down to see the cane knife, its rainwashed blade rising
above the mud.

"Oh, Lawd God, he kill her!"

Harlow sprang to his feet at the sound. Gabriel stood peering through the cane at him, his black face frozen in despair. Harlow flung the cane knife from him and ran, pushing his way through the storm-tangled stalks to the open field. After a few steps he began to scream.

The Negroes in the field saw him come stumbling from the cane. Harlow clutched at Daniel's arm. "Gabriel killed her!" He pointed, panic-stricken, behind him. "He cut her throat."

In the blood-soaked mud, Gabriel knelt over Celeste's body. He was still there when they came to get him.

XVIII

Gabriel

DINNER WAS EATEN in somber silence in the main house, and amid frightened whisperings at the quarters table. Gabriel was chained to a ring in the wall of the barn. None of the Negroes knew what would happen, and they were afraid.

The house servants went about their work in silence, even Testut and Mammy Rachel, but when Lucien rose from the dinner table, Mammy was waiting for him in the hall.

"There's a powerful lot o' scared folk tonight. Mister Lucien, what happened out there?"

Lucien shrugged. "That slut Celeste took out after McCamy again, and Gabriel got jealous and cut her up with a cane knife. At least that's what McCamy says." He started wearily up the stairs. He was too tired to care what had happened today in the rain.

Outside Paul's office, Mammy stopped and took a deep breath. She had a lot of influence in the DuMontaigne house, but this was murder, and she was questioning a white man's word. She put her hand on the knob. Come Judgment Day, the Lord wasn't gonna let her off just because she was scared to cross a white man.

"Mister Paul, can you spare me a minute?"

Paul looked up with a face nearly as fatigued as Lucien's. "I'm afraid this isn't the best time, Mammy. I've got rather a lot on my mind at the moment." Murder could not go unpunished, but Paul DuMontaigne had never hanged a slave.

"I know you does," Mammy said. "That's what fo' I come."

"All right then, sit down." Paul laid his spectacles on the desk and rubbed his forehead. "But if you're going to ask me to let him off, Mammy, you know I can't."

"No, sir." Mammy sat and looked Paul in the eye. "But I got to tell you, I ain't sure in my mind it was Gabriel what done it."

Paul looked at her curiously. Mammy Rachel hardly knew Gabriel. He wondered if she were interceding on behalf of some other slave or if she just couldn't bear the thought of one more death. "I'm afraid that he was the only one with any reason to," he said gently.

"No, sir," Mammy said stubbornly, "he weren't the only one." She paused. "Ain't no black folks on this place tonight what ain't scared," Mammy said, "an' I got to tell you, I is too. But I done thought about it an' thought about it, an' I gotta speak my piece."

"All right, Mammy," Paul said. "But I think I ought to tell *you* that Harlow McCamy saw him do it."

"He say he do."

"McCamy has no reason to lie."

"Mister McCamy, he lyin' 'cause *he* the one that done it," Mammy said.

"Now just a minute—"

"Mister Paul, I done tol' you, I done me a lot o' soul-searching afore I come in here, an' I ain't takin' it lightly, accusin' the overseer. But that Celeste, she been . . . she been *huntin'* Mister McCamy 'cause he ain't take up with her like what the las' overseer did."

"Hunting him?"

"Mister McCamy scared just about to death o' women, Mister Paul. I don' mean shy. I mean *scared*, like somethin' happen to him an' he ain't right in the head about it. That Celeste, she start workin' on him in front o' them field darkies an' Mister Lucien, an' he look pret' near crazy. You can ask Mister Lucien or that Dan'l about that."

"Whatever her motives," Paul said, "if she was flaunting herself at McCamy, that gave Gabriel a pretty good reason to kill her."

"It do, but he ain't," Mammy said stubbornly. "You ain't see the look in that Harlow McCamy's eye, like he lookin' at the devil hisself come up out o' hell. I was fixin' to come tell you you better sell that Celeste an' get a overseer what won't let them field darkies get out o' hand. That's what I was fixin' to do, afore somebody cut her up with a cane knife. An' I swear to God, Mister Paul, I believe Mister McCamy done it hisself."

Paul was silent for a long while. As long as Mammy Rachel had been with him, which was since he had married Sallie, he had never known her to lie. Mammy made her opinions on most

matters well-known to the family, but a direct accusation of this
sort was not something she would undertake lightly. And Paul's
respect for her judgment was considerable. He rubbed the palms
of his hands over his forehead again. "All right, Mammy, I'll
consider what you've said. But I don't want you talking about this
to any of your people, you understand?"

"No sir, I ain't do that." Mammy rose. "I thank you for your
time, Mister Paul."

Gabriel sat in the sparse straw on the barn floor with his head on
his arms. Celeste was gone, and there wasn't one single soul on
the plantation that was gonna take Gabriel's word over the white
boss's. Even Daniel, while he'd run the chains through the ring in
the wall and then locked them on Gabriel's wrists, had whispered,
"I ain't say I blame you—woman like that could make any man
crazy—but I cain't let you loose. It be as much as my life's worth,
I do that."

Gabriel groaned. They'd be comin' for him by morning. First
that overseer, he took Celeste, and now he was gonna take
Gabriel—gonna kill him with a lying tongue as sure as he'd killed
Celeste with that cane knife.

An' just what you gon' do about it? Gabriel's own voice seemed
to talk to him in his head. *You gon' tell master that the white boss,
he done it? If a angel with a flamin' sword was to come down an'
stand witness for you, the master, he ain't gon' believe that.*

I'm gonna die, Gabriel thought. *He done kill Celeste, an' now
he gonna kill me.* He lifted his head from his arms and sat upright,
wrapping his lean, muscular arms around his knees as if to contain
a rising fury. The chains clanked dully against each other as he
moved. Hadn't been nobody chained up in seven years, an'
nobody hung, ever, at Belle Marie. He'd been ten when his
mama, who belonged to Alouette, had died, and Mister Paul, who
had owned Gabriel's father—a pure black who had come on a boat
from Africa and could still remember it—had bought Gabriel so's
he'd have some kin. Celeste had been six then, already pretty and
a tease, and she hadn't got no better. She'd druv McCamy to it as
sure as she'd gone down to hell for her sinful ways, but Gabriel
had loved her, and he hadn't ever been able to help it.

Gabriel crossed himself, the way Father Fortier taught him. *She
ain't had no chance to repent before he kill her, an' maybe she
woulda done it. You give her a chance, Lord, an' the devil he can
have me instead.* He stood up and took hold of the chains. He

pulled with all his strength against the ring, leaning first one way and then the other. A ring that had been in the wall seven years since anybody saw to it might have worked itself loose some. Gabriel pulled at the chains again and felt the ring give slightly. Voices drifted through the night outside, and the barn door rattled. Gabriel sat down, huddled in the straw.

"I brung you some supper—master say to." Riar had a lantern in one hand and a plate in the other. She set the plate down. "I pray with you, if you want me to."

"I done prayed," Gabriel said. "The Lord knows what's on my soul."

Riar looked at him dubiously. She pushed the plate a little closer. "You eat."

Gabriel picked up the tin plate of corn bread and greens. It seemed like Mister Paul didn't want to hang him without feeding him first. He stuck his fingers in the greens. There wasn't any fork, nothing to make a weapon with. Gabriel took a mouthful and chewed. "You go on back," he told Riar.

Riar's face was troubled, her eyes sad. A man had a right to be private if he wanted to. When she had gone, Gabriel put the plate down again and renewed his battle with the ring in the wall. If he pulled it loose, there wouldn't be any way to get the chains off, and he wouldn't get far with them on. Since he wasn't planning to run, Gabriel didn't give a damn. But he figured there'd be time enough before anyone noticed he was missing to give the overseer what he had coming. After that, they could have him.

The bolt that pinned the ring into the wall slipped a little more. Gabriel braced his feet against the floor and yanked back on it as hard as he could. The ring flew loose all at once, and he fell backward, with the chains on top of him. They heavy ring landed on his foot and he yelped in pain, biting the sound back as quickly as he had made it. If anyone caught him now, they'd fasten the chains around a tree and he'd never get loose till they took him off to hang him.

Gabriel stood up and wrapped the chains around his arms to keep them from rattling. The ring still dangled from them. He limped to the door and opened it cautiously. It was quiet outside. He slipped silently through the shadows, keeping to the grass and damp leaves, away from the oyster-shell paths. He felt as if he were dead already in the still darkness.

"Sit down, McCamy." Paul motioned Harlow to a chair. The overseer was outwardly calm, but Paul thought that he looked unwell and, in the light of what Mammy Rachel had said, perhaps desperate. His skin was pale and clammy, except for two hectic spots of red on his cheeks. The skin around his pale eyes was the dark, smudged color of one who has not slept at night. In the fitful lamplight, his reddish-sandy hair seemed to lose all color, and it hung dankly above those hunted eyes.

"I would like it if you would go over everything for me one more time, McCamy," Paul said gently. "This is such a serious matter, I want to be sure I have all my facts straight."

"Certainly, Mister DuMontaigne," Harlow said. He folded his hands in his lap. "To begin with, I'm afraid that the woman rather asked for it, sir. Not to be murdered, of course, but if Gabriel had beaten her, well, I don't think I should have interfered."

"Why not?"

"She . . . she was the sort of woman who liked to have all the men run after her," Harlow said. "Gabriel, and others. She, er, she made a play for me—I rather think the last overseer encouraged that sort of thing—and Gabriel was very angry with her." Harlow pursed his lips. "She was not a moral woman, not a good example to the rest."

"A play for you? Do you mean a sexual invitation?"

"Er, yes," Harlow said.

"I would prefer that you be precise, McCamy. What exactly did she do?"

"She lifted up her skirts," Harlow said. His face flushed and then went pale again except for those two unnatural fever spots on his cheeks.

"Was that the first time she had done that?"

"No. No, she . . . she kept on . . . for . . . days . . ." Harlow's voice drifted off and his eyes stared at something apparently situated on the wall just above Paul's head.

"Why didn't you put a stop to it? That is, if you didn't want her. I would have had no objection to that sort of arrangement, you know, so long as the woman was willing." He looked at Harlow McCamy, and some indefinable gulf, unseen before, yawned between them. Paul felt an instinctive shrinking away from someone abnormal. "How long did you let this go on?" he asked.

"I didn't *let* it!" McCamy said. His hands moved restlessly in his lap. "She . . . she wouldn't . . . I . . . what has this got to do with her death, sir? Whatever the provocation, Gabriel cut her throat. Surely there is no justification for that."

"No," Paul said slowly. "No justification. I want you to tell me again how it happened."

"I don't *know!*" McCamy said. The words seemed to be wrenched from him, and Paul thought that there was truth in that. "I saw they were gone, and I went looking for them—I was going to bring them all in, there was a fearful storm, you know—and when I found them, he was standing over her, hacking at her with the knife."

"She was on the ground?"

"Yes, of course. She . . . she must have been dead already by then."

"And he was standing?"

"Yes. I mean, well, bending . . ."

"How could a man who was standing stooped over like that control his swing with a cane knife well enough to kill a woman who probably struggled for her life?" Paul kept his voice pitched low as a man would talk to any frightened thing, but his questions were insistent.

McCamy flung his head up, startled. "I—he must have been kneeling at first, and then he stood up, before I came. Yes . . . I think that that was how it must have been."

"I was told," Paul said, "that Celeste shouted at Gabriel to leave her alone, not five minutes before this happened."

"Yes," McCamy said eagerly. "Yes. I think she must have been afraid of him."

"But she went off into the tall cane with him? I find that hard to believe."

"Maybe she was trying to get away from him," McCamy said. "I think he must have followed her, and killed her while I was looking for them. He was kneeling over her, and there was blood . . . blood everywhere. Like a river. And it all washed away pink in the rain."

"I thought you said that he was standing." Paul was beginning to feel apprehensive. Whether McCamy had killed Celeste or not, there was something wrong with him.

"Yes, he stood over her." Harlow's eyes stared now at something on the floor at his feet.

"And watched the blood wash away?" Paul prompted.

"Yes."

"Mister McCamy, in that downpour, the blood had washed almost clean by the time her body was picked up. The only person who would have seen blood everywhere was the man who killed her."

Harlow looked at him blankly. "There must have been."

"Blood everywhere like a river? I'm sure there was. But by the time you got there, McCamy, if you got there when you say you did, you would not have seen it. No man describes a thing as you have done who has not seen it."

Harlow's eyes widened momentarily, and Paul saw a flash of fright in them. Then the blank look came down again, closed, secretive. "I saw . . ." His voice trailed off. Paul thought that whatever it was, McCamy was still seeing it.

Paul stood up and leaned across his desk. "Look at me, damn you!" His voice was so angry that it shook. "You did kill her. And then you tried to put the blame on a slave, and let me hang him before he could convince me you were lying. *If* he could." Paul was uncomfortably aware that he would have given little credit to Gabriel's protestations. "Answer me!"

McCamy began to shiver. He put his head in his hands. "I . . . she . . . She was unclean . . . black like the devil. Like the devil . . . she tempted me . . . and they laughed . . . all laughed." He began to shake uncontrollably. "They followed me," he whispered.

"Who followed you?"

"Women . . . witches . . . devil-things. When Mother died, I thought they would stop, but they follow me!" His voice was agonized, despairing, and Paul began to look at him with real horror. "They get into my bed at night," Harlow said. He sounded young, like a child, and horribly frightened. "Devils in the bed . . . she was one of them, wicked . . ." His voice trailed into a whisper again. "She had a knife. When they came for me, I struck with it. Struck with it. And she bled. . . ."

Paul came around the desk. He seized Harlow by the shoulders and shook him, wondering wildly what he would do if the man were hopelessly insane. But the wild, uncertain light died out of McCamy's eyes. He shuddered, looked up at Paul, and began to weep.

Paul leaned back against his desk and ran a hand through his hair. He looked at McCamy with a sympathy that was almost overpowered by disgust. "So you killed her, and then tried to hang an innocent man because no one would take a slave's word against a white man's. I want you off Belle Marie tonight. And if I ever learn that you have taken a job again where you have contact with women, or command over helpless men, I will find you and put a stop to it."

McCamy looked up at him with streaming eyes. "What will I do?"

"Clerk in a bank," Paul said. "Manage a store. Pray to God.

Anything, but go where your madness will not cause another death. I'll take Celeste's value out of your wages, but her death is on your soul." He turned to the secretary and pulled a slip of paper from a pigeonhole. "Take this to André Peyraud in the morning," he muttered as he wrote.

McCamy slumped in the chair. Paul held the slip of paper out insistently, and McCamy took it.

"Now get out. I'll send someone with enough money to get you to New Orleans. The *Sultana* is due by tonight. You can catch that."

McCamy stood up. His hair and stricken face seemed to be bleached of all color. He put the voucher in his pocket and stumbled wordlessly to the door. "God help you," Paul said as he passed through it. He thought that he had never seen a man so pursued by the hounds of hell as Harlow McCamy.

When McCamy had gone, Paul took a key from his pocket and opened the little safe hidden behind a row of books beside the secretary. He took McCamy's passage money out, wrestled briefly with his conscience, and added another five dollars. McCamy wouldn't have an easy time finding another post, and there wouldn't be much left of his wages after André Peyraud took Celeste's value out of them. He closed the study door behind him and went out onto the veranda, looking for someone to take the money to the overseer's house. Paul was not an extraordinarily squeamish man, but he couldn't bring himself to go near McCamy again just now.

A horse clip-clopped up the drive from the levee road, with a cheerfully whistling figure astride it. Paul narrowed his eyes. It was Denis, who had slipped away after dinner and whose whereabouts Paul had been too preoccupied to speculate upon.

Denis caught sight of his father and drew rein at the veranda steps.

"Where have you been?" Paul said.

"Courting," Denis said mildly.

"On Bayou Rouge, I assume." Paul wished violently that a storm would come up and wash all those Michelet sluts out to sea.

Denis took stock of his father's face, cast into angry shadows by the light of the parlor windows. "I didn't undertake not to see her, you know. I only said I wouldn't marry without your blessing." He slid down from his horse. "I'm sorry if I've caused you trouble tonight, on top of everything else."

"I've just given Harlow McCamy a voucher for his wages," his father informed him. "Less the price of Celeste."

"Jesus Christ! Do you mean to tell me *he* did it?"

Paul nodded somberly. "I don't think he's sane. I won't have him on Belle Marie."

"My God," Denis said, "has anyone told Gabriel?"

"I'm on my way to do that now. I thought it should come from me. I owe the poor soul that much." Paul dug in his waistcoat pocket. "Take this to McCamy and make sure he's put the flag out for the *Sultana*."

Denis tossed the coins in his hand reluctantly, but he didn't protest. His father had had the worst task, prying the truth out of Harlow McCamy. The least Denis could do was throw McCamy off Belle Marie for him. And when Denis talked to André Peyraud next, he was going to have a few words to say on the subject of checking hired hands' backgrounds for possible insanity. He started down the veranda steps.

"I can console myself," his father's voice remarked behind him, "with the fact that you won't have much time for courting this season. You're the overseer, starting tomorrow."

Denis stopped in midstep. He looked over his shoulder at his father. "Not," he said flatly, "unless you take Lucien out of the cane field."

Paul grunted. "That had occurred to me. All right, he comes out tomorrow."

Denis nodded. He thought the cane field might do Lucien a great deal of good, but he was damned if he'd supervise him. He dug his hands in his pockets and went off moodily toward the overseer's house. He would have precious little time to see Dinah now, even at night, until the grinding was over. Paul wouldn't hire another overseer, not while he could make Denis do the work and keep him away from Bayou Rouge. And the grinding was too important to slack on: The whole year's income hung on it.

After a moment he began to whistle again. It was hard to stay somber in a world that contained Dinah. Denis hadn't mentioned marriage to her because she would make the same objections that his mother had. But she had got used to his coming to see her now, and had evidently threatened her sisters with some dire fate, since they had taken to making themselves scarce.

The whistling died away as he came out of the shadow of the old oak that shaded the overseer's house, and stopped, puzzled. The door stood ajar and there was no light showing.

Paul took the lantern from the hook where it hung by the barn door and lit it with a lucifer match from his pocket. He pushed the

door open and stopped. The ring was gone from the wall, and the
tin plate with its greens and corn bread sat on the floor.

"Gabriel?" Paul shouted, but there was no sound. Paul pushed
the door open again, swearing, and strode down the path, carrying
the lantern. "Gabriel! Come back, you fool, we know you didn't
do it!" A dog barked, but no human answered.

Paul quickened his pace. The damn fool had run, and if the
alligators didn't get him in the swamp, weighed down with chains
as he was, the vigilante night patrol would, and if he fought them,
they'd shoot him.

"Mister Paul!" The crunch of running footsteps sounded on the
walk behind him, and Will came around the corner of the barn, out
of breath. "I jus' poke my head in to see do Gabriel be all right,
an' he *gone*!"

"I know he is," Paul said. "And what's more, he didn't kill
Celeste. I want you to ride out to Thomason's shack for me."

"Mister Paul, you ain't gon' set the slave catchers on him!"
Thomason was a local catcher, and like most of his ilk, he wasn't
choosy about what condition he brought his quarry back in.

"I don't have any choice," Paul said. "Gabriel's six feet tall,
and if he comes up to some farmer's house to steal food, he'll
scare somebody so bad they'll shoot him."

"Awright," Will said, "but me an' Dan'l, we go look for him
too. We find him, kin I tell him he won't get no whippin' if he
come back?"

"Yes, but go to Thomason's first. Thomason has dogs, and I
don't think you'll find Gabriel without them. And you tell
Thomason I said to go easy on him!" Paul shouted as Will ran for
the stables.

It was as black as a pool of ink in the overseer's house. The
curtains were shuttered, and not even a thin line of moonlight
came through them. Gradually Gabriel's eyes began to make out
shadows of table and chairs. There was a lamp in a bracket by the
door, waiting to be lit. Gabriel slipped to one side of it, holding
the chains against his chest, waiting. His heart hammered under
his ribs. Gabriel was not a man upon whom his servitude sat
lightly, but he had been conditioned all his life that to raise his
hand against a white man was the ultimate crime.

A footstep crunched on the walk outside, and Harlow Mc-
Camy's pale desperate hands fumbled with the latch. The door
swung inward, and McCamy stumbled through it blindly and
fumbled with the lamp, whimpering. All because of a black slut,

who had hunted him mercilessly. Something rustled in the room, and the fear welled up in him again. She was here! She hadn't stayed in the cane field where he had left her. Harlow screamed as hands came out of the night for him.

Gabriel was bigger and stronger, and he had nothing to lose, but Harlow had the strength of terror. He fought frantically as Gabriel's chains wrapped themselves around his throat. They staggered, chained together, across the dark room, Harlow scrabbling with his hands at the iron links, Gabriel following with the grim tenacity of avenging fury. Harlow stumbled against the bedroom door frame and was pinned against it. Gabriel grunted, took a better purchase on the chains and wrapped them one more time around McCamy's throat. A terrible rasping sound escaped McCamy's lips, and then he was silent. He slumped limply, dangling from the chains. Gabriel tightened his grasp, put a knee in McCamy's back, and snapped his head back.

Gabriel let him fall and stooped to unwind the chains. McCamy was motionless, his head lolling from a broken neck. Gabriel's breath came in gasps, and the blind fury that had filled him turned slowly to cold despair. Celeste was gone, and Harlow McCamy would keep her company in hell, but that wouldn't make anything come right again in the world, not ever. He looked dully at the body. No, one thing was right. McCamy had killed Celeste and Gabriel was gonna hang for it, but McCamy had paid up what he owed for that.

The Lord knows I done what I mean to, Gabriel thought. *I ain't gonna ask forgiveness. I 'spect He knows when a man's been lyin'.*

He sat down on Harlow McCamy's bed and waited for them to come and find him.

XIX

Adieu,

Françoise

DENIS STARED AGHAST at the body sprawled on the floor. The head was at an angle so unnatural as to make Denis's flesh creep. Moonlight from the open door flooded over McCamy's still face. Denis lit the small lamp in the bracket by the door and knelt beside McCamy. He felt for the overseer's pulse, knowing that it was no use. That twisted neck proclaimed more loudly than a stilled pulse that McCamy was dead.

Denis stood up cautiously and ran his eyes over the room.

"I be in here, Mister Denis," a voice said, and Denis snapped his head around. There was another lamp on the table and Denis lit that too, watching the darkened doorway.

Gabriel was sitting on McCamy's bed. His hands, heavy with the chains, hung between his knees. Denis backed away a step.

"I ain't do you no harm, Mister Denis," Gabriel said. "I done what I came for, an' I don't want no more on my conscience when I die. I got a powerful burden already."

"Dear God!" Denis said. Gabriel's innocence of Celeste's killing could offer him no hope now. Shouting voices outside in the night reached his ears, and Denis turned to the door. "In here," he called softly. "He's in here." Running footsteps pattered up the path.

"There will have to be a trial now." Paul and Denis sat on the veranda steps. It was nearly dawn but neither wanted to sleep—or thought that he could. "It's out of my hands," Paul said for what

243

was perhaps the tenth time, a litany of failure repeated over and over to himself.

Denis nodded glumly. A slave, or even a free black, who killed a white man, no matter what the provocation, was doomed. This was no longer a matter for plantation justice. There must be a public trial, which would be followed—neither Paul nor Denis doubted for an instant the outcome—by a public hanging. There was vengeance in that, and also example—for any other slave thinking of such a thing.

Denis stood. It would be light in a few hours, and the bell would ring to wake the field hands half an hour before dawn. "I'm going to wash," Denis said. "I don't feel clean. And then I'm going out in the field with them. Better they have work to do, to take their minds off what happened."

Paul rose with Denis and went slowly into the house. He felt cold and clammy, and his coat was damp with mist. McCamy would have to be buried in St. Louis Cemetery in New Orleans. There was no family in Vermont to send him home to—only a hometown minister who must be written to, and possibly the headmaster of his school—and it was unthinkable that he should be buried on Belle Marie, where his grave would terrify every Negro on the place. The man was a murdered murderer, a likely candidate for a ha'nting.

In the predawn dimness of the hall, he met Sallie, who was wearing a dressing gown and carrying a candle. Her face was framed in a nightcap of white lawn, and her blond hair hung in two plaits over her shoulders. She put a finger to her lips.

"I've just got Emilie to sleep. She's been having nightmares."

"I'm not surprised," Paul said. "So have I."

"Will you have to take Gabriel to New Orleans?"

"I already have." Paul said wearily. "Denis and I did it. We just got back. I wanted him out of here before the darkies got more worked up than they already are, and before someone decided just to skip the trial and lynch him. Those damn vigilantes and their idea of justice aren't any better than a mob."

"Where is he?"

"At the police prison, where he'll be a damn sight safer than he would be here once word gets around. I told the jailer to tell anyone who wants to get a head start on the trial that I will personally shoot any son of a bitch who tries to take Gabriel out of there before he's tried."

"But it's going to come to the same thing in the end, isn't it?" Sallie asked sadly.

"It must," Paul said. "There's more at stake than just Gabriel or that poor madman McCamy. A slave who kills his overseer must be a pariah. The blacks outnumber us. They must know that we are untouchable."

"Yes, I suppose so." Sallie, a slaveholder's daughter and a slaveholder's wife, knew the truth of that.

When she had gone back upstairs, Paul, troubled at heart, went into his study, prowling among his books, but reading none of them. He pushed open the windows and stared moodily into the dawn mist. Where did justice figure into it? Not the justice of the law, but the justice of what was right?

There was a tap at the door and Denis came through it before Paul could say "Come in." His boots were mud-splattered, and his clothes were wet with the mist off the river.

"I got 'em started, but I couldn't stick to it," he announced. "I left Daniel in charge. Damn it, there's got to be *something* we can do!"

"I've been uneasy in my mind," Paul said. "If you have too, maybe that's a sign that we're right. All right, then, change your clothes, and we'll go talk to Judge Craire."

Denis nodded and started across the hall for the stairs.

"Mind you. I don't hold out much hope," Paul called after him.

"Neither do I," Denis said from halfway up the stairs. He was already pulling his jacket off. "But by God, I'm gonna try!"

Paul looked down at his own boots and trousers. He was nearly as muddy as Denis from the long ride to and from New Orleans. They should have stayed the night there, but were too restless. Paul trotted up the stairs. If they hurried, they could reach the *Natchez* on her downriver run. Paul didn't think he could face another thirty miles in the saddle.

When Paul came out of his dressing room, Denis was just going down the stairs. The usual cheerful morning chatter of Negro voices was missing, and a black maid put her hands over her mouth and ran when she saw them. The aura of fear in the house was almost visible. The family was still sleeping, but when Paul and Denis entered the dining room, they found Barret prowling around the ham and eggs laid out on the sideboard by a subdued Testut.

"I thought I'd go into the city for the day," he ventured, "and stay out of everyone's hair."

Paul sighed. "We are too. I've got to do my best for Gabriel. We've had him since he was ten; I can't just throw him to the hangman. Testut!" he called. "Have someone go and wave down the *Natchez* for us."

"Yessir!" Testut's gloomy countenance brightened for a moment. Wouldn't do no good, he didn't 'spect, but it showed Mister Paul had a good heart. "I done tol' those triflin' darkies so," he muttered as he trudged to the door to find a messenger, "but they think they all gonna get whup 'cause o' what Gabriel done. Mister Paul, he know what's what. Some folks jus' askin' to get murdered, and eventual some poor soul, he come along an' do it for 'em."

His voice trailed off into the hallway. It was in this manner that Testut communicated to his master opinions that were none of his business, or that he was too well trained to offer directly.

Paul, Denis, and Barret bolted their ham and eggs and gulped the last of their coffee as a shout of *"Steeeemboat comin'!"* echoed from the levee.

"Fine day, Mister DuMontaigne," the *Natchez*'s captain commented as he welcomed them on board. "Mornin', Mister Forbes. Will you all be comin' upriver again with us tonight?"

Paul and Barret nodded, and Denis eyed Barret thoughtfully. Barret appeared to be a regular passenger. He couldn't have that much business in the city, unless the business was Claudine Belloc. Denis wondered what his father would think of that and decided that Paul didn't need any more shocks. Denis gritted his teeth. He was going to have to do something about Françoise Becquerel if he didn't want his father to get one from him as well. Today was as good a day as any. The *Natchez* wouldn't cast off until four o'clock—time enough to bid a firm farewell to Françoise and to list all his convincing reasons why she should refrain from mentioning their affair to her husband. He hoped they were convincing.

Judge Craire's clerk ushered Paul and Denis into the judge's chambers with evident curiosity. Everyone in town had heard about the murder by this time, and the judge was looking distinctly harassed when Paul and Denis came in.

"Well, you've stirred up a hell of a mess, DuMontaigne," he announced. The judge was square-faced, bull-necked, and muscular, with a flowing shock of white hair and thick white brows. "Why the hell did you have to bring that nigger into the city?"

"I assumed," Paul said, "that you would want him in your custody for the trial."

"I don't want him at all," the judge said frankly. "If you'd left him on your plantation, a few of the boys could of taken care of the problem for me and given the rest of your niggers a good scare while they were at it.''

"They don't need to be any more scared than they are. The only person at fault in this whole fiasco was my overseer. And me for having hired him. Gabriel isn't an insurrectionist, and I'm damned if I'll have him taken out and strung up by your 'boys.'''

"Suit yourself," the judge said. "But you'd save the city the nuisance of hangin' him."

"Do we *have* to hang him?" Paul asked. "There are extenuating circumstances."

"There aren't any circumstances extenuating enough to let a nigger kill his overseer," Judge Craire said. "You want to lose your election? You want me to lose mine? Hell, they'd lynch *me* if I tried to let that bastard loose."

"At least let us tell you what happened," Denis said.

"I know what happened. I read the deposition you gave the police last night. And I've had advice from every solid citizen in New Orleans since then. Starting with hanging him and ending up with old ladies who thought he ought to be drawn and quartered first."

"Silly old hens," Denis muttered.

"Well, they're just about scared to death right now," the judge said tolerantly. "There's no way I can let your boy loose. Slave uprising's not a joke, gentlemen, and your family's lived here long enough to know that."

"Gabriel didn't even try to run away," Paul said.

"But there's plenty that aren't so tame," Judge Craire said, "and we don't need to go giving them an example. Why are you so all-fired bent on keeping this one out of the noose anyway? What's one more field hand more or less?"

"You're a judge," Paul said. "What's justice, more or less?"

"DuMontaigne, we're not talkin' about justice, we're talkin' about preservation of the social order. And if you don't think that comes first here, you just test it out at the election in December."

Paul stood up. "I'm afraid we've wasted your time, Judge. And ours."

"Not entirely." Judge Craire leaned back in his chair. "Since you're here, you can make arrangements to take that damned dangerous nigger back with you. Don't tell me a man with two hundred slaves hasn't got a place to lock one of 'em up."

"I had," Paul said dryly. "It didn't prove to be very secure."

"Well, find one that is," the judge said, "if you're bound and determined you don't want him strung up premature. The chief of police, blast his pusillanimous hide, will throw up his hands like an old maid the first time the vigilantes come around."

"You know damned well he won't be any safer on Belle Marie!" Paul snapped.

"And it's also a hell of a lot less likely to start a riot if you shoot one of those fool vigilantes on your own land," the judge said. "I don't know why you've taken such a fit to keep him in one piece just so we can hang him later, but if you're set on preservin' him for the trial, you can preserve him out of my district."

"Of all the self-serving—" Denis began.

"Shut up, Denis," Paul said. "Very well, Judge, we'll take him back. I do trust you will grant me a few hours to make some arrangements? I'm not inclined to transport him aboard the *Natchez*," he added sarcastically.

"Certainly not," the judge grinned. "Aw, come on, DuMontaigne, you know I can't do anything for you. You knew it when you came in here. I'm up to my ass in frightened citizens right now. You'll just have to take a loss on this one."

"I'd like to challenge that son of a bitch," Denis muttered when they were outside, standing on the banquette along Condé Street. "What are you going to do now?"

Paul sighed. "Take him back." He grimaced. "I *suppose* I'm doing him a favor. I'm going to go and make the arrangements. Do you care to come with me?"

Denis shook his head. "Not unless you need me. I have some errands to run. Will you go back on the *Natchez*?"

"No, I'll go with Gabriel, and I'll probably wait for night. It'll be less conspicuous. When you get home, you can find a place to jail him that can't be got into. I'm more concerned with that than I am with his getting out."

"The old kitchen?" Denis suggested dubiously. "It's stone and you couldn't set fire to it." The old kitchen, which hadn't been used since his grandfather's day, was a cramped, one-room building just beyond the new one. They had played in it as children, and Lucien had locked Hollis in it once. When she had discovered that there were bats in it, her screams had been memorable.

"All right. When you get home, see if Jem can put a new door on it."

Denis nodded. He set off moodily up Condé Street. This was proving such an unpleasant day that he thought he might as well go see Françoise and lump all his disagreeable errands into one morning. He wondered what he would do if Gilbert Becquerel happened to be at home, but he never was. To be on the safe side, Denis slipped around to the bank offices and was rewarded with the sight of Gilbert himself, his florid face wearing a jaunty expression under a beaver hat, just going up the steps.

Feeling foolish, and guilty in advance, Denis ducked around the corner and walked toward Carondelet Street. Maybe Madame Becquerel would have other callers, he thought hopefully. Then she wouldn't receive him and he could tell his conscience that at least he had tried. The desire to divest himself of Françoise was almost as strong as the desire not to go near her today. He thought of praying mantises again. As a child he had watched a pair of them mate on a garden leaf. The female had bitten the male's head off in midcopulation, and its decapitated body had gone gallantly ahead with its business, unnoticing, while the female chewed thoughtfully on his head. When he had finished, she had eaten the rest of him. Françoise had the same gluttonous air about her.

Denis twisted the bell outside the Becquerel mansion and gave Michael, the black butler, his card. A man sitting on the banquette across the street, reading *The Bee,* folded it up and adjusted his spectacles.

"I see if Miss Françoise to home," Michael said.

While he was seeing, three carriages went by and a pair of schoolgirls with their mammy, arms full of brooms and dustcloths, walked toward St. Louis Cemetery. It was nearly All Souls' Day, and everyone gave the family graves a scrubbing before decorating them with candles and flowers.

By the time Michael reappeared, Denis had begun to feel that they were all looking at him and that he must have the word *adulterer* emblazoned in light across his back.

"Miss Françoise, she say come in the parlor," Michael informed him.

Denis dived through the door, trying not to scuttle furtively. Françoise was ensconced in the second-best parlor, in a morning dress of pale-green challis that Denis, unnerved, thought looked just like a mantis. A lunatic vision of Françoise chewing through his jugular and somehow consuming him whole went through his mind and he gave her a startled look.

Françoise patted the scarlet sofa cushions beside her. "Don't look so pop-eyed. Come sit down." Denis sat, and she leaned her elbow on the arm of the sofa and balanced her chin in her hand, smiling at him. "You are sweet to come and see me. You must have guessed how bored and lonely I have been, with Gilbert giving all his time to this election." Françoise pouted prettily. "But now I have my own cavalier to bear me company."

Denis snorted. That particular affectation, so beloved of Creole women, had always annoyed him. A great many things about Françoise that hadn't annoyed him the first time he had met her now got on his nerves. "Is Gilbert gone for the day?" he asked boldly. "And are you sure?"

"Of course I'm sure." Françoise looked peeved at this crass intrusion of practicality. "I would not have invited you in otherwise." Her expression softened, and she touched his cheek lightly with her palm.

"Françoise, I've got to talk to you," Denis said.

"But of course, *chéri*. We always talk, do we not?" Françoise ran a fingertip down his shirtfront. "Afterward."

"No, I meant—"

Françoise sidled closer to him and leaned her head against his chest. She began to stroke him between his thighs. Denis, jolted, hoped fervently that the servants weren't around. He wriggled away and tried one more time. "Now—"

Françoise smiled. "Ah, you are in a hurry."

She pressed herself against him in a cloud of jasmine scent. Her thick, dark hair brushed against his lips. Her fingers tickled and stroked, and she tilted her face up so that her lips met his insistently. *Maybe one last time,* Denis thought, wondering how he could want to get rid of her so badly and still be so stirred by her. His arms went around her and he bent his head to nibble at the round sea-foam swell of her breast. He knew she wouldn't listen to him now; maybe she would listen afterward. His fingers pulled at the tiny buttons of her bodice. Françoise moaned under him as his fingers ran across her nipples. Her hands slipped inside his trousers. Denis gasped while her soft, skillful fingers pressed and rubbed. He ran his tongue between her breasts. She shuddered and writhed under him, and he stood up with her in his arms.

"Are you sure?" Gilbert Becquerel pointed a finger at the man with the newspaper under his arm. "If I go barging in there and find my wife entertaining the priest to tea or one of her damned brothers and cousins, I'm going to look a fool."

"You won't," the man said. He had a round, balding head, and spectacles, which gave him a myopic expression. "I been watchin' her for weeks, like you tell me, an' I know all her brothers and relations, and I never saw no priest in a plaid waistcoat."

"Well, who the hell is he?"

"That I couldn't say." The balding man shook his head at Becquerel. "Give his card, looking over his shoulder like he didn't wanta be noticed, and after a minute the butler lets him in, and he ain't come out yet, so I don't expect it's a social call."

"All right." Becquerel swept the papers off his desk into a drawer and slammed it shut. He picked up his high-crowned hat and jammed it on his head. Françoise picked a hell of a time. "I'll be back as soon as I can," he growled at his clerk on his way out the door.

The spy with the newspaper trotted beside him. "I left a man there to be sure your boy ain't left by the time you get home," he said in an undertone when they were out of the clerk's earshot. "Big fellow, selling fish, with a cap on his head. You ask him what's up when you get there."

"Oh for God's sake!" Becquerel gave his informant an exasperated glance. "Why don't you just station a brass band outside my front door?"

"You tell us to watch her, Mister Becquerel, we watch her."

"All right, all right, get out of here. Bill Ewing'll give you your pay." Becquerel strode down the banquette, feeling, much as Denis had, that the whole city was privy to his affairs.

Outside the house on Carondelet the fish peddler was doing a brisk business. Becquerel waited, fuming, while the peddler sold a catfish to a Negress in a white turban, who seemed inclined to argue lengthily over the fish's purported freshness. Becquerel ground his teeth as they went over the disputed catfish inch by inch. When the Negress finally departed triumphant, with a picayune off the price, Becquerel stepped up before anyone else could approach.

"I sell best fish in city, me!" the fish peddler, still smarting, announced. He shoved a representative of his wares under Becquerel's nose. "Here, you smell her?"

Becquerel pushed it away. "I'm Gilbert Becquerel. I don't want your damned fish!"

"Ah." The peddler nodded knowingly. He laid the catfish down and jerked a thumb at the house. "He still in there, him." He eyed Becquerel curiously. "What you gon' do, shoot him, *hein*?"

Becquerel stalked across the street without answering. He pushed open the front door and brushed past a startled Michael.

Françoise's fingers dug into Denis's back. Her round knees gripped his buttocks, and her head was thrown back. He could see the pulse throbbing at the base of her throat and her half-closed eyes watched him appreciatively through heavy lids. He was achingly aware of the jasmine scent of her, of round, pink-tipped breasts soft under his hands, of overwhelming, almost cloying sensuality. Her soft body twisted under his, and little feet wrapped themselves around his back. He bent his head, nuzzling at the hollows of her throat, and felt her tongue flick out, licking at his ear, her breath panting and heavy.

Denis slid his arms under her shoulders and rolled over, carrying Françoise with him, so that she sat astride him, her dark hair flowing down her back. She moaned louder as he pushed himself upward, deeper into her. She braced her hands on the rose silk pillows on either side, and her hair fell like a curtain around them.

Denis squeezed and massaged her round backside, pushing her down on him, and felt her tighten around him, a wave of little contractions like ripples on water. He drove upward into her, shuddering.

After a moment, she slipped off him and curled herself under the silk coverlet like a plump cat.

"It may be," Françoise said thoughtfully, "that I will not go to Washington with Gilbert after all."

"Now wait a minute." Denis sat upright. "Françoise, that's what I came here for. I didn't mean this to happen—I mean—"

Françoise laughed, a silvery tinkle that grated on Denis's nerves. How could a woman annoy him so much and still inveigle him into bed with her? *No more,* he told himself firmly. "Ah, you never do mean it to happen, *chéri,*" Françoise informed him, "but it always does, yes? You are young, the blood runs hot. This is not so bad."

"I told you, I'm getting married. I don't intend to treat my wife the way Gilbert treats you. You don't like it. Would you wish it on another woman?"

Françoise shrugged. "That is her problem, not mine."

Denis looked at her, exasperated. "This is the last time," he said flatly.

"Denis, I warned you—"

Denis sat up and pushed the bed curtains aside. He began to put on his drawers. "You can tell your husband if you want to," he said, reaching for his trousers. "But if you do, you'll never find another lover. He'll watch you like a jailer."

Françoise eyed him with distaste. "You are growing shrewd."

Denis picked his scattered shirt studs out of the carpet. He tossed them in his hand reflectively. "Maybe I'm just growing up."

Michael watched the master take the stairs two at a time and backed out of the hall. Mister Gilbert was awful mad, and he was gon' think that Michael should of told on the mistress a long time ago. He slipped into the pantry and down the stairs that led to the winter kitchen. He thought he'd go keep the cook company.

Gilbert strode down the upstairs hall with a pistol in his pocket. He'd see how well Françoise behaved herself after he shot a man dead in her bed. No jury in Louisiana had ever convicted a man for that yet, and it would sure as hell give Françoise a day to remember. He slammed the boudoir door open and was gratified by a shriek of terror from his wife.

Denis, pulling his boots on, heard Françoise scream and looked up to find himself a reluctant participant in the recurrent drama that had haunted his dreams all during his affair with her: an outraged husband in the doorway, a cloud of brewing scandal, and an unpleasantly businesslike pistol.

"Jesus!" He snatched at his other boot, waiting with every horrible second for the impact of the bullet. Curiously, Becquerel only stood there in the doorway, his mouth open and a look of stupefaction and an odd chagrin on his florid face. Denis jammed his foot in the boot. "I suppose there isn't anything I can say, under the circumstances," he said. If Gilbert started talking to him, Denis thought, he wouldn't shoot him.

Françoise was crying dolefully, with the coverlet stuffed against her face.

Gilbert's mouth snapped shut. He took two steps toward the bed and yanked the coverlet from it, spilling Françoise onto the floor in a flurry of bare bottom and legs. She snatched at the coverlet, and he threw it across the room.

"You're mighty anxious to cover up something with which you have no doubt been dazzling half the population of New Orleans!" he informed her.

"No, no!" she said tearfully. "No, only D-Denis. Gilbert, I promise you!"

So much for her threats to tell her husband, Denis thought grimly. She was terrified. For Denis the scene had taken on the mad quality of a nightmare. He waited, frozen, for Gilbert Becquerel to remember him and shoot him.

Françoise made a grab for her petticoats and wrapped them around her. Becquerel watched her in a rage. "This one was quite

enough!'' he said furiously. "It isn't enough that you must fall on
your back for a DuMontaigne! You have to pick a puppy who's
probably my *son*!'' He shoved Denis's coat at him. "Get out
before I kill you anyway!'' he snarled, taking a certain satisfaction
in Denis's expression of horror.

XX

The

Duel

DENIS FLED DOWN the stairs and through the empty hall. Michael was nowhere to be seen. Behind him, Denis could hear Françoise's tearful voice, overborne by Gilbert's. He flung himself headlong through the door, driven more by Gilbert's parting words than by any fear for his skin. On the steps he stopped, dazed, blinking at the sunlight, and remembered to put on his coat. Across the street a man with a fish cart watched him curiously, and Denis fled in the other direction.

He walked blindly toward the levee, ashamed of himself, ashamed of Françoise, and with Gilbert Becquerel's claim burning like a raw wound. Surely Mama would never have done with that man what Denis had done with Françoise. He clutched at that thought, but into his mind crept the remembrance of the mischief-look in her eyes and the times she had gone to Becquerel's office with her canvases rolled under her arm. One encounter for each painting, and how many more without that excuse? Her acquaintance with Becquerel was of long standing, and unknown to his father. And wasn't that a trivial secret to keep for so many years, Denis thought miserably, if they never did anything but look at paintings?

The *Natchez* would cast off in an hour, and she was burning pitch pine and resin, making a tall black column of smoke as a signal to her passengers to look sharp. Denis made his way up the gangplank, pushing through the crowd of well-wishers who had come aboard to see their passengers off. He bought a glass of whiskey at the polished oak bar and settled morosely onto a divan with it.

Presently Barret appeared with his own glass and seated himself opposite. Barret looked like a man with thoughts of his own to fret over and made no conversation, for which Denis was grateful. At four o'clock the *Natchez* backed out into the river, and they steamed upstream into gathering dusk.

Two and a half hours later, with nothing settled in his mind except a growing conviction that that was not a topic that Gilbert Becquerel would lie about, Denis stepped onto the jetty at Belle Marie and trudged away to find Jem. That had to come first, he thought, and then dinner, if he could manage to eat without throwing up, and then there might be a chance to talk to his mother. And what would he say? *Am I Gilbert Becquerel's bastard?* He supposed that about covered it.

At dinner Denis picked miserably at his serving of wild turkey roasted with chestnut stuffing, trying without any great success not to look at his mother. Paul, looking haggard, arrived halfway through the meal and announced that Gabriel was locked in the old kitchen, with Daniel and Will for guards. Adele tut-tutted at Paul because he looked so tired, and Hollis and Felicie cast her looks of loathing. On that topic at least they were united. Sallie's mouth compressed into a fine line, but she made no comment, and Tante Doudouce inquired in a fluttery voice if Paul was sure that it was quite *safe*?

"Certainly, Tante," Lucien said. He patted her hand. "And we're all here to protect you if he gets any more homicidal leanings." Lucien's mood was not noticeably improved by his removal from the cane field, since Denis had informed him that it was only at his request.

"Lucien, you will not amuse yourself by terrifying your aunt!" Paul snapped.

Lucien subsided into surly silence, Tante Doudouce looked nervous, and the pall redescended on the table. Emilie looked from one adult to the other with frightened eyes, and Felicie got up and put her arms around her. "It's all right, Baby."

When the meal was over, Sallie and the girls stood up, and Denis nearly shot out of his chair after them instead of lingering with the men over wine and cigars. He caught up to his mother just as she was settling with her embroidery in the parlor, and took her by the arm.

"Mama, I've got to talk to you!"

Sallie gave him a look of concern. "You looked awful at dinner. Darling, what is it?"

"Just come out of here!"

"All right." Sallie patted his hand. "We'll go up to my sitting room." What on earth was the matter? She blanched at the sudden thought that that Michelet girl might be in the family way. She looked at Denis as they went up the stairs. He *said* she wasn't, but you never knew . . .

Denis, who had spent the evening trying to think how to ask his mother what he had to know, could find no better way when the sitting room door had closed behind them than to turn to her and blurt, "Gilbert Becquerel says I'm his son!"

Sallie sank onto the shabby settee with a faint little noise of distress, her face as white as the blank canvases on the floor. She put her hand to her mouth and looked up at him.

"Well, am I?" Denis persisted.

Sallie nodded silently, and her eyes suddenly overflowed with tears.

"Oh, Mama . . ." Denis brushed a litter of paint rags and half-finished sketches off the settee and sat down beside her. "Mama, don't cry. I'm sorry to ask you like that, but I had to know."

"No, you didn't!" Sallie said. "You *never* had to know. *Why* did he tell you?"

"Oh, God." Denis put his head in his hands.

Sallie wiped her eyes on her sleeve, no handkerchief being ready. "Maybe you'd better tell me how you found out."

"I suppose I'd better," Denis said. "I just hope I don't have to tell Papa too. Not about what Becquerel said," he went on hastily, seeing his mother's horror-stricken face. "Just about what I've done." He sat silent for a moment, and then told it to her, beginning with the day he had gone looking for his mother at the Becquerels'. "I suppose," he said dolefully, "that was why she took up with me. Revenge. She must have suspected about . . . about you."

Sallie put an arm around him and drew his head down to her shoulder. "My poor darling, I've done you such a wrong. I can't even blame you for Françoise. That wouldn't have happened if it wasn't for me."

"I don't know," Denis said with a shaky smile. "I seem to be rather susceptible." He sat up and took his mother's hand in his.

"But you— I have to know why, for my own peace. I can't go on wondering, imagining . . ."

"You probably can't imagine anything worse," Sallie said frankly. She sighed. "I don't know if I can even make you understand. I . . . Denis, when I married your father . . . when I married Paul—"

"It's all right, Mama," Denis said. "I can't think of Gilbert Becquerel as my father. I don't even want to."

"All right." Sallie took a deep breath. "When I married your father, I was so much in love with him. Believe it or not, I still am. And I thought he loved me. Maybe he did. But once we were married, it just didn't work. He . . . he doesn't give me any credit for being a person . . . for having any ideas. He hates my painting because he thinks it isn't ladylike. Because I'm not a scholar, he thinks I don't know anything. It's hard to explain, but Paul makes me feel . . . squelched. Told to run away and play, as if I were about five. I don't feel a part of his life, his real life." She stared into the clutter of rags and brushes by the easel. "And he had a mistress."

Denis nodded. "I know."

Sallie looked at him, startled. "You do?"

"Yes, I met—" He stopped.

"You didn't meet her," Sallie said tartly. "She's dead." She had come by that knowledge on the same grapevine by which she had learned of the woman's existence.

Denis looked embarrassed, but he had gone too far to cover up his blunder. "I saw her daughter," he said unhappily. "Papa's daughter, I suppose. At the Quadroon Ball."

"Oh," Sallie said faintly. "What . . . what does she look like?"

"Like Emilie," Denis said.

Sallie was quiet, digesting this, her stomach knotted into a hard little ball under her heart. "I suppose," she said finally, "that doesn't make Paul any worse than I am."

Denis hung his head. "I'm sorry I had to ask you any of this," he muttered. "We both would have been happier if I hadn't. I'm beginning to understand about you and Papa. But with all the men in the world, why Gilbert Becquerel? I could bear almost anyone better than him."

"I know," Sallie said sadly. "But that's why. I don't love Gilbert. I don't want to. I still love Paul. Damn him. I wish I didn't. But all I want from Gilbert is someone who understands

ne and treats me as if I weren't a fool. I never wanted to love him.
was just lonely."

Denis picked up a paint knife and poked moodily at the rags on
he floor with it. He was beginning to be burningly angry with his
ather, with Paul. He would never be able to think of Gilbert
Becquerel as his father, only as someone who by accident had
uddenly become related to him. But it wasn't his business to
udge Becquerel, not after what he himself had done. And if
Mama needed Gilbert Becquerel to salve her loneliness, then she
hould have him.

Denis stood up. He bent down and kissed his mother on the top
of her lace cap. "Don't worry, darling, I'm going to make it all
ight."

He disappeared before Sallie could answer, leaving her looking
fter him anxiously. But she felt leaden, too tired even to move,
nd she sat on the settee among the paint rags until Mammy
Rachel, hours later, came to find her.

"Where the hell are we going?" Lucien protested. Denis had
dragged him out of the house with only the vaguest of excuses.

Denis pushed the stable door open and picked up a saddle.
"Into the city."

"At ten o'clock at night?" Lucien balked. "What the hell for?"

"To apologize to Gilbert Becquerel for having been caught in
bed with his wife," Denis said shortly.

"Christ!" Lucien stared at him. "He'll skin you and nail your
hide up on the door."

"Well, he didn't when he caught us," Denis said. "And I've
got to apologize before he decides to challenge me."

Lucien snorted. "You embarrass me, baby brother."

"Not as much as it would embarrass Papa if I fought a duel with
Becquerel," Denis said equably. There was no way to explain to
Lucien that Becquerel wouldn't challenge him anyway, and that
what Denis wanted was to salvage his mother's relationship with
Becquerel, if possible.

Lucien picked up a saddle and suppressed a faint grin. His letter
to Becquerel seemed to have borne fruit, but it would be a pity if
Denis weaseled out of it with just an apology. It would take a
public scandal to sink Denis a few notches in Papa's estimation
and give Lucien time to ingratiate himself again.

Denis swung himself wearily into the saddle. This was his third trip into the city in two days. He felt doomed to ride perpetually between Belle Marie and New Orleans, getting himself deeper into trouble with every step. He looked at Lucien's interested, thoughtful face and wondered if he should have taken him after all. Mama's secret was something Lucien mustn't ever learn of, but surely Becquerel would have sense not to say anything in front of Lucien. The apology could be perfunctory and quickly over. Denis was almost certain that Gilbert Becquerel would prefer it that way.

They reached New Orleans in the hours between midnight and dawn. After pounding for five minutes at the door of the City Exchange, they were shown to a room by a grumpy night clerk in carpet slippers. Denis lay down on the bed in his clothes and stared at the ceiling, trying to frame some suitable remark to make to a man who had not only caught him in unlawful congress with his wife but who had proved to be his natural father. Lucien watched him with a smirk, which did nothing to add to Denis's comfort. He awoke at eight, having finally gone to sleep in the middle of one of these imaginary conversations.

Lucien was nowhere to be seen but was tracked down breakfasting in the dining room, and the two of them set out for Gilbert Becquerel's banking offices.

Denis presented his card to the clerk, Lavoie, and waited apprehensively for a roar of outrage from behind Becquerel's mahogany paneled door. Lucien stood humming "Un Petit Bonhomme" until Denis hissed at him to stop.

"À voler mes pommes quand je n'y suis pas!" . . . I'll teach you not to steal my apples when I'm not there! . . . Lucien broke off a second too late as Gilbert Becquerel came through the door. He stared at Denis, stiffly surprised, his too-brown hair standing up from his forehead as if he had run his hand through it. "What do you want?"

"Just a word with you, in private," Denis murmured. "You know my brother Lucien, I believe."

"We are acquainted." Becquerel raised an eyebrow at Lucien. "In what capacity are you here?"

"Whatever's needed," Lucien said.

"Come into my office." Becquerel stepped back through the doorway without waiting to see if they followed him. Denis gritted his teeth, but he followed and motioned Lucien to come with him. Lucien sauntered through the door, whistling the same tune, and Becquerel whirled around to face Denis.

"I find that insulting!" Becquerel snapped.

"No offense was intended," Denis said, looking vainly for some sensation of kinship with this man. He found none, but he had not come here to look for a father, only to settle matters in such a way that his mother could be comfortable again. "Your choice of music was ill-advised, Lucien," he remarked.

"Thought it was a favorite of yours," Lucien said cheerfully.

"So it is," Denis said. It was a popular song. "But the connotations just now are unfortunate, and I don't wish to give offense."

"You should have thought of that some time ago!" Becquerel snapped.

"So should you!" Denis said, goaded.

"By God—"

"Now see here, Becquerel," Lucien said smoothly, "I don't care for your tone to my brother." He had no idea what Denis was referring to, but a quarrel was all to the good.

"By God, I'll use any tone I please, you ill-mannered pup!" A shuffling noise outside the office door proclaimed that Gilbert's staff was listening with interest, and Gilbert flushed red. "Get out before I pick you up by the collar and kick you out!"

"Monsieur Becquerel, we will not stand for that tone from any man!" Lucien contrived to look self-righteous and affronted.

"Lucien, be quiet. I didn't come here to quarrel."

"What the hell did you come here for?" Becquerel demanded. "I told you to get out of my sight."

Denis stiffened. "I came, sir, to apologize for any injury done you."

"It seems to me, sir," Lucien interjected, "that now you owe my brother an apology."

"I'll see your brother in hell first!" Becquerel shouted.

A voice outside said, "Dear me," and the latch clicked. There was a quick scuffling of footsteps away from the door, and Bill Ewing poked his head in. He regarded his candidate with shrewd interest. "Dear me," he said again. "I hope I'm not interrupting anything."

"Not at all," Becquerel said. "I'm about to kick DuMontaigne's pups down the stairs."

Lucien strode forward. "Becquerel, I won't take that sort of insult from any man!" Denis, his temper deserting him fast, grasped for the last few shreds of it. "This is my quarrel, Lucien," he said stiffly.

"So it is," Gilbert Becquerel said icily. He flicked an eye at Bill Ewing and at the door behind which he knew his staff were all ears. "Name your friends, DuMontaigne."

Denis bit his lip. He had come to apologize, not to push Gilbert Becquerel to make a challenge. Somehow it had all gone wrong. Now, it was a matter of honor, and a duel was the way in which affairs of honor were settled in Louisiana. Whether Becquerel really wanted to fight him or not, he couldn't take back those words. Denis looked at his natural father. "Lucien will act for me," he said stiffly.

"Ewing?" Becquerel glanced at him.

"Glad to oblige," Bill Ewing murmured. He gave Becquerel a look that informed him that he'd better win or he was going to be a laughingstock.

Gilbert Becquerel needed no such reminder. He was too angry, and his pride was too sore to care. Lucien stood leaning on a bookcase, arms folded, smirking at him. Enraged, Becquerel turned to Denis. "The choice of weapons is yours."

"Now, now," Ewing said. "Let's observe the amenities." He glanced at Lucien. "Still time for your man to apologize, you know."

"Why, we consider that your man owes us the apology," Lucien pointed out.

"I tried to apologize," Denis said through clenched teeth. "For other matters. That's what I came here for." He glared at Becquerel. "Although in that matter also, Monsieur Becquerel's hands are no cleaner than mine. I will still apologize if he will." Pride and honor left no other option than to demand that much. He knew Becquerel wouldn't take his apology now anyway.

"Name your weapons!" Becquerel snapped.

"Swords," Denis said, and Lucien looked at him in surprise. Denis was a crack pistol shot. Lucien shrugged. So much the better. Denis wasn't quite as good with a sword.

"I have no weapon with me," Denis said, still stiffly formal, "but I'm sure one can be obtained."

"I'll hop round to Pépé Lulla's," Bill Ewing said. Lulla was among the best of the *maîtres d'armes* whose fencing schools lined Exchange Alley. "I expect he'll be glad enough to lend a blade or two."

"I expect he will," Denis said. "I studied with him."

"Ironic," Becquerel commented. "So did I."

Ewing snorted. Fencing lessons were for gentlemen. Himself, he'd of just punched a few holes in the bastard with a shotgun. "Well," he said cheerfully, "it won't take me a minute. I'll collect a doctor on the way back, and we'll all ride out to the Oaks." He consulted a fat pocket watch. "You'll be back in time for lunch. Or somebody will."

He popped through the door, and Denis bowed formally to Gilbert Becquerel. "We will meet you there."

Lucien and Denis walked along St. Louis Street in silence and collected their horses. Trotting along Esplanade Avenue out of the city, Denis wondered miserably when his encounter with Gilbert Becquerel had taken the turn from which neither could go back. There had just suddenly been a quarrel, and people to hear it, and no way out.

Denis looked gloomily through the gray November mist that still lay along the road. The Oaks were the accepted dueling ground, a stand of ancient live oaks on the plantation of Louis Allard northwest of New Orleans. On some Sundays in fair weather there had been as many as ten duels fought there in a day. Denis supposed Allard was used to it.

That was more than he could say for himself, he thought glumly. Lucien was notorious—or famous, according to one's point of view—as a hothead who often provoked a challenge out of boredom. But Denis had a strong practical streak, and all his acquaintances knew that Denis DuMontaigne was one of the best pistol shots in the city, and a very fair swordsman. Denis had never seen the necessity of putting a hole in some other idiot just to prove it.

They drew rein under the Oaks. The others were there before them. Bill Ewing was chatting amiably with a doctor in a black frock coat. Two rapiers leaned against one of the massive trunks, and Denis thought with a lurch of uncertainty that he should have chosen pistols after all. He could win with a pistol. But he hadn't wanted to kill his unacknowledged father, whatever he thought of him. A slight sword wound would be sufficient to conclude the affair with honor all round.

Ewing nodded to them. "You're in good time. You'll find my man over yonder. And allow me to present Doctor Sandoval."

Denis nodded brusquely to Gilbert Becquerel, leaning against a tree across the grove, arms folded. He extended a polite hand to Sandoval, whom he had never met. Sandoval shook it mournfully, as if he expected shortly to be feeling for its fading pulse.

"Cheerful old buzzard, isn't he?" Lucien whispered. Denis looked at him angrily. "I expect he's seen enough fools killed out here to be tired of it. I didn't want this fight, and I don't share your amusement!"

Lucien gave him a contemptuous look. "Then wriggle over and apologize."

Denis gritted his teeth. "I can't and I won't. Go tell Ewing I'm ready."

Lucien sauntered over, and in short order the four of them stood in the clearing under the spreading branches. Sandoval sat down on a rock to await the need for his services.

Ewing and Lucien made a ritual inspection of the borrowed rapiers and pronounced them to be equal in all respects. Then they backed away, their respective combatants' coats over their arms, and Denis and Gilbert Becquerel faced each other across the seared winter grass. Each had his shirt sleeves rolled up above the elbow, and had pulled off his boots to give him a better footing on the grass.

Denis lifted his rapier in salute. His father's eyes glittered angrily at him from behind his own blade. Denis wondered what Françoise would think. Would she take to widowhood? Or would she be more cheered to see Denis underground?

Becquerel advanced on him. Denis circled warily, taking the measure of his opponent's skill, as Becquerel was taking his. The rapiers clashed, scraped blade against blade, sprang apart. Denis feinted, lunged, and was gratified by a grunt of surprise from Becquerel as he parried with alacrity.

The grass was cold and wet underfoot where Denis and Gilbert Becquerel moved in the shadows, skirmishing, testing, feinting, attacking—all the tricks that Pépé Lulla had taught them both. Denis realized that Gilbert Becquerel was the better swordsman. Not much better, but enough—enough to kill him if he dropped his guard for an instant. Something in Becquerel's eyes and the grim twist of his mouth spoke of anger beyond restraint or judgment. Denis shifted his fingers on the rapier's hilt, aware that it was growing clammy in his hand.

Becquerel thrust and advanced. A faint physical resemblance to himself left Gilbert unmoved. The boy was Paul DuMontaigne's in everything but one initial tumble with Sallie on Gilbert's office settee. He had been truly angry with Sallie when she had told him woefully, well into the pregnancy, that the baby couldn't be Paul's.

Gilbert had sent her home in a fury, and she hadn't come back until well after Denis had been born. And now it was not enough that Gilbert had found his unwanted bastard in Françoise's bed, but the bastard had come to Gilbert's office and made him a laughing-stock.

Gilbert lunged savagely with his rapier and noted with satisfaction that Denis's parry came nearly too late. Denis's eyes were beginning to lose their look of confidence and had an unnaturally bright glitter. Gilbert felt his sword arm begin to ache and he pressed Denis harder.

Denis fought grimly, seeking an advantage and finding none, trying now only to tire his opponent. Youth was the only advantage he had left. He had tried to settle matters for his mother, and now they were likely to bring him home dead to her. *Don't think about that, think about what Pépé taught you. Think about the man you're fighting, watch his eyes. . . .*

Becquerel, breathing hard and tiring, lunged. For an instant he was open to attack. Denis parried and thrust. Becquerel's blade came up skillfully, swiftly, and Denis's slid along it with a grating sound. Before Denis could recover, Becquerel had struck again. Denis felt as if a hand had pushed him down. He fell backward in the grass as Becquerel's blade slid out of the wound in his chest. There was a drumming in his ears, and over it, faintly, he heard the sound of running feet and voices. Someone pulled at his shirtfront, and he had a blurred glimpse of Gilbert Becquerel looking at a red-stained sword blade with a look of unexplained fear on his face. Then a warm and comforting darkness crept over Denis, and it seemed almost too much trouble to go on looking at anything.

Gilbert Becquerel let the rapier drop. It bounced on the grass and rolled toward his feet. He backed away from it, the color running out of his face. His murderous rage had vanished, and he came to his senses with a jolt. "Is he dead?" he whispered.

"Not yet," Dr. Sandoval said. He leaned with both hands on Denis's chest, trying to stanch the wound with a pad of bandages. "You've missed the lung, but he may be on your conscience yet."

Becquerel flinched, and Bill Ewing looked at him curiously. Becquerel had fought enough duels in his day to be an odd man to turn squeamish now.

"Let me know," Gilbert said. "I want to know." He turned and strode toward his horse. He had no fear of man's condemnation, or the law's, but his earlier rage had blinded him to the prospect of another judgment. God would know, if no one else did, that Gilbert Becquerel had killed his own son. Gilbert was little troubled by conscience in this world, but his fear of hell was real.

Sandoval sat back on his heels. Denis lay on the seared grass with his shirt torn away and bandages pinned tightly around his chest. His breathing was shallow and his face was gray. Sandoval looked up at Lucien. "Where do you want to take him?"

Lucien hesitated. He hadn't thought that far, hadn't really thought what would happen if Denis died.

Sandoval shook his head. Of the pack of fools in the world, the ones who came out here to try to kill each other under Allard's oak trees were the worst. "Well, you can take him back to the city," he said. "It's shorter and might be less hard on him. Or you can take him home. They mend better at home. It's up to you."

Lucien tried to make up his mind. He didn't want the blame for the wrong decision.

"Tchah!" Bill Ewing gave Lucien a contemptuous glance. "Take the boy home, Sandoval." Ewing was used to deciding things when nobody else wanted to. "I'll help you get him in the buggy." Sandoval and Bill Ewing, who proved to be surprisingly wiry, lifted Denis between them and propped him in the back of the doctor's buggy. Ewing got in beside Denis to steady him, and Lucien, riding Molasses, led Denis's horse and Ewing's. Ewing grimaced. As a way to spend the afternoon, explaining to Paul DuMontaigne what had happened to his kid ranked pretty low on Bill Ewing's list, but he couldn't square it with his conscience to walk off now. They set off at a slow walk down the road toward the river.

It was nightfall before the buggy reached Belle Marie, and the house was in an uproar. Sallie came flying down the carriage drive as Sandoval turned into it. Testut, behind her, lifted a lantern, and its light fell on Denis's still face. Bill Ewing eased a cramped arm and helped Lucien lift Denis down. "He's not in a good way, ma'am," Sandoval said to Sallie. "Leboeuf's your physician, isn't he?"

Sallie nodded dumbly.

"You'd better send for him. I'll stay with him till he comes."

"What happened?" Sallie looked at the three grim-faced men. She caught at Lucien's arm. "Lucien, tell me!"

"Gilbert Becquerel called him out," Lucien said. "I tried to stop it, but neither one would listen."

Sallie slumped away from him. "Look out!" Sandoval shouted. He jumped from the driver's seat. Testut dropped his lantern, and they caught Sallie just before she crumpled onto the carriage drive.

XXI

Prayer

and

Seduction

SALLIE SAT, STIFF with exhaustion, in a chair by Denis's bed. They had put him in a spare room upstairs, not in the *garçonnière*, where he usually slept. Paul sat on the other side. Every so often their eyes would meet wordlessly over the still body of their son, and then each would look back to Denis's pale face, their eyes narrowed in the dim lamplight to be certain that his chest still rose and fell. They were too tired now even for words of hope and comfort.

Sallie's head nodded on her breast, and she jerked herself awake, afraid to sleep lest Denis should somehow slip away from her if she were not there to pull him back by strength of will.

Paul watched her with the same grave concern with which he watched Denis. At last he stood and came around the bed to her. He put his hands on her shoulders. "You must rest. I'll stay with him, I promise."

Sallie shook her head. "No, I won't leave. Doctor Leboeuf said the first few days would tell. I won't leave him." He had sought out Gilbert for her sake. She knew it. *Oh my darling,* she thought, watching the slow, fluttering breaths come and go, *I didn't want Gilbert more than you.* She knew wearily that she didn't want Gilbert at all now, but she would think of him later, when she could think of anything at all except Denis. Sallie knotted her handkerchief in her hands, head bowed. *Oh God, I have been wicked, wicked, but don't take my child.*

Paul left her and resumed his own vigil. He had heard the story of Denis's indiscretion from Sallie and of the duel with Gilbert Becquerel from Lucien. Lucien had done his best to imply that Denis had set out to quarrel with Becquerel, and Paul, staring miserably at Denis's still face, knew that Lucien was lying. If Denis had deliberately sought out Gilbert Becquerel again, it had been to swallow his humiliation and apologize—and Paul could think of no other reason for that than to spare himself embarrassment during the election, so Paul had his own burden of guilt to bear, along with the knowledge that Lucien would not and could not change.

Denis stirred and made a faint moan that was almost animallike in sound. Sallie bent over him, tense with fear. Denis stirred, turned his head on the pillow, and sank back into sleep. His breathing seemed to come more regularly. Sallie laid her hand on his forehead.

"He has a fever," she whispered.

"Doctor Leboeuf said he probably would," Paul said.

Sallie pressed her hand against Denis's forehead as if she could somehow hold the fever back. Watching her, Paul felt oddly envious. Sallie's love for Denis was complete and unquestioning, forgiving and forgiven. Why was it so impossible for her to love him that way? Sallie looked at him, her blue eyes circled with shadows. "Paul, I'm so frightened."

Paul got up again. He came and sat on the edge of her chair and put his arm around her. He drew her head down to his shoulder. "We must trust in God, Sallie."

They sat together until the first light of dawn crept through the shutters.

Mammy Rachel brought them up their breakfast on a tray, and stood over Sallie while she ate hers: two boiled eggs, apple cider, coffee, and Meeow's *beignets*.

"I'll get big as a house if I eat all this," Sallie protested. She didn't feel like eating breakfast anyway.

"Do you good if you do," Mammy said. She looked at Sallie's wan face and ventured a further opinion. "Keep you out o' trouble. It ain't nice, a woman your age keepin' her figger the way you do."

Sallie smiled. Mammy Rachel was as slim as her mistress, and proud of it. She picked up her spoon, and Mammy patted her shoulder.

"Thass my girl. You eat that an' then you go to bed an' sleep. I sit with Mister Denis."

"No." Sallie shook her head. "I won't leave him."

"An' when he wake up, you want me to tell him his mama sat up two days runnin' an' kilt herself? That there's my baby. You think I let anything happen to him?"

Sallie swallowed a mouthful of egg. The room felt as if it were swimming around her. "Just for an hour," she said faintly.

Mammy noted that Paul had finished his breakfast. "You too, Mister Paul. You don't look no better."

Paul helped Sallie out of her chair. He led her, unprotesting, to her bedroom, unlaced her dress and her stays, and wrapped a dressing gown around her. He laid her down on the bed and drew the curtains. She was asleep before he had finished. Curled in the big four-poster bed, with the lines of tension eased from her face, she looked no more than twenty to him. She made him think of their wedding night, five children and almost twenty-four years ago. For a few weeks, they had been so happy.

Sallie slept until nightfall and awoke to find Mammy Rachel bending over her. She sat up, her heart lurching in fear. "Denis!"

"He all right," Mammy said firmly.

"You were supposed to wake me!"

"Well, now I is. I brung you dinner. You eat it 'fore you go back in there."

"I'll eat in Denis's room," Sallie said stubbornly. She knotted the sash of her dressing gown and felt on the floor for her slippers. She found Paul beside Denis's bed again. His face was deeply lined and taut with fatigue.

"Did *you* sleep?" Sallie said accusingly.

"Some. Leboeuf was here. He said Denis is doing as well as can be expected."

"Well, what does that mean?" Sallie felt Denis's hot forehead.

"It means he doesn't know yet."

Sallie sat down by the bed and took Denis's hot hand. "I'm not leaving again." It was nearly dark. It was always in the night that death came. She looked at Mammy Rachel. "You sleep now and come back in the morning. I won't leave him in the dark."

At dawn she crept back into bed and returned with the late afternoon twilight to take up her vigil again. Sometime after midnight on the third night, Denis stirred. He looked through the dim lamplight with puzzled eyes. "Mama?"

"Here, darling."

"I'm sorry," he whispered. His eyes closed again.

"Paul!"

Paul jerked awake in the chair where he had kept watch with

Sallie. He put his hand to Denis's face, and his own broke into a smile. "Feel him!"

Sallie put her fingers to Denis's forehead. His skin was no longer burning hot. She began to cry.

Doctor Leboeuf came the next day to change the dressing again, and pronounced Denis not out of danger, but well on the way if there were no setbacks. He should eat beef broth, thin gruel, any sustaining liquids that would build up the blood. Mammy, disdainful of doctors, retired to the kitchen to brew up a concoction of her own.

Leboeuf looked after her indulgently. Open-minded in his notions, he read all the latest medical news and had caused much indignation among his colleagues by announcing that no one bled their patients anymore except for fools left over from the last century. "Your mammy's doses won't do him any harm," he said, "except, I suspect, for a nasty taste. Get all the food down him you can. And I think you may change the plaster and the dressings from now on. I'll come back in a couple of days, but send for me if he gets feverish again."

"Thank you, Doctor," Sallie said. Her voice sounded wispy even to herself.

Leboeuf peered down at her. He adjusted his spectacles and peered again. He pointed his finger at her. "Where are those daughters of yours? You've been overdoing it."

"Felicie has been running the household for the last four days," Sallie said.

"And I don't suppose Hollis has been any help," Leboeuf said frankly. "Put her to work anyway. You aren't any spring chicken, and you need your rest."

"Your gallantry leaves something to be desired," Sallie said.

"Gallantry has nothing to do with it," Leboeuf informed her. "I have delivered you of five children, which puts us, I should think, on a fairly intimate footing. I'm telling you to go to bed before you make yourself ill."

Sallie put a hand on his arm. "Doctor, tell me honestly, will he really get well?"

"God willing, and if the wound does not become infected, yes. He was lucky. His adversary missed the vital organs by the smallest possible margin."

"I see," Sallie said. "Thank you, Doctor. I'll take your advice as soon as I take care of one small matter." She marched down the upstairs hall and into her bedroom, where she scratched a few lines with her pen across a sheet of heavy cream-colored paper.

Gilbert Becquerel had nearly killed her child. She did not want to see Gilbert Becquerel again, ever. She told him so in an unsigned message he must be expecting. There was no sadness in the parting, only fury and a disgust with herself that lay heavily around her heart. Sallie gave the message to Mammy with instructions for its delivery, and lay down on her bed, unutterably relieved to have washed her life clean of Gilbert Becquerel. There was a sense of change in the air. The face that drifted across her weary mind was Paul's, as weary and frightened as her own, sitting with her by Denis's bed. Sallie buried her face in the pillow. The linen felt cool against her cheek. All that time that she had spent on Gilbert, she thought. . . . Was it even possible that if she had spent it on Paul, she might have changed things? Was it possible now, or was it forever too late because she had given up all those years ago when she should have fought? Maybe she was too tired to fight now. But at least there would be no more Gilbert.

"I am glad he is so much better." Adele's hands massaged the back of Paul's neck. "But you, you are so tired. Your shoulders are like wood."

Paul leaned back in the upholstered chair and closed his eyes as Adele's supple fingers stroked the nape of his neck. Her silk skirts rustled behind him, and there was a faint scent of lavender in the air. He knew he shouldn't be here in her room. But she had opened her door to ask him how Denis did, and he had been so tired. When she invited him to sit, he had sat, and her cool, attentive presence made the room a haven he somehow found no strength to leave.

"Such a trying time for you. So much responsibility." Adele came around the chair to kneel on the Aubusson carpet at his side. "And the worry over poor Denis." She let her hand rest lightly on his knee, and her gold-flecked eyes looked up at him earnestly and yet somehow with invitation. "*Pauvre* Paul, if only you would let me comfort you. I am so lonely too."

"My dear, are you?" Paul asked huskily. He took the hand that lay on his knee and leaned toward her. "I had hoped that you would feel that you had found your home with us."

Adele smiled. "There are times when I miss France, and Papa." She pressed his hand against her cheek. "You have been so kind to me," she whispered. "I want only to pay that back."

Her lips were parted invitingly, her eyes shone up at him. He bent his head and kissed her lips, and she responded eagerly, with a little whimper that might have been happiness—or triumph.

Adele half rose from her knees, pressing herself against Paul before he could think twice about what he was doing. Here was reason enough to surrender her carefully guarded virginity. She felt Paul's arms go around her waist, and she rose, her lips still clinging to his, and settled herself in his lap. He murmured something against her mouth and stroked her hair. Adele slipped her arms around him and tilted her head back, letting him kiss her where he liked. She felt no stirring at his touch. Carnal knowledge was a thing that a wife put up with in exchange for her position in her husband's house. She felt Paul's hands brush hesitantly across her breasts and, when she did not protest, his fingers undoing the buttons of her bodice. She gave a soft murmur of pleasure and willingness and was satisfied to feel with her bent knee the rock hardness beneath his trousers. She knew what would happen next and was pleased to find it so simple. She shifted a little on his lap, opening her legs so that he could put his hand where she knew he wanted to.

Paul was as capable of being lonely as was Sallie, and his fatigue lent a dreamlike quality to his encounter with Adele. She stirred in his arms as his hands roved beneath her flannel petticoats and came to rest against her thighs. Her skin, hot through the cambric drawers, warmed his hands as would a fire.

Adele let him do as he liked, feeling his fingers exploring her. It felt . . . more pleasant than not, but her virginity was a commodity to be bargained away only for marriage. Adele knew Paul well enough to know that that was the price he would feel he must pay.

Paul lifted her in his arms and carried her gently to the bed. The mosquito netting had been replaced with heavy gold hangings embroidered like the *ciel de lit* with white magnolia blooms. Paul drew the bed curtains closed and lay down beside her. He kissed her slowly as she twined her arms around his neck. The billowing petticoats and crinolines got in his way, and he lifted her hips to unfasten the layered waistbands of skirt and undergarments. He undid her corset strings with a practiced hand, revealing small pink-tipped breasts. His experience of women told him that she would be embarrassed, in spite of her wish to make love to him, and he handed her her nightgown, laid ready on the pillow for that evening.

"Put this on," he whispered. "You will be cold."

Adele slipped the gown over her head and braced herself for what would come next. Now that it was actually going to happen, she was less sure of herself. She watched nervously as Paul began to take his clothes off. Adele had never seen a man naked. His arms and chest were pale compared to the tan skin of his face, and his chest was matted with dark, graying hair. His dark eyes glittered with a light she had never seen in them.

Paul began to undo the buttons of his trousers. Adele put a hand to her mouth. She knew she should look away or he would think her brazen, but, impelled by dread and curiosity, she couldn't. Paul saw her expression and laughed gently. He pushed her down on the bed and bent over her, nibbling at her ears and lips so that she couldn't see what he was doing. The feel of her slim body beneath his made the blood pound in his ears.

"Adele, *petite,* are you sure?"

"Oh yes," she whispered. She knew that if she refused him now, she would never get another chance. Let him do what he wished with her, and he would marry her—as soon as his wife was gone. Adele never thought of it as "dead," just "gone." She gritted her teeth. *I can do anything if I want it badly enough.* She would be Madame DuMontaigne, rich and respected. She made herself smile at him as she felt him pull his trousers down over his hips, felt his bare flesh against hers. "Oh yes, Paul, I am sure. You would never hurt me."

"No, never." His lips moved against her throat. Between her thighs, his fingers and then something harder pushed against her. Moaning, he rubbed himself against her and pushed her legs farther apart with his hand. She lay frozen as he stroked her in her most intimate places until they grew damp. He pushed the nightgown up around her waist and knelt over her. For an instant she caught sight of his face, flushed and dark, lips parted. His eyes still had that unnatural brightness and his breathing was heavy and ragged.

"Now," he whispered. "Now, *petite* Adele, who comforts me so." She gasped as she saw the thing that stood out stiffly from the curling black hair between his thighs. It was stiff, engorged, nearly as big around as her wrist, not at all like the small appendages one saw on statues. Was he going to put *that* into her? The thought that he might be deformed flashed wildly through her mind. She stifled a cry of fear as he lowered himself upon her and guided it between her thighs.

Gasping, Paul halted there. "Don't be afraid," he murmured, holding himself in check. He thrust gently, deeper. Adele shut her eyes. She felt stretched enough to break open. There was a sharp pain, and then he was inside her, the muscles of his back shuddering with passion let loose.

"Ah, God . . ." Rhythmically, Paul drew himself in and out of her, while Adele slowly opened her eyes. *I was right,* she thought, triumphant. *It was not so bad after all*—and a small price to pay to be mistress of Belle Marie.

"Aaaahhh." Paul shuddered on top of her and lay still. Adele wrapped her arms about his back and held him tightly. He was hers now. There would be no undoing what he had just done.

Denis woke and ate a bowl of broth that night, and then slept around the clock. The next day he was alert enough to talk for a few minutes, with a desperate need to be assured by both his parents that they were not angry with him. That being promised him, he slept again and woke in good enough health to lean out of bed and tip Mammy Rachel's concoction into the chamber pot under the bed when she wasn't looking. The household returned to some semblance of order, and Sallie ceased to look hollow-eyed with fear. Word of his injury having gone around, baskets of fruit and flowers and calf's foot jelly began to arrive in profusion, and early in November Dinah appeared on the doorstep with a covered pie dish in her hands and her courage gathered to brave Denis's family and deliver it.

Testut regarded her hesitantly. Dinah had pinned her long hair up into a knot at the nape of her neck, and her dress was freshly washed and ironed, although petticoatless and much patched. She walked gingerly, as if the pair of low boots into which her feet were squeezed were unaccustomed, and possibly too small. She looked all right, but Michelets was Michelets and Miss Sallie wasn't gonna care for it.

Dinah held the pie dish out. "I bring this for Denis. She's game pie, like he like."

"I don't know. The doctor, he don't say nothing about eat no game pie," Testut said.

Dinah's face fell. "I bake her myself." She looked at Testut pleadingly. "I don' see him myself, know his mama don' like it, but you give it to him for me, *hein*?"

"I don't know," Testut began again when there was a shriek of delight, and Emilie and Charmante bounded around the corner of the house, followed more sedately by Sallie, Hollis, and Mammy Rachel.

"Dinah!" Emilie scampered over. "Did you come to see Denis? Look at Charmante, how big she's got!"

Dinah smiled. Charmante sported a red ribbon about her neck

nd smelled like peppermint oil, which was supposed to discour-
ge fleas. "She is most *belle*," Dinah assured Emilie gravely. "I
m glad you like her."

Sallie halted a few paces from Dinah and lifted inquiring
yebrows. "How may we help you, Mademoiselle Michelet?"

"I bring game pie for Denis," Dinah said, standing her ground.
'I bake her this morning for him." Her face looked strained with
vorry. "He will be all right, yes? You tell me true, please."

Sallie relented. "Yes, he will be all right. And he will enjoy the
vie, Mademoiselle Michelet." She took the dish from Dinah and
landed it to Testut. "But I am afraid he is not allowed any visitors
ust now."

"No," Dinah said. "No, I don' think you let me see him. Just
;ive him pie, yes?" She looked from Sallie to Mammy Rachel.
'Maybe you tell him I ask for him?"

Mammy inspected Dinah. Denis wasn't gonna take up with any
lo-account Michelet if Mammy could help it, but she was touched
vy Dinah's obvious devotion. The girl had been fretting herself
vith fear for Denis as much as his family had, Mammy thought.
'I tell him," she said, not unkindly. "An' the doctor say he just
ine now."

"He fight a duel, yes?" Dinah bit her lip. Over some woman,
Rafe had said.

"With swords," Emilie volunteered. "It was all about Gilbert
Becquerel's wife. I don't think Denis really likes her very much,
vut Gilbert Becquerel did, an' he fought him with a sword!"

"Emilie!"

"Miss Emilie, you git in the house this minute!" Sallie and
Mammy Rachel spoke simultaneously, and Emilie departed
.bashed.

"Well, he did," she said over her shoulder. "Everybody knows
.bout it." She didn't understand why everybody else could talk
.bout something, but the minute *she* talked about it, she was in
lisgrace.

Hollis gave Dinah a silvery laugh of calculated rudeness. "Dear
Emilie, she always knows everything—so embarrassing of her.
But I'm afraid she's right. My poor brother seems to have made a
.abit of getting involved with unsuitable women." She bestowed
pointed look at Dinah. "We comfort ourselves with the fact that
lothing ever comes of them, however."

"Hollis!" Sallie said sharply. "You will oblige me by being
ivil." She noted Dinah's stricken face and said, more gently,

"I'm afraid you must excuse us now. You were very kind to bring the pie, and I will see that Denis gets it." She sighed. "And I will tell him you asked for him."

"Merci," Dinah said. She turned and went back down the carriage drive, walking carefully in her tight shoes. She hadn't really thought they'd let her see him, but that Hollis—Hollis she could cheerfully pull limb from limb and feed to alligators in the bayou, her. Out of sight of the house, Dinah stopped and pulled her boots off, sighing with relief. Maman Estelle had got them from a gypsy tinker two years ago and they didn't fit Dinah's feet anymore. Barefoot, she went on more comfortably, thinking of the things she would like to do to Hollis.

Considering Dinah to be vanquished, Hollis gave her no more thought. She had more important matters on her mind, and she went into the parlor to think them out, waiting for Testut to bring her tea and toast. Adele, she noted with satisfaction, was nowhere to be seen. Adele had been avoiding Hollis lately, prompted possibly by the malicious look that Hollis bent on her whenever they met. Hollis settled in by the fire and smiled cozily. A very useful letter had been sent her by the parish priest of the village of St. Martin in France. Father Rosièrre was most distressed to have to inform Madame Tourneau that Adele Scarron had died of the scarlet fever almost a year ago now. Who the woman masquerading as Adele Scarron in Louisiana could be, Father Rosièrre did not know, but he felt impelled to mention that Adele Scarron had had a companion, a kinswoman of no fortune named Therese D'Aubert, only a few years older than Adele. He was distressed to think that Therese might have perpetrated such an imposture. . . . The letter was now locked away in the bottom of her jewelry case.

Mammy Rachel bustled in with a tray bearing a pot of tea and a plate of cinnamon toast, of which she had relieved Testut in the doorway. She set it on the table by Hollis's settee and stood over her, hand on her hips. "You ain't got no more manners than a alley cat," she announced. "You oughta be 'shamed."

Hollis shrugged. "You don't like those trashy Michelets either. What do you care how I talk to her?"

"Ladies is polite to everybody. Black, white, or trashy, it don't make no nevermind. You embarrass your mama, an' make yourself look no-account, that's what I care!"

"Pooh." Hollis bit into a piece of cinnamon toast. "You wait till you find out what *I* know, and you'll have more to think about than those Michelets." She smiled into her teacup. "You can worry about somebody right in this house."

"What you know?" Mammy asked suspiciously.

"Since you think my manners are so bad, I'm not telling."

"*Hmmph*. Then I 'spect you talkin' through you hat."

"Suspect anything you like," Hollis said airily. "Nobody would ever guess *this*." Hollis had no intention of telling anyone, she just wanted to divert Mammy from her tirade on bad manners. The letter would keep; it might even get more useful the longer Adele kept up her masquerade. What if she married someone, for instance?

Mammy glared at Hollis. "Somebody in this house" couldn't mean anybody but that Adele. Mammy opened her mouth to say so, and closed it again. Hollis in this mood would just delight in teasing her. "I got work to do," she announced. "If you ain't talkin' through you hat, I 'spect you'll tell me when you wants my help, that bein' the way you usually do."

She left with this parting shot, and as Hollis was pensively eating the last of the cinnamon toast, Felicie came in and began to rummage in her mother's embroidery silks.

"There's a regular parade through this parlor," Hollis said acidly. "If I want a place to think in peace and quiet I suppose I'll have to go clean out of the house."

"Go anywhere you want to," Felicie said absently. She pulled a strand of dark blue floss out of her mother's workbox and began to thread a needle with it.

"What *are* you doing?" Hollis inquired.

"Embroidering a handkerchief," Felicie said.

Hollis gave a hoot of laughter. "May I live to see the day! By the time you've stuck your finger and bled all over it and carried it around in your workbag until it's dirty, it won't be fit to clean windows with. Who's the poor soul who's going to get it?"

"None of your business!" Felicie snapped. "Why don't *you* find something to do? It might sweeten your nature."

Hollis narrowed her eyes. "It's for Roman, isn't it? What a love offering! Wait'll he sees it! Why don't you give up and go play pattycake with your dolls? You won't get Roman."

Felicie slammed the lid of the workbox shut. "Why don't *you* give it up? I haven't noticed that Roman comes to see *you*. There's nothin' more pathetic than an old widow chasin' a man who doesn't want her!"

Hollis jumped up from the settee. "An' nothin' stupider than a baby schoolgirl who can't see what's under her nose! You don't think Roman comes to see me? Roman comes to see me when you don't know anything about it.''

"No he doesn't!'' Felicie stamped her foot.

"Right under your nose,'' Hollis assured her. Her green eyes were vitriolic. "You *might* get him to come see you the same way, but I'd advise against it. *You* have to be a virgin when you get married, an' since Roman's goin' to marry *me,* that might prove to be a bit embarrassin'.''

"I don't believe you!'' Felicie felt her eyes welling up with tears and ran out of the room before Hollis could see her cry. Hollis looked after her with satisfaction.

When Roman came calling that evening, he found the parlor inhabited by all the ladies of the house, including a visibly smug Hollis and a subdued Felicie.

Roman, who generally gave the impression of having just got off a horse, was unexpectedly dapper in a dark blue evening coat and black pantaloons. He bowed formally to Sallie. "Have I your permission, ma'am, to take Mademoiselle Felicie for a short walk? No farther than down to the levee.''

Sallie hesitated. "Very well. But bear in mind that it is early yet to be making any . . . plans.'' She gave his black armband a pointed look. Roman offered Felicie his arm and she took it hesitantly, while Hollis glowered at them, and Sallie looked troubled. Roman was a good friend, but he was so *old.* Old for Felicie. Would he get bored with Felicie the way Paul had got bored with Sallie?

"And what on earth,'' Roman inquired of Felicie as soon as they were down the veranda steps, "is going on?''

"N-nothing,'' Felicie said. How could she ask him a thing like that?

"Something,'' Roman said firmly. "Let me guess. Hollis?'' Felicie nodded. "She said . . . she . . .''

"She said I had been conducting an illicit and highly disgraceful affair with her,'' Roman suggested.

Felicie, mortified and miserable, looked the other way and nodded again.

"Well, I was,'' Roman said. "I can't lie to you, honey, and I'm not proud of it.''

Felicie stared at him, appalled. "Then . . . it's true? She said—'' She wiped her eyes with the back of her hand. "She said you were going to marry her,'' she finished, feeling that she might as well get the worst over with at once. Then she could be miserable all at once too, and stop lying awake at night wondering about it.

Roman took Felicie by the arms and looked down into her face. "Not once," he said between his teeth, fighting down his fury with Hollis. "Not once since I found you. God help me, I love you. If you're willing to have me after all the things I've done, I want to marry you."

Felicie's stiff body relaxed all at once, and she leaned against his chest in overpowering relief. She didn't care what he had done with Hollis as long as he wasn't doing it now. She lifted her face, and Roman kissed her, softly, afraid to stir his own blood any more than the feel of Felicie in his arms had done already. When he took his lips from hers, he lifted her by the waist and spun her around triumphantly. He set her down, and they stood grinning at each other in the moonlight.

"I can't propose for a decent interval," Roman said, "but you may consider us engaged. Since Sallie didn't warn me off, I think they'll permit it. And you just leave Hollis to me."

"I will," Felicie said. "Otherwise, I may push her out a window for tellin' lies." She stood on tiptoe to kiss him again, then darted up the path to the house. She felt exuberant, happy enough even to be a little sorry for Hollis in a comfortably self-righteous sort of way.

Roman, following more sedately, was not surprised to see a shadow move from behind one of the slender columns that supported the veranda roof, as Felicie vanished into the house.

"Eavesdropping?" he inquired genially.

"If that is what you wish to call hearing the man whom I expected to marry me," Hollis said venomously, "betraying me with my own sister!"

"Trying for you," Roman agreed. "I daresay you'll get over it."

"How dare you! How dare you abandon me like this? After what you did!"

"Well, if you must know, I don't feel very good about what I did," Roman agreed, "but you were just too determined, Hollis, and I'm afraid my resistance wasn't very good."

"I'm sure that Papa would love to hear that as an excuse for ruining his daughter," Hollis suggested.

"I doubt that it is possible to ruin a virtue that is nonexistent," Roman snapped, "as evidenced by the things you've been telling Felicie. That will stop right now."

Hollis swung an open palm at his face, and Roman caught her by the wrist. "I'll tell Papa!" she spat at him. "He'll call you out."

"He'd have to call out every man in the parish," he said. "He wouldn't have the time."

He turned on his heel, leaving Hollis behind him on the veranda. She clenched her fists and slammed them into the column.

XXII

Tante Clélie

Takes to

Her Bed

BARRET TURNED THE key in the lock of the white cottage on Rampart Street. It was one of a row of small white houses, neatly painted, with walled gardens and curtained windows, behind which one might catch a glimpse of a gilt mirror or fine mahogany sideboard.

Claudine laughed nervously as Barret scooped her up and swept her across the threshold like a bride. She burrowed her face against his, pushing her new tignon askew. Was this how the white girls felt when they got married? Claudine doubted it. *They* were put into a big bed in their parents' house, under a new *ciel de lit* adorned with cupids and other romantic symbols, and left to stare at it while they waited for the bridegroom to join them. They were probably scared to death. *I am not scared*, Claudine told herself, but she clung to Barret a little when he set her down.

"Take a look, honey," Barret said. "How do you like it?"

The little parlor was carpeted with a thick Chinese rug and furnished with a graceful parlor set of ladies' and gentlemen's chairs in deep blue and a settee upholstered in paler blue velvet. Gaslights floated in a delicate chandelier.

"It's charming. How did you know just what I like?"

"I asked Tante Clélie," Barret said. "My knowledge of furniture extends to knowing which pieces you sit on and which pieces you eat at. My sister Alice maintains a very musty set of chairs, which were our grandmother's, and feels that what was good enough for her is sufficient for us. I'm gonna change that," he added in a mutter.

Claudine gave him a questioning look, and he put his hands on her shoulders and looked at her seriously, from a distance of about three inches, so that her eyes crossed a little. She leaned back and giggled. "I'm afraid I told Tante Clélie a whopper, honey," Barret confided. "I only took a three-month lease on this house."

Claudine's face fell. "Why? You promised Tante Clélie that you would be in New Orleans for six months out of the year and that I was to have the house. Oh, Barret, you haven't changed your mind?"

Barret wrapped his arms around her waist so that she couldn't go anywhere. "Not about you. Never about you. But the more I think about this arrangement, the more I don't like it. I want you *all* year, not just for six months, and I can't set up a mistress in Charleston. It isn't done. Alice will have a fit when I tell her I'm going to spend half my time in New Orleans, and she'll have a right to, because if I'm away that long, the plantation will suffer. It already has. I'm going to have the devil of a time when I get back to Charleston. So I have a much better idea, but I don't want you to be a goose and say no without giving it some thought, so I'm not going to tell you just yet." He kissed the end of her nose. "The house is ours for the moment, and we're going to put it to good use. Would you care to see the rest of it?"

Beginning with the bedroom, Claudine suspected. *We'll see about that.* She felt entitled to devil him a little for giving her such a fright and then being so mysterious. She made a slow, stately inspection of the parlor, then proceeded through an arched doorway into a dining room with a cherry-colored carpet and a round bull's-eye mirror that distorted their faces comically. Claudine made a face at Barret in the mirror and whisked through a swinging door into a pantry with glass-fronted cupboards displaying a Limoges dinner set. Beyond was a kitchen with a modern iron stove and a pump that drew water from the cistern. Claudine regarded these conveniences dubiously, wondering how close an acquaintance she was expected to have with them.

"I've hired a cook and a maid," Barret informed her, reading her expression correctly.

"Ah? *Bon,*" Claudine said firmly, "because I have never so much as boiled an egg, and I should without doubt set fire to myself with that stove."

Barret grabbed her around the waist. "Well, what the hell are you good for?" he inquired, grinning.

"I shall demonstrate, maybe," Claudine said, with a wicked light in her eyes. She ducked away from him. "*When* I have seen the house." She scurried through the door as Barret came after her, and fled up the stairs, laughing.

Above were two spacious bedrooms and a dressing room, and a third room, unfurnished, which had been intended as a nursery. Barret whisked her by that door. *His* children were going to grow up in *his* house. He had already decided that, but there was still the matter of convincing Claudine, and he thought instinctively that she might be more pliable after the nervousness and anticipation of their first day alone together were over. And he could probably think straighter, Barret decided ruefully. Claudine, sidetracked by the elegant furnishings of her new bedroom, was staring about her with delight.

Barret hugged her, entranced by her obvious pleasure in the room he had furnished for her. He had plenty of money. There was no reason why Claudine shouldn't have her nest as she liked it. He kissed her, poking himself in the eye with the stiff ends of the tignon. "Take that thing off."

Claudine complied, her eyes dancing. Now that the moment was at hand, she found that she wasn't frightened at all. The unaccustomed sensations that Barret provoked in her seemed to lead her on. The man in her arms was still darling Barret, humorous, kindly, and a little stocky in the middle, but when his hands roved over her back and shoulders, parts of her body that no one had ever touched cried out for *him* to touch them. He never would be a cavalier, that ideal figure of romance that her friends sighed over. There was something more real, more intimate, about Barret. She loved him with her heart; now she yearned overwhelmingly to love him with her body.

She laughed and cuddled against his chest while he pulled the pins out of her hair and draped it around her shoulders like a shawl. When he began to undo the hooks down the back of her dress, she didn't need to remember Tante Clélie's instructions that a gentleman enjoyed himself more if a lady took an active part in her own seduction. Her hands went of their own volition to his waistcoat buttons and then his shirtfront, patting, touching, exploring with interest. Barret undid the long row of buttons that closed the wrists of her princess gown, untied her petticoat strings, and peeled gown and petticoats down over her hips with a flourish. Then he stood docilely while she undid his shirt. His chest and shoulders were hard, unexpectedly muscled. While she wrestled with the buttons of his pantaloons, his fingers stroked her spine and backside in a way that made her tingle. She pulled at a recalcitrant button, and Barret ran his hand suddenly between her legs so that she jumped and flung herself against his chest.

"Tante Clélie neglected your education," he whispered in her ear. His breath was warm and his voice low, and it made her quiver. "The most important thing a woman should know is how to get a man out of his pantaloons." He undid the button himself and kicked the pantaloons off, together with his boots. They stood for a moment in their underwear, regarding each other with satisfaction.

Barret sat down on the bed and patted it invitingly. Claudine sat down beside him, her long curls falling over the ruffles of her chemise and into her lap. Barret pulled her feet up onto the bed and drew her stockings off. He bent and kissed her bare ankles.

"I want you more than I ever wanted anything else," he said, smiling, as if that idea was a pleasure to him.

Claudine scooted along the bed so that most of the rest of her was in his lap too. "Everyone always talks about love as if one became a sort of lunatic under its influence," she observed. "No one ever told me that it was *fun*."

Barret pulled her more firmly onto his lap. "It gets more fun," he assured her.

She wrapped her arms around his neck, drawing him into a deep, lingering kiss, feeling her heart thud and her body waken to new desires as his hands roved over her. He pulled at her corset hooks, at the waist strings of her pantalets, throwing each delicate scrap of silk and lace into a heap on the silvery blue, lily-patterned carpet. When she was naked in his lap, he stroked her breasts, her belly, and then very gently eased his hands between her thighs. His blood pounded in his ears, and he shook with desire, but he made himself manipulate her gently, stroking and exploring with the tips of his fingers until he was rewarded by a sigh of pleasure from Claudine, and she leaned backward in his arms, opening herself to him to do as he wished. He laid her across the watered silk coverlet, nuzzling her breasts and rib cage while he pulled off his drawers.

Claudine sighed and looked at him through sleepy-lidded eyes as he positioned himself above her. Her cheeks were flushed pink, her lips full. She looked at his naked body with curiosity and desire. There was no fear. He could enter and be welcome; it was where he belonged.

He stroked her again with his fingers, feeling the delicate wetness of her desire. With a groan he pushed himself into that welcoming place, gently but with a pent-up urgency that made her gasp. He rocked back and forth, his breathing coming faster, and buried his face in her hair.

A curious sensation began to mount within her, but a few minutes later when, spent, he pulled himself away, she winced. What she had welcomed so eagerly a short time ago seemed now to have rubbed her raw.

Barret gave her a sympathetic kiss. "One gets accustomed quickly. I promise. And then it's better yet."

Claudine laid her head against his shoulder. "I don't see how it could be." She didn't care if she was sore. "Would you think I was totally brazen if I told you that I never did anything in my life that felt that good?"

Barret shook his head solemnly. "Totally brazen. Most distressing. And I thought you were so ladylike." He grinned. "Just you wait."

"Maybe we could do it again?" Claudine suggested. "So I could get accustomed?"

Barret threw back his head and laughed. "Ha! I have you in my power." He looked at her lovingly. "My darling girl, we'll do it as often as you can stand me."

Claudine sighed. "For six months out of the year. Barret, will you write to me when you're in Charleston? You have to, or I don't think I can stand it. It is all very well to be established, but I want *you*, not just a pretty, empty house." She looked away from him as she spoke. One wasn't supposed to ask that, it was not part of the bargain, but she couldn't help it.

"I think," Barret said, "that now is the time to tell you what I've been thinking of." He rolled over and leaned on his elbows. "Now you hear me out and don't say anything till I've finished. Promise?"

She nodded apprehensively. He looked very solemn.

"I'm going to marry you," Barret said.

Claudine stared at him as if she thought he had lost his mind. "That isn't even legal," she said.

"It's legal enough some places," Barret said. "Claudine, *if* we could do it, *would* you?"

"I don't know," she whispered. "I used to think that that was what I wanted—to be like the white mademoiselles. But now— You can't have thought it through! It would ruin you!"

Barret took her hand, pulled her out of bed, and led her over to the cheval glass that stood in the corner. "Look at yourself," he commanded. Claudine's skin was as light as his own, with no telltale change in color to the palms of her hands or the soles of her little feet. Her features were finely chiseled, and her curling long brown hair was soft and wispy. "You *are* white," he said. "You are seven-eighths white."

"It's the last eighth that counts," Claudine said bitterly.

"Not," Barret said, with a strange expression, "if no one finds out. You can take my word for that."

"You mean, pass?" Claudine looked at him over her shoulder, frightened.

"It's been done," Barret said dryly. "If one black great-grandparent can make you black, then the other seven can damn well make you white." It was chilly in the room, and they were both naked. He put his arms around her, drawing her away from the mirror and back to the bed.

"My darling, I've thought and thought. I don't want a mistress, I want a wife—I want you. I love you. How can I let our children grow up as you did? And what about you when I die? I'm more than twenty years older. What kind of a time would you have of it, living alone in Charleston?"

"Barret, do you mean go home with you to *Charleston?*"

"Where else? Were you thinking I'd take you to hide on the frontier for the rest of our lives? Damned if I will!" He pulled her into his arms and held her against him. "Are you scared?"

"Yes," she said into his chest. "I'm afraid I will ruin you."

"No," Barret said. "Everyone is always very horrified by the notion, but it isn't as hard as you think. I know of someone who has done it, and no one ever found them out."

"Are you certain?"

"Yes, so trust me." He lifted her away from him and looked at her. "Here, are you crying? My chest's all wet."

Claudine sniffled and wiped her face with the back of her hand, a gesture Barret found oddly endearing. "Would you truly be happier that way?"

Barret pointed a finger at her. "If you will marry me, my darling, there is nothing that would make me happier."

"Aren't you afraid?"

Barret chuckled. Now that he had made up his mind to do it, oddly enough, he wasn't. "Only of Tante Clélie," he said. He pushed her down on the bed again and began kissing her throat and shoulders. "Now I am going to make love to you again," he whispered. "You can give me your answer when you're ready to."

Claudine's hands fluttered against his back. Barret had offered her what she had always thought she wanted and would never have. Now the idea terrified her. If she married him, she might someday cause his ruin. If she refused him, he would never be happy. She pulled his body down to cover hers. She could not say no. Better to be happy than miserable and safe.

"Happy?" Tante Clélie stared at the two of them in pure horror. She set her teacup down with a clink into its saucer. "Only a fool is totally happy, and you, M'sieu Forbes, appear to me to be a greater fool than *le bon Dieu* created room for in this world."

"Very possibly," Barret said. He wouldn't be surprised, but he didn't care. He felt a little drunk. Claudine sat beside him, looking pale and determined.

"And you, Claudine! Your position in life may chafe you, but that you would do a thing so wickedly foolish! M'sieu Forbes, she is only seventeen! She has not sense, it would appear. But you—"

"I have not sense either," Barret said. "Let us admit that. But Claudine has said she will have me, and I'm going to take her to Charleston."

"And foist her off on the society of Charleston!" Tante Clélie closed her eyes a moment in pain. "Who will of a certainty find out. And if they do not, Claudine will go in fear all her life that they will." She opened her eyes and cast a penetrating glance at her niece. "Is this not true?"

"Probably, Tante," Claudine said, her hands clasped tightly in her lap. "But I will do it anyway, since Barret wants it."

"You are not going to be afraid," Barret said firmly. "If you think as if you are white, act as if you are white, there won't be any reason for anyone to let it cross their minds that you aren't. If eveyone's sins were known, you probably *are* as white as some of them."

Tante Clélie snorted. "The possibility of a scandal of one's own does not generally prevent the mention of someone else's difficulties. *Au contraire.*"

"Without wishing to boast," Barret said mildly, "I come from a very old family. And my sister, Alice, is a formidable woman, whom it does not pay to annoy. Charleston society will be prudent enough to find other sources of gossip unless we give them a very good reason, which we do not intend to do."

"Ah, this sister. And what will she say, M'sieu Forbes, when you bring home a wife with no family?"

"A great deal, no doubt," Barret said. "But Claudine thinks she can stand her for my sake, and Alice can only push me as far as I let her, since her fortune was left in my hands unless she marries—which, at this point, is highly unlikely. You leave Alice to me." Alice had a managing nature, but Barret thought she was going to get a surprise once Claudine grew more sure of herself. His beloved, he suspected, had a managing streak of her own that might well prove a match for Alice.

Tante Clélie lifted her eyes to heaven as if imploring *le bon Dieu* to endow her niece with the good sense she was so obviously lacking, since her protector showed no signs of having any himself. "And what of Claudine's papa?"

Claudine had been sitting silently through this exchange, but now she gave her aunt a stubborn look that boded no good. "He is coming to see me tomorrow. He knows that I am spoken for, but not by whom. I will have to tell him about Barret anyway, so now I will tell him all of it."

"I'll tell him with you," Barret said.

"No. This is for me to do. And if I cannot, then how can I have the courage for Charleston?"

Barret gave her an approving nod. "Atta girl. I'll talk to Paul anyway, but I'll let you have first shot at him." Once Claudine had screwed her courage to the sticking point, it appeared that she wasn't going to let him down.

Tante Clélie gave them both a look of doom. "We may as well have tea," she announced dismally, "since it seems likely that tomorrow we shall all be thrown into the street."

Paul handed over his hat and walking stick and allowed Thomy to escort him into Tante Clélie's parlor. He thought Thomy had a skittish look about him, which was unusual.

"Miss Claudine, she waitin' for you." Thomy rolled an apprehensive eye at Paul and backed out of the parlor.

"Good afternoon, Claudine." Paul regarded his octoroon daughter with his usual mixture of affection and embarrassment. She was a very self-possessed little soul, and he never knew quite what to make of her. "Good afternoon, Papa." Claudine rose and invited him to a chair. "Will you take tea?"

Paul thought she also looked a little skittish, and he noted the absence of Tante Clélie. "Thank you," he said gravely, watching her pour for him. "Your aunt does not join us?"

"No," Claudine said. She put a lump of sugar in his tea and added a dollop of cream. "Tante Clélie has gone to bed with a sick headache and says that if I am to disgrace us all, I must do it by myself."

Paul accepted the tea with a reassuring look at his daughter. "That has an ominous sound to it," he said, smiling. "Have you refused your offer? Your aunt tells me it is a very eligible one, but I won't have you accept a man you can't like."

"No, I have accepted it," Claudine said. She began to pour her own tea and discovered that her hand was shaking, so she set the pot down. She wanted her father's approval desperately. "I have accepted, but to be married. Would you like to hear the worst now, or would you like to have tea first and brace yourself?"

Paul set his cup down. "After an introduction like that, I don't see how anyone could have tea first."

"No, I suppose not," Claudine said. "Tante Clélie says she will never be able to eat another bite again, and my death will be on her head."

Paul snorted, amused. "I assume that your aunt intended that you become a gentleman's companion. But a marriage among the *gens de couleur* is certainly no disgrace. If you feel that that would make you happier, I will talk to your aunt for you."

"He isn't of the *gens de couleur,* Papa. He's white."

"Claudine, that is not possible!" Paul was shocked.

"It's possible if I'm brave enough." Claudine's eyes welled up with tears as she looked at him. "It's possible if you don't tell on me."

"My dear girl—" Paul floundered helplessly. This was his own daughter. How could he tell her she was not good enough for any man? "It wouldn't be necessary for me to tell," he said gently. "The whole city would know."

"That isn't the worst of it," Claudine said. "He isn't from New Orleans, Papa. And he's a friend of yours."

"Good God—Barret!" Innumerable small oddities and indications now informed him suddenly why Barret had been so much in New Orleans. Paul thought of Sallie's reaction and shuddered. But as he looked at Claudine's stricken face, the thought crept unbidden into his mind that Sallie would not necessarily need to know. They would meet, of course, eventually. Was Claudine's parentage a secret that Paul and Claudine could keep forever, or would someone stumble sometime, and disaster follow?

"Does—does he intend to take you to Charleston?" Paul asked, unutterably shocked at himself for even entertaining the idea further. "And—forgive me for asking, but I must—does your wish to marry Barret stem from a wish to pass yourself for white or from love of Barret?"

"I should greatly wish to be white," Claudine said bitterly, "if I could *be* white. As it is, I shall be terrified every day of my life. But I love him, and if he wants me to marry him, I'll do it. And then my children won't have to be like me."

Paul sighed. "If no one finds out. If they do, even your marriage can be voided."

"No," Claudine said firmly. "We will go to be married in a state where it's legal. Then if all else fails, I will still have that. The children will have that."

"Mon Dieu." Paul began to understand why Tante Clélie had taken her headache and gone to bed with it. He looked at Claudine. She looked very young and vulnerable, but there was a stubborn line to her round little chin that said she was prepared to see this thing through. And if she were willing to take a risk, how could he tell her that she couldn't have what his other children were assured by their birth?

Her mother loved me, he thought sadly. *And what good did I ever do her?* Or, for that matter, Sallie. Sallie had loved him too . . . once. He got up from his chair and went and sat beside Claudine. She looked at him hopefully.

"I love you," Paul said tentatively.

"I know you do," Claudine said. "It took me a long time to understand that, after I understood how . . . things were. But I know you do. Can't you wish me happiness?"

"I do. I'm also afraid for you."

Claudine's mouth twisted a little. "And not of a family scandal?"

"Of that, too," Paul admitted. "My wife has a great deal to bear just now. But more than that, I fear for you. You will have to be so careful." He paused helplessly. There was no easy answer. At last he said, "If this is what you truly want, I won't stand in your way."

Claudine's eyes met Paul's. She smiled suddenly, her face crinkling up in happiness. "Thank you!" She put her arms out, and for the first time in their lives that Paul could remember, he held his unacknowledged daughter to his heart.

With the grinding still going on, Paul never managed to catch up to Barret Forbes—who, he suspected, was also looking for a quiet half hour with him—until the next evening after dinner, when the household gathered in the parlor. Denis was still recuperating upstairs, and Lucien had gone to play chess with him in a display of brotherly solicitude that was calculated, Paul suspected grimly, to soften his father's attitude toward Lucien himself. That still left the parlor overly full of women, and Paul and Barret, eyeing each other warily, sat down to outwait them.

Tante Doudouce was reading *L'Abeille,* the French edition of *The Bee,* and commenting cozily on the social notes therein. Paul sent Testut for a bottle of whiskey. It looked like a long wait, and Barret looked like he could use it. Neither one wanted to occasion even vague curiosity about their conversation by going elsewhere.

"Ah! Agnes Couré is to be married." Tante Doudouce peered at the paper in nearsighted interest. "To Monsieur DuPlessis from Plaquemines Parish. DuPlessis . . . let me think, didn't their cousin marry a Rillieux?"

"So did Eugene DuPlessis," Sallie said over her embroidery. "Two of them, to be exact. *And* a Couré. He's three times widowed. If I were Agnes Couré, I think I'd look a little further."

"Poor thing, I expect she has," Hollis said sweetly. "But she has such a rabbity face. Girls like that always seem to have to settle for men old enough to be their fathers." She shot a speaking glance at Felicie.

Felicie gave her a benign smile. "I expect a mature gentleman requires a wife whose head isn't stuffed with nothing but clothes and parties and how much prettier she thinks she is than everyone else. It's amazing how quickly conceited girls get that stupid look about them."

"Felicie!" Sallie said. "That was *too* rude." She eyed Hollis. "However provoked you feel you may have been."

"Well, don't think anyone's going to let you make us all look ridiculous by marrying an old widower," Hollis snapped, "because we won't!"

"Mama!"

"Hollis, Felicie's marriage, whenever it may occur, is not your business."

"Well, it's my business if everyone says my sister had to take a man twice her age because she was just dyin' on the vine! I'd be so embarrassed I'd just die!"

"Or so jealous?" Sallie suggested.

"Jealous? Of a baby-faced little—"

Felicie stood. "Hollis DuMontaigne, you're a spiteful cat!"

Paul got up. "I believe," he said, "I'll take a breath of air. Barret, would you care to join me?"

"Certainly," Barret said, rising with alacrity.

Paul collected the whiskey bottle and his glass on the way out. He wasn't sure whether he was using his daughters' squabbling as an excuse to talk to Barret, or Barret as an excuse to escape from his daughters.

Barret seemed to rather suspect the latter. "Ruthless of you," he commented as they settled themselves on the rear veranda, out of earshot of the parlor.

"Sallie can deal with them better than I can," Paul said, unabashed. He poured himself a drink. "Daughters can be the devil of a nuisance."

Barret chuckled. "Touching on which, you wish to inquire how the devil I met yours and precisely what my intentions are."

"Astute of you," Paul said. "Have a drink, Barret, you're going to need it."

"I don't doubt it," Barret said.

"Good Christ, man, you're forty years old! What the hell are you thinking of, risking your entire social standing in Charleston for a seventeen-year-old octoroon girl?"

"Damn it, Paul, she's your daughter! You can't want her to lead the kind of life those girls do!"

"The kind of life her mother led?" Paul inquired.

"To put it bluntly. How is my marrying Claudine worse than your taking her mother for a mistress?"

"Socially or ethically?"

"Ethically, blast it. I'm well aware of the social consequences."

"I'd like to be sure of that," Paul said. "I'm beginning to wonder if the pair of you haven't both lost your minds. And as to the ethics, I'm aware that I'm treading on thin ice there." Paul ran a hand through his hair. "You *do* intend to marry her? Because if you tell her you will and don't, I'll come looking for you."

"Of course I intend to marry her!" Barret shouted. He lowered his voice hastily. "Thanks to her aunt's very practical arrangements, I could have what I wanted without marrying her if I were so inclined. What kind of oaf do you think I am?"

"I don't," Paul said. "But before I lend my countenance to any such harebrained scheme as Claudine talked me into yesterday, I want to be sure."

"Well, now you are," Barret said. "Do you want to comment further on the difference in our ages?"

"No," Paul said shortly, thinking with some embarrassment of himself and Adele. "Don't, for pity's sake, mention it tonight," he went on hastily, "but I rather think Roman Prevost is going to ask me for Felicie, and if she wants him, I suppose I'll agree despite their ages. So I suppose I'd better agree to you and

Claudine as well." Paul sipped his whiskey moodily. Some unseen power seemed to have come along and stirred up his orderly world with a rake. "You met her at the Quadroon Ball, I suppose."

Barret nodded. "I'd seen her before, Paul. I couldn't get her out of my mind. Oh, Lord." A thought struck him. "Lucien arranged the introduction. I have a sinking feeling that Lucien knew who she was."

Paul stared off the veranda into the darkness. "I wouldn't be surprised. I'm beginning to realize that Lucien is like that."

"Mmmm." Barret made an indeterminate noise of agreement or understanding. "Your Denis is a fine boy," he commented. "Uh, recent peccadilloes notwithstanding." He felt entitled to poke his nose that far into Paul's business since Paul had poked his into Barret's.

"He is," Paul said. He reached for the whiskey bottle again. "Don't worry, you can just leave Lucien to me."

They sat in a meditative but companionable silence until Testut came to inform them that the ladies had all gone to bed.

"If you gemmun wants to go back in de parlor, de coast is clear."

XXIII

The

Bridge

GINGERLY, DENIS SWUNG his feet over the edge of the bed, then winced a little as he stood. He felt the bandages around his chest, but nothing seemed to be loose, so he padded across the braided rug to the armoire. Mammy and his mother had finally allowed him to go back to his own rooms in the *garçonnière* he shared with Lucien, and with no one to watch him, Denis intended to see Dinah.

He took off his nightshirt and began to pull on his drawers as quickly as possible. The mornings were cold now. He'd bet Dinah was freezing in that shanty her father called a cabin, and Denis had a warm cloak he'd begged from Felicie, which he was going to take to her. Dinah had walked all the way from Bayou Rouge to Belle Marie every day, Felicie said, braving Mama and Mammy and everyone else who didn't approve of her, just to ask how he was.

Denis pulled on a flannel hunting shirt and an old leather jacket and picked the cloak off the linen chest at the foot of his bed. Lucien was still asleep in his room across the hall, and, keeping an eye out for anyone who might decide to order him back to bed, Denis set out through the drifting mist that came off the swampland, to the back door of the stable. Will had been up a good two hours and was out in the paddock with a yearling colt. Denis got his saddle and slung it on old Butterfly's back. "Buttertub," who had been Sallie's mount for years, had a rolling gait like a rocking chair and a disposition placid enough to carry two without complaint.

The bayou land was still fog-shrouded and eerie as Denis rode Butterfly up to the Michelets' cabin. Rafe Michelet, shotgun in hand, loomed up out of the mist on the front stoop like the demon huntsman from *Der Freischütz*.

"Ha, Denis! We hear you get shot, yes," he called cheerfully, dispelling this operatic illusion. He hopped down from the stoop, his dogs at his heel. "You come see my sister, stay 'way from those city *mesdames*, you not get shot again, *hein*?"

"I hope not," Denis said, climbing down and wondering if everyone in Louisiana were so conversant with his private business. "Where's Dinah?"

Rafe obliged him with a piercing yell, which brought Dinah out of the cabin, drying her hands on her apron. Her face lit up when she saw Denis, and she ran toward him. "Can I hug you, me, or do I hurt something?"

"Carefully," Denis said. He put his good arm around her and eyed Rafe. "Go hunt squirrels," he suggested.

Rafe departed. He considered it his business to encourage Denis in his courtship. Denis brought practical presents like sacks of flour or vegetables from Belle Marie's gardens. Old Victorien had never had the urge to plant a garden, but he and his brood were happy to eat out of the DuMontaignes'.

When Rafe had vanished into the fog, Denis bent his head and kissed Dinah. Her lips were soft and warm in the chill mist, and kissing her was like holding his hands to a fire. His lips lingered, unwilling to draw away. When at last he lifted his head, his hazel eyes were serious and loving. "I missed you," he whispered. "I'm sorry I made a fool of myself over that woman."

Dinah lowered her eyes. "She is not my business, her. I don' own you."

"You're wrong," Denis said. He lifted her chin so that her eyes looked into his. "I love you. You own me lock, stock, and barrel. What are we going to do about it?"

Dinah took a deep breath. "I have an idea."

"Me too," Denis grinned. "I think you better hear mine first. But not with your brother and your sister breathing down my neck. Can you get up on Buttertub behind me?"

"I think so," Dinah said, "if Buttertub, she stan' still. This horse an' me, we understan' each other." She rubbed Butterfly's nose, and the mare whiffled at her hopefully. "I don' bring you no sugar this time," Dinah said. "You let me up anyway, I make it up to you." She held the mare's head while Denis mounted, and then put her bare foot in the stirrup and pulled herself up behind him.

"Damn it, Dinah, don't you have any shoes?"

"Not that don' pinch me, no," Dinah said.

"Well, I'll get you a pair in New Orleans," Denis said, outraged. "You can't go barefoot in the middle of winter. I brought you a cloak, too. It's tied on there behind the saddle."

"Denis, you don' need to give me things."

"The hell I don't. I'm gonna—" He broke off. He was damned if he'd propose to a girl who was sitting behind him on a horse where he couldn't even look at her. He turned Butterfly onto the path that led to the clearing by the bayou bank where the otters lived. He and Dinah ducked their heads under the bare, swinging branches as Butterfly pushed her way through, then Denis drew rein and let Dinah slide down before he dismounted. With only one arm, he didn't feel very gallant, letting his beloved climb on and off horses by herself, but Dinah didn't seem to mind. Denis dropped Butterfly's reins, and she nosed contentedly for a few sprigs of withered grass. He held out his arms, and Dinah came into them.

He held her for a moment, drinking in the fresh rainwater smell of her. All the other women he knew always smelled like lavender or lemon verbena or jasmine. Dinah just smelled like Dinah. He rubbed his face against her brownish-gold hair. It was thick and newly washed, and it slipped from the two hairpins she had put in it and tumbled around his hands. Dinah sighed contentedly, pressing herself into his arms, and somehow, before he knew it, they were lying in the damp pine needles. If his chest hurt, his mind was taking no notice.

Dinah lay on her back in the pine needles, looking at him. Her dress, much washed and patched, was a fine French calico in a palmetto leaf pattern that someone must have given her. It was too tight across the front, and the shape of her breasts showed tantalizingly through the cloth. Like the rest of the Michelet women, Dinah wore no corset. She probably didn't own one. She touched his cheeks with the palms of her hands. "Me, I love you too," she whispered. Whatever he wanted, she thought, she would give to him. And if he didn't want her anymore after that, at least she'd have this time. It wouldn't be long before they married him with some New Orleans plantation girl, not a Cajun girl with no shoes.

Denis leaned over her, his hands tangled in her hair. His head was swimming, whether from his own infirmity or from the proximity of Dinah, he didn't know. It didn't matter. There was a strange air of witchery about the clearing, of mist-shrouded bayou

magic. He fastened his lips on Dinah's warm, inviting ones and
felt her fingers brush the back of his neck and her slim young body
move under his. She shifted to cradle him in her arms, and the
calico skirts fell away from her knees. Denis had a glimpse of
smooth white calf and bare knee dappled by the shadows of the
trees and the dancing light off the water. His heart thudding, he
cupped one kneecap with his hand and ran his fingers lightly down
her shin to caress a slim ankle.

"Je t'aime," Dinah whispered, and Denis shivered, overcome
with longing, and let his hands go free to explore those bare
shade-dappled legs, upward to cool white thighs hidden beneath
calico skirts, upward still into warm and secret places behind the
soft brown-gold smoke that was the color of fallen leaves. The
shadows wavered before his eyes, and Dinah smiled out of them at
him. Half-unconscious of his own actions, he pushed her knees
apart and laid his body on top of her.

A feeling of fulfillment, of belonging, came over him, followed
by a light-studded darkness that swam in his eyes. He laid his head
on Dinah's shoulder and sank into it.

He awoke to find Dinah bending over him, half laughing, half
frightened. "Denis! Ah, *bon*, you wake up. I am afraid I kill
you."

"What happened?"

"You pass out," Dinah said severely. "Also you are bleeding
again, like a pig, yes. I take your handkerchief an' make new
bandage, an' I think she is stop now, but—"

Denis groaned. He sat up and inspected the bandages on his
chest, now bared. "It's all right, it's healing nicely. Leboeuf said
so. I've just opened up one of his sutures." He put his head in his
hands. "Dinah, can't I ever do anything right with you? I didn't
mean to do that at all, and then I pass out in the middle."

"I *think* you had finish," Dinah commented.

Denis chuckled weakly. "Maybe I had, at that. Dinah, I'm
sorry."

"For what? For make love to me or for pass out?" Dinah
inquired.

Denis put his arm around her with caution. "Both," he said
ruefully. "My darling girl, forgive me. I didn't bring you here to
seduce you, but you're so—you're so beautiful," he said huskily,
"and I don't think I'm quite right in the head."

"I don' think is seduction if I think of it too," Dinah offered.

"That's beside the point. I'm older than you, and I ought to
know better. I came here to propose to you," Denis said. He

grinned at her. "And then afterward, well, maybe . . . But I meant to propose first."

"Now I know you not right in the head," Dinah informed him severely. "An' all your brains they leak out with the blood maybe."

"Maybe," Denis conceded, "but not where you're concerned. Can't you say anything more romantic than that?"

"Non," Dinah said firmly. "Or I get to thinkin' as crazy as you, maybe. Nobody gon' let you get yourself married with me."

Denis tightened his arm around her possessively. "Watch me."

Dinah shook her head, her brown eyes welling up with tears. "You get yourself married with me, how you gon' show me to your friends? I can be no lady, Denis. My family live always since a hundred years on the bayou, and always we is like this. How I'm gon' change, *hein*?"

"Honey, I don't want you to change." Denis looked at her gravely. "I'm in love with Dinah, remember? Not with a fancy accent."

"You don' think about it," Dinah said. "The way you think, she is crazy, yes. All the time I embarrass you, me. An' you friends, they laugh, and nobody they are receive us, no."

Denis pulled her head down onto his shoulder and thought about it for a minute. She was right about that; he was just too damned pigheaded to care. But Dinah would care, and she wouldn't be happy. He started to say that he would teach her, but he couldn't teach a girl the things she would need to know. The answer leapt into his mind, and he took her by the shoulders and kissed her, his eyes dancing. "I've got it! Don't you worry about a thing. You meet me here tomorrow, and tell your mama you're gonna be gone a few days." Her mama probably wouldn't even notice, he thought, angry that no one had ever taken proper care of Dinah. "I'll bring you some clothes to wear tomorrow, and then I'll buy you things when we know what you'll need."

"Denis, what you thinkin' of?" Dinah eyed him suspiciously. "I think you crazy as a loon, you. You have still these fever from sit on wet ground."

Denis just smiled mysteriously. "It's a secret. You'll see."

"Denis, who is it that live here?" Dinah looked at him nervously as Denis twisted the bell of the pale yellow house on Toulouse Street. He was still wearing his mysterious expression when he had met her in the clearing that morning and handed her a dress and bonnet and mantelette of Felicie's, and a pair of boots,

which, he told her chuckling, he had filched from Hollis, because
Felicie's looked too small. Dinah shuddered to think what
Mamzelle Hollis would have to say to that, but presumably Hollis
had so many pairs of shoes, she wouldn't miss one.

Dinah looked down at her feet admiringly. They were encased
in a pair of neatly laced, soft ankle boots made of bottle-green
kidskin. Never in her life had Dinah worn anything so fine as
those boots, or the green challis gown woven with little yellow
flowers, the camel's-hair mantelette, and the bonnet of brown
shirred silk. Denis had turned his back gallantly while Dinah had
dressed herself in this finery, and then they had ridden Butterfly
double to a woodyard along the levee where the steamers sometimes put in, and given the woodyard man a picayune to stable
Butterfly until Denis came back. Then they had flagged down the
Belle Creole, the packet steamer that meandered up and down the
river above New Orleans carrying passengers and light cargo. The
Belle Creole in itself had been an adventure, and Dinah had been
too excited to do anything but hold Denis's hand and stare.

Now she gathered up all her courage to keep herself from
bolting like a rabbit away from this tall yellow house with its
graceful wrought-iron balconies and air of formidable grandeur.
She tugged his arm again. "Denis—"

"You'll see," Denis whispered. The door swung open to reveal
an elderly Negro in a cutaway coat, to whom Denis presented his
card, with a request to know whether Mademoiselle Claudine was
receiving today. Her address had not been hard to discover with
discreet inquiry. He wondered if she might not refuse to meet him.
He gave the butler a hopeful smile. "I have a favor to beg of her."

Thomy took the card warily. Mademoiselle was within, certainly. Since she and Monsieur Forbes had conceived a notion of what
was to Thomy the utmost madness, she had ceased to use the new
house on Rampart Street, lest anyone should see her there with
him and inconveniently remember it later. Whether she would
wish to receive Monsieur Denis DuMontaigne was entirely
another matter.

Claudine, when consulted, looked puzzled, and Tante Clélie
threw up her hands and rolled her eyes heavenward. "Ah! Already
it starts. He has come to threaten who knows what if you marry his
papa's friend!"

"I dunno, Miss Clélie," Thomy muttered. "He got a girl with
him. Not one o' his sisters, neither."

"A girl?" Claudine looked baffled. "Papa promised me he
wouldn't tell his children. Thomy, you had better show them in."

Denis and Dinah; admitted to the parlor, stood staring, Dinah at the opulence of French silk hangings and ormolu mirrors, and Denis at his half sister.

"You do look like Emilie," he said suddenly. "And I am very happy to meet you." He held out his hands and smiled, and his hazel eyes exuded such genuine friendliness that Claudine relaxed.

She gave him her hand. "May I present my aunt, Madame Belloc."

Denis took Tante Clélie's hand in turn and kissed it. He turned to Dinah. "And may I present Mademoiselle Ermandine Michelet. Dinah, this is my half sister Claudine Belloc and this is her aunt, Tante Clélie."

Dinah, who by this time could be surprised by nothing, curtsied first to Claudine and then to Tante Clélie, whose darker skin tone proclaimed without words the nature of Denis's relationship to her niece. She found Tante Clélie terrifying, but Claudine was more reassuring. Her round, pretty face bore an air of friendly inquiry.

"Enchantée," Claudine said gravely. "Do sit down. Will you take a glass of Madeira?"

"Thank you, no." Denis sat Dinah down in a chair upholstered in moiré silk, where she perched uncomfortably on the edge. Claudine and Tante Clélie looked equally perplexed. "I am going to marry Dinah," Denis announced. "There has been, er, a certain amount of argument on the subject."

"These argument, she come from me too," Dinah said firmly. "Denis marry himself with me, I make him embarrass, all the time."

This speech left no doubt in either lady's mind as to what the objections had been. Tante Clélie said in a not unkindly voice, "You are quite right, child. There are some rules of society that it is not for us to go against." She followed this with a speaking look at her niece.

"Nonsense," Denis said briskly. "The only thing Dinah needs is knowledge. And for that, all she needs is a good teacher."

Claudine broke into laughter as the light dawned upon her. "And you want *me* to teach her? M'sieu DuMontaigne, that is more ironic than you know."

"Maybe," Denis said stubbornly. "I know that the ladies of your world have an excellent knowledge of how to go on properly in company. Better manners than my sisters, probably. Dinah needs to learn a better French accent, and English entirely. She needs to know how to dress and how to make conversation and how to go on at a dinner party. Now you tell me who's better qualified to teach her all that.''

"Mon Dieu," Tante Clélie said faintly. She looked at Dinah. "Are you willing to learn all these tedious things, child?''

Dinah looked admiringly at Denis. "I think is very good idea, me. An' I won' marry with him otherwise, even if his mama, she let us, which she is not do anyway maybe, but I try. Denis," she explained gravely to Tante Clélie, "he say he don' care how I talk, or how I am act at these dinner with his friends, but *I* care, me. So if you teach me, I am learn them.''

"You have good nerves, at any rate," Claudine said. She smiled, and Dinah smiled back shyly. Really, she would be beautiful with a little care, Claudine thought. She had a wild, wood-nymph grace, and her devotion to Denis was obvious. Claudine looked at Tante Clélie helplessly. Denis would most certainly recognize her if she was introduced to him in the future as Barret's wife. If she taught his Cajun sweetheart to hold her own in the society the DuMontaignes moved in, he might be grateful enough to keep her secret.

"It is most unorthodox," Tante Clélie pronounced. Denis, grinning, knew that was an understatement. "But possible. Stand up, child." Dinah obediently stood. "Now walk across the room. Ah. *Bon.* Now turn. *Non, non!* Not with the arms out stiff like a gingerbread man! Pretend you are holding a bouquet. Relaxed, graceful. You are not a weathervane. Ah, better. Better. *Bon,* you may sit.

"Oui, c'est possible," she informed Denis. "But it will be a matter of much work. And also I must ask what arrangements are you prepared to make for all this?" Tante Clélie had not become as rich as she was by not counting her picayunes.

"Any that seem fair to you," Denis said. "I shall require your advice on the matter of her clothes as well.''

"You are wise to leave that to us. Men do not understand dress." Tante Clélie bent an appraising eye on Dinah. "She has good bone. That, at least, will not be a difficulty. Claudine, you will take Mademoiselle Dinah to your sitting room while I discuss business with M'sieu DuMontaigne. Then we begin this evening with this transformation. But we are not wizards, M'sieu. It will take time.''

"Now then, you may show M'sieu Denis what you have learned in a week.''

"Oui, Madame Belloc." Dinah waited while Denis held Tante

Clélie's chair for her, and then smiled shyly over her shoulder at him as he seated first Dinah and then Claudine at the table. Dinah wondered if he would approve of the change in her, and if it was worth the inordinate amount of money she thought he must be spending. A modiste of Tante Clélie's had come to the house and sewn furiously, and Dinah was elegantly and unfamiliarly attired in a low-necked dinner dress of oyster-color satin trimmed with bronze ruching at the hem and Mechlin lace at the neck. When Dinah had protested the cost of the latter, the modiste had turned pale and Tante Clélie had informed her firmly that a lady was known by the genuineness of her lace and the genuineness of her diamonds. Dinah had acquiesced before Tante Clélie suggested the diamonds as well.

Dinah saw Denis grinning broadly at her from across the table and lowered her eyes, embarrassed. That dress showed her whole front. She noted that it was no lower than Claudine's or Tante Clélie's, however. Although there were only the four of them, Tante Clélie had ordered a dinner of the utmost elegance, composed of sufficient courses for a formal party. Tante Clélie was dressed in ruby-red velvet trimmed with quantities of jet beading, and displayed among the jet was a brooch of rubies and diamonds. Claudine wore a gown of seafoam-green moiré, and her maid, Delilah, had dressed both her and Dinah's hair in the latest style from France, combed into smooth bands over the ears, with long ringlets arranged just below a knot of hair at the back of the head and ornamented with twisted strands of pearls and silk flowers.

Dinah looked at the bewildering array of china and silver flatware set before her and closed her eyes a moment, trying to remember Tante Clélie's instructions. Ah, *bon!* That was it. One simply used the implement on the outside and worked one's way in. If one did that, one should come out even with one's dinner. She picked up her soupspoon and beamed at Tante Clélie's approving nod.

Denis took a mouthful of soup, a cold vichyssoise, and raised his eyebrows. Tante Clélie's cook could have held her own in any house in the city. As the sole gentleman present, Thomy presented Denis with the wine. Denis sipped the splash that Thomy poured into his glass and gave his approval.

"And why is it that the gentleman always tastes the wine first?" Tante Clélie inquired of Dinah.

Dinah laid her soupspoon down in her bowl, then snatched it up and rested it on her plate instead. "To . . . to be sure it is good, not soured, and that it is not . . . corked?"

"*Bon!* She has an excellent memory," Tante Clélie informed Denis. With considerable interest, Tante Clélie had heard Dinah's history and come to the same inescapable conclusion that Denis had: that there was no way under heaven that Dinah could have been sired by Victorien Michelet. Tante Clélie thought that it would be very interesting to know who *had* fathered Dinah. Somewhere she was sure she had seen that color hair before. Tante Clélie gave up this line of speculation as she noticed Dinah looking with dismay at a plate upon which rested a whole lobster.

"And how does one deal with a lobster?" Tante Clélie resumed her lesson.

Claudine giggled. She had had a great deal of trouble in her schoolgirl days in dealing with a lobster herself.

"At home we hit him—it—with a hammer," Dinah said. "But I do not think that is *comme il faut*."

"Only at a picnic," Tante Clélie informed her. "And then you require a gentleman to do it for you. At the dinner table one uses a sharp knife, which you see before you, and one's fingers, only the tips."

"Followed," Claudine said, "by Thomy picking it up off the floor."

"Followed," Tante Clélie said reprovingly, "by the lobster fork. Mademoiselle Dinah has not the time to learn as you did, with lobsters in the lap."

Dinah took a deep breath and picked up her knife. She saw Denis watching her with amusement and shot him a baleful look. *I cut my fingers off maybe*, she thought, *but I open these lobster without he fall off the plate*. She colored as she saw Tante Clélie also watching her. Sometimes she thought that Madame Belloc read her thoughts, and Dinah was not allowed to think in anything but the proper French and English, which Tante Clélie and Claudine had been relentlessly instilling in her. *I will learn. Not "I am learn," but "I will learn."*

Dinah gripped the lobster with her fingertips and sliced quickly down the tail of the lobster. It opened into two perfect halves on her plate, and she laughed delightedly.

"Very neat," Tante Clélie said. "Next time it will help, however, if you do not look so determined, as if you are about to fight the bullfight, first."

* * *

"One, two, three! One, turn, three! *Don't* look at your feet."

In Denis's arms, Dinah spun around the parquet floor of Tante Clélie's parlor. They had rolled back the rug, and Claudine, at the pianoforte, accompanied their dance.

Denis guided Dinah around the room with a practiced arm. "You're doing fine, honey," he whispered.

"Madame Belloc says that when I have practiced enough, I will forget about my feet," Dinah said carefully, "and they will do what they are supposed to, without my thinking about them. Myself, I do not see how one is supposed to dance and talk and breathe at the same time. I am wear . . . *ing,* one of Mamzelle Claudine's corsets," she confided. "It has a board down the front, and I do not like this at all."

Denis sighed. "I know. You feel just like a beetle in a shell."

Dinah chuckled ruefully. "Or the poor lobster. There are so many things to wear under a dress like this. Madame Belloc, she say, says, I need camisoles and drawers, but I am not to mention them to you. It is indelicate."

"I see," Denis said. "Well, I won't tell on you. I feel sure she'll mention them herself." Madame Belloc had certainly mentioned everything else a young lady of fashion could possibly need, beginning with dress goods from Woodlief's and Barrière's, and lace from Mr. Syme on Royal Street, and *mantillas* and *visites* from Madame Frey, and ending with *chapeaux* from Olympe, whose bills were always as astronomical as her creations were ravishing.

Dinah looked up at him doubtfully. "Denis, this is cost you a great deal of money, yes?"

Denis swirled her past Tante Clélie with a flourish. "Fortunately for us, I *have* a great deal of money." He didn't mention that even his generous allowance was being rather strained by Olympe. His father would increase it upon his marriage. The fact that Paul might not increase anything if he didn't approve of the marriage was not something Denis felt inclined to consider just now. He felt too happy, and unaccustomedly reckless, to let money intrude upon his pride in his Dinah's accomplishments.

Claudine finished her piece and turned around to applaud the dancers.

"*Très bien,* we make progress," Tante Clélie said. "M'sieu Denis, you will leave her with us a few more days, and then we will send her home for a week and see if these things that we cram into *la petite*'s head will stay there."

* * *

Adele saw Denis coming along the bayou road and flattened herself against a tree trunk in the shadow of the leafless wood. He rode by without seeing her, and she thought, *He has been to see that girl on Bayou Rouge, and he has been out all night. If he gives me difficulties, I will tell his papa on him.* Adele made it her business to know where everyone on Belle Marie was. When Denis was out of sight, she slipped from the wood into the narrow road again. Just beyond, where the cane field ran down to the water, there was a deep, fifteen-foot-wide ditch, cut to keep the rise and fall of the bayou and surrounding swampland from flooding into the cane. It was nearly full of murky green water, and a low plank bridge crossed it to the road on the other side. Beside the road, leafless willows trailed their strands in the water. Adele hurried toward the bridge, her walking boots kicking up clumps of the damp, dead leaves that buried the road. She neither rode well nor liked horses, but she had begun to take a constitutional walk every morning before her breakfast. No one ever came this way, with one exception—Sallie DuMontaigne on her morning ride. Adele intended to be home and at the breakfast table before Sallie set out.

Adele walked to the center of the bridge and knelt down, feeling carefully along the underside beneath the rough planks. There were two planks rotted through, just in the center of the bridge, and Adele had contrived a way to put them to use. With exploring fingers, she found the braces that supported the center planks, took a hammer filched from Jem's workshop from the black sateen pocket that hung from the waist of her dress, and stretched herself full length across the bridge so that she could peer under it.

The green water was slimy and bubbled with the gases of decaying muck on the bottom. Adele regarded it distastefully and reached her arm, hammer in hand, under the bridge with caution. There were alligators in the swampland, a horror that Adele felt she was unlikely ever to become used to. The sort of murky, greasy water that ran in the ditch was just what they liked.

She swung the hammer against one of the center braces. It shuddered and moved a little, and she hit it again. There was a satisfying crack, and the wood split along its length. One more blow, and the brace hung useless. The same treatment sufficed for the second brace and left the rotting planks supported only at their ends. Adele scrambled to her feet and backed cautiously away from the middle of the bridge, dropping the hammer into her pocket.

* * *

There were home-cured bacon, steak, and buckwheat cakes for breakfast. They filled the dining room warmly with a beckoning aroma. Adele, who had carefully brushed the leaves and mud from her skirt, sat down to a plate of cakes and new eggs with a sense of having somehow crossed the Rubicon. For a moment there was a flash of sharp triumph on her face. When Sallie came down for breakfast in a riding habit, the look intensified, victorious and secretive as she watched Sallie out of the corners of her eyes.

She thinks she get Mister Paul to herself all mornin', Mammy Rachel thought, shepherding Emilie along behind Sallie. *She get a surprise when she find out he gone into New Orleans again to talk to Judge Craire 'bout Gabriel.* Mammy sighed. She didn't hold out much hope for Gabriel, but Mister Paul was a purely good man for tryin'.

Sallie ate a buttered egg, drank a cup of coffee, and stood up from the table again before the rest had finished. She was one of those people who either ate breakfast at one gulp, having other, better things to do, or lingered leisurely over it for an hour with the morning paper, depending on her mood. This morning Briar Rose was saddled and waiting for her, and Sallie wanted nothing so much as to get out of the house before she slapped Adele Scarron's sly face.

Adele watched her go with a furtive pleasure. The riding habit Sallie had chosen was a new one, of dark blue *gros de Naples*, with trousers underneath and a high crowned hat with a green *barège* veil to keep off the sun. The skirt was full, long, and heavy, and had to be carried over the wearer's arm when she was not mounted. Weighed down with that, Adele thought with satisfaction, she would most certainly drown if she unaccountably failed to break her neck.

"I am so happy to make your acquaintance, madame. Would Monsieur care for a cordial? It is so unseasonably hot just now, is it not?" Dinah gave her hand to her imaginary callers and fanned herself with a palmetto leaf. *"Bonjour, monsieur. Oh!"* She snatched the falling dictionary, which she had been endeavoring to balance on her head. It slithered from her grasp and thudded into the wet leaves. Dinah retrieved it and set it upon her head again. Madame Belloc maintained that such exercise improved the posture: "A woman who moves always as if she had a book upon her head cannot slouch."

Dinah sighed. She supposed that she would learn all this in time. For the moment she was just glad, yes, not to have a board down the front of her dress. She and Denis had agreed to leave her nice things with Madame Belloc because Maman would ask too many questions, and Sukie and Tassie would laugh. Already they were laughing at her for practicing Madame Belloc's lessons, and so Dinah had come out by the bayou, where she could have a little peace.

The hammering of hooves sounded behind her, and Dinah stepped hastily out of the road. She raised her hand shyly as Madame DuMontaigne galloped by on her little sorrel mare, but Sallie didn't even see her. Perched on her sidesaddle, Madame DuMontaigne rode as gracefully as if she were part of the horse, but Dinah caught a glimpse of her face as Briar Rose thudded past. *She is very angry,* Dinah thought, and prayed that it wasn't at Denis.

Sallie kicked Briar Rose down the road toward the ditch, furious at Adele for that sly, smug look, and at herself for caring. The heavy thud of hooves on wet leaves changed to a clatter on the bridge. In two strides Briar Rose went down in a tangle of flailing hooves and jagged splintered wood. Frantically Sallie wrenched her foot from the stirrup as she pitched forward. She landed heavily in the water, against piling, and clung to it, trying to drag herself back up. Briar Rose, thrashing and whinnying in fright, half in the water and half on the bridge, kicked out with an iron-shod forefoot and caught Sallie across the wrist. Excruciating pain ran up Sallie's arm, and her fingers opened and slipped from the piling. The green water was already dragging at the heavy skirts of her habit. Sallie clawed frantically for a handhold on the slick, wet wood, but the movement of her arm sent another wave of pain through her, and she slipped deeper into the water, carried by the current away from the shattered bridge. Inside tightly laced stays, she fought for enough breath to swim against the weight of her skirts and the slimy green murk in the ditch. The water was icy, and she felt frozen, as heavy as an anvil. She tore at the waist strings of her habit skirt, but they were stiff, swollen with water. The pain in her left arm was almost unbearable, and darkness, studded with pulsing lights like fireflies, swam in her eyes. She choked on a mouthful of the green water. Something pulled at her shoulders, and she lashed out at it in terror.

"Don' you fight me, you drown us both!"

Sallie opened terrified eyes to see Dinah shivering in the water beside her. Dinah's hair was dark and plastered to her face with swamp water, and her teeth chattered. She got an arm around

Sallie's waist, thankful to be wearing nothing herself but her old calico dress.

"Don't try to swim," Dinah gasped. "Jus' float an' don' fight me, I think I get us to the bank."

Sallie nodded. She took as deep a breath as her stays would allow and fought down panic and the urge to thrash in the water. Dinah began to swim, letting them drift with the slow current, making for the nearest bank. The ditch was choked with waterweeds, which pulled at their feet. Willows overhung the water, and Dinah grabbed at them with her free hand, pulling herself and Sallie toward the steep side of the ditch. At the bank, she scrabbled upward for a handhold in the black wet dirt, but it came away in clumps in her fingers. Dinah tugged at the willow branches, trying to drag herself and Sallie upward. The willows bit into her hands like wire, then snapped. Frightened, Dinah looked at Sallie's white face. It was unnaturally pale, her lips bloodless, nearly blue, and her eyes glazed. *I don't get her out of this water, she die,* Dinah thought. She snatched at a willow branch, strong enough to hang onto but not to climb, and stuck it in Sallie's hand.

"You hold this. Don' let go."

Sallie nodded. Dinah began to scrabble with both hands at the bank. The top was more than two feet above her head. She kicked and wriggled and managed at last to hook her elbows over the top. Another heave and she was out of the water and leaning down for Sallie. Sallie's head drooped sideways, and as Dinah reached for her, the willow branch slipped from her hand. Dinah snatched at Sallie's arm and pulled frantically, but it was no use. Sallie was deadweight, and the black mud of the embankment was as slick as grease. There was a heavy stick on the ground by the trees, some flotsam dropped by the last flood, and Dinah tried to get Sallie to grasp it and climb, but her fingers uncurled and slid away.

She floated with the current and drifted against a tangle of willow roots, her face barely above the water. Dinah jumped up and pushed her way through the undergrowth by the ditch. She leaned down above Sallie's pale face. A ripple cut the water against the current, and a dark, triangular head rose above the water and regarded them curiously. A cottonmouth! Dinah screamed and slid into the water again, beating at it with the stick. The snake's jaws opened in a hiss, showing a cottony pinkish-white mouth and elongated poison fangs. It reared up above the water, and Dinah, in pure terror, swung the stick at it again. The stick cracked into the cottonmouth's skull as it swayed forward to strike, and the snake slipped limply into the water. Not at all sure that it was dead, Dinah slipped the stick under the undulating body and flung it downstream with all her strength.

Sallie's eyes were half rolled back in her head, and her breath seemed to Dinah unnaturally slow and infrequent. Her skin felt like ice. Dinah saw with another lurch of fear that a cut on her injured arm was slowly seeping blood into the water. Dinah pulled Sallie's face as high above the water as she could and huddled with her under the overhanging willow branches. Given enough time, the blood would bring 'gators.

XXIV

Sallie

and

Paul

TWO HOURS GONE and Miss Sallie wasn't back yet. Mammy fought down her fear as she waited for Will to harness Peaches, one of the big roan work mules, to the spring wagon. Mister Paul was gone to New Orleans, and the four older children were not in the house. Remembering Adele Scarron's look of secretive triumph, now given a new and sinister meaning in Mammy Rachel's mind, Mammy hadn't wasted time trying to find them, or in questioning Adele, who would keep her from going after Miss Sallie if she could.

Will tightened the last buckle on the harness, and Mammy clambered up on the wagon seat beside him. "You drive," she commanded. "You drive like the devil was chasin' you!"

After some hesitation, Will took the levee road first, downriver toward Alouette, to where the Bayou Rouge road ran into it. Sallie always took the same ride, along the levee road, up beside the bayou, through the back orchards, and home, but there was no way of telling how far she had got.

The levee road was deserted, except for one of Roman Prevost's darkies exercising a colt.

"You seen Miss Sallie this mornin'?" Mammy shouted. When he shook his head, puzzled, Will whipped up the mule, and the wagon rumbled past.

At the Bayou Rouge road, which was really no more than a cart track, Will looked at Mammy. "You wanta turn here? Maybe she go on down to Alouette."

313

Mammy shook her head. "Not without tellin' me, she don't."
And Adele wouldn't have known it either. The look on Adele's
face was too clear in Mammy's mind. "You turn here."

Dinah stared, frozen with fear, at the long, knobby head that
floated just above the water, its snout making little ripples against
the current. A yellow eye stared at them, and Dinah held her
breath. The 'gator stopped. It knew enough of men to be afraid of
them, but it was hungry.

Sallie, who Dinah had thought was unconscious, stirred,
prodded to consciousness by the pain in her arm, which Dinah had
raised above the water in the hope that it would stop the bleeding.

"Paul?" Sallie whispered.

"He come," Dinah assured her. "You rest, keep that arm out o'
the water. I think maybe she's broke, and the cold, she's bad for
her." Dinah didn't know if that were true, but Sallie seemed to
accept it. Dinah turned Sallie a little in her arms and kept talking
so that Sallie shouldn't look up and see the 'gator. "You rest, they
come for us. I think maybe I hear them now, maybe they come in a
minute. . . ." Dinah cradled Sallie, trying to put what little
warmth was left in her own body into Sallie's icy one, holding her,
talking, keeping her turned away from the 'gator. There was no
way to escape when it got up its courage to come for them, but
Sallie needn't see it first.

The wagon rocked dangerously along the narrow bayou road.
Will was going a little faster than was safe, but Mammy Rachel's
expression had put the fear into him, too. The leafless branches
and a few low, scrubby swampland pines loomed over them. The
road was too thickly overlaid with leaves to see whether a horse
had passed that way recently or not. The woods ended abruptly on
one side as they came to the cane field, and Mammy scanned its
empty reaches anxiously.

"There she is!" Will shouted, pointing.

Mammy squinted through the cold sunlight and saw Briar Rose,
her saddle askew, cropping grass by the ditch. The mare walked
with a lurching limp that made Will swear and shake out the reins.
He sawed frantically on them when he saw the gaping hole in the
bridge. Mammy jumped down before the wagon rumbled to a
stop. She peered into the deep ditch fearfully and spun around as
Will yelled, "Over here!"

"Mother o' Gawd!" Will said. Dinah and Sallie clung to the
crumbling bank on the far side of the ditch, their heads barely

above the water. Neither moved. Will began to climb cautiously over the remaining supports of the broken bridge, making for the other side. Mammy picked up her skirts to follow him.

"Go back, you fool woman!" Will shouted at her. "How you gonna get 'em back across? Take that mule down to the north corner bridge an' bring them over!"

Mammy ran back to the wagon. Will clambered hand over hand, on his knees, past the broken planks. Slipping in the mud, he ran along the ditch to the women huddled in the water below. "Miss Sallie!"

Dinah looked up and tried to focus her eyes on him. "She fainted long time ago," she said wearily. "I lift her up an' you pull, but be careful. I think her wrist she is broken." Dinah's teeth chattered. "I start to think no one ever come."

Will got his hands under Sallie's arms and pulled. She was as cold as a tombstone. "She ain't dead?" he whispered.

Dinah shook her head. "No, but maybe if you don't come when you do . . ." Will laid Sallie on the bank and held out his hands for Dinah. Dinah scrambled shakily up the bank. "There is 'gator over there," she said, pointing to a bumpy gray-green shape just breaking the surface of the water. "He is watch us last ten, fifteen minutes." She shuddered.

The creaking of wagon springs and the thud of the mule's hooves sounded behind them, and Will picked Sallie up. "Miss Dinah, kin you walk, or you want me to come back an' carry you?" Will asked with real respect in his voice.

Dinah took a step and stumbled, but managed to stay upright. "I can walk."

Will lifted Sallie into the back of the wagon, and Mammy Rachel wrapped a blanket around her, thanking the Lord that she'd had the sense to bring one. She looked at Dinah's wet, bedraggled form and held out her hands to her. "You come up an' sit under this blanket, honey. As Gawd's my witness, I take back every bad thing I ever thunk about you."

Dinah climbed shivering into the wagon, and Will turned the mule back the way it had come.

Sallie opened her eyes as the wagon jolted over the cane stubble.

"You jus' hol' on, baby," Mammy said. "We be back on the road in a minute."

"Dinah," Sallie whispered. "Where's Dinah?"

"I'm here," Dinah said.

"Denis," Sallie said. "You . . . marry Denis. I've been

stupid, but I'm not ungrateful." She looked at Mammy. "She killed a cottonmouth. With a stick."

"You sure you think the same when you feel better?" Dinah asked. "I know my family she's not good." But her heart was thudding eagerly. "I can learn," she said with assurance. "So I don't embarrass you."

Sallie winced as the wagon shuddered over a low bank onto the road, but she smiled at Dinah. "I'm sure you can." Dinah's new-taught accent, which had deserted her in the water, had begun to return. "Who's been teaching you? Denis?"

"*Non,* it is Madame Belloc. Denis says—" Dinah clapped her hand over her mouth, remembering who Madame Belloc's niece was.

"It's all right," Sallie said weakly. "I know about her. It was all a long time ago." She realized that she didn't give a damn about Claudine Belloc's mother, who was dead anyway. If she wanted to worry about Paul's amours, she could worry about Adele Scarron, who was, she thought viciously, unfortunately still among the living. "That was resourceful of Denis," she said with a weak chuckle. "I think he deserves to have you."

Dinah looked doubtful. "Will Monsieur his father think so too?"

"You leave him to me. You nearly drowned yourself for me. I hope all my children find someone that brave."

"*Merci,*" Dinah whispered. "Oh, *merci.*"

The wagon jolted off the bayou track and onto the levee road. Sallie opened her eyes again. "Will, where's Briar Rose?"

"I send a boy back for her soon's we get home," Will said. "She got a sprained foreleg, but she be all right."

"Good." Sallie's eyes closed again. She hardly woke, even when Will carried her into the house and Mammy stripped off her sodden clothing and put her to bed with a hot brick wrapped in a blanket, and a shawl around her shoulders.

Two hours later, Paul flung himself off a lathered horse and took the stairs up to the second floor two at a time. Will, leading Molasses and riding Denis's gelding Jack, had caught up to him when the *Belle Creole* had stopped downriver to take on more passengers.

Adele met Paul in the hallway upstairs. "She is sleeping," Adele informed him. "*Monsieur le docteur* informs me that it is not serious. I am surprised that Will would bring you back from an important errand, but he is stupid like the rest of them. Would you like something to eat?" Adele smiled solicitously at Paul and hid her fury at Sallie for not having drowned.

"No, not now." Paul brushed Adele aside, leaving her, flushed and furious, in the hallway. Mammy, Barret, and all five children were clustered in the hall outside Sallie's bedroom door, with Doctor Leboeuf in their midst. Paul grabbed him by the arm. "How is she?"

"She's all right," Leboeuf said. He noted Paul's strained face and something very close to terror in his eyes and said gently, "I'm telling you the truth. You were lucky, Paul. It was a close thing, but she'll be fine now."

Paul followed him into Sallie's room, and the door closed behind them. Adele stared balefully at the closed door, but all thought of her had gone out of Paul's head.

When Sallie awoke, it was to find a lamp lit in the afternoon dimness of her bedroom and Paul in a chair by her bed, his face etched with strain and fatigue and much the same expression that he had worn at Denis's bedside.

He's worried about me, Sallie thought with mild surprise, and she put out her good hand to him. She vaguely remembered Doctor Leboeuf coming to put a splint on the other one. "How long did I sleep?"

"It's four o'clock," Paul said hoarsely.

"Have you been here all that time?"

He nodded and took her hand, turning it over in his, looking at her fingers and not at her face. He seemed hesitant, as if unsure that she would want him there.

"You needn't have been so worried," Sallie said gently. "I've only got a sprain."

"You were cold to the bone," Paul said. "I was terrified." He lifted his eyes to hers, and she saw that he meant it. "Leboeuf said another hour in that water and you would have died. Dear God, Sallie, to come so close to losing you! All I could think was that if I did, I would deserve it. I—I want to talk to you, when you are feeling stronger."

"Help me to sit up," Sallie said. Paul in this mood was something new to her. She didn't want him to leave. She wriggled up against the pillows Paul propped behind her, and leaned back on them, her eyes searching his face. "Talk to me now."

"It's hard to begin," Paul said miserably. "When we married . . . Sallie, you loved me then, I know you did. Where did we lose it?"

"Did we?" Sallie whispered. Her face was nearly as white as

the pillows, worn with aftereffects of shock and exposure and the pain in her wrist, but her cornflower-blue eyes were gentle.

"I don't know. I know you haven't been happy, not for years, maybe. I think that's been my fault."

Sallie lay silent, almost afraid to speak. She watched him with questioning eyes.

"I went up to your studio," he said abruptly. "After Leboeuf left. He told me he'd seen one of your paintings. A friend in Mississippi had bought it. I didn't know you'd been selling them, and I was furious, but Leboeuf was impressed with it. So I tried to look at them with his eyes. If I hadn't known they were yours, I would have seen from the start how good they were. I've let the fact that you're my wife—and that your painting didn't accord with my notions of a wife—well, it's all clouded my judgment. It has also occurred to me since then that if I had a talent like yours and no one would let me make use of it, that would be pretty nearly unbearable."

Sallie smiled crookedly. "I could have explained that to you, I think, if I had tried hard enough. It would have served more purpose than throwing paints." Sallie paused, her throat constricting. "But I had myself convinced that since you didn't love me anymore, I didn't care. That was less painful."

Paul sighed. "I've always loved you. But I haven't done a very good job of showing it. I know why you thought I didn't. Will you let me explain about Justine? The explanation I should have given you years ago?"

Sallie nodded.

"I didn't love her," Paul said slowly. "I was fond of her. But she loved me. When I married you, it seemed wrong to make her so unhappy, just because *I* had found my happiness elsewhere. I settled money on her, of course, but it was *me* she wanted. I told myself that since the arrangement in no way took away from my love for you, it wasn't your concern. That that was the way that things were done here. I think I knew even then that it wasn't fair. God forgive me, I was relieved when she died."

"For you to talk to me about this . . . it's hard for you, isn't it?" Sallie said.

"Yes." Paul gave her a wry smile. "But I want your forgiveness. I want your love, if there's any still there."

"You've always had my love," Sallie said. "And forgiveness isn't as hard to come by as you think." She knew jubilantly that there was no need to mention Adele Scarron. If Paul really meant all that he was saying, Mademoiselle Scarron would shortly get an unpleasant surprise. She took a deep breath. "But you're going to have to forgive me for something too."

"If you love me," Paul said huskily, "anything."

"I hope so," Sallie said. She looked him in the eye. "I've been unfaithful to you." If he could swallow that, she thought, then he meant what he had said.

Paul blinked in surprise. That had never occurred to him, fool that he was, though why it hadn't, he didn't know. Sallie, having steeled herself to make her admission, now looked so stricken with terror that he couldn't find it in himself to be angry, only sad over all the wasted years. "Are you still?" he asked her. He could bear anything but that.

"No," Sallie said. "Not for some time. And never again."

"Is it someone I know?" Paul asked.

Sallie gritted her teeth and lied. "No." The desire to cleanse her conscience of Gilbert Becquerel was strong, but the truth wouldn't do Paul or Denis any good. "No," she said again. "You never knew him."

Paul got out of his chair and sat on the edge of her bed, looking at her. "Maybe he was my fault too."

Sallie shook her head. "No, not your fault. Mine. Paul, forgive me."

"My darling." Paul's voice sounded choked. "My darling, anything, so long as things come right between us." He bowed his head, and Sallie thought that he looked as if he had been through some forcible physical transformation that had left him torn and exhausted and slightly strange to her. "I was afraid you would die," he said. "I couldn't imagine being without you. Or rather, I could imagine it, but I couldn't face it."

Sallie wriggled over into the middle of the bed and pulled him closer to her with her good hand. She leaned against him, soaking up the warm feel of him next to her. "I don't think we've ever talked like this," she said. "Truth-telling. If we had, we mightn't have got into this mess."

"We'll talk from now on," Paul said. "I'll talk you to distraction. I never knew how much I leaned on you, how much I needed your companionship. I've always loved you, but the years have made you part of me, and I didn't know it."

Sallie put an arm around his neck possessively, with a little triumphant flame in her eyes. "Where's Mammy?" she whispered.

"Sitting in the next room like a watchdog," Paul said. He

chuckled as it dawned on him what Sallie had in mind. "You'll scandalize the old soul."

Sallie giggled. "Carryin' on in the daytime like no-account shanty folk!" she said, mimicking Mammy's disapproval. "Let's."

Paul slid down in the bed beside her. "What about that sprained wrist?" he said huskily, his eyes dark and eager.

"I'll use my other arm," Sallie said. "Just don't you bounce." She wasn't at all sure this was going to work, but she'd be damned if she'd give up without trying. There was too much at stake. If Paul made love to her now, she knew he'd never get in Adele Scarron's bed again. Sallie wasn't sure that he had, but she was almost willing to bet on it. She lifted her lips to meet his and gave a little murmur of contentment as he kissed her.

Paul's hands roved over her nightdress. He was almost afraid to make love for fear of hurting her, but he wanted her desperately now. He wondered briefly, as his hands caressed her, who else's hands had done the same, and decided that he didn't care. How could he ever have acted as if he owned Sallie, he wondered. Sallie belonged to herself. She lay in his gentle embrace now because she loved him, and that was infinitely better than ownership. His lips brushed against her throat, and his hands lifted the nightdress above her waist, burying her breasts and shoulders in a froth of lace and pin-tucking.

Paul surveyed her ruefully. "That is a most inconvenient garment. How am I supposed to lay my hands on all of you at the same time?"

Sallie sighed, but her eyes were amused. "I know. But it won't come off over this arm." Paul got off the bed, to strip off his shirt and pantaloons where he wouldn't jostle her, and she watched him with amusement. She stretched her good arm over her head and gripped the cherrywood post behind to keep from jiggling as Paul got gingerly into bed beside her. The bandaged wrist was supported in a sling made from one of her silk scarves, and it was certainly tender.

"I feel very much as if I shouldn't be doing this," Paul said, but one look at him told her how much he wanted to.

"Just be careful," she whispered.

"As cautious as a pair of porcupines," he assured her, straddling her with his knees and nuzzling her throat and ears. She wished she could fling her arms about him and hold him to her. But there would be many more times for that now; as many as she wanted. Beneath his bookish mien, Paul was a passionate man, and he was about to learn that his wife could be so too when there were no troubles between them to cloud her pleasure.

Paul slipped his hands under her buttocks, lifting her gently and positioning her. He slipped between her outspread knees. His staff was rigid, and his breath came in hot, hurrying gasps. Sallie lifted her slim waist and cool white hips to meet him and gave herself to him with an urgency that surprised him.

"Aaahh!" She bit her lip, not in pain but in pleasure, as he entered her and looked at him with heavy-lidded eyes over the froth of ruffles and lace of the nightdress that was bunched beneath her chin.

Afraid to put his weight on her, Paul held himself off the bed with his elbows. He wriggled deeper inside her, throbbing now with desire. Sallie whimpered under him, her face flushed now, her cool skin grown hot to the touch. Paul drew back so that he knelt above her. He fastened his mouth on her lips and leaned forward, reentering her slowly, tantalizingly, deeper into that warm embrace, while Sallie leaned back her head, gasping. The hand that had been braced against the bedpost clutched at his back, and she quivered as wave after wave of mounting pleasure washed over her. Paul's breath came raggedly now, quick and panting, until with a final gasp he too shuddered and lay still.

He moved off her, still panting, and looked at her anxiously. "Are you all right?"

A sleepy, satisfied smile answered him. *That,* she thought, *was for Adele Scarron.*

Paul lay down beside her, straightened her nightdress, and drew the coverlet over them both. He turned his head on the pillow and nuzzled at her ear. "If things are going to go on like this, I'm going to move in here. I refuse to tiptoe down the hall in my nightshirt every night. It's not decent."

"We'll scandalize our children," Sallie chuckled. "People's parents aren't supposed to be still doing that sort of thing."

"The hell with our children," Paul said. "How do they think they got here?"

"Not like this," Sallie said. "We haven't made love like this since before Lucien was born. Not since before—"

"Before we messed everything up," Paul said. "Well, we will now, so I'm moving in. We'll just be a scandal."

Sallie's eyes were jubilant. "Yes, won't we? Help me to sit up, Paul. I may have done something awful to this wrist after all. It feels better when I'm upright." He pushed the pillows back into place for her and helped her scoot up against them.

"I ought to go away and let you sleep." Paul started to get out of bed.

"Not on your life." Sallie grabbed his hand. "I want to talk to you while you're feeling mellow. About little Dinah."

"The Michelet child? Will said she kept you from drowning. Anything you want to do for her has my approval, you know that."

"Good," Sallie said. "Because I want her to marry Denis."

Paul gave her a startled look. "I thought you said over your dead body."

"Well, it nearly was," Sallie observed. "It would have been if it weren't for Dinah, and God knows I owe her gratitude. But it isn't just that, Paul. The girl has character and a good heart, and she loves Denis; she's no opportunist. You'll see that if you talk with her. I don't think she has the temperament to put on an act. She's a straightforward little soul."

"She may be," Paul said, "but how will she ever fit in here without making herself a laughingstock, and miserable as a result?"

"As to that," Sallie said, laughing, "*Denis* says that all she needs is the right education, and it seems that he's been seeing to that."

"Indeed?" Paul gave her a wary look.

"Yes, he took her to an expert," Sallie said, her eyes dancing. "Clélie Belloc. And yes, I know who *she* is."

"Mon Dieu!"

"Don't look so horrified," Sallie said. "I think it was clever of him to think of it, although I suppose *they* were probably as shocked," she added, kissing his bare chest.

"Not in light of, er, recent developments." So long as Paul loved *her,* she could put up with his octaroon woods colt.

Paul looked at her affectionately. There was a great deal more resilience and wisdom in Sallie than he had given her credit for.

"They are teaching the poor child to balance a book on her head," Sallie elaborated, "and learn proper French, and eat lobsters, and wear a corset. She was rather bitter about that last, and I can't say I blame her. In another ten years, Paul, I'm going to get fat and wear a *blouse volante* and just give up corsets, I warn you."

Paul laughed and put his hands around her trim waist. "Then I'll make the most of the next ten years," he said suggestively.

Sallie giggled. "I feel like I'm on my honeymoon. But you just contain yourself a minute, because I want to finish talking to you about poor Dinah."

"Bother poor Dinah," Paul said. "If you want her to marry Denis, then I expect she will. But she's awfully young." He slipped his hands under Sallie's nightdress.

"She's hardly younger than Felicie," Sallie pointed out, "and you're going to let *her* marry Roman Prevost. Aren't you?"

"Yes, yes," Paul said, feeling that he was going to have to settle the future of all his children before he was going to be allowed to make love to his wife again. He sighed and withdrew his hand. Maybe now was the time to drop his own bombshell. "As long as you're feeling tolerant, we'd better talk about Claudine."

It was Sallie's turn to look suspicious. Sallie had let Paul know that she knew about her, but it was the first time either of them had mentioned the girl by name. "There aren't any more, are there?" Visions of a chocolate-colored horde of brothers and sisters crossed her mind.

"No," Paul said. "Claudine is all. But your childhood chum Barret wants to marry her."

"He *what?*"

"The loon wants to take her home to Charleston and pass her for white, and he's convinced Claudine that it's feasible."

"I think he's one brick shy of a load," Sallie said.

"Are you shocked?"

"Well of course I'm shocked, but not as shocked as his sister Alice is going to be if she finds out. Paul, what are you going to do?"

"Damned if I know," Paul said, encouraged by the fact that at least hysterics had not been forthcoming.

"Lord have mercy." Sallie leaned back against the pillows and appeared to be mulling it over. "I'll tell you, Paul," she said finally, "I don't think there's much you *can* do. After never marrying all these years, Barret must be head over heels to do a thing like that, and he'll do as he pleases. It would be cruel to give them away."

"You're taking this remarkably well," Paul ventured.

"I wouldn't take it nearly so well if it were Denis," Sallie admitted. "Dinah Michelet is about all I can swallow. But my grandmother always said there was an odd streak in the Forbeses."

"What sort of odd streak?"

"I don't know. She was always hinting at something, but she never would come out and say it. Some shocking old scandal, I suppose."

"I find this shocking enough," Paul said. "I'm glad you aren't angry over it."

"I couldn't wish ill to a child of yours." Sallie kissed him. "Truly."

Paul leaned his head against hers. This intimacy was new to him, and there was a great deal of comfort in it, a solace for his troubles.

"You never got to see Judge Craire today, did you?" Sallie said suddenly. "You came back because of me."

Paul shook his head. "It wouldn't have done any good, honey."

"They'll try Gabriel. When?"

"In two weeks."

"And hang him."

"Oh, God, Sallie." Paul buried his face against her hair. "He hasn't a prayer, and I can't bring myself to look on it as justice." There was relief just in unburdening himself to her, and in a moment he went on. "If he were white, he'd get off." He spread his hands, palms up on the white coverlet, in a helpless gesture. "Sallie, I don't know what to do. I'm almost at the point that I'd turn him loose, but they'd only catch him again, and it would be worse for him."

Why, he's asking me, Sallie thought. Paul asked her advice on domestic matters, never on a thing like this. This was new. She bent her mind to the problem, unwilling to disappoint him.

"Paul, there's only one way that I know of to get Gabriel out of here, and I'm a little frightened even to be thinking about it. But my conscience won't be any clearer than yours if we let them hang him."

"What is it?" Paul said.

"The Railroad," Sallie whispered. "But if they catch us, we won't be much better off than Gabriel."

Paul looked at her intently. "You would do that?"

If my nerve doesn't fail me, Sallie thought. She nodded slowly. "Would you?"

An hour later Mammy Rachel opened the door a silent crack. She had a tray of chicken and rice in one hand, but after one look she backed out again, grinning. It was dark in the bedroom except for the shaded light of the bedside lamp and the red glow of sparks from the sugarhouse chimney that fell through a half-drawn curtain into a bar across the floor. Miss Sallie sat propped up in bed, and Mister Paul was next to her. His bare chest and shoulders proclaimed to Mammy's great satisfaction what had occurred.

Mammy set the tray down on the table in the hall. There was one more thing she had to take care of, and this looked like a fine time to do it—all the residents of the great house would be dressing for dinner. With fire in her eye, Mammy Rachel made for Hollis's room.

Hollis, in a camisole and pantalets, was drying her face and arms at the blue china bowl that rested on a cherrywood stand next to her dressing table. She hung the towel on the bar beside the bowl as Mammy came in.

"Where have you been?" Patience had never been Hollis's best quality. "I rang and rang. You know I need you to lace me up another half inch so I can wear that green silk." Hollis pointed accusingly at the moiré silk that lay in a pile of sea-green ruffles across the bed.

"I been takin' your mama her dinner," Mammy said. "An' you oughtn't to be wearin' colors anyhow."

"It's been over a year," Hollis said. "An' if I see another purple dress, I'm goin' to die. Now you come lace me up."

"I lace you up in a minute," Mammy said. "I wanna talk to you first."

Hollis looked at her suspiciously. "What about?"

"About that Adele Scarron and whatever it is you done found out about her."

"How do you know I found out anything?"

" 'Cause you done tol' me, mighty big an' important like you is, that's how."

"I was just funning you," Hollis said, determined to tell Mammy nothing.

"Now you jus' listen to me," Mammy said. "That Adele done tried to kill your mama this mornin'. She done somethin' to that bridge, I knows it. I seen her lookin' sly and pleased with herself jus' like a weasel when you mama go out to ride this mornin'. But I cain't prove nothin', and your daddy, he ain't gon' believe me without no proof. So you take whatever you knows about Adele an' you fix it so she don't never go near your mama again."

Hollis stared at her. "*You* must be funning. I never heard anything so silly."

"You put it past her?" Mammy demanded.

"I wouldn't put anything past that mealymouthed, two-faced cat," Hollis conceded. "But I don't think she's got enough sense to fix a bridge, so don't wait for me to waste my time on her."

Mammy Rachel grabbed the wet towel off the washstand. "Hollis DuMontaigne Tourneau, you're jus' so plain mean-spirited you don' wanta give up that secret you been so bigheaded about, that's what!"

"I am not!"

"You is too!" Mammy snapped the wet towel at Hollis's legs, thinly protected by muslin drawers. "You near let your mama get drowned jus' 'cause you too selfish to tell what you know 'bout that woman!"

"Ow!" Hollis danced out of reach. "How dare you!" She gave Mammy a furious green-eyed glare. "You aren't too much of a pet to get a whipping!"

"Neither is you!" Mammy snapped the towel again, this time at Hollis's backside. "I done raise you from a baby, an' no chile o' mine is gonna act like you is!" The towel connected with Hollis's bottom again, and Hollis retreated, pursued by Mammy. "You let that woman hurt your mama, you gonna go to hell sure. Iffen you don' wanta burn with the worst sinners they is, you make that foreign woman leave your mama and your daddy alone. Or I'm gonna smack you with this here towel till you cain't sit down!"

"Ow!" Hollis retreated behind the bed, and they glared at each other across it. Hollis rubbed her smarting buttocks. A wrathful Mammy Rachel was perhaps the one thing in the world that gave Hollis pause. If Hollis had a conscience, its name was Mammy Rachel.

Mammy smacked the towel across her pink palm and started around the bed.

"All right," Hollis said angrily. "All right. You just leave me alone. I'll fix that Adele."

Mammy folded her arms. "Thass my girl. You got it in you to do right when you has to. Now you come over here, an' I lace you up some, so's you can get in that dress."

Hollis gripped the bedpost sullenly as Mammy tightened her corset strings, but she didn't say anything further.

Mammy tied off the corset strings, and Hollis let her breath out. At the door, Mammy fired her parting shot. "You leave your sister and Mister Prevost alone, too—'cause if you ain't, I'm gon' tell your daddy jus' what you been up to, even if it break my heart to do it. It gon' pret' near break his too, I 'spect, but you can bet he ain't gon' take you to no parties in Washington iffen I do, so you jus' think about *that*.''

Getting no more than a malignant look from Hollis, Mammy retired victorious, leaving her charge to nurse her stung backside and her injured ego.

XXV

The

Railroad

HOLLIS CONTEMPLATED ADELE Scarron across the dinner table. Since Hollis had gone back into colors, Sallie had ordered some of Hollis's half-mourning dresses made over for Adele. Adele appeared tonight in a gown of deep purple cut low across the shoulders, with a little fichu of lace to lend it a modesty suitable for the bereaved. Hollis was charmed to find that it made Adele's skin look sallow. The conniving, whey-faced little cheat! How dare she think Papa would ever take up with the likes of her? Mammy Rachel had forced the role of avenging angel upon Hollis, but, seeing the smirks and simpers that Adele was directing down the table toward an embarrassed Paul, Hollis began to feel that she was going to enjoy it. She laid her fork down and said thoughtfully to Adele, "If I were you, I don't think I should have gone out of black quite so soon."

Adele opened gold-flecked eyes wide with every evidence of innocence. "But why not? It has been nearly a year, and if Madame DuMontaigne feels that it is proper—"

"Well, for one thing," said Hollis, sweetly helpful, "purple is *such* a tryin' color to wear. Especially when a girl has any yellow in her skin. I'd be glad to help you pick out somethin' more becomin', if you like."

Adele bridled. Emilie put her napkin to her mouth and giggled. Felicie, willing to call a temporary truce with her older sister in order to discomfit Adele, added brightly, "I'm afraid Mama was tryin' so hard to be nice, an' save you the expense of new clothes, that she just didn't stop to think about the color not suitin'."

329

Adele, simmering at the wreck of her elaborate scheme, and the dreamy look she had caught on Paul's face as he emerged from his wife's bedroom, felt herself tried beyond endurance. "I do not require *help* from either of you!" she snapped, stabbing at her meat with such force that the knife grated with an angry sound across the plate.

Lucien grinned and Tante Doudouce looked puzzled. "I'm sure they were just trying to be nice, dear," she faltered. To her guileless ears, they had *sounded* nice, and certainly purple wasn't a color at all *séduisant* on the poor child. But something in the malevolence of Hollis's smile and the amusement of Felicie's and Lucien's led her to feel that there were unsuspected depths here. Tante Doudouce looked helplessly from Adele to Paul.

"I'm sure Adele is capable of choosing her own clothes," Paul said with a quelling glance at Hollis. He was fairly certain of the reason for his daughter's dislike of Adele and sufficiently ashamed of himself to be embarrassed by it. "Let us change the subject," he said in a voice that brooked no argument. "Denis, I wish to speak to you after dinner. And don't look so nervous," he added in a whisper. "Your mother has been pleading your cause." Paul glanced at Barret and decided that he might as well kill two birds with one stone. "Barret, I expect you'd better join us." If Denis were going to continue "educating" his Dinah at Madame Belloc's, it would be as well if he knew how the land lay.

Adele, in a cold fury, was eating the rest of her dinner, and Hollis, resting an anticipatory gaze on Adele, returned to her own, content to bide her time.

Since Sallie wasn't present, Hollis signaled the ladies to retire as soon as Testut began to clear the dessert dishes. Hollis waylaid Adele at the parlor door. "Let us leave my sister and my aunt to themselves for a moment," she suggested.

"I am not obliged to speak with you!" Adele snapped.

"Well, that's a pity," Hollis said, "because I was hopin' you could tell me about a friend of yours. Her name was Therese D'Aubert."

Only a small, startled breath gave any indication that Adele knew what Hollis was talking about. "I do not," she said distinctly, "remember anyone by that name."

Hollis tut-tutted at her reprovingly and linked her arm through Adele's. "Well, why don't we just step into the best parlor an' let me jog your memory."

Adele withdrew her arm with distaste, but she followed Hollis into the unused best parlor, her purple skirts making an angry little swishing on the oak floor.

"That was what I meant about your not goin' out of black so soon," Hollis remarked. "I thought you might want to do a little mournin' for Therese . . . since you might in a manner of speaking say she died in France."

"You take too much on yourself!" Adele hissed. She was blazingly angry, but Hollis noted that she was taking pains to keep her voice low.

Hollis settled herself comfortably in a chair. "What did you do with the real Adele?" she inquired. "Did you murder her too, like you tried to murder my mama?"

"It was scarlet fever!" Adele clamped her lips together and regained control of herself. "Therese died of it," she said. "She was my companion."

"I thought you said you didn't know her."

"One forgets."

Hollis folded her hands in her lap. Her green eyes contemplated Adele in a businesslike fashion. "I haven't thought much of you since you got here," she remarked. "I never could bear a two-faced woman. So I wrote your Father Rosièrre at Saint Martin." Hollis made a pious face. "He was awfully upset. Said he wouldn't have thought it of you. I'll bet Papa wouldn't either," she added reflectively. "He purely can't abide a liar."

Two crimson spots of fury splotched Adele's cheeks. "How dare you! I've seen you—running around after Roman Prevost and every other man in this place. You have the morals of a mink! How dare you make wild accusations about me?"

"I never tried to murder anyone," Hollis observed. She was beginning to enjoy herself. "You better sit down, honey, or you'll bust your stays, and that dress has been let out about all it'll stand for."

"You are a slut," Adele spat at her.

Hollis lifted one elegant shoulder. "At least I'm not a no-account poor relation tryin' to make out she's better than she is! An' since you aren't even *our* poor relation, you better sit down an' listen to me before you find yourself set out on the levee road with your little threadbare carpetbag in your hand."

Adele gritted her teeth. Her immediate inclination was to slap Hollis's face, but the fear of exposure was beginning to get the better of her. To have come so far and then lose it all because Hollis had written to that meddling little priest!

"If you think your father will believe one word of this—" Adele began.

"I think he'll believe every word, when he reads that letter," Hollis said. "An' don't go thinkin' you can drown *me* in a ditch, because there's somebody else who knows, too."

"What do you want?" Adele was sure that Hollis wanted something. Otherwise, she would simply have taken the letter to Paul. "Your papa most certainly will not believe that I would do your *maman* any harm," Adele said flatly. That must never be admitted to. "But it is possible that he would believe that lying little priest, so we will talk if you wish it."

"How sensible," Hollis drawled. She was enjoying this feeling of power over Adele, especially after the recent interlude with Mammy Rachel. Hollis got down to brass tacks. "You stay away from my papa. No more smarmy looks, no more little hand holdin' an' bringin' him his newspaper. An' no more writin' his letters for him either, you hear? You just stay plumb away from him. That's the first thing. The second is, if anything more than a mosquito bite happens to my mama, I'll see you end up in a paupers' house without a picayune to bless yourself with. You think you have all that?"

Adele's expression told Hollis that she did and that furthermore she would cheerfully have seen alligators pull Hollis limb from limb if it could have been arranged.

"Don't look so down in the mouth, honey," Hollis said. "You noticed I haven't said anything about Lucien."

"Lucien?"

"I saw you chasin' him when you first came here. My, I never *saw* such a desperate woman. You only took after my papa when you couldn't get anywhere with Lucien. Well, here's my advice: You go back to your first idea. You land Lucien an' I won't say one li'l bitty word. I kind of think you deserve him."

Hollis rose, satisfied. She considered herself to have a happy knack of turning a situation to her advantage. The letter was still a potent weapon when she needed one. If Adele got Lucien, it could be awfully useful later. "Pleasant as this has been, I do have a few other things to see to," Hollis said.

She sailed out, and Adele, longing to send the gilded clock on the mantel flying after her, balled her hands into fists and beat them against each other. Paul's voice in the hallway sent a stab of fear through her. Had Hollis told him anyway? She backed toward the far door, but it was too late. At this point Adele would put very little past Hollis. She looked at Paul with a white, taut face, and Paul, oblivious to the recent scene, looked back at her guiltily.

"My dear, I must speak to you."

Adele realized that he was embarrassed, and a wave of relief flooded over her. She would have a way out after all, a way to comply with Hollis's commands, in which she had no choice, and still keep herself like a lead weight on Paul's conscience. She smiled warmly at him. "Of course."

"Adele . . . my dear, I have done something dreadful, to you, and to myself. I think that in these last few weeks I must simply have gone mad."

Adele allowed her face to fall. She looked at him sadly. "You do not want me," she whispered.

"My poor child," Paul said. "I broke my marriage vows, which do mean much to me, and I injured you. I had no right to do either, and it mustn't happen again. I can only hope that you won't think too harshly of me." He was beginning to think that Adele's moods adapted themselves to her purposes with too great a facility, but after what he had done, he had no right to judge her. "If you will think about it," he said gently, "I think you will find that you do not want me, that you deserve better. I am married, and I can offer you no future. You must have a man who can." He came forward and brushed her cheek lightly with his hand. "It would be a dreadful thing if I were to stand in the way of that."

Adele sniffed. She gave him a look of pained courage and a little smile. "I understand. I think I knew even then that happiness of the sort I found with you could not last." A wan, sad expression crept over her face. "I will try to do as you say, although it may be that no man will have me now." She raised her eyes tremblingly to his. "But always I will know in my heart that those few weeks were worth it." With a strangled sob, she picked up her purple skirts and ran from the room, leaving Paul behind her with his insides twisted into a leaden knot in his chest.

Lucien, glowering at the world from the veranda, saw her purple dress flash by the window and, with a sullen satisfaction, noted his father's stricken face, lamplit in the empty room. So they'd had a quarrel, he thought. How nice. Why should he be the only one balked of his sport? Paul, his interview with Denis and Barret completed, had cornered Lucien and informed him in no uncertain terms that as permission had been given Denis to marry Dinah Michelet, Lucien was to refrain from embarrassing the family by visiting her sisters. It was not a request, it was an order, and Paul had made it plain that the consequences of disobedience would be unpleasant.

Adele, since she had begun her pursuit of Paul, had had little time for Lucien, but in light of what he had seen through the window, Lucien was not overly surprised three days later when she smiled prettily at him from the balcony of the second-story veranda and requested his help in dislodging a handkerchief that the winter wind had snatched up into the bare branches of an oak tree. Lucien had been careful never to mention matrimony, which was what Adele had so patently wanted in the first days of their acquaintance, but since she had been willing to be his father's mistress, she had obviously lowered her sights a little—in which case Lucien was happy enough to renew the acquaintance. He was still angry over Paul's edict concerning Tassie Michelet and her obliging sister Sukie. Stealing his father's mistress as a replacement would afford him great satisfaction. He grinned up at her and mounted the curving stairs to the balcony, using his walking stick to fetch down the wayward scrap of lace.

Adele tucked it into her pocket. "You are most adept." Gold-flecked eyes considered him thoughtfully, and a suggestive smile curved her lips.

"I'm always happy to oblige," Lucien assured her.

"One does not usually see you staying so close to home," Adele said thoughtfully. Since Paul had released him from the cane field, Lucien had spent most of his time in New Orleans, leaving Denis to oversee the grinding without his assistance.

"I saw that you were . . . unattached today and found I was unable to tear myself away," Lucien said with mock gallantry.

"How kind of you," Adele said. "I trust you do not wish to show me the sugarhouse for entertainment. I have seen it."

"So have I," said Lucien. "I had in mind something more entertaining. A picnic perhaps, with champagne and oysters and some of Meeow's eclairs. Just the two of us, I fear, since everyone else seems to be so busy."

Adele rested a speculative gaze on his face, seemingly studying what his motives might be. Apparently she decided that they accorded well enough with her own. She nodded her head. "But is it possible that it will rain?" She looked at the sky suspiciously.

"It's always possible here," Lucien said cheerfully. Adele, he had discovered, disliked being wet as much as a cat. *You really are going to be a great deal of trouble to seduce,* he thought.

"We'll take the closed carriage," he told her reassuringly. He gave her his arm. "Shall we?"

They descended the steps together. They made, Adele decided, a handsome couple. Hollis was reclining with *Godey's Lady's Book* in a chaise on the veranda. She raised her blond head slightly from the cushion, and Adele was aware of her amused expression. She swept by Hollis with no comment, still puzzled and suspicious that Hollis should abet her in a pursuit of Lucien.

"You and Hollis have another spat?" Lucien inquired when he had charmed an exquisite picnic out of Meeow and settled Adele in the carriage, with one of Will's stable boys to drive them. "She looked mighty full of herself just now."

"*Non*," Adele said firmly. "We have not spoken today." She smiled brightly at him as he tucked a carriage rug over her lap. "It is much more interesting to me to speak to you than your bad-tempered sister. Tell me where we are going for this picnic."

"There's a little cove I know of," Lucien said, "with a road that runs right up to it, not too narrow for the carriage. If it rains, we can watch the water from inside. Ladies are said to admire the view."

As he could have predicted, it did rain. Lucien, charmed at this happenstance, ruthlessly sent the stable boy back on foot for more blankets in case Mademoiselle should feel cold, and uncorked the champagne with an anticipatory air.

"This does not seem to me to be proper, without servants," Adele ventured, seeing how the land lay.

Lucien's eyes glittered brightly. "We are family, are we not? Courtesy cousins?" He handed her a glass of champagne, and his fingers brushed hers.

"So we are." Adele took the champagne and sipped it. She watched with interest while Lucien displayed the contents of the picnic hamper. He appeared in no hurry, but almost certainly he had sent the boy away on purpose. Lucien provided her with a plate of oysters and crabmeat salad, and a dark, sweet pumpkin bread. He in turn watched her intently while they ate, thinking that this was the closest Adele had let him get to her since he had made it clear that he wasn't the marrying sort. It appeared that she didn't care anymore. He reached out a hand for the curtains that were looped back beside the carriage windows. "Are you through admiring the view? It looks frightfully dreary out there to me." He let the curtains fall closed without waiting for her answer, but she made no protest. "Are you perhaps also through with that sticky plate?"

"*Oui.* That was an excellent lunch." Adele handed Lucien her plate, to be stowed away in the picnic hamper, and leaned back against the velvet upholstery of the carriage. She laughed a little. "How can I thank you?"

Lucien untied her bonnet strings and put a hand under her chin. "Oh, I think you know." He knelt on the carriage floor and put his hands about her waist. "You look most elegant today, Miss Scarron. Ravishingly so. My sister is right. Black is a much better color on you than purple. You don't really expect me to resist temptation?"

Adele licked her lips. The glitter in Lucien's dark eyes seemed brighter, unnaturally flickering and reckless. "That depends upon what it is that you are tempted to do," she whispered. She began to feel a current of danger in the carriage, not from their situation but from the intensity of Lucien's passions. It was not a sensation she had felt with Paul.

"Why, I don't know yet," Lucien said, smiling. "I like to . . . improvise." He put his hands to the onyx buttons of her bodice and pulled them open with a jerk. Adele gasped in surprise. "Now don't tell me you haven't been thinkin' the same thing," Lucien murmured. His hand crept inside her bodice, and she gasped again as he yanked corset and corset cover downward together and lifted one breast over the top of it.

Adele's face was scarlet with embarrassment, and Lucien chuckled. "Now who's goin' to see you, honey, exceptin' me?" He cupped her breast with his hand and bounced it on his palm.

"The stable boy!" Adele protested, mortified. "He will be back."

"Not if he knows what's good for him," Lucien said. He tweaked the nipple with his fingers, not tenderly, and pulled the other breast out. Her outraged expression only seemed to amuse him. He leaned forward and took the other nipple between his teeth. Her breasts were small compared to the voluptuous Tassie's, and blue-veined, not so much to his taste, but there was an excitement in her obvious dislike of what he did. He wondered why she was here. To spite his father, maybe.

Adele gritted her teeth as she felt his hands beneath her crinoline. His fingers pushed between her legs with sharp prods until she opened them trying to wriggle away from him. "That's better," Lucien said indistinctly, his mouth still around her nipple. He rubbed his hand between her thighs and bit down on her nipple with a slow, relentless pressure until she yelped. Lucien laughed and sat back. "Stand up and turn around," he commanded.

She turned, eyeing him with a dislike that wasn't lost on Lucien. He pulled at the hooks of her skirt and the ties of crinolines and drawers. In horror, Adele felt skirts and pantalets yanked ruthlessly to the floor of the carriage. She knew it would do her no good to protest now. A hand slid down her buttocks and between her legs, pulling her against him. She could feel his organ through his pantaloons, stiff against her. With the other hand, he bent her forward and pulled off the bodice of her gown.

Adele looked at him over her shoulder. Lucien's eyes were half-closed, reckless with passion, and he was smiling. She was acutely aware that he was still clothed while she wore only a much disarranged corset and camisole, and her stockings. Lucien sat down on the opposite seat and pulled her onto his lap, turning her so that she landed facedown across his knees.

"What are you doing?" Adele kicked in protest, but he held her still with one hand. He was unexpectedly strong. With the other he began to peel off her black lisle stockings. "Undressing you," Lucien said. "But if you feel your stockings afford you a certain modesty, I'll leave them on." His hand brushed lightly over the backs of her legs and began to rub her buttocks instead.

Adele kicked her feet again, bouncing futilely on his lap. Lucien's open palm smacked down hard across her buttocks, and then he proceeded to rub them again. "Don't do that," he said.

"Let me up!"

"No. I'm enjoying myself. Quit being embarrassed, and you will too."

"I did not think," Adele said in a tight-lipped fury, "that this was the way a gentleman made love!"

"Well, I don't often make love to ladies," Lucien conceded, "so I haven't had much practice."

"You prefer sluts like those Michelets!" Adele's voice was muffled against his leg and the carriage upholstery.

"Let us say I prefer the unusual," Lucien said. He was perfectly willing to have her fight him all the way. If she had thought she was going to enjoy the sort of namby-pamby lovemaking she had indulged in with his father, she was in for a surprise. He squeezed her buttocks vengefully, enjoying the way she bucked under his hand. Strong fingers probed between the white cheeks, sliding downward until he found the moist opening he was searching for. As she gasped in outrage, he slid first one finger and then two inside her. Holding her down with the other hand, he began to push them rhythmically in and out. "I told you, if you will just forget that you are lying bare-bottomed in my lap, and how mortifying that is, you might begin to enjoy yourself.''

When we are married, Adele thought viciously, *I will never let you in my bedroom.* He twisted his fingers inside her, tickling and probing deeper, and a new sensation began to come over her. Her face felt hot. She moaned, no longer wishing to struggle.

Abruptly the fingers were withdrawn. Adele gave a little cry of disappointment and found Lucien was laughing at her. Robbed of her pleasure, she glared at him furiously as he swung her off his lap so that she knelt on the floor in front of him. Deliberately he began to unbutton his pantaloons.

"Now I am going to teach you something else." He cupped her chin in one hand, his fingers gripping her tightly, and drew out his organ, stiff and alarmingly large, with the other. He pulled her head toward him.

Adele's eyes widened in alarm. Lucien clasped both hands behind her neck so that there was no escape. He rubbed himself against her lips. His saturnine face was flushed, and his lips were open a little, showing the glitter of white teeth. "Open your mouth."

"No!" she said from behind clenched teeth.

"Pleasure for pleasure, Adele," Lucien whispered. "If you want anymore from me, then do what I tell you."

Adele closed her eyes. *When we are married,* she thought, *I will see that he has a mistress. I can bear anything once.* She opened her mouth.

Lucien began to rock back and forth while she fought down her revulsion. But as his breath began to come in increasingly shuddering gasps, she drew back in alarm. No! He must not! He must do the other thing—it was what she had come here for.

Lucien chuckled, misinterpreting her fear. He didn't want her hysterical, and that might be just too much. "Lie down," he ordered. "On the seat."

Adele obeyed, watching him wearily, but he only stripped off his coat and pantaloons and then began to stroke her breasts with his hands.

"That seat's too narrow," he said after a moment. "Get on the floor."

Adele's indignation at these unloverlike commands was plain, but she slid onto the floor and did not protest as he pushed her thighs apart roughly. His fingers began to massage the source of her pleasure, and she whimpered. She was aroused in spite of herself, and at the same time terrified of what he might do next.

Lucien knew it. He reached into the picnic hamper and brought out a heavy pistol-handled knife. As she stared at him, horrified, he reversed it and began to rub her with the broad, round end of it: up over her belly, across her breasts, down between her legs again. "You don't know much, do you?" he said. "It's time you learned things."

The cool metal of the knife drew away from her, and he leaned over her. He took her black-stockinged legs in his hands, holding her by the ankles, and braced them against the opposite seats of the carriage. His fingers gripped her breasts painfully, and she struggled to catch her breath, still laced tightly into the corset, which he had pulled down only enough to expose her breasts. "Now," Lucien said. "Now it's time."

He plunged into her, and she moaned, aroused beyond humiliation now, wanting only the ache inside her satisfied. Her breath came faster as the feeling within her intensified. Lucien hammered at her, rocking back and forth. Her hands clawed at his back. His eyes were locked on hers. She stared into them, hating him for the final humiliation of making her want him, even as pleasure exploded within her.

As it ebbed, those dark eyes still held her. There was a dancing, demonic light in them as he pushed her hard against the floor of the carriage and shuddered into climax on top of her.

A moment later he lifted himself off her and began to button his trousers. Adele sat up and gave the back of his shirt a baleful stare. She tried to feel some difference in her body, other than the mixture of pleasure and indignation that Lucien had aroused in her. When did you know if you were with child, she wondered, thanking *le bon Dieu* that she had not got that way with Paul. But now there must be a child, even if she had to do this with Lucien again until there was. Lucien would feel no remorse for that, but Paul would, and Paul's conscience would drag Lucien to a priest for her. Adele began to pull her clothes back on, unassisted by Lucien, who had gone to sit on the driver's box and smoke a cigar. She ached all over, and she was beginning to be a little afraid of Lucien. *When we are married,* she thought, *there will be a lock on my bedroom door.*

As November wore on, so did the grinding and the preparations for the election and holiday parties. If the master and mistress spent much of their time in each other's company, the house servants, who generally knew everything, thought no more of it than that Mister Paul and Miss Sallie were happy together again, bless the Lord, and that Miss Adele, she'd got just what was coming to her.

But there was more than companionship in Sallie and Paul's whispered conferences. Late at night toward the end of the month, the back door of Belle Marie creaked softly as Paul swung it open. He caught and held it for Sallie, so it wouldn't creak again. Testut, if he heard, would make it his business to investigate, certain of catching some thieving darky in his pantry. Paul felt rather like a thief. He wore a shooting jacket with a pistol in the pocket, and Sallie had put on an old black linsey dress that hung petticoatless around her ankles. The November wind rustled the dead leaves around her feet, and an owl hooted somewhere in the pecan trees.

"Are you sure you can handle Molasses?" Paul whispered.

"Don't worry. I'll meet you on the old road." The old road ran north from Belle Marie to skirt Lake Ponchartrain, and then into the swamps, to end at the ruins of the first house that Paul's Grandpère LeClerc had built in the wilds of Louisiana, its land now largely reclaimed by the water.

Sallie disappeared into the moon-dappled darkness of the back garden, and Paul made his way cautiously toward the old stone kitchen. The solid wooden door that Jem had put up was locked with a heavy bolt, and Paul pulled the key out of his pocket, looking guiltily over his shoulder. He had sent Will, who always slept in the stable, to Alouette with a mare that Paul wanted bred to one of Roman Prevost's stallions and instructions to stay the night there. No other darkies were allowed out at this time of night, but there was always the chance that one of them—or worse yet, one of his children—should have chosen tonight to do some illicit moonlight courting. What Paul was about to do was a secret, with which he wished neither to trust nor to burden anyone else. That Sallie should come with him was different. Sallie had thought of it, and he needed her. As he fiddled with the lock, it occurred to Paul that he had begun to look at his wife with a vastly different eye.

The bolt slid open, and Paul slipped inside.

"Who that?" Gabriel sat up on his cot in one swift motion, his manacled hands raised to ward off whoever might come after him.

"It's me," Paul whispered. "Be quiet."

Gabriel stared at him in the darkness. A thin line of moonlight coming through the open door fell across Paul's face. Gabriel sat back on the cot. "I thought you was vigilantes," he said. "Thought they might hurry up the job." He looked somberly at

Paul. "I don' 'spect it make no difference, but I'm skeered of 'em, skeerder 'n I is of the hangman."

Paul closed the door silently. "Nobody's going to hang you," he said. He flung the tattered blanket off the cot and onto the floor and pulled a pair of metal cutters out of his other pocket. "Hold still." He felt for the manacles around Gabriel's ankles. Gabriel flinched as the cutters bit through.

"You figgerin' to set me free, why don' you unlock 'em?" Gabriel said nervously as Paul reached for his wrist.

"Vigilantes wouldn't have a key," Paul muttered, working on the wristband. "And I won't be able to show my face off my own land if they pin this on me." He chuckled in the darkness. "If vigilantes got you and you gave 'em the slip, that's not my fault."

"You gon' turn me loose? I ain't get two miles," Gabriel said. "I'm skeered enough to try it, but I ain't gonna make it."

"You aren't any more scared than I am," Paul said, "so get moving." He dropped the last chain on the blanket and motioned Gabriel out the door before him. "This way," Paul whispered.

"How come you do this?"

"A bad conscience," Paul said. "Mine."

Gabriel followed him. The night looked fearful and filled with ghosts and far too open and uncertain for a man who had never been free in his life. Freedom had come too suddenly on him. They had walked for a half a mile when suddenly three horses and a rider loomed up out of the shadows by the old road.

"Anyone see you?" Paul whispered.

"No," Sallie whispered back, "but I'm purely glad to see you." There was something eerie and foreign about the old road by night.

Gabriel saw that the rider on the horse was mounted sidesaddle. *"Miss Sallie?"*

"Hush and get on the horse," Sallie said. Briar Rose was still lame, so she rode Denis's Jack, who threw up his head and snorted at Gabriel.

"I ain't never rid no horse in my life!" Gabriel protested.

"Well, now you're going to." Paul held Butterfly's head while Gabriel put his foot in the stirrup. He pulled himself up and sat uncertainly, holding the saddle. "You just hang on," Paul said. "I'm going to lead her." He swung up on Molasses, and they set out at a trot with Sallie ahead of them.

Sallie had tied rags around the horses' hooves and bridles, and they moved like ghosts in and out of the moonlight, through the shadowy depths of trees. A ground mist floated along beneath them so that the horses' feet disappeared into it past the fetlocks. In the distance to their right they could see the gleam of moonlight off the lake. The old road, overgrown, went nowhere except to a house long since abandoned. Low-hanging branches, to which a few withered leaves still clung, raked at their hair and faces. Denis's Jack, unaccustomed to a sidesaddle, curvetted, snorting at ha'nts or whatever it was that might be abroad in the night. An owl floated past on silent wings, and deep in the dark swamp a fox barked.

An hour into the swamp Sallie drew rein cautiously and pointed. Paul brought Molasses up beside her. "He's there," she whispered. A dim light glimmered through the trees where the moonlight showed an old stone chimney rising above the mist-wreathed ground.

"You stay here," Paul said. "I want to make sure." The man they were to meet was a stranger and, except for tonight, an enemy. He wouldn't trust Paul any more than Paul trusted him, and mistrustful men carried guns. Paul dismounted and pushed his way through a tangle of wild berry vines and pine saplings. Paul, peering through the dimness under the trees, saw a man standing beside the chimney, on what had once been the hearth of Paul's grandfather's house.

"DuMontaigne?" A voice spoke quietly in the darkness.

"Yes." Paul stopped where he was.

"You bring him?"

"Yes."

"Then let me see him. And anybody else you've got with you."

"Just my wife," Paul said. "Bring Gabriel, Sallie," he called softly.

Sallie and Gabriel came forward on foot, and the man by the chimney put up a hand when they drew abreast of Paul. "That's close enough." His face was shadowed in darkness. It had taken nearly two weeks to get in contact with him, cautiously and through many middlemen, in a search that had begun with a preacher in Baton Rouge. Paul didn't know this man's name and never would, or even if he was black or white.

"Show him to me," the voice said from the shadow of chimney.

Sallie lifted the lantern that she had carried slung from Jack's saddle, and Paul struck a lucifer match to light it. Sallie held the light so that it shone on Gabriel's face. Gabriel stared fearfully, not understanding, into the darkness of the ruined house.

"All right," the voice said after a moment. "Put the damned light out." Sallie obeyed.

"DuMontaigne, you *believe* in slavery, don't you?" the man in the shadows asked abruptly.

"Yes," Paul said.

"And you'd catch any abolitionist you could lay your hands on and string him up on a tree with all the runaway darkies, wouldn't you?"

"I believe abolitionists are meddling in matters that are not their concern," Paul said. It was an odd, surreal conversation, and Paul wondered what its purpose was.

"*We* believe that any man who is not free is *God's* concern." The man's voice was resonant with his conviction.

"Then I suggest that you leave the matter to God," Paul said.

"Why are *you* here, DuMontaigne?"

"I won't see Gabriel hang," Paul said. "A matter of justice, if it is your business."

"Everything's my business when I put a man on the Railroad," the voice said. "That's why I know you and you don't know me. You have the reputation of being an honorable man, DuMontaigne, so I'll take this one to freedom for you. But I warn you, the day will come when we will take them all." He lit his lantern again so that Gabriel could see the way. "All right, send him across."

Gabriel had been standing silent, listening to the two men speaking in the dark. Now he cast a hesitant look across the wild vines and undergrowth to the shadow by the chimney. He had heard of the Underground Railroad in secret whispered conversations in the quarters—a route of safe houses and secret trails north to freedom. Freedom! He had longed for it, dreamt of it. Now that it was here, he was almost afraid of it. Sallie put a gold piece in his hand and closed his fingers around it. She gave him a little push.

"Go with him, Gabriel. He'll see you north. If you can ever send us a message saying that you made it, do."

"Come along, Gabriel." The voice from the shadows was unexpectedly gentle. "You'll come to no harm with us."

Gabriel cast a last look at Sallie and Paul, and then across the darkness to freedom. *I got no choice,* he thought. *Even if they wasn't gonna hang me, I got to go an' see how it is.* Gabriel took a deep breath and began walking through the undergrowth, toward the future.

The light by the ruined house went out again, and Paul took Sallie by the arm. At the sight of her moonlit face, pale against the old black linsey dress, he felt his heart turn over with love and a respect for her that was new to him. There was courage in Sallie that he had never known was there.

Paul pointed silently at the horses, and she nodded. Gabriel and the man from the Underground Railroad wouldn't move until they had left. Paul looked back once over his shoulder. Men like that were called "conductors" by the abolitionists, and they led lonely, dangerous lives in defense of principles that Paul considered indefensible. If they were caught in a slave state, they would die. If Paul and Sallie were known to have consorted with one—much less to have freed a slave, even their own, who had murdered a white man—they would be outcast from their own kind forever.

Nevertheless, as he boosted Sallie into her saddle and picked up Butterfly's trailing reins, Paul's heart felt lighter than it had in weeks.

XXVI

Election

Day

"WHY THAT LOW-down, slimy son of a *bitch*!" Denis rocketed through the door of his father's hotel room and slid to a halt in front of Paul. "Do you know what he's *done*?" It was the second day of December, election day.

"Who's done?" Paul asked, as Barret Forbes looked up from the armchair in which he had been dozing with a newspaper over his face.

"Gilbert Becquerel! Damn it, he's convinced the court that a carriage is enough proof that a man's a property owner, and a carriage *license* is enough proof of the carriage! And now his men are handing out carriage licenses to every layabout in town who'll vote for the bastard Becquerel for the price of a drink!"

The Democratic party advisers appeared in a herd, drawn by Denis's indignant tones. They clustered around Paul, muttering anxiously, while Denis paced and swore.

"Calm down before you burst something," Paul said. The look on his own face was furious, but he got a grip on his temper. He looked to the agitated knot of party men. "What do we do now?"

"Ain't nothin' we can do about them carriage licenses now," one of them said. "You oughta be out on the street, givin' the boys the glad hand, Mr. DuMontaigne. Maybe it'll turn the tide some."

"Like hell it will!" Denis said after his father had left, accompanied by a somber following. "After all the work my father's done, that bastard's gonna *win*!" He stood grinding his teeth while Barret laid down his newspaper, amused, in spite of

345

his sympathy for Paul, by the transformation in the normally equable and even-tempered Denis.

"I'm afraid there's not an awful lot you can do about it now," Barret ventured.

Having considered, Denis looked at Barret with a gleam in his eye. "Don't bet on it." He picked up Barret's coat and thrust it at him. "Meet me on the levee where the boats-for-hire dock."

Denis disappeared out the door, and Barret pulled on his coat. He hadn't the faintest idea what Denis had in mind, but whatever it was, Barret didn't think he wanted to miss it.

He arrived at the levee to find Denis and a Democratic party man, who was introduced as Pierre LaFourche, shepherding a straggling line of men up the gangplank of a dilapidated steamer. The name *Bayou Rose* was painted in fading letters across the paddle box, and the owner-pilot, named Ovide Landry, who had a dark, inquisitive Cajun face, leaned out of the pilothouse above. He was conversing with two other pilots, presented to Denis as "my brother-in-law what married with my sister Onesia, an' my cousin on my mother's side, who is call Tee Joe."

Tee Joe took off his cap and announced that he also had a boat— "fine boat, only a little bit old"—for hire. Barret eyed it and a third boat, belonging to the cousin who had married Onesia, with a shudder and decided that if he were going to join this expedition, he would stick with Landry and the *Bayou Rose,* which at least looked like it wouldn't sink.

Pierre LaFourche darted through the crowd on the levee, pushing them toward the boats. He had acquired several runners from somewhere, who vanished and reappeared again regularly, each time with more men in tow. When *Bayou Rose* finally steamed into the river, with the other two boats behind her, she was jammed on both decks, and Denis was grinning broadly.

Politics in New Orleans afforded a fertile imagination a scope not generally available elsewhere, but in this instance Barret was baffled. "I hesitate to inquire," he said, "but what in hell are you doing?"

"Voting where it'll do some good," Denis said. "The Whigs are going to take the city precincts anyway."

"You mean you can vote anywhere you want to?"

"As long as it's in your county," Denis said cheerfully. "And Orleans County covers four parishes. There're some precincts down in Plaquemines Parish where they're lucky if a frog comes in to vote."

"If Becquerel has more voters in New Orleans, I still don't see the point."

"That's the beauty of it," Denis said. "The man who wins is the man who takes the most precincts. There's nothing in the rules that says he has to get the most *votes*."

Barret thoughtfully digested this oversight on someone's part while *Bayou Rose* steamed downriver. Below the bend called English Turn, Orleans Parish ended, and Plaquemines began. In area, Plaquemines was by far the largest parish in Orleans County, but the most sparsely populated. It was a land of freshwater swamps and open, sunlit salt marshes, whose few trees grew in twisted and agonized shapes like tree demons set to warn the traveler of the elemental forces into whose domain he had ventured. This was tornado and hurricane country. It was no wonder, Denis assured Barret solemnly, that no one but the Plaquemines Cajuns, who were reputed to be amphibious anyway, would live in Plaquemines, because the hurricanes left everything torn apart, drowned and buried.

The first stop on the itinerary was Woodville, just below the county line. Here they deposited two hundred men, as befitted Woodville's superior status and proximity to New Orleans. At the next point, after hurried consultation between Denis, LaFourche, and Ovide Landry, only fifty men disembarked, because, as Landry informed them, "Nobody she don't ever come here since Alec Thibodeaux he die an' his store she is all closed up." Barret decided that a flat-roofed building with a weathered and unreadable signboard, at the head of the point, must be the store. There didn't appear to be anything else in the vicinity bigger than an outhouse.

The Democratic party voters moved on, alighting in small bands at Poverty Point, Fort St. Philip, Fort Jackson, and every hamlet in between, most of them no more than a cluster of weathered, gray houses built on stilts above the encroaching swamps. Finding his passengers growing restive, Ovide Landry declared it to be long past lunchtime and hailed a passing shrimp boat, whose owner, so he said, was another cousin, this one in the second or third degree on his grandpère's side. Denis thought the man had more relatives than a rabbit, but he was perfectly content to tie up at Belize, at the delta's mouth, and be fed a jambalaya of shrimp, rice, and tomatoes concocted in a monstrous cauldron by the boatman's wife, and a homemade whiskey of hellish strength that made his eyes water. Denis paid the cook with a five-dollar piece, which she tucked into her blouse before her husband saw it, and complimented her with French gallantry on her culinary skill. As an afterthought, he bought three more jugs of whiskey from her husband. It was a long way home.

On the return trip, Tee Joe's boat, none of whose passengers had yet voted, cut across to the coast at Plaquemines Bend to make the rounds of the population along the Bayou aux Chenes, Bayou Terre aux Boeufs, and Bayou Chersonese, and finish off their jug. At each point they had visited on the way down, the *Bayou Rose* and her companion boat docked, and Denis and Pierre LaFourche alighted and inquired genially of the precinct workers how many folks had been in to vote today. If Becquerel had more votes than Denis and Pierre liked, a few of the Democrat voters they'd been keeping in reserve on the boat were trotted out to put Paul ahead in the voting.

"Is you nearly finish with these voting?" Landry inquired as they all trooped back on board for the twentieth time at a ramshackle cluster of cabins above Poverty Point. "Because she is gon' rain like hell in a few minutes." The sky above was cold and wet looking, and the wind was beginning to blow nippily, bending the salt-marsh grass flat along the ground by the jetty. As he spoke, a spatter of rain struck the windows of the pilothouse, and it became evident that what little roof there was leaked. A howl of outrage arose from the passengers on deck.

"Damn!" LaFourche said. "Is there any more whiskey?"

Denis consulted his stores. "Half a jug."

"Well, give it to the ones that ain't voted yet," LaFourche growled.

Barret, who was enjoying himself immensely, pulled his hat down over his eyes and went to get the whiskey, while Denis and LaFourche put their heads together over the precinct list.

They made a final stop at Woodville, where they turned loose any man who hadn't voted yet and any who thought he could get away with voting twice, and steamed upriver into New Orleans as the last twilight darkened into night. It was pouring rain.

In the morning, *L'Abeille*, and its English-language twin, *The Bee*, announced in large headlines that Paul DuMontaigne had won. It was, as Barret said between whoops and laughter, the damnedest reform election he had ever seen.

Paul accepted the congratulations of his party (who were soothing their self-esteem with this victory since their incumbent presidential candidate, Van Buren, had lost resoundingly) and bent a steely eye on Denis. "The next time you want to help, I would take it kindly if you would tell me what you're doing."

"You'd have told me not to," Denis said unrepentantly. "And it wasn't as bad as what Becquerel did."

"That is beside the point."

"No, it ain't," one of the party men said, grinning. "And *you* didn't have any hand in it. But I tell you, DuMontaigne, if you ever want to give up politics, we'll run this one in your place." He slapped Denis on the back. "He's got a natural turn for it."

"I'd do it," Denis said, "if that son of a bitch Becquerel were running." He was still inclined to outrage at how close Becquerel had come to winning. "And if he wants to challenge me again over this one, you tell him that's just fine—I'll be glad to shoot the bastard any place he picks out!"

A strong hand clamped down on his shoulder, and Denis turned to find his father looking at him. Paul's lips were twitching, but he said firmly, "Go home, before he shoots *you*."

"But—"

"Go home," Paul said, exasperated, "or *I'll* shoot you and put you out of commission." He wouldn't put it past Becquerel to challenge Denis for his bright idea. There were always eight or ten duels after an election. It would be a good idea, Paul decided, if Denis stayed at Belle Marie until Becquerel had cooled down some.

Christmas in Catholic Louisiana was almost strictly a religious holiday, with gift-giving reserved for New Year's Day, although all the children, white and black, hung up their stockings from the mantel in the big house on Christmas Eve and in the morning found them filled with peppermints and candy hearts and blueback spelling books from Papa Noël.

On Christmas Eve there was eggnog, hot and liberally laced with whiskey, to fortify everyone for the long cold ride to midnight mass. That duty being done, the children and the quarters folk were packed off to bed, and the adults of the family settled thankfully in the parlor for a last glass of eggnog by the fire. Also present were Dinah, who had come to spend the holidays; Barret, who was still making mysterious travel plans that everyone tactfully forbore to inquire about; and Roman Prevost, who, Paul thought wryly, had begun to live at Belle Marie. Roman and Felicie had gone to mass together in Roman's carriage, and Roman was now showing every sign of looking for a quiet word with Paul. Sallie, taking due note of that, collected Felicie and bore her off to her bedroom.

Paul, more than somewhat amused by the state of nerves that his old friend appeared to be suffering, invited Roman into his office and closed the door. "These are trying times," he observed.

Roman chuckled. "You've had your hands full at any rate. At least Judge Craire has ceased battering at your door about that missing darky."

"I *told* him not to send Gabriel back here," Paul said. "And I *told* him that old kitchen wasn't proof against those jackasses who were threatening to lynch him."

"I expect it was the fact that they apparently *didn't* lynch him that upset the judge," Roman said.

Paul snorted. "If he got away from them, more power to him." Judge Craire had been voluble on the subject, but Paul remained adamant throughout the resulting furor that if the citizens' vigilante committee, which he referred to as "those night-crawling idiots," had taken the law into their own hands and made a mess of it, he did not find himself in any way responsible.

"I don't suppose anyone has come forward yet," Roman said.

Paul snorted again. "Would you? What they were doing was illegal in the first place, and, judging by the fact that no one's found a body, they made awful fools of themselves into the bargain. *I* don't know who they were, and I don't want to. All I saw was a lot of hoofprints in the morning. If I'd got close enough to the bastards to see who they were, the judge could have identified 'em by their corpses." Paul decided this line of conversation had gone on long enough. He eyed Roman benevolently. "Roman, you've heard all this, so I know damn well it isn't what you've been perishing to talk to me about all evening."

"Er, no," Roman conceded.

Paul offered him a cigar from the silver humidor that Lucien had brought him from Paris and lit one for himself. "Shall I guess?"

Roman looked exasperated. "No, damn it, you know perfectly well. I want to marry Felicie. As soon as it's respectable, I mean."

"She's awfully young," Paul said.

"She makes *me* feel young," Roman said. "Paul, you don't know what it was like, all those years with Eugenie."

Paul sighed. "In a way, I do. Sallie tells me you're the right man for Felicie, incidentally, and *le bon Dieu* knows I've never had a better friend. The prospect of having you as a son-in-law is a little unsettling."

"I could," Roman suggested, "call you Papa."

"I'll throw you in the river," Paul said. "Assuming, however, you feel you can maintain a proper respect for my gray hairs and yours, you have my blessing."

"What did you want to talk to me about, Mama?" Felicie plopped herself down in the bed and smiled sunnily at Sallie, exceedingly wide awake for three o'clock in the morning.

"If, as I expect, Roman Prevost is down there proposing to your father that he be allowed to marry you," Sallie said, "there are certain things we need to discuss."

"Clothes," Felicie said dreamily. "An engagement ball."

"Not exactly," said Sallie. "There's more to marriage than a trousseau and a little innocent handholding in church. . . . *I* saw you, and so did Father Fortier."

Felicie blushed.

"Now, my darling girl, you listen to me." Sallie sat down beside her and took her hand, their bright taffeta skirts rustling against each other. "When I got married, I didn't know anything because my mother couldn't bring herself to talk about it. It was a dreadful shock, I can tell you, as much as I loved your papa, and I made up my mind that my girls were going to be prepared." She paused. "I don't want to upset you by bringing up something dreadful, but you had that awful experience with that boy last spring—I don't know how much you know about what he was trying to do. . . ."

"Well . . ." Felicie grimaced. Her cheeks flushed fierily, and she looked down at her lap. "I've seen horses," she said, embarrassed. "Is it anything like that?"

"Well," said Sallie, "there *are* parallels."

"Oh," Felicie said faintly. She tried to envision Roman in the context of her father's stallion Molasses, and her eyes grew wide with alarm. The only thing she could think of to say was, "Why?"

"Babies," Sallie said firmly. "And, er, other reasons. Now listen carefully while I explain, because I only have the gumption to do this once with each of you." She wondered if she'd have to tell Dinah too. She rather suspected not, considering Dinah's family. There might be advantages to that, Sallie thought, blushing herself. She hadn't had a more embarrassing conversation since she'd explained it all to Hollis. "The first thing to remember is that Roman loves you, and he wouldn't do anything that was wrong," Sallie began. If she could make this take long enough, Roman would be gone by the time she was through. After the shock Felicie was in store for, Sallie thought it might be just as well for their romance if she didn't encounter Roman for the next few days.

The next day, Paul, attired as Papa Noël to the general amusement of his older children, handed round the stockings to Emilie, Mimsie, and the children from the quarters. After Christmas dinner—roast goose in the main house and roast chicken in the quarters—had been served, the gentlemen retired to easy chairs to sleep it all off, and Sallie, Felicie, and Dinah figuratively rolled up their sleeves and continued with the plans for New Year's Day.

A ball had already been settled on to celebrate Paul's election, and now it would serve as the announcements for two engagements as well: Denis's to Dinah, and Felicie's to Roman Prevost, who had talked Father Fortier into putting up the banns at a date that the good father considered scandalously early, but that Roman said was as late as he was willing to stand for. Considerably more latitude was allowed to a widower than a widow, as Hollis pointed out acidly.

Sallie, who wanted reliable assistance, decided not to bother Hollis or Adele. Preventing Tante Doudouce from helping was trying enough; the last time Tante Doudouce had helped, invitations had gone out to a number of people who had been dead for years, only Tante Doudouce hadn't noticed. But Dinah was a godsend. She remembered every item of Sallie's lengthy lists and made herself a favorite with the house servants by consulting them seriously on difficult questions. She quickly became "Miss Dinah" and not "Mamzelle Michelet."

"I'm going to learn to be a lady if it kills me," she confided to Mammy after painstakingly addressing the two hundred cards of invitation, which would all be delivered by hand.

"You is got more nerve than I is," Mammy said. But she peered over Dinah's shoulder and inspected the fine copperplate inscriptions with approval. "I 'spect you is gonna make it, though. What you want done with all them trees?" Daniel and Will were laboring through the open front doors under a staggering armload of pine boughs.

Instinctively Dinah said the right thing. "Well, they're to make garlands for the ballroom, but you know better than I would how Mamzelle Sallie likes them hung. *Would* you see to it?'' She looked hopefully at Mammy.

"Folks allus think a body ain't got anythin' else to do," Mammy grumbled, but she bent down and kissed Dinah on the forehead. ''Don' you worry, honey, I take care o' them garlands." She bustled off to arrange the decorations to her liking and to inform Testut, who was directing the placement of the musicians, that Miss Dinah wasn't too proud to ask for help when she needed it, unlike *some* folks.

All during the week between Christmas and New Year's, delivery wagons came and went and steamers from New Orleans stopped to unload. There were French wines and cheeses from Loveille; a hundred gilt side chairs from Seibricht; bandboxes from Olympe and the mesdames Pluche and Frey; and mysterious packages from Hyde and Goodrich, the jewelers—one containing Denis's New Year's present to Dinah, an engagement ring set with topazes the color of her hair.

Dinah had been in a quandary about presents. She had no money of her own and would have died before she let Denis and Sallie give her any. It had been all she could do to prevent them from ordering her so many new gowns and bonnets and ball dresses as to make her ashamed. But money—*non*. At last Dinah had hit upon the expedient of salvaging every scrap from the mountain of sewing that was being done in preparation for the ball, and for Sallie and the girls she had created three beautifully hand-embroidered satin reticules bordered in velvet; for Paul a spectacle case of brown watered silk embroidered with his initials; carpet slippers for Denis; and for Lucien and Barret notecases neatly stitched with sprays of violets. For Emilie, she thought, inspecting her hoard of fabric pieces by candlelight when everyone else had gone to bed, she could make a dress for the new doll Sallie had bought. After a moment's further thought, she decided upon serviceable reticules made of calico and trimmed with bright grosgrain ribbon for Mammy and Meeow and for Junie, who had been assigned to wait upon Dinah as well as Adele, and who, if Dinah had only known it, prayed every night to *le bon Dieu* that Mister Paul would give her as a wedding present to darling Miss Dinah.

The New Year tree, a cypress dragged from the swamp, stood proudly in the best parlor; a second tree for the slaves had been erected on the lawn at the rear of the house. Beneath the inner tree, family presents were opened first: a new black cashmere cloak and an evening cap abob of pearls for Tante Doudouce; the historical works of Voltaire, bound in red kid, from William McKean's bookshop for Paul; a necklace of pearls and sapphires for Felicie, from Roman, opened amid much giggling and comment; and Denis's ring for Dinah, amid the welter of other presents. Shyly Dinah presented her own offerings, and Paul kissed her soundly and slipped his spectacles into their new case. If Hollis felt compelled to remark, by way of thanks, that "At least you embroider better than my sister," Dinah had the satisfaction of seeing Denis slip his feet contentedly into the slippers, and Emilie hold the spangled gauze dress up to her new doll with delight. There had even been enough time left to make a second dress for Mimsie's wooden doll, and seeing Mimsie's wide brown eyes glowing with pleasure, Dinah was glad she had done it.

"My dear child," Sallie whispered in her ear, "when did you sleep?"

"I was too excited to sleep," Dinah whispered back. Not even in the luxury of the huge four-poster bed with its silk hangings had Dinah been able to stop thinking about all that had happened to her so quickly. She looked down at the soft cashmere shawl that lay in her lap, a present from Sallie, and her eyes misted over. Dinah was beginning to grow comfortable in these grand new clothes, but never would she forget the kindness that lay behind them. She touched Sallie's hand. "Thank you again."

Sallie knelt by Dinah's chair and put an arm around her shoulders. "It was worth falling in that water to learn what you're really like. I nearly made a dreadful mistake. And you must stop thanking me. I owe you the thanks."

Dinah nodded and brushed her hand across her eyes, but she didn't think so. She had an essentially practical nature, and she thought that it was one thing for someone to save your life. It was another to have someone in your family for the rest of it.

Charmante, now almost full-grown, was rolling playfully in the tinsel and ribbons and colored paper strewn on the carpet. Her black beady eyes peered at them from under a layer of crumpled wrapping, and her ringed bushy tail stuck out the other side.

"Now we know what to give that critter for *le jour de l'an* next year," Sallie said. "All the trash!"

A hubbub of voices on the back lawn proclaimed that the Negroes from the quarters had arrived for the next stage of the celebration. Paul rose from his chair. Denis brought him the old hunting horn that hung on the wall of Paul's study, and they went out onto the back veranda, followed by the rest of the family. Paul put the horn to his lips and blew three deep blasts, and the milling Negro children ceased shrieking and chasing each other and galloped toward the veranda steps.

A pile of gaily wrapped presents lay on the floor of the veranda. The children crowded forward, amid shouts of *"Bonne année!"* and their parents followed, sifting through the milling throng for their offspring.

"Bonne année! Bonne année!" They waved and shouted at the family on the veranda, and the DuMontaigne children shouted back. Paul and Denis began to distribute the presents, assisted by Mammy Rachel, Testut, Meeow, Mimsie, and Junie, who had opened theirs with the family that morning. Junie was resplendent in her new red taffeta dress and gave her relations from the quarters such a sassy, satisfied look as she bustled about that her mother came up the steps and took her by the ear. "Don' you git uppity with me. Mister Paul don' stand for sassin' of ole pussons, not by no sixteen-year-old house nigger what can allus go back to the field!"

"Yes'm." Junie, chastened, rubbed her ear.

Each family came forward as their names were called. For Daniel, a new suit of clothes. For his wife, Riar, a new dress and neckerchief. For their brood of children, shoes and clothes and wooden toys. Will got new boots, and his wife, Salome, who had become a mother again during the past year, got two dresses. Incentives were always combined with the holiday presents. Pots, pans, stockings, a red bonnet . . . the gift-giving went on until each slave had something according to his needs, his desires, and how hard Paul considered him to have worked over the past year.

Sissie, the kitchen maid, with a new calico dress clutched in one hand, hammered on an iron triangle with the other, and the slaves hurried to the tables set up under the New Year tree, while the DuMontaignes retired to their own breakfast. On New Year's Day morning, the slaves dined on grits, thick loaves of French bread, fried oysters and shrimp, eggs, gravy, milk and butter. The DuMontaignes' table was even more heavily laden. The same rule and superstition held at both: Eat well, because if you have a thin meal on New Year's Day, you will be hungry every morning until the next.

After breakfast, preparations for the ball went into full swing. Guests who lived at some distance had already begun to arrive at noon, by steamboat or by carriages that drew up to the front door as deliveries of ice and shellfish and other easily spoiled delicacies arrived at the back. There was to be a ball for the slaves in the sugarhouse, which had been swept and cleaned of the last debris of the grinding.

By nightfall, the house was ablaze with candles, and a new steamboat, which at Paul's insistence had been christened the *Belle Sallie,* was tied up at the jetty, her decks ablaze with colored lanterns. For the young and adventurous, there would be a moonlight cruise after supper.

Dinah came down the stairs, clutching Felicie's hand, with her heart fluttering under her stays. The house seemed to be overflowing with people in holiday clothes, laughing, drinking champagne, catching up on the news with old friends. There was silence and then a burst of applause and congratulations as the brides-to-be descended. Felicie, her eyes sparkling, presented her cheek to be kissed by old ladies, her hand to be kissed by gentlemen, and accepted their best wishes with enthusiasm. Dinah followed, dressed in rose-colored ribbed silk trimmed with butter-colored ribbons and Brussels lace and draped over an extravagant crinoline. Butter-colored satin dancing slippers covered her feet, and Mammy and Junie together had dressed her heavy hair into a chignon and a mass of curls, then threaded it with pink and yellow roses from the hothouse. Denis, seeing her terrified smile, pushed his way through the crowd to her, and tucked her hand into his. Well-wishers crowded around them, exclaiming sentimentally.

"*Enchantée,* Mademoiselle. Denis, you have caught a beauty!"

"So you are to marry our Denis! But I remember him when he was only so high!"

"Ah, yes, and naughty! Well do I remember the New Year's he put the frog in the eggnog! But he is changed now, and so grown up, *n'est-ce pas?*"

Old ladies with peppermint breath patted her hand, and old gentlemen with a gleam in their eyes patted her cheek. Dinah was relieved to discover that no one seemed to find fault with her accent or be inclined to remark upon her family. She smiled a little more easily as Denis steered her toward the dance floor. Denis, beaming at her proudly, was aware that many of the people in attendance tonight were laboring under the impression that Mademoiselle Michelet came from somewhere upstate, Baton Rouge perhaps, making no connection between the elegant girl on his arm and the Michelets of Bayou Rouge. Old Victorien

Michelet and his appealing brood had been dissuaded from attending the ball by the dispatch of a wagonload of food and a barrel of whiskey to their cabin, where they could toast the bride in absentia with the rest of their raucous clan and not start a scandal that wouldn't die down until doomsday.

The musicians, hired for the occasion from New Orleans and dressed in eighteenth-century livery and powdered wigs, struck up the first waltz, and Roman and Denis led their fiancées onto the polished oak floor. The two couples circled twice around the ballroom to the applause of all the guests before being joined first by Paul and Sallie and then by a host of other laughing, whirling couples.

Dinah, spinning in Denis's arms, remembered her sisters' taunts about Cinderella waiting for her prince and closed her eyes happily. She no longer needed to mind her steps; they came naturally to her with the music, and she had found her prince after all.

Felicie, in a gown of blue slipper satin with a delicate overskirt of embroidered, paler blue gauze, leaned back in Roman's arms and smiled up at him blissfully.

"Happy, *p'tite*?" Roman brushed his lips across her forehead.

"Yes." Felicie's eyes danced with pleasure. Having had a week to digest her mother's information on babies and their origins, and to consider the pleasant tingling sensation that came to her when Roman put his arm around her, Felicie had decided that the whole process might not be as peculiar as it had sounded at first. It was, Sallie had assured her, fun when you got used to it. Gazing dreamily at Roman, Felicie decided that it might be fun getting used to it, too.

Only Hollis viewed this romantic spectacle sourly. She too was wearing a new gown, of a soft green velvet that made her eyes as green as grass, and trimming of blond lace and violets, and she was undeniably the prettiest woman present, but the expression on her face was making even her most devoted beaux wary.

Finally Mammy Rachel, circulating with a tray of little glasses filled with the ladies' favorite anisette cordial, took Hollis by the arm with every intention of giving her what-for.

"Don't you come lecturin' me," Hollis forestalled her. She shot a malignant look at Felicie, around whose white throat Roman's sapphires gleamed conspicuously. "I'd like to choke her with that silly necklace!"

Mammy gave Hollis a look more sympathetic than she had

intended. "Honey, you don' want him. Every other man in this here room what ain't too old to walk would jump at a chance to marry you."

"They're all so insipid," Hollis said. "Or they're as old as Methuselah an' just about as lively." She tossed her head. "Anyway, I'm not sure I *want* to get married again." She wouldn't have admitted now that she had wanted to marry Roman, not for anything.

"Well, you better, afore you has a accident," Mammy said under her breath. "Now you jus' think a li'l," she went on cagily. "You Papa, he's gonna take you to Washington, an' there ain't many insipid mens what makes it into the guv'mint."

Hollis looked thoughtful. "I wasn't sure whether I wanted to go, but I believe I will. I don't think I could abide to stay here with the four of them drippin' sugar all over each other. I 'spect you're right, Mammy." Men in Washington had power. They did things. They appreciated a woman who wasn't a namby-pamby schoolroom chit.

"Thass my baby." Mammy patted Hollis's arm, satisfied. And Mammy was gonna tell Mister Paul he better take *her* along too. She knew better than to mention it to Hollis just now, but Mammy had no intention of turning Hollis loose in Washington without a watchdog. Studying Hollis's beautiful, calculating face, Mammy Rachel decided that she'd better get Miss Hollis married again as soon as she could.

Paul, accepting congratulations on his children's engagements, his own election, and the success of his ball, saw Hollis bestow a smile and an elegantly evening-gloved hand on young Alain Rillieux for a quadrille and breathed a sigh of relief. His willful eldest daughter could be delightful company when she chose and a hellcat when she didn't. Sallie was dancing with an ancient second cousin, who was clad in a pair of knee breeches and silk stockings, which he had apparently brought out just for the occasion. He was deaf, and her voice could be heard cheerfully shouting pleasantries at him over the music. Paul smiled at her, and she smiled back over her partner's shoulder. When Paul turned back to the men with whom he had been conversing, he found Adele at his side instead.

"If Messieurs will forgive me," Adele said, "I must speak with Cousin Paul a moment."

Her face was expressionless, but Paul made his excuses to his companions warily. Adele had avoided him, as was perhaps to be expected, ever since their interview in the best parlor. Now her gold-flecked eyes were not hesitant or tearful, but somehow triumphant behind her masklike expression. Paul followed her uneasily as she drew him into a little alcove off the ballroom, which was used mainly by ladies who were feeling faint or by courting couples when someone's *maman* was not sufficiently watchful. Adele's hair was dressed in an elaborate series of loops and braids that Paul thought were not particularly becoming to her.

"What is it?" he asked her. "I mustn't stay away from my guests."

"I am *enceinte*," she said flatly.

Dear God in heaven! Paul put out a hand to steady himself, and Adele looked at him mockingly.

"It is not yours. It is Lucien's."

"Lucien's!"

Adele's face, slightly swollen with her pregnancy, was complacent. "You may see in what manner your family has treated me," she informed him. She did not appear embarrassed, but, Paul thought, rather businesslike, a woman who had achieved her goal.

"Have you told Lucien?" he demanded.

"*Non.* Lucien will do as you bid him," Adele said with certainty.

Paul groaned. He knew, with a sick knot in his stomach, what he had reluctantly begun to suspect weeks ago, that she had not loved him so much as coveted him. But after making love to her himself, now to have her pregnant by his son! It would make an unbearable scandal for which everyone in the family would suffer. Nor could Paul bring himself to condemn Adele to the life she would lead if he did not intervene. He looked at her despondently.

Watching his face, Adele thought jubilantly, *I was right. His conscience will win.* A wave of nausea passed over her. She was not only certain that she was with child now, she was sick with it. She focused her eyes on the glittering ballroom. It still seemed a small price to pay. *I will have one child,* she thought, repeating the credo that had brought her this far. *I can do anything once.* "What will you do, now that your family has disgraced me in this manner?"

Paul held back the things he wanted to say. If she was to be his daughter-in-law, however unwanted, there must be at least the pretense of acceptance. Lucien had brought this on himself. Lucien had always taken advantage of people. Now a craftier person had taken the advantage of him, and there was no way out.

"Lucien will marry you," Paul said, his face rigidly controlled.
"As soon as possible."

"Thank you," Adele said.

"I wouldn't," Paul said. "I fear you're going to discover you deserve him."

Paul pushed his way through the thronging ballroom in search of Lucien. Paul found him with three of his cronies in the garden, tipping the last of a bottle of champagne into his glass.

" 'Fraid we've run out." A young man in lime-colored pantaloons and a dashing waistcoat peered dolefully into the bottle. "*Bonsoir*, DuMontaigne," he added as Paul approached. He waved his hand at the lantern-lit garden. "Hell of a party."

"It's turning out to be," Paul said. "Come into the summerhouse, Lucien. I want a word with you."

"That was embarrassing," Lucien said, as his friends shrugged and went in search of further champagne without him. "I don't deserve to be hauled away by my father like a brat of Emilie's age." He had committed no sins tonight and felt self-righteous about it.

"You deserve to be thrashed," Paul said, "but what you're getting is worse." He eyed the weaving trio disappearing toward the house. "They're so drunk they wouldn't notice if hobgoblins came out of the night and got you," he said disgustedly. "I expect you aren't much better."

"A trifle under the weather," Lucien said. He raised his glass in a mock toast. "Drinking to the family's health."

"Then allow me to sober you up!" Paul snapped. "You're getting married. As soon as I can decently arrange it."

Lucien lowered his glass.

"To Adele," Paul added grimly. "Who is pregnant with your child."

"That conniving—"

"I don't know which of you is worse," Paul said. "But you don't have an out, Lucien. You will marry her, or I'll disinherit you."

Paul turned and strode back toward the party. Behind him, Lucien slumped against a post of ornamental iron, from which streamers of colored lanterns dangled. He stared blankly at his father's retreating back.

On the veranda, Paul took a deep breath. The party was in full swing now. Laughter and candlelight overflowed the ballroom into the garden, where the night was mild and the *Belle Sallie* hooted an invitation to cruise the Mississippi by moonlight. Paul had an insane urge to stop the music and announce this third, unlooked-for, betrothal. He felt drunk himself, and galled and angry. He looked up at the moon, sitting fatly in the bare trees. A fine night for traveling. His spirits lifted a little at that. At least his left-hand daughter, beloved but never to be claimed or acknowledged, was happy tonight. Paul wondered if any of the dancing throng in the ballroom had noticed that Barret Forbes was not among them.

XXVII

A Service
of Marriage

CLAUDINE CLUTCHED BARRET'S hand tightly as the preacher, solemn in his black frock coat, read the service of marriage over them. Assured that Claudine was of age and that the proper New York license had been procured, the reverend Mister Fordhook had raised no objection to uniting two runaway Southerners in matrimony. As a staunch Methodist, he had even accepted with a certain approval Barret's glib explanation that his intended's family, being Roman Catholics, had not approved of her union with a Protestant.

Claudine felt lightheaded, but she spoke her responses readily. Having decided to leap the hurdle of race, a shift in religion seemed unimportant.

They had come from New Orleans first on a steamboat and then by the railway, stopping at a hotel in New York City only long enough for Barret to change his soot-stained clothes before he had gone out in a determined search for a preacher. While he was gone, Claudine had exchanged her brown serge traveling suit for a gown of light blue satin and a white lace mantilla for a veil, then sat down to wait.

Now, in the warmth of the little parlor, the Reverend Fordhook thought he'd never seen a bridegroom who looked quite so certain of what he was doing and so happy to be doing it.

"You may kiss the bride, sir," he prompted. Barret pressed his lips to Claudine's while Fordhook beamed at them. He was a romantic man and was happy to have assisted Cupid as well as to have rescued a soul from the toils of popery.

Mrs. Fordhook, a round and motherly body who had played "My Faith Looks Up to Thee" with verve on the pianoforte, pressed Claudine's hand and whispered, "God bless you, my dear. That's a good man. You can tell by looking at him."

"If the dear old lady had known what I was thinking . . ." Barret shook his head. "Most improper for a preacher's parlor."

Claudine laughed. "I expect she did. I rather think a preacher's wife must know a good deal about things, whether she wants to or not." Claudine was beginning to relax in the comfortable anonymity of New York City and the restaurant where Barret had taken her for a wedding luncheon. In a gilt mirror opposite them, she caught sight of her reflection, oddly unlike herself in a shirred blue silk bonnet with a plume. *I will never wear a tignon again*, she thought. *How strange*.

After luncheon, they went back to their hotel room, where Barret had already registered them, with a flourish, as Mr. and Mrs. Barret Forbes of Charleston. As the door closed behind them, he pulled off her new bonnet and sent it sailing across the room. As proof of his devotion, Barret had promised to take her to the opera at the Park Theater that night, and he had every intention of claiming his reward in advance.

Claudine sank happily into his arms, and then into the featherbed. No one slept in featherbeds in semitropical New Orleans. She sighed contentedly as this one engulfed her warmly. It was snowing outside.

"Maybe we could just spend our honeymoon in this bed," she whispered, snuggling under the down coverlet and warming her cold hands on Barret, who yelped.

Barret detached his beloved's icy fingers from his back and rubbed them between his palms. "If you keep that up, Mrs. Forbes, I shall tell my sister Alice to get separate rooms ready."

"I thought that was what people got married for," Claudine murmured contentedly. "To have somewhere to warm their hands. My feet are cold too."

"I'll buy you a warming pad," Barret said. "Come here." He kissed the hollows of her throat with mounting enthusiasm.

Claudine abandoned herself to his attentions. They would have a week in New York for a honeymoon. She could start being afraid of Charleston after that. For now there was the featherbed and Barret, who had stopped kissing her throat and was now kissing her toes. Claudine giggled. "I thought one became respectable when one got married. That is not respectable!"

"I'm going to get less respectable as I go on," Barret said. He sat up cross-legged on the bed with her foot in his lap. "If you don't let me kiss your feet, I might develop some sinister fetish for your corsets, until you can't take me out in public."

He tugged suddenly on her ankles, and Claudine slid down in the bed toward him with a gurgle of laughter.

"I've thought about this every minute since we climbed on board that damned railway car," Barret said. "For you I have had my tailbone compacted into my upper vertebrae for two days and got soot in my eyes. I shall graciously allow you to leave this bed to go to your horrible opera tonight only upon the condition that you get back in it within ten minutes of the final curtain."

Claudine held out her arms to him, and he stretched himself on top of her. "I love you more than anything I ever saw," he whispered.

Claudine nuzzled at his ear as his hands stroked her, exploring places he already knew by heart. She twisted her hips under him, reveling in the warm feel of his body as it lay on hers. She pulled him closer, locking her arms possessively around his bare back. Barret continued to explore her with mouth and hands, slowly, tantalizingly drawing her to the peak of desire. Claudine watched his face change from the genial, solid-looking man who had sat opposite her in the restaurant to the embodiment of passion, face flushed, eyes heavy-lidded, mouth full and sensual. She wondered if she underwent a similar metamorphosis when they made love. Her fears, her hidden parentage—all were forgotten as she opened her body to Barret and welcomed him into it.

Two weeks later they stepped off a sailing packet in Charleston. Claudine still clung to Barret's hand, but the week in New York and the days aboard the packet had been a turning point. No one had suspected her as a fugitive from her birth, no one had questioned that she was white. And because the world had assumed it, Claudine had begun to feel inside that it was so.

Charleston was cold and damp, but the houses overlooking the river harbor were touched with winter sunshine. They sat like a row of belles at a party, adorned with white lace balconies. A black coachman waved his hat wildly at Barret and Claudine from among the throng of carriages that crowded the dockside.

"Mister Barret!" The coachman shouldered his way through the crowd and beamed at them. "Sure is good to have you home! Everybody's about fall down dead o' surprise when we hear you bringin' home a wife! You sure is took your time, but you sure is got a pretty one!"

"This is Jonah, Claudine," Barret said. He gave Jonah a stern look that broke up involuntarily into a laugh. "Never you mind how long it took."

"Miss Claudine, you is just what Mister Barret been needin'," Jonah assured her. He hefted a trunk onto each shoulder. "You all jus' follow me an' git comfor'ble in the carriage, an' I git the rest o' you things."

"I'm afraid they're all going to have opinions on my tardy nuptials," Barret said ruefully as he tucked Claudine under a rug in the waiting carriage. "They've all been trying to marry me off for years; they're tickled pink."

Claudine hoped his sister was going to be tickled, although she doubted it. Alice had sent a letter to the hotel address in New York that Barret had given her, expressing her dubious congratulations and the hope that he had not, "at his age," done anything foolish. His young wife would doubtless "want to make all manner of modern changes in the old house, but I suppose I must leave that all to her, as I am only your sister," had been her concluding sentiment.

The drive from Charleston to Goose Hill, the Forbes family plantation beside the Cooper River, took only a little over an hour, but Claudine was nearly asleep when Jonah drew the carriage up outside a graceful red-brick house with a serpentine brick walkway that meandered toward the river from a white columned portico. It was well after dusk, and the lights were lit at either side of the door and along the carriage drive. At the crunch of wheels the door burst open, and what appeared to Claudine to be a flood of black faces poured forth, followed by a white woman in a gray silk housedress and a cap. She had Barret's sandy hair and gray eyes, and a face that appeared ready to disapprove of everything.

She consulted a watch on a chain about her neck. "You're very late, Barret."

"Now, Alice, you know I don't sail the ship." Barret climbed down and helped Claudine to alight. "Claudine, this is my sister Alice. Alice, this is Claudine, and we are very tired and hungry."

Alice sniffed. "I don't doubt it, traveling on those nasty railway cars and staying in hotels."

"That was a week ago," Barret said, as Claudine smoothed her travel-rumpled brown serge and murmured that she was *en-chantée*. "All that ails us is having missed our dinner, knowing that you would have one waiting at home." Barret kissed his sister on the cheek. "And if we *hadn't* been hungry, you'd have been highly insulted."

"Come inside then and don't keep Claudine standing in the night air." Alice swept her gaze over the slaves who were gathered around for a good look at the new mistress. "And you all get to work. You can gawk at the poor child in the morning." She inspected Claudine. "You're very pretty, and I don't suppose you're a day over eighteen, if that. I can't imagine why you wanted to marry my brother, but we'll do our best to make you welcome."

With this pronouncement, Alice swept them all together up the steps. Barret looked at Claudine to see how she was taking all this and was relieved to see that Claudine's mouth was twitching with suppressed amusement.

"I think you must be a great trial to your sister," Claudine whispered to him as they stepped into the warm, candlelit entrance hall.

"I'll take you up to your room in case you want to use the convenience before dinner," Alice announced. "It's a very wet walk to the privies just now, and Peter killed a snake there yesterday. I told you you ought to build them closer to the house, Barret, but you never did listen. I expect you'll see to it now that you're married." She started up the stairs, and Claudine, with a grin over her shoulder at Barret, followed.

Barret watched them go with mingled amusement and relief. If Claudine could handle Alice, she could certainly hold her own with his friends and neighbors.

Claudine waved her handkerchief at the carriages disappearing down the drive. Barret, standing beside her in the portico, slipped an arm around her waist and kissed her cheek, tickling his nose with the Mechlin lace evening cap that sat in matronly propriety atop her curly brown hair. "Happy?"

"Blissful," Claudine said. "I like your friends the Longworths. The Hollises too, although I felt a little odd around them." The Hollises were Sallie Hollis DuMontaigne's family. "I felt I was knowing them under false pretenses." Claudine sighed.

"Everyone operates under false pretenses," Barret said cheerfully. "We pretend to be sympathetic when we're not, congratulatory when we're really jealous, content when we're dissatisfied."

"All except Alice," Claudine chuckled. "Dissimulation is not Alice's habit."

"No," Barret conceded, "but that's only because she knows of no reason for it." He drew Claudine into the house. "And if Alice has gone to bed, I think it's time I showed you something."

Claudine followed him, puzzled, into the first-floor library, where he struck a match and lit a china lamp on the heavy library table. He stood on a three-step ladder and pulled a leather-bound volume from the top shelf. The spine was lettered in gold: *S. N. Doyle*.

Claudine gave Barret a baffled look as he laid it on the table.

"Samuel Nathaniel Doyle," Barret said. "A distant uncle on my father's side. These are his sermons. He had them bound himself. So far as I know, no one has ever bothered to cut the pages, much less read them." He blew the dust from the book. "It has made an admirable hiding place."

"For what?"

Barret smiled, an odd expression Claudine had never seen on his face before. "For an old disgrace."

He opened the book and took from between the uncut leaves a portrait in miniature, unframed and pressed flat between the pages. The face in the painting was a woman, very beautiful, in a gown of the style worn before the War of Independence. Framed in a powdered wig, her face smiled out sweetly at them, but the dusky bloom of her skin and the curve of nose and lips spoke unmistakably of her bloodlines.

Claudine stared, first at the face of the portrait, and then at her husband.

"My great-grandmother," Barret said. "My father's mother's mother. She was a quadroon. I never knew her, and no one in the family ever spoke of it, but my father thought I should know." He closed the leaves again on the sweetly smiling face and bent and kissed his wife. "No one ever found my grandmother out, so I guess we'll do all right."

At Belle Marie, the holidays were over, the grinding done, and the cycle begun anew. Following behind the plow, the slaves had begun to lay the seed cane, saved from last year's harvest, into the black earth. On a drizzling day in late January, Paul assembled his wife, his aunt, and children, and Dinah, Roman, and Adele, who were all to marry into the family soon, in the parlor. Sallie knew what was coming, but the others exuded curiosity and puzzlement.

"I have made my will," Paul said. "Or rather, I have remade it. And since I will be in Washington four months out of the year at the least, I have decided to put some of its terms into effect now."

Lucien's hands clenched where they rested on his knees, and Roman looked slightly uncomfortable, as if he felt that his friend's domestic arrangements were not something he should be hearing.

"The terms will affect all of you," Paul said, noting Roman's constraint. "Some to a lesser degree than others, but I thought it best to explain them once to everyone, so that there are no mistakes or misunderstandings. And if you're going to be in the family, Roman," he added dryly, "you may as well know it all."

"Very well," Roman said. "If the patriarch of the family wishes it, I'll stay."

"You're only two years younger than I am," Paul said testily. "If you keep on treating me like Methuselah, I'll leave you a picayune and my curse."

Roman chuckled. He knew Paul had no intention of leaving him anything. He suspected that his main purpose was that of disinterested witness.

Paul adjusted his spectacles and consulted the notes in his hand. "Felicie is already provided for in her dowry," he began. "And so was Hollis, when she married her late husband." He glanced at Hollis. "If you marry again, Puss, I'll make you a present for form's sake, but you have your fortune in your own hands now, and it's more than enough to live on handsomely. When Emilie marries, her dowry will also be paid from Belle Marie, at the same amount as her sisters, and Tante Doudouce will naturally be provided for." He cast a reassuring glance at Tante Doudouce, who fluttered her hands to indicate that she understood nothing of money matters but was sure that Cousin Paul would do the right thing. "In addition," Paul went on, "each of the girls will have an inheritance from their mother in time, and should I predecease you, Sallie, you will have an income from Belle Marie for life."

Sallie nodded. They had worked out the details of all this between them.

"As to Belle Marie itself . . ." Paul paused and looked at both his sons. "I have never approved of splitting estates, but in this case I feel that I have no choice. Lucien, I can neither entrust Belle Marie to you nor bring myself to sever my eldest son from the land he has been brought up to expect."

Lucine's face went rigid with anger. Paul looked from him to Denis, who sat quietly but with his heart in his eyes. "Denis, you of all my children, I think, love Belle Marie the best. I can't give it to you wholly, but you are to have half, and Lucien the other, with a common residence in this house—unless one of you feels impelled to build another at his own expense."

Denis's face split into a grin. "Except for Dinah, that's the best present you could have given me. Thank you, Papa."

"There is one proviso," Paul went on. "And it's written into the will with the rest, because I felt I must. Look at me, Lucien."

Lucien raised his eyes to his father's. Paul's were implacable.

"Denis is to run Belle Marie. Completely, and with no questioning of his decisions. If you, Lucien, interfere in any way, you will forfeit your half. Leave business matters to Denis and you may live as you choose in all other respects."

Lucien's face was white—mortified and outraged. He stared at his father for a long moment, but didn't speak. Then he stalked from the room, leaving Paul looking sorrowfully after him.

Adele regarded Lucien's disappearing back with disinterest. They were to have half of Belle Marie, and half of everything was riches beyond even Adele's requirements. If Lucien was humiliated by his father's terms, that did not concern her.

Dinah smiled shyly at Denis, pride lighting her face. Denis loved Belle Marie, thus Dinah did too. It was nice to be rich, but they would have been that anyway. It was the land that Denis had wanted, and what Denis wanted, Dinah wanted for him.

"I think," Paul said, in the embarrassed silence that followed Lucien's exit, "that I have said everything. I told all of you because I want my wishes to be unmistakable, but I will be very displeased if this is spoken of outside the family." He was beginning to feel like the headmaster at a school. He took off his spectacles and slipped them into the case Dinah had sewn for him. He grinned, and there was a general murmur of relaxation and assurances.

Paul took Felicie by the hand. "Let us go on to weightier matters," he said. "I understand that there is a certain difference of opinion as to the most propitious spot for the wedding." The family had agreed on a triple wedding, but Felicie and Adele were deadlocked on the garden versus the best parlor for the ceremony. Dinah, as Paul was aware, would have got married in a pirogue so long as she married Denis.

"You might as well try to stuff everyone into a molasses barrel as get them in the best parlor," Felicie protested.

"It will rain," Adele countered with assurance. "It always rains."

No one looked as if they cared very much if Adele got wet, but that was certainly a consideration for the guests. Paul rubbed his chin. Since he was in the way of making pronouncements, he might as well go on. "Allow me to settle your difficulty," he said.

"You will get married in the ballroom. Roman, I want to show you a horse." He made his exit before anyone could think of further objections, and was followed with alacrity by Roman.

Having won his bride, Roman now found himself drowning in a sea of silver patterns, Great-Grandmère's lace tablecloths, and the advantages of floral canopies versus shirred silk. "When you've finished showing me your horse," he offered Paul, "I'll show you one."

Sallie, having gone to see if it was possible to make a triple wedding in the ballroom look like anything other than a performance of *Figaro* in an auditorium, saw Paul and Roman striding across the lawn and looked after them with a troubled gaze.

Mammy Rachel came in with an armload of Emilie's starched and pleated pinafores, which she permitted no one but herself to iron, and Sallie jumped.

"You looks like the hoo-doos is after you," Mammy observed. "Time you get all these chillun married off, you gon' need a rest in the 'sylum."

"Mammy, he's giving half of Belle Marie to Denis," Sallie said.

Mammy didn't ask who. "An' a mighty good thing," was her opinion. "Mister Lucien, he ain't fit to run it, an' he ain't gon' be. It's a sorrow to me, but that's the Lord's truth."

"I know, but . . ." Sallie twisted her hands together.

"You ain't tol' him Mister Denis ain't his," Mammy said. She met Sallie's startled gaze. "I kin count as well as the nex' woman, an' I knows when you has your time, which Mister Paul don't necessarily."

"You knew? All this time, and you never said anything?"

"I ain't seen no point in it," Mammy said. "I loves Mister Denis same as the res'." She fixed Sallie with a stern eye. "You ain't fixin' to tell Mister Paul an' ease you conscience, is you?"

"I don't know," Sallie whispered. "I never meant to, but I never thought he'd leave the land to Denis."

"You tell me who gon' do a better job with this here land than Mister Denis."

"No one." Sallie put her hands to her face. "But before God, Mammy, it is on my conscience that he's not Paul's son."

Mammy put her arm around Sallie's shoulders. "You got a conscience what crop up at the wust times. You just looka there." She nodded at the window, through which Denis could be seen conversing with Paul and Roman, running his hands over the shoulders and forelegs of a big bay mare that Paul had bought in Kentucky. "Who you gon' do any good to if you tell? Mister Denis may be off o' the wrong side o' the blanket, but that boy's the most like Mister Paul of all your chillun, down in the heart where it counts. You go fin' a priest an' ease you conscience there, an' let Mister Paul be happy."

The ballroom was tented over with a pink silk canopy, from which hung garlands of roses and hothouse lilies, and it was ablaze with candles, which Sallie, eyeing them nervously, hoped didn't set the canopy alight. No Creole with any pretensions to gentility was ever married in the daytime, since it was considered embarrassing to have the bridal couple about all day after a morning marriage. As a result, no Creole was ever married at Nuptial Mass either, which the Church did not permit to be said after noon. Monday and Tuesday were considered the most fashionable days, and the DuMontaignes had settled on a Tuesday in mid-February to marry three of their offspring in one swoop. The house had been full of guests since morning, and some of them, Sallie knew, wouldn't go home for a week.

Sallie made one last inspection of the bridal party, gathered in the entrance hall: Felicie, in a cloud of white silk muslin with orange blossoms in her hair, clinging to Paul's arm; Dinah, in white tulle, on the arm of a neighbor, Valcour Aimée; and Adele in lavender, on the arm of Paul's factor, André Peyraud, a concession to her continued mourning and to Sallie's adamant refusal to have a daughter-in-law whom she knew to be *enceinte* go brazenly down the aisle in white. Sallie wished violently that Paul's conscience could have found something else to do with Adele than marry her to Lucien, but she couldn't honestly think what. She must be satisfied to be joyful at two of tonight's three marriages. And at her own. Sallie smiled mistily at Paul, remembering their own wedding so many years ago in Charleston. What a long way they had come to reach tonight. Was there any hope that her children, embarking on the same path tonight, would find the way less hard? Did anyone's children, ever?

I'm looking at the next generation, Sallie thought suddenly. Oddly enough, the thought didn't make her feel old, but only content. Hard on the heels of that came another: *That girl is carrying my grandchild.* Sallie looked at Adele again: Her sallow face was grimly triumphant under her tulle veil. Sallie thought, *He won't make her happy. She's going to be sorry she's done it.* And again, *But that's my grandchild.* She nodded her head briskly, as if at some decision. Sallie kissed Felicie and Dinah and crossed the hall toward Adele. She took Adele's hand while Adele regarded her warily. "God bless you tonight," Sallie whispered.

In the ballroom, Denis, Lucien, and Roman were waiting on the dais, where Father Fortier was murmuring a heartfelt prayer that in the excitement of the moment he would not lose his place and marry anyone to the wrong party. Denis looked joyful, Roman Prevost proud. Lucien had the ears-flattened-back look of a horse that is where it does not wish to be. It was the opinion of Father Fortier, who was a more perceptive man than his bishop and his parishioners frequently gave him credit for, that each half of these three bridal couples fully deserved the other.

Sallie nodded to the nervous young third cousin who awaited her in the doorway and gave him her arm. The music of a pianoforte came jauntily through the open doors, and the wedding guests craned their necks around. As the mother of one bride and two bridegrooms, Sallie was escorted in state to her seat in the front row of gilt chairs that filled the ballroom. The music swelled joyfully, and she rose and turned to watch the next generation follow after.

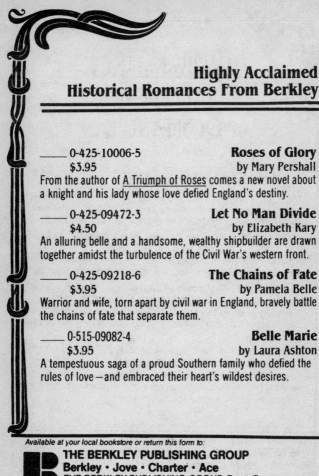

Highly Acclaimed
Historical Romances From Berkley

_____ 0-425-10006-5   **Roses of Glory**
$3.95   by Mary Pershall
From the author of A Triumph of Roses comes a new novel about
a knight and his lady whose love defied England's destiny.

_____ 0-425-09472-3   **Let No Man Divide**
$4.50   by Elizabeth Kary
An alluring belle and a handsome, wealthy shipbuilder are drawn
together amidst the turbulence of the Civil War's western front.

_____ 0-425-09218-6   **The Chains of Fate**
$3.95   by Pamela Belle
Warrior and wife, torn apart by civil war in England, bravely battle
the chains of fate that separate them.

_____ 0-515-09082-4   **Belle Marie**
$3.95   by Laura Ashton
A tempestuous saga of a proud Southern family who defied the
rules of love—and embraced their heart's wildest desires.

BESTSELLING TALES OF ROMANCE

___ 0-515-08977-X **The Rope Dancer** $3.95
by **Roberta Gellis**

The magical story of a spirited young woman and the minstrel who awakens her to the sweet agonies of new-found love amidst the pomp and pageantry of twelfth-century England.

___ 0-441-06860-X **Blue Heaven, Black Night** $3.95
by **Shannon Drake**

A passionate tale of the bastard daughter of Henry II and his fierce and loyal knight—set in England's most glorious age.

___ 0-515-08932-X **Crown of Glory** $3.95
by **Rosemary Hawley Jarman**

The saga of beautiful Elizabeth Woodville, who captures the heart of Edward IV, King of England, during the bright days of chivalry.

___ 0-425-09079-5 **A Triumph of Roses** $3.95
by **Mary Pershall**

Betrothed to the powerful Earl of Pembroke against her wishes, the raven-haired princess of the roses is caught in a struggle where surrender means love.

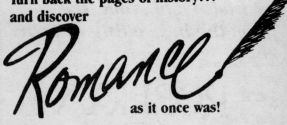